ALSO BY T/

JUST FOR HIM

Bad for the Boss

Undone by the Ex-Con

Sweet on the Greek

Work for It

THE BROWN SISTERS

Get a Life, Chloe Brown

Take a Hint, Dani Brown

RAVENSWOOD

A Girl Like Her

Damaged Goods, a bonus novella

Untouchable

That Kind of Guy

DIRTY BRITISH ROMANCE

The Princess Trap

Wanna Bet?

STANDALONE TITLES

Merry Inkmas

UNDONE BY THE EX-CON

JUST FOR HIM BOOK TWO

TALIA HIBBERT

NIXON HOUSE

UNDONE BY THE EX-CON: Talia Hibbert

Copyright © 2018 Talia Hibbert

Print ISBN: 978-1-9164043-8-0

Ebook ISBN: 978-1-913651-02-2

Credits: Cover by Cosmic Letterz

Published by Nixon House.

For all my brothers and sisters. I love every one of you.
And for the others; my siblings in chronic illness, disease or disability.
Your body is not your enemy. It just feels that way sometimes.

CONTENT NOTE

Please be aware: this story contains scenes of homophobia that
could potentially trigger certain audiences.

PROLOGUE

JULY 2017

"THIS ISN'T LEGAL."

Lizzie was sitting in the window seat of her Parisian apartment, feeling as frigid and fragile as the glass behind her. But she couldn't allow anyone to see that. She'd rather die first. And so, she kept her voice steady and her gaze uncompromising as she launched one final, desperate attack.

"I could sue," she continued. Even though the words felt like ash in her mouth, she forced herself to say, "My parents are very powerful."

Powerfully vile.

"Lizzie," Ellen said. "Please." There was desperation in her voice. She was afraid, then. How satisfying.

But Lizzie's old friend and roommate was not the most important person in the room. That honour went to Mariella Rossi, the company's ballet mistress. The woman who quietly choreographed every step of the inner workings at Paris House, no matter what her job description might say.

The woman who was ruining everything.

She stood before Lizzie, her feet tucked into fifth position, her face grim and unyielding. "*Elisabetta,*" she sighed, and even her frustration was graceful. "Please do not become hysterical."

Hysterical. That was an interesting word. Lizzie *should* be hysterical. She should be horrified, devastated, holding back tears.

Instead, she felt only a detached sort of outrage. And shame, of course. Always shame.

You've failed. Even in this, you have failed.

"We are not sacking you," Mariella was saying. Her voice sounded like an echo, like the distant racket of a train through a dark tunnel. "It has simply been suggested that you take a break—"

"A break?" Lizzie interrupted, her voice sharp. Somewhere in the corner of her mind, she heard her mother's severe tones: *Elizabeth. You are losing control.*

Didn't matter. All of a sudden, Lizzie was quite sick of control. Simply look where it had gotten her in the end.

Nowhere.

"A break," she said again, huffing out a bitter little laugh. "Every dancer knows what that means." She shot to her feet, anger burning through the fog of detachment. "I've gained... what, three inches at the waist? Four at most." *Five.* But who gave a fuck? "I am still the best dancer here, and you know it. There will be no *break*, Mariella."

"Ah, Betta," the ballet mistress murmured. The low words might as well have been a whip crack, so attuned was Lizzie to this woman's voice. "You misunderstand," she said, her lyrical accent stretching out each word. "Some things are more important than the way you look."

Lizzie couldn't hold back her laughter at that outright lie. "We all know that's not true, Mariella. No need to be delicate about it. If you want me to lose weight, say so." Lizzie's mind ran through calculations that had become painfully familiar in the past few months. She considered carbohydrates, calories, practice sessions... "I'll need time," she finished. "That's all."

But Mariella was shaking her head. "Time will not heal your sickness," she said gently. It was the gentleness that hurt the most.

Lizzie sucked in a breath, ignoring her mother's voice—*school your emotions, child*—as the implication of those words sank in.

2

She turned accusing eyes toward Ellen, who was blushing fiercely.

"You told?" Lizzie demanded.

Despite her red cheeks, Ellen refused to back down. "I had to," she insisted. "I'm sorry. You aren't looking after yourself."

Hearing those quiet, hopeless words was like taking a fall mid-pirouette. Like a blow that snatched the air from Lizzie's lungs, and the fight from her soul. "I'm trying," she whispered, her voice cracking. Breaking. Crumbling like everything around her. "You don't understand—"

"It's difficult," Mariella said, her voice soothing. She approached Lizzie slowly, as one approaches a wounded animal. "Diabetes is a serious condition. You must think of your health first, Elisabetta." She rested a cool hand on Lizzie's shoulder. "Your body is different now. You must relearn your limits."

Her words, her touch, should have been calming. Instead, they acted as another reminder that Lizzie had failed.

She had failed to maintain physical perfection. And now, even worse, she had failed to adapt; failed to overcome. Everything Mother had taught her, everything they'd prepared for over the years… it was all coming to an end. Because Lizzie's body couldn't care for itself alone, and she hadn't worked hard or fast enough to make up the difference.

Shit. Shit, shit, shit.

Tears pooled in her eyes, and for a moment, Lizzie felt the urge to accept Mariella's comfort. To turn and seek out an embrace, to cry in the woman's arms like a common fool.

The impulse passed as quickly as it had come. In its place, Lizzie saw her mother's lipsticked mouth forming the familiar words: *Perform, Elizabeth.*

Well. It was too late for a true performance: she had been found out. Her so-called-*friend* had betrayed her, and Mariella had pity in her eyes, and everything was falling apart.

But at the very least, Lizzie might maintain her dignity.

"I have discussed it with the director," Mariella was saying. "And we both agreed that you should take some time off."

The words echoed like a death sentence. Like the last cry of hope as it fell screaming from a cliff.

Her career was over.

So why did she feel… relieved?

Lizzie pulled herself together, cradling her battered pride to her breast like a crying babe. She thought of her mother's frigid, blue gaze, of her father's dismissive arrogance. And she channelled them both, wielding her heritage like twin blades, her only weapons against the threat of humiliation.

"No time off," she said coldly. "I don't need it. I'm leaving."

"Betta," Mariella murmured, her lyrical accent pampering the word. "That is not necessary."

"I've had an offer," Lizzie lied. "Back home, in England. I intend to go soon."

There was a pause. Mariella pursed her lips, raising her hand from Lizzie's shoulder. "I see," she murmured, the way one panders to a screaming child before laying them down for a nap. "Well… we wish you luck, of course."

"Thank you," Lizzie said. *Chin high. When the sun rises, you become a swan.*

And none of this will matter.

Mariella turned with her usual grace, gliding out of the room as thought the bare floorboards were a stage. But Ellen, the traitor, hovered awkwardly behind, her face a pale moon beneath the flames of her tumbling, red hair.

Lizzie cast a venomous glare at her former friend. "I require privacy," she said acidly.

"Liz," Ellen whispered. "I really am sorry. But I'm worried about you—"

"You are worried about the fact that my star rises with each day while you remain in the *corps* with no hope of ever becoming a soloist," Lizzie snapped. Some distant part of herself knew that she was lashing out unfairly, but she couldn't help it. She had trusted Ellen. She had ignored her mother's training and confided in someone outside of their family—and look at the result.

Lizzie had been a fool. But it wouldn't happen again.

4

Ellen's face fell, and regret prodded at Lizzie's heart. She opened her mouth, ready to take back the cruel accusation—but no; that wouldn't do. Instead, she visualised Mother's face over her own in the mirror, forcing Lizzie's springy curls into a bun. With each painful, imagined twist, Lizzie's grip on her self-control tightened.

There. The regret still prodded, but she could hardly feel it now.

"Leave," she said icily.

And, with a sigh, Ellen obeyed.

As soon as the door closed, Lizzie rushed over to the bedside table, pulling her phone from its charger. She sat down on the bed, her knees unsteady. She would allow herself one moment of weakness. Just a second. Just for now.

Her hands shaking, Lizzie dialled a number that she'd called less and less these past few months, praying that he would answer.

With each ring came a new worry. *He won't pick up. He's busy. You shouldn't be calling, anyway. Are you a child again, running to him whenever disaster strikes?* The phone rang and rang, and she almost gave up. But then, finally, she heard his familiar voice.

"Keynes," he answered, because that was what everyone called him. Everyone but her.

"Olu," she said, taking care to keep her voice steady. They hadn't spoken in so long, and yet there was no need for preamble and politeness with him. "I need a favour."

He saw through her facade immediately, of course. Probably because he knew how to command such deception himself; after all, they'd learned falsehood and performance together

Only he'd never needed to use them. He was braver than her.

"Lizzie?" She could hear the frown in his voice. "Is everything okay?"

"It's fine. I'm fine. I just... I need you to do something for me. That's all." She patted her head absently, her fingers gliding across the smooth waves of her scraped-back hair. Everything was still in place. She was in control now. She could do this.

"Well... Alright," came his doubtful reply. "If you're sure." And then, perking up at the prospect of helping—how Olu loved to help—he added, "Anything for my baby sister."

"Thank you," she whispered. And then she cleared her throat and began spinning stories.

She'd always been an expert at that.

CHAPTER ONE

THE AIR in the gentlemen's club was as stale as the institution itself. Throughout the luxuriously appointed rooms, light were dim and voices were politely low. Haughty men sat about in expensive suits, congratulating each other on having entered the world with piles of money and illustrious bloodlines already waiting for them.

At least, that's what Isaac assumed they spent their time discussing. This was England, after all.

And here he sat, a hawk amongst the swans. Sullying their cocaine-pure society.

Opposite Isaac, in a plush leather chair of his own, lounged one of those very swans. Mark Spencer: posh twat, family man, and founder and CEO of Spencer Publishing. This man had changed Isaac's life forever. Dragged him up from the gutter and into the limelight.

Before Mark had transformed an abandoned diary into a best-selling prison memoir, the name Isaac Montgomery had been synonymous with the lowest of filth. And now? Well. Isaac's soul could never be washed clean. But he was filthy fucking rich and over the course of the last three years, he'd confirmed what he'd always suspected: money *could* buy happiness. Or safety, at least, which was close enough.

Thanks to Mark Spencer, Isaac would never go hungry again. His future children would never shoplift their dinner or sit in the dark to hide from the bailiffs. He would never be powerless. For that, he owed Mark the debt of a lifetime.

But, he reflected, watching Mark the way he'd watch a rabid dog—that didn't mean he had to roll over for the fucker.

Isaac took a slow, measured sip of his port. It tasted like his gran's perfume, but if he'd ordered a pint in this place, he might have been crucified. Setting down the heavy glass with a clink, he glanced at the wad of crisp paper in his hand: the contract.

"What do you think?" Mark finally asked. Was it Isaac's imagination, or were his cultured tones a little harsher than usual? A little more... desperate?

After a second's thought—a moment's analysis of the sharp glint in Mark's rain-cloud eyes—Isaac made his decision.

He released his grip on the contract and watched dispassionately as sheets of paper fluttered through the air, scattering like snow.

No; like ruffled feathers.

Neither man moved to pick them up. But Isaac was willing to bet that as soon as he left, Mark would be scrabbling for each scrap of that bullshit.

"What happened to the old contract?" Isaac asked, his voice empty as ever.

Mark leant back comfortably in his seat, taking a moment to answer. Trying to regain the upper hand. But that didn't faze Isaac; he knew more about power plays than this wealthy twat with his slick hair and sharp suit ever could.

"Things change," Mark finally answered. "Our standard approach has been updated to suit the times. You're an intelligent man. I'm sure you understand."

Intelligent? Nah. Isaac was sharp. He could smell bullshit from a mile away. See, Isaac was simple. His books sold to other simple men—and, of course, to the rich and witless desperate for a second-hand thrill. The contract he'd just dropped was way beyond his understanding, and that was a purposeful move on Mark's part. Business wasn't Isaac's area of expertise, but he'd spent enough time on the streets to know bullshit when he smelled it.

And right now, something stank.

"You're quiet," Mark murmured. His thin, white fingers fluttered slightly before he reigned them in, gripping the arm of his chair. But Isaac saw it. Isaac saw everything. "If I didn't know better, I might be worried," Mark chuckled.

Isaac's jaw clenched. "Worried? You think I'm gonna flip on you?"

A trembling bead of sweat emerged from Mark's pomaded hairline, tracing a shimmering trail down his brow. Once upon a time, Isaac would've found that satisfying. These days, it simply pissed him off.

Taking pity on the man who'd changed his life, Isaac sighed. He may not like people, but he owed this one. "Whatever. Just send me a copy. Yeah?"

"You could always sign now—"

"Send. Me. A. Copy. No; two." Because he'd have to show Kev. Kev was the one who saw through the fancy words and layered meanings, who sliced right to the heart of all that crap.

There was a pause. Mark's blank gaze slid over Isaac's body; probably cataloguing every flaw, from the twice-broken nose to the plain T-shirt and work boots. As though anyone could miss the fact that Isaac was common as shite. As though Isaac didn't feel every inch of his oversized frame in this elegant room.

As though he'd ever give a damn.

"Email?" Mark acquiesced finally.

"Paper."

Mark gave the pages littering the floor a significant glance. But he didn't say a word—he knew better. "I'll have it courier'd," he said blandly. And then, his tone a touch brighter: "And you're ready for the trip next week?"

Isaac shifted in his seat, which was bad. A tell. He needed to lie more; clearly he was getting out of practice. "Yep," he said, his voice carefully flat.

"We'll have a grand old time."

Right. A retreat for Mark's best-selling authors, in the fucking Alps, of all places. To *ski*. Isaac wasn't sure he even knew where the Alps were. He'd never thought about it. He'd never wanted to. Leaving England's cold embrace to go somewhere even colder and far more expensive had always struck him as utter foolishness.

But all he said was, "Yep."

As always, his silence made Mark nervous. Men of a certain class, Isaac knew, were raised to talk as much shit as possible; to pour bollocks in each other's ears as a mark of respect. In Isaac's world, respect was a far more complicated matter, and silence was golden. Not to mention safe.

Some may say that he should adapt to the glittering society he'd been thrust into. He'd rather eat his own fist.

Nodding tightly, Isaac rose to leave. The soft, Italian leather of his chair was making him itch. Or maybe it was the room in general that grated. Either way, he was ready to get the fuck out of there and breath some good, old-fashioned, polluted London air.

Except Mark's voice stopped him, delaying sweet freedom.

"My wife's been missing you, Montgomery. And my girls."

At the reminder of Mark's three daughters, Isaac felt his lips twitch—which was as close as he ever got to a smile.

"You're invited for dinner on Saturday," Mark continued. "Sunday dinner, really, but we have it on Saturdays. Clarissa spends the Sabbath at the spa. Will you come?"

Isaac shifted. "Thought you didn't want me near your girls. Not since—"

"Nonsense!" Mark breezed, cutting him off. Smoothing it over. Which, of course, made Isaac's skin crawl. The guy had treated him like a pariah for the last six months, but now that there was a contract to renew, Isaac was a family friend again? Wasn't that always the fucking way.

His temper flaring, Isaac finished the sentence, forcing out the words that Mark obviously found inconvenient. "Since I beat the shit out of that reporter," he said slowly. "I thought you said it was best if I stopped coming over."

Mark's jaw hardened, and Isaac could almost hear the internal monologue. *Why can't you just let things pass? Be tactful, be polite?*

Fuck that. If the rest of the world could spread the rumour, why couldn't Isaac?

The older man's eyes flickered with distaste, but all he said aloud was, "Not at all. I simply thought it best while things died down. Of course, if you'd deign to tell me what, precisely, happened on that day..." He trailed off hopefully.

Isaac simply stared.

"Right. Well. Anyway..." Mark adjusted his razor-sharp cuffs. "Now that you're behaving..."

Behaving. Isaac certainly was—because Jane, the publicist he'd hired after that summer's fiasco, had him by the balls. Which he didn't mind, exactly, since she spoke plain and watched his back.

"You will come, won't you?"

Truthfully, the last thing Isaac wanted to do was spend his Saturday at the Spencer mansion. But it had been months since he'd seen the girls, and he liked them. You always knew where you were with kids. Besides, they thought of him as a friend. Friends didn't just disappear.

"Alright," Isaac said finally. God, he was soft as shite.

"We're eating early. Around three. Come over beforehand and we can discuss this matter further, perhaps." Mark waved a manicured hand expansively, encompassing the paper on the floor. Reminding Isaac that he was just as out of place here as those scattered pages were against the varnished wood.

"Maybe," Isaac said. He turned, more than ready to wind his way quickly through the maze of chairs, desperate for freedom. But Mark must have sensed his need like a shark scenting blood because the fucker called him back again.

"Isaac," he called, and his voice was soft, but somehow piercing. "Don't forget; we need each other, you and I."

What the fuck was that supposed to mean? The words sank

into Isaac's skin, burning as they went. He didn't like the way that sounded. Didn't like the implications.

He'd learned a long time ago that it was best not to need anyone.

But men like Mark didn't know how to speak; how to ration out their words, how to walk the line. They just threw out any old phrase, because they'd never had to face the threat of blood when a mistake was made.

And so, Isaac let his anxiety fade away. Unclenched his fists. Kept his back to Mark's watchful eyes.

Walked. And walked. And walked.

Because when it came down to it, that's all life really was: putting one foot in front of the other.

———

BY THE TIME Isaac got home, the sour taste in his mouth had almost faded.

He lived in a flat, just as he always had, but things were a little different now. As a kid, he'd lived on the twelfth floor of a high-rise block owned by the council. The building was grey, the walls were graffitied, and the elevator smelled of piss. The stairwell smelled of shit. You carried a knife, or you suffered for it. Every week, his mother would make him walk to the fire escape with his eyes closed, checking he remembered each step by heart. *"You won't be able to see if there's smoke."*

His mother would have loved this place, he thought, as he nodded at the security guard by the front desk. Just four floors. A private fire escape outside every flat, like they had on TV. The elevator played soft music and its buttons lit up bright white, but Isaac took the stairs. There was no stench. No junkies lurked in the stairwells.

He let himself in without watching his back, opening the front door wide without worrying that someone would force their way in from behind. Then he entered a space that was solely his, a space where he was utterly free. And it had been years since everything changed, but this wasn't routine to him. It would never be routine to him. He was grateful every fucking time.

Hanging up his jacket, Isaac pulled out his phone and headed to the kitchen. As he put the kettle on, he pulled up Kev's contact and hit 'call'.

The phone rang, and rang, and rang. It was evening; should be a good time. But if Kev was in a tight spot—

"Ay up." Just as Isaac began to give up hope, his friend's voice came loud and clear through the phone's little speaker.

"Kev," he said, relieved. "How are you, mate?"

"Not bad, not bad. You?"

Isaac plopped a tea bag into his favourite mug and picked up the steaming kettle. "Fine. Got a bit of work for you."

Kev tutted. "*Work.* I'll do it for free."

"No, you won't. Listen; it's a contract. For my next book. Different this time."

"Oh yeah? Trying to fuck you over, are they?"

"Maybe."

Kev chuckled. "They'll soon see their mistake."

"No," Isaac said mildly. "Jane."

"Oh, of course." Kev's voice shifted into a higher key, dripping with mockery. "Mr. Lah-Di-Da's got himself a publicist now. Can't be misbehaving anymore." Dropping back to his usual smoker's rasp, Kev snorted. "Load of rubbish. Don't know why everyone went mad. You don't talk about a man's—"

"I'll post it," Isaac interrupted. Because he couldn't have this conversation. Because his blood still boiled every time he thought about that summer's day six months ago. And even though Kev had helped him resolve the situation, that didn't make the topic any easier.

"Alright mate." And then, through the phone, Isaac heard a familiar series of banging knocks, the kind that boomed between connected cell walls. A warning. "Shit, gotta go. Warden's coming."

"See you."

Kev hung up without replying, which was understandable. He'd have precious little time to hide the Nokia his Mrs. had smuggled in for him. Speaking of, Isaac owed Lisa and the kids a visit. He'd put it on his to-do list.

CHAPTER TWO

SHE WAS awake when her alarm went off.

Lizzie's head was pounding, and her mouth was dry. She'd been lying on her back for at least an hour, staring up at the artfully bare beams of her little cottage's ceiling, telling herself to get up. Reciting her doctor's words: *Routine is everything. But you'll be used to that, I'm sure!*

Oh, yes. She was very used to routine. And sick of it.

But she was sick of her own petulance, too. Heaving out a sigh, Lizzie threw off her covers and dragged herself out of bed. Every movement sent a slash of pain through her tender skull. She didn't need to take a test to know that she was high, but she'd do it anyway.

Just like every other room in this cottage, her en-suite was gorgeous: a chic mix of modern and traditional aesthetics that reflected the house as a whole. The slate walls and chrome fixtures interspersed with splashes of royal-blue should have delighted Lizzie—in fact, they usually did. But right now, all she could see was the wall of glass behind the bathroom's chrome counter.

Her reflection stared back at her in all its mocking glory. The face she knew so well was present and correct. Which was hardly surprising; faces didn't tend to go wandering about in the night.

But it disturbed her, sometimes, that even though everything about her life had changed... she still looked exactly the same.

She shouldn't look the same, should she? She shouldn't look like *Lizzie*. But she most assuredly did.

Shaking her head, Lizzie jerked open the drawer beneath the sink, producing a little plastic box. She popped it open and found exactly what she needed, falling into the rhythm of the ritual.

Wash your hands. Grab a needle. Then a test strip. Ready the metre.

There. She pricked her finger, let the drop of blood fall on the test strip, and the metre flashed. High. She'd known that, but she hated the sight.

With a sigh, Lizzie dropped the damning metre on the bathroom counter and pulled her pyjama top over her head. She allowed herself a minute of vanity, studying her body in the mirror. No professional company would take her at this size, and Mother would be horrified at the appearance of stretch marks on her daughter's once-tiny hips—but Lizzie found her plumpness... Satisfying. At least she liked *something* about herself these days, even if it was shallow.

How refreshing it felt to let her body exist without conforming to anyone else's standards—functional or aesthetic.

Still... pursing her lips, Lizzie forced her focus onto the area she *didn't* like: her stomach. Or rather, the mottled bruising that marred her lower belly. Bruising that she was about to add to.

Falling into a deep plié, Lizzie opened the mini-fridge beneath her sink's counter. It was probably the best purchase she'd made since moving in, but she resented the little appliance almost as much as she appreciated it. Her feelings were annoyingly illogical these days; it was one of the many things she disliked about this new version of herself.

Biting down on the inside of her cheeks, Lizzie grabbed her insulin pen and rose to prepare it. While she went through the now-familiar steps, her nerve-endings dulled as if wrapped in cotton. When she pinched the skin of her stomach, her fingers felt numb. When she positioned the needle, a low whining began in her ears. When she pushed its sharp point into her own flesh, she felt the rope that tied her to the body she lived in. It had been fraying for some time now. She didn't know what would happen if it snapped.

But she'd have something to write in her journal for the morning. She was taking care of herself. She was following the routine.

So she hadn't failed today. Yet.

———

LIZZIE LOVED FROST.

Frost carpeting the grass underfoot; frost webbing the trees' bare branches; frost hanging in the air like a fog, condensing with each breath. She loved every inch of it.

She let the icy air scour her lungs as she walked, tracing the winding barrier of the grand wall that surrounded her workplace.

Workplace. That word felt good. As a child, she'd dreaded growing up to face a world where *work* meant something other than *dance*. Of course, all that had changed when Mother sent Lizzie away to train. To become a professional.

How foolish childish imaginings could be.

Now, *this?* This was more than she'd ever hoped for. To dance without having to perform. To dance for joy. To share the magic that ran through her body with every step and turn, without the pressure of being the best.

She was blessed, and she knew it. She felt it. Even now, when her mother's voice nagged at her mind.

Wasting your time and talents on children. After all I did to make you worthy of the family name—

Lizzie pushed the whisper away, focusing on the soft, fluting calls of the nearby wood pigeons. The voice in her head could bitch and moan all it liked, but she didn't have to listen.

By the time she reached the gates of the Spencer house, hefting her bag over her shoulder, she was in a damned good mood. She slid into the back garden with a smile on her face. A lone gardener haunted the lawn, a woolly hat tugged down over his ears and thick, muddied gloves protecting his fingers.

"Mornin', Lizzie!" he shouted cheerily.

"Good morning, Mr. Brown," she waved back, speaking at a volume and with an enthusiasm that her mother would've chided her for. But Mother wasn't here, was she?

The reminder put a spring in Lizzie's step as she let herself into the grand house, passing Barbara in the hall.

"Off to see the misses?" Barbara asked, smiling from behind the plumes of her feather duster.

"I am. How is your grandson?"

Barbara huffed out a sigh, rolling her eyes. "Causing trouble as ever."

"Give him a biscuit on my behalf, then."

"You're cheerful this morning!" Barbara laughed, swatting Lizzie's behind with the duster.

Lizzie grinned as she danced away, heading toward the back stairs. "I certainly am." How could she be anything other than happy? It was 9.50 a.m. on a Saturday, and in just ten minutes, she would dance. There would be no audience and no expectations; just music and movement and three students to share that pleasure with.

"Goodbye, Barbara!" She waved over her shoulder as she began jogging down the stairs.

"Ta-rah, darling!"

Yes. Today would be a good day. Lizzie could feel it.

Absolutely nothing would go wrong.

CHAPTER THREE

MOZART'S *GAVOTTE* filled the wide, open space of the studio, its bouncing charm bringing a smile to Lizzie's lips.

"Again, girls. To the corner. Ava first." She walked over to the stereo and started the song once more, waving her hands to hurry her grumbling students into place.

Well, only two were grumbling. Ava and Alexandra, the younger girls, muttered resentfully between themselves, tired of the endless repetitions. But the eldest of the sisters, Audrey, was already in position, practically vibrating with excitement. Lizzie knew that giddy energy well. Even now, months after leaving Paris, its ghost still haunted her.

But Audrey would go last. As the eldest, she must. And anyway, anticipation would only sharpen the girl's performance.

"Ava!" Lizzie called over the *Gavotte's* opening chords. "You first. Prepare. And—" On cue, the thirteen-year-old began. Her opening *chassé* was perfect; smooth and light. The *pas de bourrée* that followed was not so impressive; its *relevé* was… half-hearted, to say the least. Ava's efforts improved with the two *glissades,* and Lizzie felt the crawling discomfort that sloppy dancing brought upon her slowly recede.

But then came the *grand jeté*. Ava's leap was more of a bunny hop. When she landed, her turn-out all but disappeared; instead of graceful lines rotated at a ninety-degree angle, Ava's feet were clumsy and flat.

Unable to take any more, Lizzie paused the music and crossed her arms, spearing the girl with a glare.

"Ava," she said. "What is my rule, please?"

Ava sighed, rolling her eyes gloomily. They were heavily lined with a black kohl that did little for the girl's pale colouring. Clearly, Lizzie would have to have another word with their mother.

"Dance with the heart, or not at all," Ava parroted, her tone casually mocking in the way that only a thirteen-year-old girl's can be.

Lizzie nodded grimly. "So you haven't forgotten. And yet, you give me nothing."

"I'm *tired*, Lizzie," Ava whined. "Why do we *all* have to take Saturday classes? Only Audrey wants them."

Lizzie pursed her lips, then turned to look at Alexandra. The mousy middle sister was plucking at the tight cotton of her leotard, staring down at the floor as though force of will could induce it to open wide and swallow her up.

"Is this true, Alexandra?" Lizzie asked. "You don't want to take part in the extra classes?"

"Ummm..."

Lizzie had witnessed this slip of a girl command an Arabian stallion with nothing more than a twitch of her knees. But when faced with direct human contact, Alex became a toddler peering from behind her mother's skirts.

Or, more typically, her little sister's. There was a year between the two, but the way they behaved, onlookers might be forgiven if they judged Ava to be the elder.

"Not really," Alex admitted, her voice almost a whisper. She blushed, the poppy-red stain creeping up to her hairline, and Lizzie took pity.

"Alright," she relented. "I'll speak with your mother."

She heard Ava's satisfied murmur of "*Yesssss*," across the bare floor. Then the little terror said, louder now, "Can we finish for the day?"

Resigned, Lizzie pinched the bridge of her nose. "Fine."

Ava clapped her hands excitedly.

"But first," Lizzie added, "we must allow Audrey her turn."

"Oh, alright." Ava walked over to the room's mirrored wall, leaning against the barre as she prepared to watch her sister. Alex scurried off too, leaving Audrey—the eldest, at sixteen—to stand alone.

Ah, Audrey. The real reason that Lizzie was here, in this grand house's private studio, tutoring three pampered sisters in the ageless art of ballet.

Audrey was a principal in waiting.

Audrey was a star.

She stood tall—or as tall as a girl of five feet and three inches could stand, her body an elegant, never-ending line. Her little feet were tucked neatly into fifth position, the posture appearing effortless. But it was not. Lizzie knew that every muscle in the girl's body was engaged, straining, put to use for the ultimate human purpose: beauty.

Her body humming with anticipation, Lizzie reached for the stereo and started the music one final time.

The violins began their cheerful tune, and Lizzie watched as— with every movement, every look, every breath—Audrey's body told a story so convincing that the studio transformed.

Gone were the blank walls and floorboards of the purposefully ascetic space. In their place lay rolling hills of summer grass, and never mind the harsh winter they all knew waited outside. No; it was July, it must be, and here was Audrey: not a wealthy, sheltered girl who'd never known a day's labour, but a blushing shepherdess chased by her first love. She *chasséd* and Lizzie saw dandelion seeds floating through hazy sunlight. Next came the *pas de bourrée*, so joyous in its precision, like the geometry that allowed a church spire to touch the sky's very soul. The *glissades* were light as air. And the *grand jeté*— oh, that clever girl. *À la* Don Quixote—Lizzie hadn't told her to do that. But it was perfect, of course it was, even if she faltered slightly at the landing. After such a feat, Audrey deserved to slip.

There. The opening sequence was done. Next would come—

"Isaac!"

Lizzie jumped, the sudden cry startling her out of her dream-like state.

She turned to find Ava and Alex barreling into the arms of a huge man, one she'd never seen before. His face was obscured as the girls leapt at him; even Alex had abandoned her usual shyness for a whoop of excitement.

Lizzie stared, stunned by the spectacle. Then she turned back to Audrey and found the girl standing awkwardly in the middle of the floor, which was once again plain wood. No rolling hills of verdant grass here. And no effervescent shep-herdess. Audrey was just a teenage girl now, small and distracted—and longing to join her sisters, if the look on her face was anything to go by.

Defeated, Lizzie gave a dramatic sigh. "Go," she said, waving her hand toward the gathering by the wall as if it were beneath her notice.

Audrey gave her a grateful smile and—bless her—a lovely curtsy, leaning into each delicate motion. Then she ran off like a puppy in a leotard.

Good Lord.

Lizzie crossed her arms and took her time cataloguing the scene. The girls were gushing over this mysterious man, and now that they'd stopped hugging him—as though they were his darling daughters and he some naval officer of old, returned from a round-the-world trip—Lizzie could see his face.

It was… interesting.

He had the kind of tan that was hard-won, a breath away from burning, as if he'd been forced to stay overlong in the sun. Though where he'd come across sun in England at this time of year, Lizzie couldn't fathom. His hair was sandy, and his eyes were some light, piercing shade—blue, or green, or grey, perhaps. She couldn't tell from this distance. But men with coloured eyes were trouble. Her own notoriously charming brother was proof of that.

His colouring wasn't unusual in a white man, though. His face, however...

She supposed, when studied bit by bit, there was nothing especially disturbing about it. His eyes, his nose, his mouth—they were all present and correct, situated in a perfectly ordinary fashion. But the lines of his features were blunt and harsh. His brow was so very foreboding, and his mouth was almost... cruel, somehow. Firm and unyielding. His nose had been broken at least once, clearly; it was slightly crooked, with a bump in the bridge. Somehow, she doubted it had occurred by accident

He was tall, though not unusually so—with the girls crowding around him as a measuring stick, she could see that. And yet, he seemed intimidatingly huge. Perhaps it was the breadth of the shoulders, or the way his biceps bulged beneath the sleeves of his plain, white T-shirt. But more likely, it was the air of danger that hung about him like cologne. He seemed like a man who cared little for anything in this world and was very aware of the power that gave him. She hadn't spoken a word to him, yet his mere presence set Lizzie on edge—not only because he was so obviously coarse, but because something about him made her... Aware. Aware of her body, aware of the air in her lungs and the blood in her veins, but most of all, aware of him.

She didn't like that. She didn't like that at all.

Grinding her teeth, Lizzie hurried over to the place where she'd slung her bag, her satin slippers padding softly against the floor. She rifled through the holdall, until she came up with an oversized hoodie and—oh, yes. A carton of orange juice. She'd better drink that.

Her discomfort mounting, Lizzie slid on the hoodie and zipped it right up to her chin. She'd danced before thousands wearing next to nothing, but this man's presence made her leotard and leggings seem indecent, somehow. Feeling slightly more secure beneath her hoodie's thick fabric, Lizzie popped the straw into her juice. She took a breath. She took a sip. And then she turned her attention back to the mysterious newcomer and his adoring fans.

"Behave," he was saying, and his voice was low and raw and rough as gravel. Its easy cadence sent a thrill through her belly—and now she was *really* pissed off. Because how dare this rude bastard burst into her class, distract her students, ignore her, take up all that space with his ridiculous shoulders—frankly, it was impolite of him to be so very *solid*—and then, to top it all off, have the voice of sex itself?

Oh. Now she was thinking about sex in public. Yet another reason to despise this man.

"I've interrupted," he muttered, and Lizzie wanted to shout, *Yes! You have!* But he wasn't talking to her; he was talking to the girls. And at his words, they erupted into a chorus of *No*s and *Don't be silly*s that made Lizzie grind her teeth. Even Audrey was smiling at the man with adoration. *Audrey*, for goodness sake!

He looked up and finally—*finally*—seemed to notice her. His gaze settled on Lizzie with all the weight of a boulder, and she felt her cheeks heat. Had she really wished that he would acknowledge her presence? She'd changed her mind. All she wanted was for him to go away.

But he didn't, of course. No; he stood there as though he owned the place, studying her with calm insolence. "Friend, Audrey?" he asked with a jerk of his head.

Well! Lizzie felt her jaw drop. Which was absolutely mortifying. Just as quickly, she schooled her expression into careful boredom—but inside, her fury burned bright. A *friend?* Of the *girls?* Audrey was sixteen, for heaven's sake!

"No, silly," Ava giggled. "That's Lizzie. She's our dance teacher. You'd know that if you ever came to see us."

"Ah," he replied. He wasn't smiling, not really—he hadn't since the moment he'd come in. But his lips twitched, and his face was so severe that the expression might as well have been a grin. "She's very young to teach you."

Good Lord. That was absolutely outside of enough. Lizzie

knew her cheeks had always been plump, but she was twenty-five years old!

"Girls," she snapped. "Class is dismissed."

The three of them blinked at her, no doubt startled by the harshness of her tone. But Lizzie couldn't help it. She was uncertain, uncomfortable, adrift—and that was one thing she could not abide. Regardless of who it belonged to, this was *her* studio. She was its mistress. And no stranger was about to walk in here and steal her hard-won control without feeling the sharp edge of her tongue.

"You may leave," she continued.

The girls' eyes dimmed as they responded to her words. Hurrying toward the centre of the floor, they lined up neatly like China dolls before curtseying. Then they pattered out of the studio together, one pink little piglet after another.

Leaving Lizzie alone with the big bad wolf.

He surveyed her as though she existed solely for his perusal. His air was infuriatingly, effortlessly arrogant, as if he didn't realise how utterly he took up every inch of the room. And yet, she sensed a rigid control in his body that most probably wouldn't recognise. To the average person he might seemed perfectly relaxed, completely at ease—but she saw the way his muscles were coiled, ready to spring. She saw it, and she wanted to know why.

That was how she recognised him, in the end. Not by his face, which had graced enough front pages to enter the nation's consciousness—but his body. His posture. His aura. It had been strong enough to shine through on grainy tabloid photos. Now, confined to this little studio, its intensity was a slap in the face.

Here stood the nation's beloved criminal. Their dark angel.

Isaac Montgomery.

CHAPTER FOUR

ISAAC LEANT AGAINST THE WALL, dragging his gaze over the iron-jawed beauty on the other side of the room.

She was an interesting character.

At first glance, she'd blended in with the girls. But it hadn't taken more than a second for him to realise that she was most certainly a woman. A woman with searing eyes and a cut-glass accent who stood as though wearing a crown.

She was actually wearing nothing more intimidating than a grey hoodie with PARIS HOUSE printed along the bottom right hem. Her hair was scraped back into a severe bun, dark and gleaming and bigger than his fist. She was drinking from a child's juice carton, for Christ's sake—and still, he felt as if he should bow down before her. Not because she was anything special, he told himself; simply because the air of control that she wore like a cloak demanded it.

But Isaac had never responded well to demands.

They faced each other as though preparing to duel, each eyeing their opponent with little curiosity. The woman was bold, he'd give her that. Most people struggled to meet his gaze; she crashed into it with her own, fierce and defiant. Her plump lips spread around her straw like a kiss, and despite himself, Isaac watched. Closely. Even felt himself entering a mental danger zone as his imagination took over—it always *had* been overactive—and replaced the straw with the image of his...

Ah. She bit.

Hard.

For a moment, a smirk sharpened the smooth lines of her face. Then he blinked, and it was gone, replaced by a studied blandness that in some circles might seem polite.

But Isaac knew exactly what nothingness meant. He often used it himself.

And he knew how silence could become a weapon.

Well, call him a lamb to the slaughter. Because as the quiet stretched between them, Isaac found himself desperate to reign it in.

"I'm Isaac," he said.

Her teeth released the straw, replaced once more by soft lips. She sucked, slow and delicate, the fine column of her throat shifting as she swallowed. God, he should stop looking. But he couldn't.

Finally, she let go of the straw and spoke. Her voice was as blank as he'd always wanted his own to be. "I am Elizabeth."

The girls had called her Lizzie. Had acted like they knew her. Could a man ever really know a woman like this? Or would learning her mind become a walk through a hall of mirrors? He didn't have the time to find out. He didn't want to know. He couldn't care less.

She swept her gaze over him as though he were dust to be brushed aside. He watched as she catalogued every inch of him in the way those people had—and she was definitely one of *those* people. He saw it in her stance; he heard it in her voice; he felt it in her fearlessness. Here was a woman who had never struggled for anything. She expected the world, and through sheer force of will, she would have it.

He knew this in an instant, and he hated her for it. And yet, once again, Isaac felt himself moved to speak. As though she could pull words from him with just a flick of her honeycomb gaze. That gaze was the exact same shade as her skin, and the effect was strange. Fascinating. Something like a sunset. Why couldn't he stop looking?

"I..." He cleared his throat; felt rust crumble away as rarely used words prepared to emerge. The phantom taste was sharp. "I'm a writer. Mark—"

"I know who you are," she interrupted. And how could eyes like hot treacle be so very cold? "Isaac Montgomery. You wrote *Catching Time*."

He winced. "I hate that title." *Why did you tell her that?*

She popped her straw between her lips and did not reply. They stood there in silence

And she continued to say nothing else. Absolutely nothing. Why bother talking to someone so far beneath her, right?

The thought—the understanding of what this twisted interaction really was—had Isaac clenching his fists. Here he stood, making a fool of himself, throwing words like confetti at a beautiful woman, and for what? For the chance to run his hands over the muscles of her thighs? To see how her face softened when that fancy hairdo came tumbling down? As though he couldn't find a girl on any council estate in the country with just as much beauty and far more charm. A girl who didn't think that he was shit beneath her shoe.

He should be used to this by now. In fact, he *was* used to it. He simply wasn't used to caring. And holy shit, did he care. Scorching shame, a brand whose cruel touch he hadn't felt for years, burned through his abdomen. Why should this single snob, of all the snobs he'd come across, make him give a shit? His teeth clenched; his ire rose. And words fought their way from his throat before he could draw them back, powered by the force of his resentment.

"Know me?" Never before had his stilted speech been so screamingly obvious to his own ears. It was her fault. She was making him hear himself the way *they* did. She was making him feel the thickness of his own stupid tongue. He never wanted to see her again. But he already knew that he'd fantasise about her tonight, whether he wanted to or not.

"The nation's bad boy," she said, tongue and teeth owning every single syllable. "Our dark angel. I'm sure you're recognised every day, Mr. Montgomery."

"You read about me. In the papers." *What do you think you know? I don't care. I don't care. I don't care.*

She studied him as one might study an ant. "Are you so invested in your own notoriety, then?"

He wanted to say, *I hate it*. He wanted to say, *I deserve it*. He wanted to say, *if it weren't for people like you, there wouldn't be people like me*.

He said, "It sells."

And she said, "It's vulgar."

He almost choked. When was the last time anybody spoke to him like that?

Since he'd entered this glittering, monied world, he'd become used to people who hid their derision behind smoke and mirrors. People who delighted in disrespecting him *just* enough to provoke a response—but not enough to seem like the aggressor.

This woman had no problem being the aggressor. He liked her for it, almost as much as he hated her.

Like a magnet, she drew him closer. Isaac stalked forward and was gratified to see her step back, just a touch; she felt the energy tingling between them, and it pleased him to know that he wasn't alone. He was even more pleased when she met his gaze without fear. Did this woman even know what fear was? Probably not. In fact, after that first stumble, she stood her ground. Planted her feet and set her jaw, and he saw...

He saw himself.

Which was entirely impossible. He was drunk on those whiskey eyes; that was all.

Drawn short by his own wild thoughts, Isaac stopped in the middle of floor. And still, he needed to drag more of her into the light. He needed to feel the lash of her tongue, the bite of her indifference, again and again. All of a sudden, he was exhilarated; he was *feeling*. He'd wasted countless days and thousands of pounds on thrill-seeking and foolishness to cut away the scar tissue of numbness that surrounded him, and all he'd gotten for his troubles was a bloody reputation and a hundred tabloid articles. But now? Now, he felt like he could pick up a pen and write for hours, thanks to ten minutes with this awfully beautiful, silently vicious woman. He wanted to see those pretty lips form more insults. And she looked happy to oblige.

"Vulgar," he echoed, his tone thoughtful. "Me. I'm vulgar." He stepped closer. "True. I'm common. You see it. Don't you, *Elizabeth*?" Her name was acidic on his tongue. Unsweetened lemonade. How did she draw words from him in a way no-one else could? There was only a metre between them now, yet she looked right through him. Infuriating. "Or is it the headlines?" he prompted, moving further into her space. "The things they say? Or my past? My record. Is that it?" And then, frustration burning away his sense, he growled into her silence: *"Tell me."*

She continued to behave as though he wasn't even there—right up until the moment when his space and hers merged, when he stepped within a breath of her. Then, her choices narrowed radically: she could look at his chest, or at the floor, or into his eyes. She chose the latter. And so, when she spoke, he saw the length of her dark lashes. He saw the trio of tiny little moles beneath her right eye. And he saw her disgust.

"It is vulgar," she said, "that you killed a man, and now you profit from it."

Fuck.

If she had said anything else—anything at all—he could have turned away. Written her off as one of many; a beautiful bitch who didn't know if she wanted to step on him or sit on his face. She'd have been filed away with the wealthy women who'd asked to hire him for a night, or to bring him home to punish Daddy-dearest. And he'd have gone back to his flat and hate-fucked his hand thinking about the state of the world as represented by one vile angel.

But of all the things she could have done, she just *had* to echo the thought that haunted him with every breath.

You killed a man, and now you profit from it.

Isaac stepped back abruptly. What the fuck was he doing? Playing with fire as though the tabloids didn't burn him every other week? As though the whole world didn't watch him spend his money, live his life, enjoy everything he'd ever missed out on, and judge him for it?

Seconds ago, he'd been on the edge of enjoying himself—it was rare to find a snob so passionate in her hatred. He'd always liked a challenge, a taste of aggression. But now she was something more than the box he'd put her in. Now she was someone he'd remember forever.

She was the first person to tell him the truth.

He spun away, dragging a hand over his face. "Fuck," he breathed.

"Are you alright?"

He turned to glare down at her, wondering if he'd misheard. "What?"

"Are you alright?" She peered up at him. "Your breathing—I thought... Is something wrong with you? Do you need help?"

"What the hell is that supposed to mean?" He scowled.

Her gaze shuttered, that momentary flash of concern hidden behind concrete-thick disdain.

"Nothing, I'm sure," she murmured. But somewhere beneath the pounding of blood in his ears, he heard a voice whisper: *The ice queen can care.*

About what, he had no idea.

It didn't matter now, anyway. She was frosty as ever, and clearly done with him. Graceful steps took her across the room, achingly elegant and yet so quick, he'd barely noticed that she was moving.

Isaac blinked, tracking her as she walked away. He would swear she was running, with the speed she travelled, yet every motion was fluid and controlled. In the blink of an eye, she was sliding through the studio's back door without another word. And he hadn't even moved to stop her.

How the fuck had she done that? Like a cat, she was, all subtlety and silken fur.

He bloody hated cats. Give him a dog any day.

CHAPTER FIVE

CLARISSA CALLED it the rose parlour. Isaac called it another useless fucking room.

It was easy to forget, out here in the bountiful hills of Oxfordshire, that England was only an island. That there was a housing crisis. That people were going hungry.

And here was Isaac, his belly full, his glass empty, and his arse parked on a cream, velvet sofa in a fucking rose parlour.

Ah, if Mam could see him now. She'd smack him upside the head.

"Don't be tedious, darlings," Clarissa was saying. "You know I only want the best for you."

Her daughters crowded round her, and it was like seeing a woman hold court with her past selves. The girls were lucky; they had nothing of their father's unsettling looks. They were all respectably plain, just like Clarissa, with rosy cheeks and gentle chins and sky-blue eyes and sandy hair. They were little, taking up no more space than was proper, and when they spoke or smiled or entered a room, it did nothing to cause unease.

Oh, yes; they were so lucky. Imagine if they'd been like their father.

The man in question sat opposite Isaac now, watching his

family with something that masqueraded as fondness. But it was a touch too cold and calculating to pass muster.

It had taken Isaac a while to see beneath Mark's veneer—it was so refined, compared to those found on the streets—but now that the veil had been lifted, Isaac's unease grew every day.

He'd sent the contract to Kev. It would be a while 'til the other man could go through it, maybe a while longer before he offered feedback. But Isaac knew in his gut that something was up.

Or maybe the churning waves within him were remnants from his conversation with the dance teacher—if it could be called a conversation. It had been more like a princess slaying a dragon.

God, he hated the way she hated him. Why couldn't she be uninspiring and simple like everyone else? Why couldn't she judge him for his rough hands or his blunt words or his background? Why did she have to be *right*?

"Let's ask Isaac," Mark said, his voice breaking through the fog in Isaac's head. "Here, Montgomery—my daughters want to alter their schedule. Ava and Alexandra don't like extra dance classes on Saturdays."

Isaac had seen the girls' schedule, a long time ago. It was a physical thing, a whole whiteboard put up in Clarissa's study, filled with the many activities and tutoring sessions and other obligations designed to make them true ladies.

Clarissa was the third daughter of a baron, see. Isaac hadn't known all that shit still existed before he met Mark. But it did, and evidently it produced children with painfully high standards for their own offspring and the cash to do something about it.

The girls were looking at him with wide, pleading eyes. He had no idea what the right answer was here.

"Audrey," he said. "You?"

"I want to go," Audrey said. "But alone. Ava and Alex don't take it seriously. Ava isn't even *en pointe* yet."

"That's not my fault!" Ava cried. "Lizzie says I have naturally weak ankles."

"Lizzie's just being nice. You're lazy."

The idea of Elizabeth—he supposed her nickname was a privilege for the privileged—being *nice* made Isaac want to snort in disbelief. Only, the last time he'd made an 'indelicate' noise in front of Clarissa, she'd looked ready to faint.

"Alex," he said, swallowing his reaction. "What about you?"

Most people were content to allow Ava to speak for Alex. Lord knew, talkative little Ava was happy with that arrangement. Perhaps Alex was too. But for some reason, Isaac enjoyed pulling the gentle middle sister from her shell. Probably because he knew firsthand how easily silence became an unwanted habit.

She chewed her bottom lip, her expression solemn. After a moment of thought—always thinking, was Alex—she gave her verdict.

"We like dancing. And we like Lizzie." Again, Isaac found himself baffled. "But I think the extra classes only really help Audrey. She's the one who wants to—"

"*Shhh*," Audrey hissed sharply, as though the whole room couldn't hear her.

Alex clamped her jaw shut, looking guilty. Which was unnecessary. Everyone already knew that Audrey wished to be a dancer.

But maybe hearing the words aloud would make the dream too real to handle. It happened that way, sometimes.

Mark was still staring with his colourless eyes. Like a shark's skin, they were. Clarissa was awaiting Isaac's judgement in that birdlike way she and her daughters shared. This house was full of tiny, twitchy, sharp-eyed females, it seemed.

Although the sharpest of them all had appeared to be the softest, physically. Unbidden, a memory of Elizabeth—fuck it, *Lizzie*—floated to the front of Isaac's mind. Curves, curves everywhere.

Not that he cared. Not that it mattered. Women who flashed like police lights over shattered glass were not the kind of women he wanted.

"Isaac," Ava laughed. "You've gone all quiet. Is it so very hard to decide, then?"

Shit.

"No." He cleared his throat, tapped his fingers against the

heavy, crystal glass in his hand. "Let Audrey take the class. Alone."

The girls erupted into victory cries while Clarissa rolled her eyes at their exuberance.

"Alright!" she called finally. "I'll let Lizzie know. Now make yourselves scarce. You must have homework of some sort, I'm sure."

"They ought to have a pile of it, the amount we pay for that school," Mark muttered. Ever the exasperated father. But something about the way he shook his head mockingly, the way he grinned, was off. It was a performance.

The only problem was, Isaac couldn't figure out why.

Had the man always been this way? Had Isaac simply been too grateful over the past few years, and too busy coping with his own growing success, to see it?

Or was something different?

Perhaps it was a combination of both.

The girls left grudgingly, with many a sigh and a huff, and then the adults were alone. Without the easy energy that children always brought to a room, Isaac felt a familiar anxiety tighten his throat. Now, there would be conversation. Direct questions, and no tactless interruptions or childish quarrels to take the spotlight off him. But Mam had always said that he had to push past. That if he forced himself to speak, it would become easier.

It never had. But you don't disobey your mother. He'd learned that lesson, eventually.

"Cracking dinner," he forced himself to say, nodding at Clarissa.

"You're a darling," she smiled. "I'll tell Lena you said so."

Ah. Yes. Because this woman didn't slave away over the stove when it was time to entertain; she paid other women to do that for her. He was always forgetting the rules of this new world, always embarrassing himself.

"Right," he muttered. "Cheers for having me, anyway."

"Oh, nonsense. The girls adore you, and so do I. You haven't visited in so long!"

He shifted, brought his gaze fully upon Clarissa's face. Stared in silence for too many seconds and watched a delicate flush roll over her cheeks. *Oops.*

But he was confused. Was this politeness? Or was she unaware of Mark's informal ban?

Isaac twisted the ring on his little finger, caught himself, stopped. "Well," he said. "After the summer—"

"Never mind all that nastiness!" she trilled. "I don't believe a word of it."

And he didn't believe a word of *that*. The 'nastiness' had been the scandal of the summer—even though no-one would admit to seeing a thing, and the journalist himself wouldn't talk. Everyone knew what that meant, didn't they?

No doubt it was easier for Clarissa to ignore Isaac's supposed guilt. That was how these people operated: they did whatever suited them, and for now, ignoring Isaac's nature suited them. They'd transformed him from a criminal to an angel, made a tragic sob story of him—one that relied not on his humanity, but how very worldly it made them feel to pretend to understand. And all the while they thought of him as a wild beast on a leash. Poverty porn 2.0. It made him fucking sick.

But there was a dance teacher with burning eyes and scalding words who thought he was the scum of the earth and didn't mind telling him so. Why did that knowledge ease the pressure in his chest?

"Have you taken another look at that contract?" Mark asked, standing up abruptly. Clarissa was smiling expectantly, and now Isaac felt bad. She wasn't a terrible woman. She wasn't the worst of them. And it wasn't her fault that her husband was a snake in a suit.

Mark strolled to the sideboard at the back of the room, and Isaac resisted the urge to turn around. Letting a man get behind him went against his every instinct. Only, this wasn't a fight in some dingy bar; it was his publisher's family home, and he was in no danger. At least, that's what Isaac told himself. But his sixth sense, the one that he'd relied on all these years, appeared to be screaming otherwise.

No time for paranoia, now. He pushed it firmly away.

"Not yet," he finally answered. "Sent my advisor a copy."

"Ah, yes; your mysterious advisor. More port?"

"No, thanks."

"Sherry, Clarissa dear?"

"Please, darling. Oh, but you know I can't stand to talk business." She fiddled with her skirts, rearranging them neatly over their frothy petticoat. A Saturday evening at home and she was decked up fancier than the Duchess of bloody Cambridge.

"Sorry, my love." Mark came to sit back down, passing his wife a glass of the amber liquid. The sun-shot, mellow brown reminded Isaac of something, but his mind wouldn't let him focus.

Then Clarissa said, her tone artificially airy, her society smile in place: "The girls said you met Lizzie, earlier!"

Fuck.

"Yes," he said, doing his best to sound neutral. It shouldn't have been hard; he almost always sounded neutral. And yet, to his own ears, the single word was packed with feeling.

But no-one else noticed.

He hoped.

"What did you think?" Mark grinned. "Clarissa loves her, don't you darling?"

"Oh, yes. I saw her dance, years ago, in Denmark. And again, last year, in Paris. We know her brother, don't we Mark? Or you do, rather."

"Yes, I do," Mark said. "She's from a very good family."

Oh, Isaac bet. The woman walked as though the whole world lay at her feet. Fuck, it probably did.

"She's a God-send, truly." Clarissa took a fortifying sip of her sherry. "A while ago, Audrey began complaining that the dance school we sent the girls to wasn't *stretching* her. She asked to go to London, didn't she darling? To *audition*." Clarissa's voice lowered, as though the word were scandalous. "She wanted to join one of those *awful* colleges. Well, we couldn't have that. And then Lizzie's brother called and said that she was back in England and accepting students. It was fate! Wasn't it, darling? The stars aligned!"

"They certainly did," Mark murmured, nursing his port.

"Of course, she was *very* in demand. But we wanted her here, didn't we darling? So that the girls could train every day. That's what I did when I was a girl. Ballet is absolutely vital in developing the proper grace a lady requires."

"Quite," Mark agreed. Then there was a moment of silence as they both looked at Isaac expectantly.

"Yes," he said quickly. *I really couldn't give a fuck.*

At least the girls didn't seem to hate this particular obligation—though he didn't know how, with a teacher like that. But then, Lizzie was what they'd one day become, wasn't she? Or what they were expected to become. Cold. Controlled. Superior.

Maybe Lizzie had once been as exuberant as even Ava. Maybe joy had been drained from her drop by drop, like blood.

Not that he cared. *Poor little rich girl* never made much sense to him.

"So what did you think?" Mark said again.

"She's fabulous, isn't she?" Clarissa gushed. "I saw her in *The Nutcracker*. Her Dance of the Sugar Plum Fairy... Oh, she was divine."

Hm. Lizzie hadn't struck him as particularly fairy-like. But then, what did he know?

"Yeah," he mumbled. "She… she seems great."

"She certainly puts the girls through their paces," Mark said, his tone jovial. But his eyes were sharp, so sharp. Two pale, grey spotlights, watching Isaac like CCTV cameras. They flicked down to Isaac's hand, and he realised with a start that he was gripping his glass too tightly. Way too tightly.

He loosened his grip, took a deep breath. Fought back his resentment—both at her for being so fucking righteous, and himself for wishing that she were wrong. For wishing that he could've tasted her intensity on something other than a wave of disdain.

Pathetic. He was who he was, and nothing would change that.

"Anyway," Mark said suddenly. "Never mind all that. I actually have some news for you, Clarissa."

"Oh?" She turned toward her husband, her blonde hair shimmering as the setting sun poured through the windows.

"Mmm. I've been thinking about the trip on Wednesday. I was rather dreading leaving my ladies, you know."

"Really?" Clarissa said dryly. "I'd have thought you'd be happy for a rest."

"Bah! A rest!" Mark waved one manicured hand. "I'll be managing the egos of my best sellers for a week. *Rest* is not the word." He flashed a debonair smile at Isaac, as if to say, *Ah, writers, eh? So very high maintenance.*

And now another worry set up shop in Isaac's head. He hadn't even considered the presence of the other writers on this retreat, but he should have. Because he'd have to be around them, wouldn't he? Have to interact. Shit.

"I'm very jealous," Clarissa was saying. "Did you know that I'm to be left behind? Since it's a *professional* trip."

"Ah. That's a shame." He meant it. If Clarissa wasn't coming, the girls weren't either. And so he'd spend the week avoiding people and trying not to freeze his own bollocks off. Bloody fantastic.

But then Mark said, his pink lips curling into a smile, "Actually, darling… I've reconsidered. I think you ought to come."

"Oh!" Clarissa cried. "Do you mean it?"

"Yes. And the girls, of course."

Just like that, Clarissa's smile vanished. "Oh—the girls? But they've only just gone back to school. And they have their—"

"Not to worry," Mark said. He swirled his port, and then his gaze slid to Isaac.

That couldn't be good.

"We'll have a few of their tutors set extra work. Mrs. Brandt, for Mathematics, I think, and young Thomas for their English and history. A week off will do them no harm."

"Well," Clarissa relented. "If they're to continue studying…"

"And, of course," Mark added, "We'll bring Lizzie. You know Audrey would only fuss if she missed a week of training."

"Oh, yes," Clarissa trilled. "You're quite right! Now, I must go and tell the girls…" She stood, and Isaac stood with her. Not out of politeness, no; more because his body was filled with the sudden, uncontrollable urge to get the hell out of here.

Now.

"I-I'd best get off," he choked out.

Clarissa looked at him with concern. "Oh; are you certain?"

"Yeah. Need to get back to London. Before the rush hour."

Nobody pointed out that it was always rush hour in London.

"Well, alright then, dear," Clarissa said. She gave him one of her beautiful smiles; the kind she saved for hellos, goodbyes, and special occasions, because they were so very lovely. Because they transformed her pleasant face into something like art.

They must teach that kind of smile at private schools.

Isaac found himself wondering if Lizzie had a smile like that. Then he crushed the thought ruthlessly. It was pathetic. And anyway, he doubted she ever smiled at all.

But that would make her just like him, wouldn't it?

"Leaving so soon?" Mark asked, all concern. "Shall I see you out?"

"No," Isaac replied, his voice raw. He tried again, and the words were more human this time: "No. Thank you. Speak later."

And then he hurried from the room as though the hounds of hell were snapping at his feet.

Of course, because he left in such a rush, Isaac failed to notice the smile on Mark's face.

But if he had, he would have been worried.

Because it was the smile of a predator.

CHAPTER SIX

TWO DAYS.

Lizzie lay in bed, staring at the lock screen on her phone. At the letters just beneath the time, forming the word 'MONDAY'.

They were leaving in two days. The Spencers were off on some business-family-trip, and they'd pay her handsomely to follow, and they were leaving in two days.

So by Wednesday afternoon, Lizzie would be in France again. Perhaps the thought should devastate her, should act as a reminder of the way her life's goals had been snatched away.

It didn't—and she was reluctant to analyse that fact.

But it did remind her of the way she'd failed, the way she'd let her body's needs spiral out of control. The fact that people had felt *sorry* for her. The memory of Mariella's pitying gaze made Lizzie's stomach burn, humiliation bubbling like acid. No, this trip to Mont-Blanc would not be easy.

And Isaac Montgomery would be there, to boot. Of-fucking-course.

Clarissa had told her so just yesterday, over the phone, gushing out the words. *You met Isaac, didn't you Lizzie? Isn't he wonderful? Isn't he so deliciously coarse?*

As though the man were a slab of steak. Ha. If only. He was more like a raging bloody bull.

Lizzie pushed back the covers, welcoming the cool air of her cottage. She kept the heat low, to keep herself sharp. It wouldn't do to sink into laziness. She had a routine to maintain.

Of course, it was altered slightly. Once upon a time, she'd have woken up and been at a barre minutes later. Now, she had no such freedom. There was blood sugar to test, medicine to take, meals to eat—oh, she'd learned the hard way about meals. No more dancing on an empty stomach for Lizzie, as delightfully airy as it may feel.

She was never empty these days. Never pure. Never perfect. There was always something her body needed; self-sufficiency was a foreign word.

She'd bet Isaac fucking Montgomery was self-sufficient.

As she went through the motions of her morning, Lizzie allowed her mind to sink—just a little—into recklessness, like it was a feather bed. To run through memories that she'd rationed out over the last couple of days for sanity's sake.

Isaac Montgomery. The way he looked at her as though she were some creature both fantastic and terrifying. The way he baited her, and the way he filled a room. His stony face and the pressure of his gaze—dark blue, she'd noticed, like an ocean's depths...

And the way he'd reacted to her final words, as though he'd taken a fatal blow. The way his breathing harshened and his colour weakened. For a second, she'd thought he was ill. For a moment, she'd thought he was ashamed.

But he wasn't. He couldn't be. Lizzie told herself that as she took her insulin, adding bruises to bruises. As she chewed her granola like a cow with cud. As, finally—fucking *finally*—she grabbed her pointe shoes and wrapped the familiar ribbons tightly round each ankle. Whether it was shoes, hair, or self-control, tighter was always better. She pushed the sofa in her cosy living room against the wall, and she told herself: *If he were ashamed, he wouldn't have done it.*

She slotted her phone onto the speaker and chose her morning playlist and thought: *If he were ashamed, he wouldn't swan about like the king of the fucking world.*

She took her position by the window, its ledge serving as her barre, and thought: *If he were ashamed...*

Well. If he *was*, she'd said a rather awful thing, hadn't she?

Perhaps they called him 'angel' for a reason. Perhaps there was more to the story. Perhaps she'd been just like her father, judging those around her based on bits and pieces, fragments of fluff.

But he had killed a man. Hadn't he?

All this and more passed through Lizzie's mind, *Allegro*. Faster than her footwork had ever been.

And then, blessedly, her music began with the meek opening chords of Chopin's *Piano Concerto*. Just like that, her mind—and its thoughts—disappeared.

She was only a body now. How beautiful that was.

———

SILENCE WASN'T hard to come by in the country. The little cottage that Olu had found for her was as secluded as it was cheap, so Lizzie often spent hours practising, interrupted only by her body's nagging needs—and if she was lucky, not even that.

But after just eighty minutes of exercise, she was disturbed. The sound of envelopes flopping onto the hallway floor shattered her peace and piqued her curiosity. Slowly, keeping her core contracted, Lizzie lowered her right leg from its position above her head. The quiet trill of Chopin's *Piano Concerto* played on as she padded out of the living room, cool sweat trailing down her back.

She never had letters. Well; *never* was an overstatement. But Olu insisted on paying her bills, mumbling something about the fact that he never saw her, that it was the least he could do. And she supposed that taking his money, which came from their parents, technically contravened her vow to never touch her own trust fund. But really, principles aside, money didn't grow on trees.

So most of the post she should receive was directed to Olu's assistant, Jared. As Lizzie bent to pick up the white envelopes spilling across the hallway tiles, she frowned. Not one, but two letters; both identical. They were slim but heavy, the envelopes thick and creamy with delicate, winding vines embossed in gold down one side. The stamps were similarly decorated and the addresses on both of them were typed rather than written.

Of course, they had both been sent to her home. But the first was for 'Elizabeth Adewunmi Olusegun-Keynes,' while the second was addressed to 'Olumide Akin Olusegun-Keynes, care of Elizabeth'.

Lizzie bit her lip as she ran her gaze over her brother's name. Whoever sent these letters clearly knew that he was essentially unreachable and must have assumed that she'd be closest to him. Eighteen months ago—a year ago, even—they would have been right. But somehow, without Lizzie realising, their bond had stretched thin as a cobweb. Now they barely clung together, happy memories trapped and dying in the mess of what was once a real friendship.

He was only her brother now. Just as their parents were only their parents. And she knew it was her fault.

Setting Olu's letter aside, Lizzie headed to the kitchen and pulled a butter knife from the drawer. She could almost hear her mother's voice scolding her: *Just go upstairs and fetch the letter opener, Elizabeth! You lazy child.*

But her hands were beginning to shake, and she suspected that she hadn't eaten quite enough this morning. Grabbing a banana from the fruit bowl, Lizzie hopped up onto the cream kitchen counter and opened the mysterious envelope.

Her trepidation dissolved into joy as she slid out the letter, recognising the purpose of its heavy weight, its cream and gold motif. It was a wedding invitation.

Jennifer Abigail Johnson and Jyu Theodore Chamberlain cordially invite you to celebrate the joining of their lives.

Lizzie kicked her heels excitedly against the cupboard beneath her. *Theo's getting married!*

Theo Chamberlain and his little sister Yen had been the bright spots in Lizzie and Olu's youth. Their prestigious private school wasn't attended by many ethnic minorities; even fewer who were British nationals without bodyguards. So their parents had pushed them together, and while Yen and Lizzie had maintained an easy friendship, Theo and Olu had become brothers in all but blood.

The Chamberlain household was everything Lizzie had ever wanted. As a child, it had been one of the few places she could relax, could let go of the polite mask Mother always insisted on. When Theo and Yen's father had moved the family to another city, following his work, Lizzie had been devastated. Of course, she'd ended up moving away herself, just a year later…

Munching happily on her banana, Lizzie scanned the invitation for details. The wedding would take place in mid-March, at—good Lord—an island resort in Greece. Olu had something to do with that, no doubt; he had friends in Greece, she remembered. God, he had friends everywhere.

She'd never met Jennifer, but she'd heard all about the woman from Theo's sister, Yen. Apparently, Jennifer Johnson was some kind of angel walking the earth. Then again, Yen liked everyone. She was kind of a sweetheart.

But Theo was far more reserved. He'd only known this woman five minutes, yet he wanted to marry her. She must be something indeed.

Lizzie turned to put the invitation down, and her gaze caught on the open envelope. It had something else inside, a corner of paper peeking out. With a frown, she slid out the folded scrap. She opened it to find a note scrawled inside, the handwriting bold and angular, veering wildly as though each line was on the verge of taking off.

Hi!

Jen's maid of honour here. I'm in charge of invites! Apparently you and your brother are Very Important and I should send his invitation to you. So I did that. Anyway, if you need to, call me!

Aria xox

P.S. Yen said to tell you your parents aren't invited.

Below, she'd written her phone number. Biting down on a smile, Lizzie traced the digits. *Very Important*, hm? And their parents weren't invited. Thank God.

No doubt Theo had told Olu all of this over the phone—in fact, Olu was almost certainly the best man. But she should ring him anyway, to tell him that she had his invitation. At that thought, the bubbles of joy in her chest coalesced, thickened, became storm clouds. *Fuck.*

Another stilted conversation with her own brother. Her best friend. The one who'd done everything for her, who'd used his charm to protect her from the worst of Mother's wrath, who'd cheered her on despite Father's indifference. The one who'd moved halfway across the country when Mother sent her away, just so Lizzie wouldn't be alone.

What would he say if she told him? If she told him that her career was well and truly over, and that she wasn't sure she minded? If she told him that being ordinary felt better than being a star?

If she told him that she'd be sick for the rest of her life?

She knew what he'd say. *It's alright, Liz. You'll be okay, Liz. We can get through this, Liz. Together.*

And then he'd pack up his lifelong world tour, leave freedom behind, and move into her spare room. Schedule her shots. Test her every five minutes, scold her when she overworked. Call in a favour here and there from his never-ending Rolodex of powerful contacts; get her the very best doctor, the best trainer, the best dietician.

He would fix everything. He always did.

He was the person she could count on. She was the weight dragging him down.

She couldn't tell him.

But as long as she lied, they would remain broken.

CHAPTER SEVEN

LIZZIE LEFT home at 1.15 p.m., giving herself just enough time to walk the short distance to the Spencer house.

She'd had a good morning. And her journal looked positive; her levels were balancing out, becoming predictable. She was getting the hang of this whole *diabetic* thing. In fact, a small part of Lizzie dared to hope that she might continue like this forever: quiet and forgotten, coping, dancing for her own pleasure and relearning her body.

But, like clockwork, Mother's chiding tones slithered into her mind. Moments ago the icy wind had seemed harmless; now it carried whispered insecurities. *What do you have to be happy about? You have thrown away the only thing that made you worthwhile. You are the shame of the family. And now you will return to the country where you were once adored and triumphant... as nothing but a* teacher. *Practically a servant.*

Lizzie reached out to pluck a frosted leaf from a nearby bush as she passed, her firm tug shaking the whole branch. The leaf resisted for a split second before it broke off in her gloved fingers. It had been so pretty, pale green burnished with ice.

But she'd crushed it into shattered pieces, now.

Setting her jaw, Lizzie picked up the pace, her leisurely stroll becoming a determined march. This was ridiculous. She hadn't seen Mother in years—only heard from her every birthday. Touring Europe had its perks.

For a few years, Lizzie had almost eradicated the echoes of Mother's voice in her mind.

She'd had everything under control.

Then, early last year, she'd fallen ill. Quickly been diagnosed. Retreated into denial. And that fucking voice had returned. As if adjusting to diabetes wasn't difficult enough without Mother's imagined commentary.

There was no reason for these twisted thoughts. She knew that, logically. But for some reason, at the minute, she felt on the edge of chaos all the time, no matter how much she told herself that everything was under control. No matter how tightly she pulled back her hair or tied up her pointe shoes, Lizzie always felt like she was falling apart. Unravelling. Coming undone.

And that reminded her of days best left in the past. The days when she'd been firmly under Mother's perfect thumb.

Lizzie arrived at the house a few minutes early, thanks to her punishing pace. The brisk walk and biting cold had scoured away her miserable thoughts; she made her way through the luxurious house with a freshness of air and attitude that only January weather could bring.

She should be happy. How many people in her position, suddenly out of a job, could have landed on their feet like this? For God's sake, she was about to take a trip to the Alps for work. Yes, Lizzie had grown up filthy rich, but she wasn't completely oblivious. This was the definition of a dream job.

She pulled off her scarf and gloves as she jogged up the side stairs. No hat, despite the weather: it would only make her hair frizz.

Sliding out of the stairwell, she let herself into the house's west wing. Just a few doors down the long, richly appointed corridor, and—here. Coming to a stop in front of Mark's door, she rapped smartly against the dark wood.

"Enter," his familiar voice called. Lizzie did so with a smile on her face, shutting the door behind her. Mark took his privacy very seriously.

"You wanted to speak with me?" she asked.

He looked up from his desk, where he was studying what appeared to be four separate documents at once. "Ah, Miss Keynes. Yes, please sit down."

Ignoring the bastardisation of her last name, Lizzie came forward and settled into one of the chairs before Mark's desk. Automatically, she folded her hands in her lap and crossed her ankles demurely. It was a posture that Clarissa was always nagging the girls to adopt; one Lizzie's own mother had beaten into her well over a decade ago. Mother would say that Clarissa was soft, asking instead of telling.

But Lizzie rather liked Clarissa.

Mark put down his pen and folded his hands, matching her smile with one of his own. He was so kind to her; so welcoming. People always were, when they knew she was Olu's sister. Everybody loved Olu.

"Lizzie," Mark began, leaning forward in his seat. "Where to begin? It's always a pleasure, employing people like you."

Despite herself, Lizzie felt a flush of pleasure creep up her skin. There was nothing better than a job well done.

But then he continued: "People that I can control."

Her smile faded. Confusion took its place. "I—I beg your pardon?"

"I think you heard me," he said. Had she always thought his grey eyes so expressive, his narrow face so open? All at once they seemed sinister. Twisted. She felt goosebumps break out on her arms, beneath the warmth of her jacket.

"I knew I'd find some use for you eventually," he went on, his tone as friendly as always. As though this were just another casual conversation, like the many they'd had since she began working for the Spencers months ago. "But I never thought you'd have such potential." Adjusting the cuffs of his suit—always, he wore a suit—Mark leant back in his leather throne, steepling those long, thin fingers.

"You see," he purred, "I have a particular talent. You'll think me immodest, I'm sure, but it simply cannot be denied: I am an expert at identifying people's weaknesses." He reached for a nearby paperweight, a glass sphere filled with swirling colours, and weighed it in his palm. "I'll admit, I struggled a little with Isaac—"

"Isaac?" *Montgomery*. It had been days since she'd seen the man, and still he disturbed her peace. But for his name to come up in a conversation like this…

"Yes, Isaac. He's a difficult one. He gave me some worry, in fact. But then I overheard the two of you in the studio last week…"

"You—you did?" Her mind raced back to that brief meeting. She'd have noticed, wouldn't she, if someone else were there? If this man, this spider-like creature, were spying from the labyrinthine halls?

She thought and thought, but all she could remember were calloused hands clenched into fists, a gravelly, stilted voice, and ocean eyes. *Shit*.

"I did," Mark said. And she believed him. "It came to me, as I watched him spit around you like a tomcat. Our diamond in the rough has a weakness for the finer things in life." His eyes travelled boldly down her body, and despite the layers of clothing she wore, Lizzie felt suddenly naked. It wasn't a pleasant sensation. She resisted the urge to cover herself, or shrink back into her chair, or get up and leave the room—despite the fact that her instincts were demanding all of this and more.

She was Elizabeth Olusegun-Keynes, and she did not back down.

The control that had evaded her for weeks suddenly returned, like a faithful hound sensing its owner's need. Lizzie steeled her spine, as the familiar, ice-cold tendrils of restraint wrapped around her like a lover. "Speak plainly," she demanded, her words sharp.

The transformation was clearly noticeable. Mark shifted for a moment, his eyes flickering nervously. But then his surety returned, and he murmured, "As you wish. I have a task for you, Lizzie. I believe that during our upcoming trip, you above all people will be best placed to extricate... certain information from Isaac Montgomery."

"Information," she repeated slowly. Because her mind was moving faster than her lips ever could.

"Yes. I'm rather fond of information. I trade in it, actually."

"You mean the kind of information that you can hold over his head." Her voice was flat.

"Clever girl."

"Isaac Montgomery is a convicted killer," she said, speaking clearly, as though to a child. "He has presented every sin he's ever committed within the pages of his books. You're the one who published all his dirty secrets for him. What could there possibly be to find?"

Mark smiled. It looked more like a beast baring its teeth before opening its jaw wide, but if she were being sensible rather than fanciful, she would call it a smile. Lizzie was hurtling toward hysteria, and that simply wouldn't do. She kept her face blank and her gaze dead and her ankles demurely crossed, and she remembered who the fuck she was. The daughter of Olatunde Olusegun. And the ice princess to her mother's queen.

"Not all of his secrets are common knowledge," Mark was saying. "Have you read his books? Isaac is a very private man. There are... *gaps* in his life story. For example, the incident that occurred during the summer. Did you hear about that?" His voice came at her as though through a tunnel. Her skin crawling, Lizzie nodded slowly. "A mystery, isn't it?" Mark asked. "By all accounts, Isaac beat a popular journalist almost to death. And yet, Mr. Wright refuses to press charges, or even speak a word of the incident. But if he were to bring Isaac's loss of control to the authorities..."

Of course. Isaac was a convicted killer. There would be no leniency.

"I've exhausted my resources where Mr. Wright is concerned," Mark continued. "I need something directly from the source.

And if that particular incident does not prove useful, well, I'm sure a man like Isaac has an endless supply of secrets. We need only to tap into them." His eyes lit up, as though this conversation were exciting. Invigorating. "Simply *imagine* the possibilities, my dear."

Lizzie pointed her toes inside her soft trainers, harder and harder, until the familiar ache came and sharpened her cotton-wool mind. When she spoke, her voice was frostier than the Spencer lawn on a January morning.

"Why?" she demanded. "What do you want from him? This all seems so—"

"Elizabeth," Mark interrupted dryly. "This is an issue of some delicacy. Hence, you are not required to be the brains of the operation. Consider yourself a foot soldier with breasts."

There were so many things wrong with that statement, she didn't even know where to start.

"And why," she challenged, "would I possibly take part in any sordid little scheme of yours? If you think I need this job so badly, you are quite mistaken."

But Mark did not appear disconcerted. That maddening smile of his didn't slip. If anything, it widened.

"I was waiting for you to ask," he said slyly. Then he reached down and opened one of the drawers built into his old-fashioned desk. And she remembered what he'd said: *I'm rather fond of infor-mation. I trade in it, actually.*

But what could he possibly hold over her? She had no secrets, not really. Open secrets. Half-secrets. Nothing that might cause her trouble. Certainly nothing that could induce her to blackmail a man who might not be innocent, exactly, but had certainly done his time.

And so she watched with smug confidence as Mark produced a slim dossier and tossed it across the desk. It slid toward her, and she reached down to pick it up with nothing more than mild curiosity.

Lizzie opened the file and looked at the first of its pages.

And the blood drained from her face.

She stared down at the image before her. Two men: one pale, one brown, both naked.

The pale man's face was out of frame; he was the one taking the picture. But the brown man was fully visible. He knelt at his lover's feet, his hands standing out against the other man's bone-coloured thighs. He wasn't smiling for the camera, as he usually did, but Lizzie recognised him in an instant.

She couldn't look at the photograph any longer. She certainly couldn't go through the rest of the images. For one thing, they were private.

And for another, the sight of her own brother in the throes of passion was making her feel slightly sick.

Lizzie closed the dossier, her movements slow and precise. She did not speak.

But Mark did.

"I understand that your father is quite vocally homophobic," he said. Which was an understatement, to say the least. No doubt he knew that.

She remained silent, staring at the slim, brown folder. It seemed so innocuous now, its secrets once more hidden from the world. Secrets her brother wasn't ready to share.

Secrets this man had stolen.

"Keynes travels the world on an allowance from your mother's estate, I know," Mark added. "Thirty-six years old, and the man's never worked a day in his life! My, my. I wonder how he'd fare if his income were to… disappear?"

Lizzie didn't bother to correct the viper sitting before her. She didn't tell him that her brother was the hardest worker she knew; that he travelled the world to help those in need; that he'd practically raised her, following her across the country when she was just fourteen, bandaging her bleeding feet after each class.

She didn't tell him any of that. He didn't deserve to hear it.

Instead, after a long minute of thought, she looked up. She let him see every inch of the hate in her eyes. And she said simply, "Tell me what to do, and I'll do it."

So he did. He told her exactly what to do, in minute detail. He heaped every expectation upon her in plain language, just as Mother always had. It was almost familiar, really.

And when he was done, Lizzie nodded, and stood, and left the study with determination coursing through her veins.

This would be the best fucking performance of her life.

It had to be. Because for once, Olu needed her help. She would protect him as he'd always protected her. She would guard his privacy and his livelihood.

If her brother ever shared himself completely, it would be *his* choice. His decision. Not anyone else's.

And certainly not fucking Mark's.

CHAPTER EIGHT

"HERE WE ARE, *Monsieur*. Welcome to *Charmonix-Mailet*."

Isaac stared at the grand hotel from behind his taxi's window. It rose proudly up into the sugarplum sky, a stone structure that was somehow as elegant as it was monstrous. A few lit windows stood out brightly, outshining the lazily setting sun, and silhouettes moved within. Couples and groups armed with huge skis and snowboards marched into its vast entrance, bundled up against the cold.

Isaac still wasn't convinced that this trip was a good idea, but his publicist had insisted he accept. And he'd thought, on the plane ride over, that nothing could possibly make this week worth the monstrous waste of money it must be. Isaac might be wealthy in his own right, but he still heard his mother's voice tutting every time he switched the heating on before November.

Right now, though, Mam's voice was silent. Because even she would agree that a sight so beautiful as this—the blood-red sun glinting off snowcapped mountains, the pristine white blanket protecting the frozen earth, undisturbed for miles into the distance…

Well. It was absolutely fucking priceless.

"Thanks," he said. There were a thousand words running through his head, and his fingers itched to pick up a pen and pour them onto a page before they escaped him, but all his useless mouth could bear to say was *Thanks*.

Still, the driver didn't seem to notice how woefully inadequate the response was. He simply got out before Isaac could protest and unloaded his luggage with a grin. Isaac tipped the guy and trudged off into the hotel, shaking his head when eager staff leapt to assist him. He made his way through the luxurious foyer alone, passing a roaring fire on his way to the huge reception desk.

The place had clearly been decorated with 18th century opulence in mind. After collecting his information and room key, Isaac was led through dimly lit, luxurious corridors by a man whose uniform looked like a designer outfit. Even the staff here were painfully sophisticated. Who had the fucking time?

The guy opened the door to Isaac's room and stepped aside, running through a spiel that probably included valuable information. Isaac should definitely pay attention to the lightly accented words, but he couldn't. He was too busy staring in astonishment at the outlandish display before him.

This place wasn't a room at all, but a suite. There was a kind of sitting room with its own fireplace, along with a writing desk tucked into the corner. Separated by a short hallway was a bedroom decorated in cream and burgundy, with a beautiful view framed by heavy, velvet curtains, and walls that appeared to be covered in fucking silk.

And of course, there was a bathroom. He couldn't even bring himself to look in there. It probably had a golden bloody toilet seat.

"Your party has full access to the chateau's amenities, of course," the Frenchman—Luc, according to his name tag—was saying. "And access to a private parlour for the duration of your stay." What the hell was it with rich people and parlours? "As per the request of your party's leader, the room number of each party member is contained within your welcome packet." He nodded toward the sleek file that had been pressed into Isaac's hand downstairs.

"Right," Isaac murmured, still slightly stunned. "Cheers." He put his crap down on the nearest flat surface and tipped the guy. It might not be the done thing in a place like this, but fuck it. Tipping politics was hard enough without taking into account the fact that this was a foreign country.

Finally, Luc left, shutting the door behind him, and Isaac sagged into a chair that looked like it had been pulled directly from Marie Antoinette's palace. Then he stood up again, because he wasn't about to sully the fancy furniture with his ripped jeans and battered jacket.

Fuck this.

With a resigned sigh, Isaac headed over to the window, staring out at the magnificent view of the slopes. He hadn't come here intending to ski, but frankly, the outdoors looked a lot safer for a guy like him than the lavish decor in here. He wondered, on a scale of 1 to 10, just how embarrassing it would be to let three teenage girls teach him how to ski.

Probably pretty fucking embarrassing. But they'd enjoy it, and it would get him out of here.

Anyway. He'd better get a move on; he was late. He'd booked an afternoon flight because sleeping in was one of the few luxuries he allowed himself, and nothing was going to get in the way of that indulgence. But he should probably get washed up—if this place had anything so mundane as a shower—and head down to that private parlour. Yeah. That sounded about right.

CHAPTER NINE

AFTER THE MOST aggressive power shower he'd ever experienced—clearly the plumbing was bang up to date, unlike the decor—Isaac dressed and checked his phone. There was nothing new to see, bar an email from Jane. Something about a particularly inquisitive blogger. Apparently, he had a fan site now. Fucking hooray.

Jane would fix it. She always did.

Setting his phone aside, Isaac pulled out the little map from the back of his welcome package. Despite the size of the hotel, everything was laid out fairly logically. Within ten minutes, he found himself entering the private parlour.

It was, thankfully, on the smaller side. It was annoying to realise he had a grasp on the average size of a parlour, but he did. This one was cozy, with masculine decor. The walls were plain, and a fire burned merrily in the stone grate. The room was littered with the kind of deeply comfortable chairs a man actually felt confident about sitting down in—despite the obviously high-quality leather with which they were upholstered. All in all, this was a room Isaac might safely occupy.

Predictably, since he'd rushed down here, the place was almost empty. The girls were nowhere to be found; even Mark was absent. The only occupants of the room were two women curled up near the fire, talking quietly amongst themselves.

One woman—though she was more a girl, really, with cheeks like ripe plums and wide, dark eyes—was facing him, but the other was sitting at such an angle that he mostly saw the back of her head. They were laughing amongst themselves, chattering rapidly, but when the first girl saw him, she fell silent.

And wasn't that just the effect a guy wanted to have on innocent young women? *Sigh.*

As he approached, the dancing flames dragged shadows across the other woman's profile. She turned, following her friend's gaze, and, too late, Isaac recognised her. He stared, unable to hide his confusion.

Lizzie.

The stuck-up ice princess had... friends? Or at least, people she spent time with, who talked to her willingly? That seemed to imply she was capable of being pleasant.

Who the fuck saw that coming?

But it made sense. Of course it did. There was nothing wrong with her, not really. It was him. It was always him.

It was far too late to turn around and disappear, as much as Lizzie clearly wanted him to. The graceful line of her jaw was even sharper than usual, and her brown eyes flashed with an emotion he couldn't quite identify—but he'd bet his balls it was a negative one.

Still, she stood up and gave him a polite, if hollow smile. Always the lady. He didn't know how these women did it—whether it was through training or simple birthright, they always maintained a vague air of control. Or, in Lizzie's case, an absolutely stifling air of control.

Isaac tried to imagine his mother smiling like this at someone she despised. Tried, and failed. He'd take her unrepentant honesty any day of the week.

"Hello, Isaac," Lizzie said levelly. She took her friend by the arm and led her forward, a lamb to the slaughter. "Do you two know each other?"

The girl shook her head solemnly. Everything about her, from the way she moved to the smile on her face, was hesitant. Isaac found himself in the uncomfortable position of wanting to put another person at ease while barely managing to feel at ease himself.

"Hello," she said softly.

He held out a hand for her to shake and said, "Isaac Montgomery"—because he was all about full disclosure. Plenty of people didn't want to associate with someone like him.

For example, one particularly infuriating dance teacher.

But this girl either didn't recognise him or didn't care about his reputation. She shook his hand, her grip gentle, and murmured, "I'm Candice. Candice Cooke. But everybody calls me Candy."

The name triggered a faint memory. He frowned. "As in, Aunt Candy?"

"Oh, yeah." And though her dark skin might hide it, he'd swear she was blushing. "That's me."

This was Aunt Candy? The famous online relationship expert —the one who'd gotten a deal with Spencer Publishing after her blog took the Internet by storm, or something like that? She couldn't be more than 20 years old. She certainly didn't resemble the stylised cartoon that adorned the cover of her book. *That* Aunt Candy was at least thirty years older and much homelier.

Isaac found himself looking at the girl with something close to admiration. However few years she had under her belt, there were clearly more than enough brains in her head.

"Candy," Lizzie said brightly. "I don't suppose you could hunt down the girls for me, could you? They're probably still in their suite and I'm sure they're at each other's throats as we speak."

"Oh, yeah," Candy smiled. "I bet they are!" Her accent, he noticed, had none of the effortless precision Lizzie's held. She spoke like a normal human being. Somehow, he'd never expected to see Lizzie smiling at anyone who didn't talk like the Queen.

But that was unfair of him. It was probably just criminals she had a problem with.

Candy tripped out of the room with a little wave, and Lizzie watched the younger woman go with what appeared to be fondness. But then her gaze turned to Isaac, and he watched its warmth disappear. It was strange how her eyes could be soft as melted honey and hard as stone all at once. She was a woman of contradictions.

And he didn't like that at all. He *didn't*.

"Smart move," he heard himself say—and then came shock. Because somehow, his mouth had spoken without permission from his brain. Usually, he had to force his voice out into the world, and now it was taking solo trips? What the fuck?

She arched a brow, folding her arms over her chest. She was wearing an oversized jumper that drowned her figure, hanging almost to her knees. Thank God. Because the last time he'd seen her, her thighs had been worryingly distracting.

"What do you mean?" she asked innocently.

"Sending your friend away. She seems too sweet to survive five minutes with me." His tone was as close to scathing as it ever would be. She seemed to get the message. She shifted her weight uncomfortably, and her lips parted. Her pupils dilated. Fear?

Then she said, "Is it hard?"

For some reason, the question pointed his twisted mind to the state of his cock—which was starting to take a disturbing interest in the conversation.

But she didn't mean that. She couldn't. Unless she was one of those women, the kind he'd come across more and more as his reputation grew. The kind of woman who would happily fuck someone they considered subhuman, just for the thrill of it.

And though he'd thought he despised her already, somehow the thought of Lizzie being like *that* made him absolutely furious.

"Is what hard?" he asked through gritted teeth.

She smirked. "Convincing yourself that you're the centre of everyone's universe."

Ah. Direct hit.

There she stood, her skin shining in the firelight like topaz, her dark hair pulled back in a way that should've looked awful, but only emphasised the loveliness of her features—those full lips, that broad nose, her wide eyes. Now, at the precise moment when he disliked her most, the fact of her beauty—that thing he'd tried so hard to ignore since the very first moment he saw her—hit him harder than ever. Jesus fucking Christ, even her ears were adorable. And that was just unfair.

"You're pretty fucking bold," he said through gritted teeth. Because it was true, and he wasn't sure if he admired or despised her for it.

She arched a brow—and then he had to wonder if she was reading his mind, because she said, "Does that bother you?"

He spoke without thinking. "*You* bother me."

"And God forbid anything get under your skin," she whispered. It was treacherous, that whisper. It made him want to lean in. To watch the way her lips kissed each consonant.

"Bet I bother you too," he whispered back. "People like you— you don't like it when guys like me end up on top."

She smiled indulgently. "Oh, my darling. Is that where you think you are? On top?" She shook her head, taking a step toward him. "No. You're a tool. Mark's tool, actually. Maybe one day you'll be someone else's. And I'm sure they'll pay you handsomely for the pleasure, just like Mark does, but you'll still be a tool."

Fury shooting his control to pieces, Isaac surged forward, crowding her. So she thought he was a monster, and a fool besides. Let her have it, then. Let her have just what she wanted. No doubt she always did.

He stood over her, looking down into her pretty face, his breath raw and ragged and loud in the silence of the room, and he waited, studying her bottomless eyes for… something. Satisfaction. Vindication. Even fear. Anything, anything at all, as long as it meant that she *saw* him.

There was a smile tugging at the corners of her lips. It was soft, and it was mocking, and it was a lie. He knew because her eyes were shuttered completely—but back in Oxfordshire, they'd displayed her hatred clear as day.

She was hiding. He had no idea why. And that shouldn't have intrigued him, but it did.

"You are the best torturer I've ever known," he said softly.

Maybe he was imagining it, but her eyes sparked a little at that.

"I learned from a great teacher," she murmured. That threw him. Who in this woman's pampered life could possibly have shown her this—how to reduce another person to dust with nothing but a glance? "Are you trying to scare me?" she asked.

"No." A moment ago that would have been a lie, but now it was true. Suddenly, Isaac realised what he was doing, and hated himself for it.

His size was intimidating; he knew that. Once upon a time, using it to his advantage had been a necessary habit. But there was no need for that now. And using prison tactics against somebody half his size was nothing more than the work of a coward.

He took a breath, stepping back. Let his eyes slide closed for a moment so that he could concentrate on the floor beneath his feet. It would do. The fire helped. But he needed to get outside, and soon.

He opened his eyes and forced himself to meet her gaze. "Sorry," he said. "Shouldn't have done that. Won't do it again."

She arched one delicate brow. "Do what?"

So she wanted to make this difficult. Well; that was her right. "I won't... lose my temper."

"Is that what just happened?" She cocked her head. And then, to his surprise, she stepped toward him. Closer and closer until there was nothing but a breath and a foot of height between them. Until she rose up and up and up, onto her toes, and even their height difference was obliterated. Suddenly her face was so close that he'd only have to lean down—just a touch—to kiss her.

Which he absolutely was not going to do.

"I think I like your temper," she said simply. "It's adorable, really." Her quicksand eyes captured his, and he finally saw something other than blank dismissal in their depths. Something he'd never expected to see, not in a thousand years.

Lust. Lust that burned hotter than the flames crackling behind them.

Suddenly, Isaac was afraid.

"I'm guilty," he said. "I'm guilty of every crime I've ever been convicted of."

"I don't doubt it." Was it his imagination, or was she moving closer, leaning into him as slowly as the earth span?

He tried again. "A man is dead because of me."

"I am aware," she murmured.

"I won't meet your parents. You can't use me to make your mother hysterical."

"My mother is never hysterical."

"No, I bet she isn't. I bet she's just like you."

For a moment, the flame of her lust flickered, threatened to die. "She is nothing like me," Lizzie said, frost creeping into her voice. But then her face cleared, and she spoke again. "Have you ever smoked a cigarette?"

"I started smoking when I was ten," he admitted, just to see judgement flash across her face. To remind himself of why he should leave. Now.

But the judgement never came. Instead, she smiled. "I started when I was twelve. To stay thin."

Isaac blinked. *Huh.* Who'd have thought childhood smoking was something they had in common?

"Did you quit?" she asked.

"Had to. Couldn't afford it when I…"

"When you were in prison." She almost said the word without flinching. Impressive, all things considered. "Well, I quit too. I realised after a while that my lungs were more important than my waistline. But sometimes… when I really need it—"

"When you have to," he said, understanding dawning.

"Yes," she nodded. "Sometimes you have to. And there's no point beating yourself up about it."

"It's not like it's a habit anymore," he said.

"Exactly. And they say each one takes five minutes off your life, but…"

He leaned down. Just a touch. His hands went to her waist. Her hands went to his shoulders. And he said, "What's five minutes, anyway?"

"Nothing at all," she whispered.

He kissed her. He kissed her, and she was right: it was nothing at all.

He kept repeating that to himself, in time with the rapid rhythm of his own heartbeat.

It wasn't the moment of coming home after a long, cold, day, shutting the door on winter and sinking into your favourite chair. It wasn't the fantasy of a soft pair of hands and a smile to greet you when you arrived. It wasn't even the memory of a home to go to, one full of love instead of things.

It was absolutely nothing at all. If anyone asked him, that's what he would say. Because how the fuck could a woman who held herself so stiffly feel like pure summer melting in his arms? How could a woman who despised him make him feel like a king with nothing more than the brush of her lips, the flick of her tongue, the pull of her hands on his shirt?

How the fuck could this woman, out of every woman on earth, be the one he'd waited a lifetime to touch?

Their mouths danced, advancing and retreating in a teasing rhythm that echoed the way she toyed with his emotions. Just like her words, her touch was laced with challenge. She took from him without remorse, her tongue hot and demanding, her body pliant against his, and Isaac thought he might do anything—anything at all—to get her into bed. Because holy shit, if she could own him so thoroughly with just her mouth…

He was doomed.

As suddenly as she'd come to him, she took herself away. Pulled his slice of heaven from his hand, and really, at this point in his life, he should expect that, shouldn't he?

He'd once thought that she didn't seem fairy-like, but in this moment, she was all magic. She stood panting and wide-eyed, with her lips parted from his kiss and her fingers pressed to her cheek.

She was regretting it already. She must be. But it had been so perfect while it lasted. Just like the single cigarette you had to have.

Then she whispered, "The girls are coming." And the sounds of the outside world filtered through his lustful haze. He heard familiar voices, unrepentantly loud in the way only a kid's can be.

Isaac sobered instantly, adjusting the erection straining against his jeans and wondering exactly what he'd done to make fate treat him so cruelly.

Oh, wait; he already knew the answer to that.

"I'm going to dress for dinner," Lizzie was saying, touching her hairstyle self-consciously. Smoothing what was already smooth, as if her hair would be so foolish as to disobey her.

"Dress?" he echoed. Really, it was no wonder people suspected his work was ghost-written. What was it about conversation that erased his ability to string a sentence together?

But she said "Yes," as if she understood exactly what he meant. "There's a dress code." She headed for the open door, her steps quick and light. "Didn't you read your welcome package?"

"Ah…" Not really. But his answer didn't matter; she was already gone.

If it weren't for the sound of the girls cooing her name as they passed her in the hall, he might think she'd never been there at all.

CHAPTER TEN

ISAAC MONTGOMERY COULD WEAR the shit out of a suit.

Which, Lizzie told herself briskly, was not something she should notice. Her task didn't require admiration; only the imitation of it.

But Jesus Christ; the way his roughly hewn jaw and sharp eyes contrasted with the sleek, black three-piece? The way those impossibly broad shoulders filled out his suit jacket? There wasn't a soul on earth who could avoid noticing that. Even surrounded by vast, glittering chandeliers, facing the floor-to-ceiling windows that lined one side of the chateau's Michelin-starred restaurant, it was Isaac that drew Lizzie's eye. His body, his beauty, and his utter separation from everything around them. He may as well have been a thousand miles away.

"You alright?" Candy muttered under her breath, stabbing awkwardly at the leafy garnish on her plate.

"Fine, darling. You don't eat that part, by the way. It's for decoration."

Candy's lips twisted wryly. "Why's it on the plate if I can't eat it?"

"Don't ask me." Lizzie nibbled delicately at her sea bass, hiding a smile.

"Whatever. What did you and Isaac talk about, earlier? After I left?"

That wiped the smile right off Lizzie's face. Chewing carefully, she let her gaze travel slowly around the table, avoiding Candy's knowing eyes. As it was the first night, Mark had arranged for them all to eat together. That gave Lizzie plenty of faces to study as she avoided her new friend's question.

Beside Lizzie sat the girls, who had been giggling amongst themselves throughout the meal. On the other side of Candy was Sir John Barrett, a gruff, old military man whose non-fiction tomes were apparently quite popular. His greying eyebrows were bushy enough to match his impressive moustache, and he held himself with a conscious care that Lizzie respected. His piercing, blue eyes and red-tinged cheeks gave him the appearance of an especially grumpy and grizzled Santa Claus.

Next came Kate Winters, a bubbly woman in her mid-thirties with glossy, dark hair and unnaturally white teeth who wrote yummy-mummy cookbooks. She appeared to be unimpressed with French cuisine, thus far. If Lizzie recalled correctly, Kate fed her three children a vegan, gluten-free, plant-based diet. The poor woman was glaring at her lonely plate of sautéed mushrooms with something close to murder in her eyes, but what could be done? The French, behind all their sophistication, were a nation of comfort eaters. Kate, it seemed, was not.

Beside Kate sat Clarissa, who was sparkling and vivacious in a lavender-grey gown that matched the restaurant's icy decor. Had she come down earlier, to coordinate her outfit? That was what Mother would do. Lizzie was impressed. Echoing one's surroundings was key to the art of effortless belonging.

Mark sat with his wife, directly across from Candy. He matched the room too; or rather, his cold, colourless gaze favoured the silver waistcoats worn by the restaurant's waiters. His tie and pocket square were of the same shade. As Lizzie watched, he turned to the man on his right and murmured something under his breath with a charming smile.

The man on his right was Isaac.

The display of camaraderie sent disgust crawling over Lizzie's skin. Mark was plotting to destroy this man—to blackmail him into submission for some nefarious purpose—yet had the audacity to behave as though they were friends.

But then, she was just as bad. Wasn't she? Lizzie bit her lower lip as Isaac grunted in response to Mark's words. God, the silent, brooding man was infuriating. His scowling presence was like a thunderstorm settled directly over their table; he'd barely deigned to say a word all evening. His reticence grated against every inch of Lizzie's society-trained nerves. She could quite happily throw her salad fork at his head.

And yet, just an hour ago, she'd kissed him.

God, what the fuck had she been thinking?

Without warning, Mark turned his head, catching Lizzie's gaze like a sprung-trap. His eyes bored into hers, and she knew exactly what she *should* have been thinking: *Protect Olu.*

Only she hadn't been.

Isaac shifted uncomfortably, as though the furniture was too delicate for his large frame. And that single movement reminded Lizzie of what had truly passed through her mind as she'd brushed her mouth against his.

That if his presence alone could make her feel so much, surely his touch would set her alight.

"Lizzie?" Candy prompted, nudging her beneath the table. "Are you listening to me?"

Crap. Tearing her focus from the men across the table—her demon and her soon-to-be-shame—Lizzie pinned her smile firmly in place as she faced Candy again. But then she saw the knowing arch of the younger woman's slim brow, and she let her facade drop.

She'd been doing that a lot, recently. She had no idea what it meant.

Except weakness.

"We can't talk about it when he's sitting right there," she murmured.

"Why not? He can't hear us."

"How do you know?"

Candy smirked. "He's not paid attention to a word said all evening."

Ah.

"Because he's been so busy trying not to stare at you."

Wait. What?

"I—I beg your pardon?" Lizzie stuttered.

Candy chuckled. "You sound like the bloody queen sometimes, you know."

"Sorry. But what do you—"

"Don't bother being all coy. Just give me the gossip."

Shaking her head, Lizzie sighed. "I don't know," she whispered. "He's so… grim. And anyway, Isaac is not interested in me. He thinks that I'm… stuck up."

"You are," Candy said immediately. "But that doesn't mean you're not a nice person. You just have to work a bit harder at it."

Laughing despite herself, Lizzie rolled her eyes. "My, how you flatter me."

"Someone's got to tell you the truth. But listen—I think you're wrong about Isaac. I think he's very interested in you. And you should trust me on that. I know things."

Lizzie picked up her napkin, patting gently at the corner of her mouth to hide a smile. For someone so young, Candy was rather decisive. Which was probably how she'd achieved success early in life. Lizzie had often found that being sure was half the battle, in most situations.

And Candy, it seemed, was quite sure about the inner workings of Isaac Montgomery's mind.

At least someone was.

———

SHE WAS TRYING to kill him. It was the only explanation. He would die, and it would be all her fault. She just had to come down here looking like gilded fucking sin.

Lizzie leaned forward, closer to Candy's ear, and the weight of her lush cleavage pushed threateningly at the neckline of her glittering, forest-green gown. It hung off bare shoulders, swirling elegantly around her body like a stormy sea. He had no idea what that kind of dress was called, but he wanted to buy her one for every day of the fucking week.

Only she wouldn't need him to buy her shit, would she? She probably had more money than he'd see in a lifetime, even though he was a rich motherfucker these days.

Her hair wasn't scraped back into its typical bun. Instead, it was pulled up tight in an elaborate, high twist that left the sloping lines of her face as bare as usual. She should have had huge ears that stuck out like jug handles—that would've been fair—but of course, she didn't. Her ears were small and neat, as though they knew their owner often had them on show and wanted to please her. The whole world must want to please this woman. How humiliating that he'd joined their ranks so quickly.

Isaac gripped the arms of his rigid little chair, holding himself perfectly still as he strained to hear Lizzie's conversation. Snatches of words floated to him over the quiet cello music filling the restaurant; words just interesting enough to fill him with frustration.

"Isaac…"

There. Lizzie's voice, plummy vowels and all, murmuring his name as she gossiped with the little agony aunt. Her tone was loaded enough to make him wish he could move closer, could go to her and hang on her every word the way he suddenly wanted to. The way her secret smile commanded him to.

And he'd thought he hated commands. Right now, it was entirely possible that just a word from her could send him to the moon.

She must be some kind of spy. An assassin. A demon. Something, no matter how outlandish, that would explain the transformation her kiss had wrought in him. She must've curled a pill beneath her tongue and slipped it between his lips—a pill that stole his good sense, maybe. Drugs, or magic. Those were the only things that could have him panting after a woman he fucking hated.

Because he did hate her, even now. He had to. She was a toff, and up her own arse besides, and she blew hot and cold, and she thought she was better than him, and she was right.

He absolutely hated her. He wondered what she looked like when she came. Which had nothing to do with her being his mortal enemy.

Wait—why was she his mortal enemy, again?

Effortlessly, Lizzie switched from her conversation with Candy to engaging the table at large. She let out a tinkling laugh at something the cookbook author, Kate, had said, and even the grim-faced Sir John looked thoroughly charmed. While Isaac sat there like a silent fool, his tie a silken noose, Lizzie lit up the room.

And it was fake. It was all fucking fake.

Everyone was taken in by Lizzie's smiles, by her demure words and artfully lowered lashes, by the way she wielded beauty and charm with razor-sharp precision. They probably thought their admiration of her was organic. That it was all their own; that they had free-will where she was concerned. They were wrong. Lizzie wasn't a sparkling young socialite. She was a con-woman. Isaac watched in fascination as she brought her wine glass to her lips, her slender fingers caressing the delicate stem. She pressed her mouth to the glass in perfect tandem with Clarissa, yet she didn't appear to be looking at the other woman.

But she was. Somehow, she was. And when Clarissa lowered her glass, so did Lizzie. The faint, red outline of her lipstick had smudged across the rim. Perhaps that was enough to distract the table from the fact she hadn't swallowed a fucking sip. But it didn't distract Isaac.

See, what was really pissing him off—what had Isaac absolutely *furious*—was that, even though he could see right through this performance of hers... he didn't want it to stop.

It was brilliant. It was magnificent. She was flawless, perfect in her falsehood. And perhaps he only grasped that because he'd seen her as she really was, utterly guileless in her disdain for him, achingly real in his arms. Maybe if she hadn't been so blunt the day they'd met, he'd be sucked in by her wiles along with everyone else. Whatever the reason, Isaac felt like he was watching the table from a distance, some omniscient overseer laughing at the foolishness of mere mortals. Mortals who thought they'd ever understand a woman like Lizzie.

Hating her and wanting her was bad enough. But now he hated her, he wanted her, and he grudgingly respected her.

This would not end well.

A small hand tapped Isaac's thigh, and he almost leapt from his chair. Almost. But at the last second, he remembered where he was, and who he was with, and his brain overruled the ingrained responses of his body. He turned to find little Ava smiling up at him, her eyes sparkling with mischief.

"Isaac," she stage-whispered. "Why are you growling?"

He blinked. "Not."

"You are," Alexandra said, her head popping out from behind her sister's. "I can hear you from here."

"And you've been frowning all night," Ava added.

"What are you all talking about?" demanded Audrey. Audrey, who was sitting right next to Lizzie. Shit. "I can't hear!" She pouted, and Isaac held his breath, waiting for the commotion to draw Lizzie's attention. He didn't know what he would do if the realest woman he'd ever met turned her grand facade his way, but it wouldn't be polite.

But for some reason, Lizzie didn't react to the noise at her left. She must be aware of it—Isaac was beginning to suspect that she noticed everything. Just like him. Yet she didn't turn around.

Maybe she didn't want to con him anymore than he wanted to be conned.

"You're like Mr. Darcy," Ava chirped, ignoring her oldest sister's whining.

Isaac tapped his fingers against the table. "Who?"

"You know? *Pride and Prejudice*? He's very grumpy and hand-some..." She trailed off, a blush staining her cheeks.

Isaac made a show of looking off into the distance, across the restaurant. Then he turned his attention back to Ava and said, "What? Didn't hear you."

"Oh!" Relief smoothed her features. "Nothing. Isaac, I was wondering..." The sentence hovered in the air for so long that even Isaac felt compelled to help the poor girl finish it.

"Yeah?" he grunted.

"Well. Are you shy?"

He couldn't have been more surprised if she'd tossed her champagne flute of apple juice at him. "Uh..."

"Because I've been thinking, and I believe you are. You're just like Alex, you see? You're very nice, only nobody knows because you won't show them!"

Feeling heat rise in his cheeks, Isaac grabbed his expensive beer—he could tell it was expensive, because it tasted like smokey piss—and took a sip, trying not to choke.

"It's okay if you are, you know," Ava said. "I'm helping Alexandra. I could help you, too! We could have lessons!"

His throat working convulsively, Isaac put down his beer. "Um..."

"Or you could ask Lizzie, if you want a proper teacher. Her grandfather is a viscount."

Of course he was. Jesus Christ. Isaac shook his head. "No. Thanks. Not shy. Just quiet." Which was a lie. His mother had called him shy. When he was a kid, she'd stroke his hair and say to people, "My Isaac, he's right shy bless him. Loves his mam, don't you babe?" And she'd look down at him, and he'd nod stiffly, even though what he really wanted to do was sink into the floor.

"Are you sure?" Ava asked, all innocence. Had he been like this, at thirteen?

No. No, of course not. At thirteen he'd been running drugs on his bike.

He forced himself to nod, just like he used to.

"Well, all right then," she said doubtfully. And she turned back to her sisters. Which was both a blessing and a curse. Now he was free of interrogation. But he was also free to stare at Lizzie.

Throughout the rest of the meal, Isaac watched her

like a hawk. He knew that he was behaving badly—grunting at anyone who spoke to him, barely even pretending to eat the fancy food. He didn't know what half of it was. Never ingest unidentifiable substances; that was his cardinal rule.

By the time the plates were collected, and the final drinks served, Lizzie's image was seared onto his retinas. Why did she have to be so damned beautiful?

She looked up suddenly, catching his eye, and the effortless charm she'd displayed for the past hour slid away. In its place, he saw a flash of something real, something vivid. She was so intense when she looked at him.

Because she hated him. Passionately. He had to remember that part.

But for some reason, he realised, Lizzie was the woman he'd break his rules for. He would never deny her. If she'd only fucking ask for it, he would be her delicious taboo, her dirty little secret, just because he wanted her so much. That knowledge was galling enough in itself.

The worst part was the fact that she wouldn't ask. Because she didn't want taboo; she didn't want a thrill, and her attitude was just fine. She simply didn't like him. Not because she was prejudiced; not because she was used to having her way. She didn't like him because he was a bad person. She didn't like him for him.

And it was becoming obvious that in another life, he could really fucking like her.

"Montgomery!" Mark snapped his fingers in front of Isaac's face. "Come on, man. Do you hear me?"

Jolting to life, Isaac turned to find Mark standing up. The rest of the table was preparing to leave, most of them looking at him strangely.

Except Lizzie. She wasn't looking at him at all.

"Sorry," Isaac muttered.

"Not to worry," Mark said. So fucking magnanimous. "Bit too much to drink, eh?"

Takes more than a pint to get me bladdered, pal. "Maybe. Might go out."

"Out?" Mark echoed.

"Oh, not in this cold, darling," trilled Clarissa, adjusting her ivory wrap. "We're going back to the drawing room for chocolate. Will you come?"

"No. Thanks. Need to clear my head."

"Ah, leave the man be," Mark said. "He's knows what he's about."

Right. Nodding, Isaac turned and sped through the restaurant as though there were engines in the back of his fancy shoes. Rude, probably. Necessary, definitely. The spider-fine weight of eyes on him, creeping across his skin all at once, was too much. He needed to get outside and look at the sky and feel the cold and touch the earth. Or the snow. Whatever. Something.

But first he'd get this awful bloody suit off.

Then he'd feel better. Then everything would be fine.

CHAPTER ELEVEN

COLD HAD A SCENT. It had a taste. Some people didn't realise that, but Isaac had grown intimate with the cold in its many forms, years and years ago. Once upon a time, it had ruled his life each winter. Mam would put him to bed early for the cold, hoping sleep would protect him from the chill she couldn't afford to fend off. And for the cold he'd stay awake, frozen despite his nest of blankets—even as he closed his eyes and slowed his breathing so that she'd never know.

These days, it was just another temperature. Just another feeling. Another scent, another taste.

And it was beautiful. Like the ghost of blood on your tongue after a long run tore up your lungs.

He should write that down. Might be able to use it somewhere.

Isaac stood alone in snow level with his boots, his hands shoved into his pockets and his chin tucked close to his chest. He ignored the frigid air and stared into the distance, at the point where icing-sugar inclines became jagged mountaintops. He could see the ski-paths tracing up and down each slope, and the ski-lifts above them like the ghosts of ley lines over cracked earth.

Only, he couldn't see earth; not for miles. Usually, that would bother him. Would make him itch. But the pine on the wind and the savage cold was close enough, it seemed. His breathing was even; his soul was soothed; his mind was as quiet as it ever fucking got. Quiet enough for the fragments of poetry that chased him to capture the whole of his attention.

He hadn't wanted to write poetry. He hadn't wanted to write at all, when he was young. He'd been so stuck on what 'real men' did, on what was for 'bitches' and what wasn't, that he'd denied himself.

But then everything had changed, and nothing had mattered, and he had written and written and written.

Thank God that prison warden had passed on the journal to a friend of a friend, instead of the shitty poetry—those pathetic lines he'd stuttered over like a baby bird trying to fly. If they ever faced the light of day—

Wait.

Isaac paused, quieting his wandering reminiscence, letting his other senses take over until his sight was a mere blur.

Hearing. That was the sense he needed now. Someone was behind him.

The soft crunch of snow under heavy boots floated to his ears. So soft, the walker might be trying to silence their footsteps. Trying and failing.

Not that he was paranoid. Just… alert.

Isaac held himself perfectly still, every muscle wound up tight and ready to snap to attention. Calculations ran through his mind; not numbers—he'd never trusted their black and white nature—but instincts, subtle and shifting and layered. He judged weight and gait and intention, running through options, potentialities, until he found one that seemed to fit…

There was a crispness in the air that had nothing to do with frost. And light as the steps were, they didn't lack surety. They weren't hesitant, but fluid as any movement could be through a foot of snow. In an instant, he knew. Or did he hope?

"Hello, Isaac."

Her fucking voice. So soft, so sharp. Deceptive. Seductive. Did she even know? Was she even half as fascinating as he imagined her to be? Surely she wasn't. Surely it was all in his head.

Then he turned, and the dam of anticipation broke, and tension flooded free, and he had the answer to his question.

It wasn't in his head. Not at all.

She was beautiful, as she had been at dinner, but in a different way. The vestiges of whatever dark makeup she'd worn were smudged around her eyes. Her brown-sugar skin was squeaky-clean and shining, and the end of her snub nose was red-tinged. She was all wrapped up in designer ski gear, though he couldn't imagine her skiing. But she must. That sort always did, didn't they? Her gloves were so thick, she could barely move her fingers. Fluffy, pink earmuffs protected her ears, and despite himself, he was charmed. He wouldn't expect her to own a thing like that. But then, she was a ballerina, wasn't she? She probably lay down to sleep each night beneath a pink princess canopy.

He studied her, and she studied him. They stood apart, she hovering at the edge of the salted path and he out in the untouched snow, his big footprints damning evidence. He'd destroyed fresh purity for a better view, and he gave not one single fuck.

"Your hair," he said, his eyes going to the familiar bun. The elaborate style she'd worn earlier had disappeared.

She rolled her lips in, touched a gloved hand to her head, and he thought she might be self-conscious. But he must be mistaken.

"I don't like being all done up," she said. "But since it was our first night…"

"So you took one hairstyle down for another?"

She shrugged, her shoulders artificially inflated by her jacket. "It sounds silly when you put it like that."

And now he was sure: she was uncomfortable. He didn't know *how* he knew—her voice was crisp as ever, her eyes cold stone—but he knew. Maybe he was getting used to her. Wasn't that a terrifying thought?

"Why did you come?" he asked, turning back to his view. To his peace. Only he couldn't find the feeling anymore; something bright and unsettling shimmered in its place, something that had him deliciously on edge. Perfectly present. He heard her moving closer, crushing snow beneath her feet.

"I wasn't looking for you," she told him. Her voice was so carefully steady when she said it, he wanted to call her a liar. Except he knew she always sounded that way. The usual cues, the hints he'd learned to notice, didn't apply to her. She added, "I like a little exercise before bed. Something to wear me out."

Like a rocket, his thoughts were thrust into dark, desperate places. Shadowy corners of his consciousness were set alight by her words, images flashing before his eyes. He could wear her out before bed. Was she hinting? Was she asking?

Of course she wasn't. But that didn't stop his pulse from rising, or his cock from swelling beneath all the fucking thermal layers he wore. Shaking his head, Isaac turned to look at her—because that would fix things. She'd be staring at him with all of her disdain, or looking on him as some animal of lust, and it would drain the desire right out of him.

Except things didn't go to plan. They never did, with her. He found her paces away, her gaze soft on him, her face open. The way it had been back in the drawing room, right after she'd…

"Why did you kiss me?" he blurted out.

And just like that, warm eyes turned cold. She was suddenly stiff again, her movement toward him slowing, becoming robotic.

"I don't know," she said slowly. And that just pissed him off. She was infuriating and impossible and sexy as hell for reasons he couldn't define; she apparently controlled both his mood and his fucking cock; and she claimed she didn't know why she'd started him down this pathetic path? That wasn't good enough.

"You don't know?" he gritted out, facing her fully. "You don't know? I thought I was *vulgar*. I thought you hated me."

"You are vulgar," she said, lifting her booted feet high as she moved deeper into the snow. "You are rude and coarse, and I don't appreciate your tone at this minute, thank you very much. But—"

Just steps away from him, she stumbled. Maybe she lost her

balance; maybe some dip or root beneath the snow tripped her up. Whatever the reason, she was falling.

So Isaac caught her.

———

LIZZIE PANTED, her heart thumping in her chest. She was hovering over the ground, arched as though in dance—and that must make Isaac her partner, because one of his huge hands was splayed against the small of her back, and the other wrapped firmly around her forearm. She could feel the heat of him burning through the thick, sheepskin layers of her coat, and the firm pressure thrilled her to the point of indecency. So many good intentions, she'd had, coming here. How in control she'd felt. And now it was ruined, pushed aside in an instant by the wildfire surging through her veins.

Infuriating man. How typical of him to be so awfully divine.

Their faces were close, so close, as he leant over her. The vast sky stretched out behind him, and his eyes matched the inky-blue night perfectly. Stars twinkled from afar and from within his gaze, and Lizzie let every detail of her plan fade into the mists.

It wouldn't work with him. It had to be real.

He pulled her up, drawing her close, bending slightly to meet her. His lips were just a breath away when he murmured, voice low and urgent: "But what? You hate me, I'm awful—but what?"

For a second, her mind stuttered like a record. Her carefully prepared script was useless now.

"But you make me feel like myself again," she said. And then she winced, embarrassed by how breathless she sounded. Even more embarrassed because she was telling the truth.

Since everything changed—her health, her career, her friendship with her brother—Lizzie had become someone she didn't particularly like. Someone pathetic at the best of times and empty at the worst, who performed more than she lived. It was like being at home again, confined by Mother's expectations, but it wasn't Mother at all. Lizzie was doing it to herself, and she knew it, and she couldn't stop.

Unless she was around this man. Something about him—about his intensity, his abrasive nature—revived the woman she used to be. Razor-sharp, proud, forceful, unafraid. Some might say those were not qualities to aspire to. Her parents always had.

But she didn't give a shit.

They were *her*, and she had been missing them, and around Isaac Montgomery, they all came flooding back.

"That's a good fucking reason," he said softly. She blinked. He hadn't heard her meandering thoughts—couldn't have—but he was looking down at her as though he had. As though he knew everything about her.

"Why did you let me kiss you?" she asked. Which was ridiculous; she already knew why. She'd orchestrated the whole thing, after all; become the kind of woman he would want.

But she hadn't been faking it. Not for a minute.

He paused for a moment. She didn't mind. She knew, as silent as he was around everyone else, that he would speak.

Finally, he said, "Trade, yeah?

"Yes. Question for question."

"Right." When he spoke, she felt each puff of air against her lips; saw it coalesce before her eyes. They were still so close. He held her comfortably now, cradling her, and she relaxed in his arms despite herself. As though it were normal that he hadn't let go, that he drew her into the comfort of his broad chest so intimately. They were dancing without movement. Static, like characters in a music box waiting to be wound up.

Then he said, "Because you're beautiful. And I like the way you hate me."

"What does that mean?" she whispered. "You like the way I hate you?"

He shrugged. "You don't hate where I come from. You don't hate my family or my accent or the place I grew up. You hate the things I've done. You hate me for me."

"Ah," she murmured. And somehow, that twisted justification resonated within her. Still... "I wish I could say the same for you."

He jolted, as if startled. Frowned down at her. Said, "Explain."

"Well," she said. "You hate where I come from. You hate my family and my accent and the place that I grew up. Don't you?"

"No," he said, shocking her. Because he wasn't lying. She could tell. "Wanted to. But no."

"Then what?" she asked. "What is it?"

His wide mouth quirked, and her heart jumped at the threat of a smile. But no; false alarm. He was back to his usual scowl. "Why do you think I hate you at all?" he asked, his tone oddly light. For him, anyway.

"I see it when you look at me." With burning eyes. Burning and blue. An ocean aflame.

He shrugged. "You're confusing. Don't act the way you should. Can't place you; don't like it. But mostly it's because... you were right about me, the day we met."

Lizzie blinked. Of all the things she'd expected to hear, that certainly wasn't one of them. And it emphasised a crack in her logic, a question that had been nagging at her for a while.

"Isaac," she said carefully. "I know what they say about you. And I know why you... Why you went to prison. But I'm starting to wonder if I really understand what happened. What happened with the man you—"

He stepped back, his touch becoming instantly impersonal. No longer did he hold her; now, he merely offered stability, a courtesy. Startled, Lizzie regained her footing—which wasn't difficult, considering her excellent balance—and pulled back too. God forbid she hang on to him like a puppy.

Over the last few minutes, he had bloomed under the moonlight like an evening primrose. Now, she expected him to close up again, to slam his walls back into place so fast and so hard that they'd graze her damn nose. But he didn't. He seemed to be struggling, true; the harsh lines of his face became even tighter, and his muscles quivered with that instinctive awareness she'd noticed about him before. But there was a battle taking place behind his eyes, rapid and too bright to understand, like lightning.

Then his face relaxed, as much as it ever did, and the crackling air around them became still.

"Enough," he said. "Let's race."

She frowned. "What?"

And he repeated, "Let's race."

And then… Lord, then. He smiled. She'd never seen him smile. And although she'd noticed the lack, Lizzie had never dreamed that his grin, when it finally came, would be so breathtaking, so unexpectedly sweet. Adorable, unguarded and surprisingly mischievous, as though there was a little boy hiding somewhere inside that terrifying mountain of man.

"All this time," she said. "You've been glaring and moping and brooding in silence, and all this time you had a smile like that?"

And now, God help her, he looked embarrassed, and that was so bloody cute she might just die.

He leant in close, and her breath hitched at his nearness. He murmured in her ear, "Secret."

She said, "Tell me."

"Can't smile in front of people. I get nervous."

And then, before she could fully register the enormity of what he'd just revealed, the little cheat turned away and jogged off toward the hotel. He was starting the race without her.

Indignant, Lizzie began chasing after him, trudging through the snow as quickly as she could. "That's not fair!" she cried. "Where is your sense of sportsmanship?"

"Ain't got one," he called back.

He was moving insultingly slowly. No doubt, he thought that she'd be easy to beat. Well. She'd soon disabuse him of that notion.

Gritting her teeth, Lizzie forced her way out of the snow, reaching the salted path where she could move unhindered. Isaac, with his greater weight, had already broken free of the snow's grasp and was at least ten metres ahead. Determination rising,

Lizzie put on a burst of speed, gratified to see the distance between them shrink rapidly.

He took a casual look over his shoulder, and the shock on his face when he saw her sprinting toward him was hilarious. To her satisfaction, he immediately sped up. He didn't intend to let her win, then.

But she still might.

She didn't doubt that he was fit—his muscular frame hadn't happened by accident. But he was huge, and that would slow him down. She, meanwhile, was strong, and fast. Fast enough to cross a stage in seconds; fast enough to beat him to the hotel's front steps.

She gained on him slowly but surely, pushing herself to the absolute limit, and never mind the nagging worry that her body would make her pay for this later.

But she didn't win, damn him. No; when they finally arrived at the front of the hotel, near-hysterical with laughter, panting and breathless, he was a good few metres ahead of her. She didn't mind; not really. He bent over and slapped his hands against his knees, and she pressed her palm to her heaving chest, and they chuckled and choked and regained their breath, the air turning silvery with the clouds of their fatigue.

His laughter was even better than his smile. Lizzie's heart swelled curiously as she watched him, her own smile fading.

He was shy.

She'd been wrong about him. He was shy.

What else had she been wrong about?

He straightened up, his breathing even now, and moved toward her with heated intent in his eyes. She stepped back once, twice, until her back bumped gently against the hotel's wall. The steps leading up to the grand entrance were at her right, but the doors were closed and no-one was around. He probably knew that—had probably taken in the entire scene at a glance before he came to her with seduction written all over his face.

He pressed his palms against the wall on either side of her shoulders, and the movement sent a heady thrill through her, tearing her breath away once more. His eyes focused on her mouth, and then his tongue slid out to wet his own lips in a move that had Lizzie clenching her thighs. When she'd left the hotel in search of him, she hadn't known how things would go. In fact, she'd been horribly anxious.

And yet, she thought she'd earned an inch of his trust tonight. Because when he looked at her, there was no lingering resentment in his eyes. There was nothing but desire. And as he leant down to kiss her, she thought: I *could do it. I could have him.*

Just like someone had her brother.

Jesus Christ. She was complete and utter scum.

"What's wrong?" he whispered, his breath warm against her wind-chapped cheek. And that just made it worse; because she thought she'd remained perfectly still, and yet the second her thoughts turned dark, he knew.

Something connected her to this man. This man she should never have met. Fate was hilariously cruel.

"Nothing," she lied. God, even she could hear that her voice was stiff.

He straightened, pulling away from her. And she wanted to say, *No. Come back. Fill up my world again.*

But leading him to his doom was bad enough. She couldn't ask him outright.

"Okay," he said. Clearly dubious. "Should I walk you to your room?"

It was unreasonable, but his response—the fact that, despite everything people said about him, he was a fucking gentleman— made Lizzie suddenly angry.

She rolled her eyes. Knew she was about to be awful. Suddenly, recklessly, didn't care.

"I'm not a child," she said acidly. Waiting for him to pull back. To lose his temper in turn. To hate her all over again.

But he folded his arms and eyed her calmly and said, "Wouldn't know, with the tantrum you're throwing."

Her mouth working silently, Lizzie stared up at him. He remained silent in the face of her outrage, impassive.

Finally, she let out a huff of frustration—which she immediately wished to take back, because now it really *was* a tantrum.

Ugh.

Clenching her fists, she gave him a cool nod before turning to climb the stairs, her head held high.

When she reached the top, she looked back, stealing a glance at him.

And the awful man was leaning against the wall, a smirk on his face, staring at her backside.

"I changed my mind," she shouted down. "I do hate you."

"No you don't," he said mildly.

Lizzie stormed inside.

CHAPTER TWELVE

THE ELEGANT PATTERN of the cream *fleur de lis* on his carpet receded, grew closer, receded again. Isaac grunted as he ground out his last few push-ups, sweat blurring his vision. And probably staining this obviously expensive rug. Oh-fucking-well.

He didn't always push himself this hard. He had his routine, devised over years of mind-blowing boredom in shitty cells, and he stuck to it. But when his thoughts took on a life of their own, Isaac had to scour them from his mind. Even if that meant punishing his aching muscles until he wanted to throw up.

Only it wasn't working. Jesus fucking Christ. How long would he torture himself over Lizzie?

Sighing, Isaac flopped onto the floor, rolling over to stare at the ceiling. It was perfectly smooth and blindingly white, just like the untouched snow outside his window, glinting in the morning sun. Mark had already knocked on his door and invited him out to ski, about an hour ago. Isaac had told the man he'd rather fucking die.

Wait; no. He'd just said, *No thanks.*

But it was all in the tone. That's what Mam used to say.

He wondered if Lizzie was skiing. He wondered if he should've dragged himself out there and strapped those ridiculous things to his feet for the chance to speak with her again. Not because he was some smitten stalker. No; he just wanted to test out his theories. It was practically scientific.

See, he'd spent half of last night held prisoner by unfulfilled lust, and during that time, Isaac had come up with three explanations for Lizzie's behaviour.

1. He was projecting his sexual obsession onto her, and she actually found him hideously unattractive.

Isaac would like to think that option number one was unlikely, but the fact was, his social instincts left a lot to be desired. Of course, she *had* kissed him first. But maybe... maybe she'd changed her mind. And he just hadn't caught up.

The possibility stung. He'd move on, for now.

2. Lizzie was a manipulative, spoilt brat with poor impulse control, torn between the attraction they shared and the fact that he wasn't good enough to lick her boots.

This theory *should* seem likely. It happened a lot, after all. Half the women he met these days were guilty of similar internal conflicts. But then, none of those women had made him desperate for their touch. None of those women had been Lizzie.

Which left him with the final theory:

3. Lizzie's hot-and-cold routine was actually a defence mechanism that she pulled up when things got real.

See, he knew more than a little about that third option. And, truthfully? It was his favourite. Because walls could be torn down.

Not that he'd be the man to do it.

Ah, who the fuck was he kidding? It was pathetic enough that he'd spent so long mooning over the woman; he might as well stop lying to himself. He wanted her. He wanted everything about her. Badly.

Tutting at his own foolishness, Isaac sat up, his abs screaming at the movement. He'd already torn them to shreds this morning. And that was after all the damn squats.

He'd better shower and eat. If the portion sizes at dinner were anything to go by, he'd need three helpings for breakfast. And it was already past 10.

Mopping his brow with a discarded T-shirt, Isaac heard his phone ring from somewhere on the bed, the sound muffled. He tossed blankets and pointless pillows around until he located his battered old smartphone.

It was Kev. Finally.

Bringing the phone to his ear, Isaac answered, "Yeah?"

"Morning, you grumpy bastard." Kev's hoarse words were predictably sarcastic, but his tone was off. Far too serious.

Isaac frowned. "What's up?"

"Nothing we didn't expect. Finally got the contract—they took their bloody time screening it."

"They don't like you working."

"It's not work. It's a favour for my mysterious benefactor."

Isaac rolled his eyes, heading toward the bathroom. "Not your benefactor."

"My wife and kids are living in a house you bought. You're my benefactor."

Isaac simply grunted.

"Listen; you were right about this contract."

Coming to stand before the bathroom mirror, Isaac stilled. "Yeah?

"Yep. There's a shit ton of bullshit hidden in here. Starts at II, 4. a) 1—"

"Kev. English."

The other man sighed down the phone. "He's having you over, mate. By the way, this kind of shit is why you need an agent. But I already know you won't listen, so let me shut up. Sign this, and you give up all rights to the last two books along with the next."

Frowning, Isaac dragged a hand over the thick scrub of his stubble. He should probably shave. In fact, he thought, remembering the delicate skin of Lizzie's cheeks, he should definitely shave.

Wait. Focus.

Turning away from the mirror, Isaac leant against the bathroom's marble counter. "Right. So we…?"

Kev puffed out the air from his cheeks, a familiar habit. Isaac could almost see his old cellmate now: his narrow face would be pensive, his bulging eyes wide. "I don't know, mate. Could draw up a counter-offer. But the way he's shafted you here, I don't see as you'd want to keep working with him."

Isaac clenched his fist, then released, feeling the stiff joints ease up. "Who else?"

"What, you ain't got any fancy writer contacts? No publishing buddies? All these bloody soirees you go to, mate; you gotta start making connections."

Isaac snorted. "Don't like 'em. Don't speak. You know that."

"True. Alright; what about this publicist woman. Jane. You like her, eh? She must know someone who knows someone."

Jane. At the thought of her—she of the iron hair and steely spine—Isaac brightened. "Yeah," he agreed. "She'll help."

"Good. Cuz this contract's a pile of wank. Cheeky bloody fucker. But listen—don't have him out, yeah? Not until you finish this little holiday. I know what you're like. Keep it light, mate."

Isaac grunted.

"I need a yes on that one, son. Behave yourself. Alright?"

Isaac rolled his eyes skyward. But he felt himself smile, just a little. "Alright."

"Good. Now, how's things? Been skiing, your highness?"

"Nope."

Kev chuckled. "Don't blame you, mate. T'ain't natural. You enjoying yourself, anyway? Anything kicking off?"

Isaac thought of melting eyes and warm lips and wide hips. He thought of easy laughter and easier words.

He said, "Nope."

"Thought not," Kev muttered. "Bunch of boring pricks."

"WELL DONE, AUDREY. YOU MAY GO."

Her skin rosy and glowing, Audrey sank into a swan-like curtsey that looked out of place in the small, modern sports hall. The hotel was so elegant, Lizzie had assumed there'd be a studio somewhere in the building. But no. The Spencers had to hire out one of the gym's private rooms, bursting with high-tech exercise machines.

Call Lizzie old fashioned, but she preferred bare wood and a barre. Still, at least there was a mirror.

"Thanks, Lizzie. I'll see you later!" Audrey glided off in her practice skirt and leotard, happy to roam the halls barely dressed. A year ago, Lizzie would have done the same. But once she'd left Paris, modesty had crept up on her like a hyena in tall grass. A lifetime of being forced to strip in the wings had been erased within months. Shaking her head, Lizzie threw on her hoodie before packing up her little portable speakers.

At least she'd gotten to practice with Audrey. Teaching the girls together was fun, but teaching Audrey alone was especially satisfying. Demonstration yielded swift improvement, as well as allowing Lizzie to work on her own technique. And God, there was nothing better than dancing in tandem with another brilliant body, sharing every *assemblé* and pirouette.

Heading to her room, Lizzie planned the rest of her day— which was gloriously free. She couldn't ski, of course, and she'd told Audrey the same. They'd both be fools to risk their ankles. But the hotel had many facilities hiding within its elegant rooms, and she'd have plenty of time to explore them.

For now, though, Lizzie had a simpler pleasure in mind. Finding her room, she slid her keycard into its slot and entered the luxurious little space.

She was on a lower floor than everyone else, which meant a smaller room. Didn't matter; she was staff, after all. Even though everyone thought Mark terribly thoughtful for bringing her, the truth was that it had been an afterthought; a last-minute plot devised to fit his twisted needs.

And it was working beautifully. After a single day, Lizzie had wormed her way into Isaac's good graces. Who knew she'd be so sickeningly good at falsehood?

Actually, it shouldn't be a surprise; as anxious as it made her, Lizzie had always been a performer. Around Isaac, though, the lines between masquerade and reality blurred. When she was with him, she didn't experience that familiar anxiety. She didn't *feel* like she was faking it.

But she was. Wasn't she?

She had to be. That was the bottom line.

Pausing in the middle of her room, Lizzie was struck by a sudden thought: if she did this—if she trapped him, betrayed him —Isaac would never forgive her. He would never look at her with openness in his eyes, never laugh with her. Never kiss her again.

Just as quickly, Lizzie pushed those thoughts away. Nonsense. Utter nonsense. She didn't want his laughter or his kisses; what she wanted was her brother's security. And for that, she would commit any crime.

Her good mood evaporating, Lizzie made her way to the room's mini-fridge, which hid behind a lemon cupboard door. It was almost lunchtime. She needed to eat, and she was pushing it, time-wise. The signs were easier to recognise, now. Now that she was used to them.

Next time, she wouldn't get carried away. She'd follow her routine to the letter, to the second. That was important, she knew, if she wanted to maintain her level of activity; if she wanted to keep her strength and avoid the kind of complications that might stop her dancing completely. She wasn't a child, to hurt herself in an act of pointless rebellion.

This Lizzie told herself, again and again, fighting the resentment that still clung to her soul.

After testing and noting down her blood sugar, Lizzie undressed and took her insulin. She'd had a discreet word with the hotel manager yesterday afternoon; now her little fridge held a variety of small sandwiches, their crusts daintily removed. Lizzie set a timer, and when her fifteen minutes was up, she devoured seven of those ridiculous little sandwiches without pause.

She waited. She tested again. And then, finally, she ran herself a bath.

God, she loved baths. Showers were delicious, refreshing and invigorating, but baths—baths were pure decadence. Or at least, they were the way Lizzie had them. She turned the taps on full blast, pulling out a dedicated little wash bag from her luggage. Bath salts, bath bombs, little scented samples of bubble bath, shimmering body wash, various lotions and oils; she laid them all out meticulously on the bathroom counter, dashing some of their bright, glimmering contents into the tub as needed. She found her other wash bag—there were three in total: body, hair and face—and pulled out a tub of deep-conditioner and a wide-toothed comb. Might as well.

With a sigh, she faced the mirror, reaching up to tug the hair tie from her bun. Off it came; and then she rolled her hair out from around the soft, spongy donut that gave it shape, until only a long, twisted ponytail remained. One of the many reasons she kept her hair up: no tangles. It made wash day that bit less painful.

She took out the ponytail holder, but her hair remained comically in place, as usual. It would be trapped in the ghost of a style until water hit it, and then the tight curls she'd brushed out would spring back into place. Lizzie filled the sink with cold water. Then she dunked her head.

Ah.

Something about that freezing shock made the warm bath that followed a thousand times better. Maybe she was strange. Olu always said so. Whatever. She didn't care; it felt good.

Holding the weight of her wet hair, Lizzie wrung out the dark mass. Then she opened her deep conditioner and slapped it on haphazardly before winding her curls up on top of her head. It'd hold.

And now, everything was in place. Her satisfaction rising, Lizzie stepped into the steaming water, clutching a rose bath bomb. Sinking into the luxuriously wide tub, she plopped the little pink ball down and watched it fizz. She still smiled like a child at the sight—the way the pink bubbles popped and spread, the way the bath bomb zipped around the surface of the water as it dissolved. Her aunt used to buy these, her father's sister. But

Auntie had married an American years ago, a man whom Father described as *a disgrace*. There had been no visits.

Of course, Lizzie thought, she was a grownup now. Her parents had no control over her. She could do whatever she wanted, including locate her aunt.

Maybe she'd call Olu about it. Eventually. When talking to him felt less like choking on her own lies.

Then again, he'd been hiding things too, hadn't he?

As soon as that poisonous thought whispered its way into her mind, Lizzie felt guilty. It wasn't the same. It wasn't the same at all. She was choosing to work through her diagnosis alone—but Olu likely felt he had no choice whatsoever. He must have been hiding from their parents, burying pieces of himself, before she was even old enough to speak. Lizzie couldn't imagine what that was like.

Maybe it had become a habit. At least, she hoped that was it. She hoped that was why he hadn't told her. Because surely —*surely*—he couldn't think that she'd react the way their parents would.

Surely he must know that it was he and Lizzie against the world. No matter what. Always.

Closing her eyes, Lizzie sank further into the tub, letting the rose-tinged vapours melt her frown away. There was no use thinking about it. She would do this for her brother, and she would use the information she gained to win back those pictures. She would destroy them. And then, she swore to herself, she'd tell Olu the truth about her illness. They'd rebuild their relationship. She would let him try to fix things, the way he always did, because that would make him feel better. And maybe, one day, he'd tell her about his sexuality simply because he wanted to.

Maybe.

"Having a good time?"

Her heart rate rocketing, Lizzie sat upright, water splashing everywhere. The thick twist of hair atop her head began to unravel, but she barely noticed as she wrapped an arm around

96

her chest, staring wide-eyed at the man who had broken her peace.

He stood in the doorway, leaning against the frame as though he had every right to be there. As though it were the most normal thing in the world.

Mark.

"What the fuck are you doing?" she hissed, her voice sharp as ever. But she wasn't angry. She didn't have room for anger. Because she was terrified.

He walked into the little room, trailing his fingers along the counter, casting a smile over her crowd of toiletries. "How sweet," he murmured.

"If you touch me," she said, "I will carve out your eyeballs with a dessert spoon."

He looked at her, apparently startled. "Oh, Lizzie. No need for dramatics. I assure you, I have no interest in…" He let his gaze drift over her body, his lip curling. "That."

"Good." She gave him a level stare. "Because I'm not joking."

He rolled his eyes. "I'm sure. Now, onto more important things: why is Isaac having lunch with my wife and daughters while you hide away in your room?"

"Mark," she replied, her voice just as light as his. "How the fuck did you get in here, and when will you leave?"

He arched a brow. "I paid for your room, my dear. Did you really think I'd have no way to access it?"

The last of her bath bomb fizzed through the water in front of Lizzie. As fury finally overcame fear, she grabbed the pink clump and threw it at him. It hit him squarely in the chest, sliding wetly down his slick, grey suit.

He looked up at her with murder in his eyes. "I hope you haven't just stained my Costello."

"Buy another," she said. "It's not like you can't afford it."

Something in his reptilian gaze flickered. His thin lips set. He remained silent. And realisation dawned.

"Unless you can't," she said slowly.

He stiffened. "Elizabeth. Focus, please. While Isaac, for whatever unfathomable reason, seems to find you… compelling, I'm sure you'll need to put in some work to complete your task. Lying around on your back won't help unless Isaac is also present. So get a bloody move on." After snapping that last sentence, he turned and stalked out of the room. Moments later, she heard the soft click of her bedroom door shutting.

Lizzie lay against the hard porcelain, the water feeling suddenly cool. A dried rose leaf brushed past her ankle, and she held back a shriek before realising what it was. Jesus. Fuck. Her heart was in danger of cracking her ribs.

Biting her lip, she slid beneath the water, feeling her hair spread out like a tangle of weeds around her head. She hadn't even combed it. Didn't matter.

Her hair could wait.

CHAPTER THIRTEEN

"SURE YOU DON'T WANT to join us, old chap?"

"Nah." Isaac gave Sir John what he hoped was a friendly look. The older man appeared unimpressed.

"Good for the constitution, is skiing," John insisted. "You ought to see the slopes with us."

Us being Kate and Mark, two people Isaac hardly wanted to spend time with. They hovered in the hotel's vast foyer, wrapped up in thick, protective gear, their skis in hand. Clearly, they were ready to leave. But Sir John had caught sight of Isaac wandering the halls after lunch, and apparently the old veteran had taken a shine to him. God knew why.

"Tomorrow," Isaac lied. "Busy right now. Need to call my publicist." Which, now he mentioned it, was true enough.

John's moustache trembled dismissively. It was a very expressive moustache. "Publicist! Bah. Glad I'm not a young fellow anymore, or I'd be in the papers like you."

"Yeah," Isaac said wryly. "Maybe."

"Tomorrow, then! I'll hold you to that!"

Isaac waved the older man off, shaking his head. Perhaps he was being paranoid, but he had a sinking feeling that Sir John really meant that.

Jogging up to his room, Isaac thought for the thousandth time that this 'writer's retreat' wasn't much of a retreat at all. In fact, he'd never been so distractingly surrounded by people.

Lunch with the girls hadn't been too bad. Even Clarissa didn't grate on his nerves too much. But being stuck in this stiflingly opulent hotel wasn't doing shit for his temperament. He could always go outside—but then he might be forced to ski.

Of course, there was every chance he'd orchestrated his own doom in talking to Sir John just now. But the older man was too genuinely congenial to ignore. It was rare that people actually seemed to *like* Isaac, and call him pathetic, but he kind of enjoyed the unfamiliar feeling it gave him.

Isaac entered his room with something approaching a smile, pulling his phone from his back pocket. He wouldn't call Jane after all; he'd had enough verbal interaction for the day. But he'd text her, check his emails, try to write something. Follow his routine, let the written word and the bliss that was silence wash over him. He'd been sociable today; he deserved an afternoon of seclusion.

The little email icon on his phone was red and blinking, so he opened that first. Huh. There were a few from Jane, which was unusual—but she'd have called if something was wrong. Wouldn't she? Frowning, Isaac opened the first one—it'd arrived yesterday, apparently—and scanned the contents.

Persistent blogger... Repeated attempts to reach you... Losing her temper...

Isaac relaxed. Nothing was wrong. Jane was fine. Just pissed off by one of his... fans. God, that was a weird word to use, but it was the only one that fit. Apparently, certain people found convicted killers with an attitude problem worthy of fan-worship. And Tumblr blogs. Or whatever the fuck they were called.

A knock sounded at his door and Isaac put his phone down with a frown. Unexpected knocks made him anxious. They reminded him of bailiffs and police raids. Those things were hardly likely here, but his alarm bells still went off.

Old habits died hard.

Isaac strode across his suite and yanked the door open in one swift movement, a scowl twisting his face. "Yeah?" he demanded, ingrained distrust pushing its way to the fore. His eyes settled on the wall across the corridor before lowering to find the person who'd disturbed him.

Ah. Fuck.

It was Lizzie.

She arched a delicate brow as she pushed past him, sauntering into the room. "Charming," she said. "Do you always greet visitors that way?"

He turned his head to gape after her. There she stood, running her fingers over his furniture, eyeing the room as if she were conducting an inspection. *Lizzie*. In his hotel room. Why the fuck...?

"Close the door," she ordered. "And your mouth. You'll catch flies."

Isaac clamped his jaw shut with an audible snap. Then he slammed the door with a single push.

She didn't jump. Didn't even flinch. Just looked at him as if he were a toddler throwing a tantrum, a slight smile curving her lips. Her *red* lips. She was wearing makeup again, the kind a man noticed—it made her eyes darker, smokier, and her lips even fuller than they already were. Her clothes were simple; a cable-knit jumper and thick, woollen leggings. Completely appropriate for an informal afternoon. It wasn't her fault that the material clung to every single one of her curves—and there were many. She couldn't help the way she looked. She couldn't help the fact that her breasts, her hips, her thighs, the softness of her belly, looked like they were made for his hands.

So he should stop thinking about how good she'd feel under him.

Right now.

Clearing his throat, Isaac followed her into the room. He tried to seem calm. Casual. Unaffected. "You okay?"

"Yes," she said simply. She came to stand before his desk, her eyes flickering over the notebook and pen he'd abandoned there.

But she didn't ask; she simply brushed them aside, then hopped up and settled her arse on the wood.

He'd been moments away from sitting down at that desk before she arrived. What he wouldn't give to sit there now, in front of her, and spread her legs and—

"Concentrate," she said, every syllable sharp as a knife.

He shook his head, thoughts scattering. "What?"

"Stop thinking about fucking me. Concentrate." Her voice was deliciously low, husky. The way it might sound just before she came. The word *fucking* should've sounded strange, coming from her lips. It didn't. It just sounded sexy as shit.

"I don't... I'm not... I wasn't thinking about that." He moved toward her, his words as slow as his steps. He felt like he was in some sort of trance. This was a fantasy. Right? Or maybe a dream. Maybe he was sick, and he'd passed out and smashed his skull on the way down. Maybe he was in a coma.

She raised her leg, stretching it out before her in one long, elegant line. The tip of her foot collided with his stomach, stopping him in his tracks. When had they gotten so close? He could reach out and grab her. Pull her to him and take her mouth the way she obviously wanted him to. How the fuck had he ever thought that this was in his head? That she didn't want him? Because now she was here, looking at him with those knowing eyes, and there was absolutely no doubt in his mind.

He was not alone. Lizzie felt this too.

"What are you doing?" he rasped out.

"I've come to torture you," she said. "I think you'll like it."

His cock, already stiffening, became hard as stone. He wrapped a hand around her ankle, desperate for something—anything—to ease the flames she'd stoked with nothing more than her words.

But she shook her head, the fine curve of her nostrils flaring. "I didn't say you could touch," she admonished.

He let go.

"Good." She smiled again, and then she moved her leg. She didn't lower it—no, she brought it up higher, the movement almost unconscious, and held it there casually. She wasn't even wearing shoes, he realised; just thick, fluffy socks with little pom-poms hanging off them, dangling above her head. Pink, like her earmuffs last night. Adorable. But she wasn't adorable right now. She was a goddess.

"Come here," she said, her eyes burning into him. And Isaac obeyed, couldn't even imagine refusing her. He took two more steps until he was almost on top of her, and yet he remembered the rules. He didn't touch. She must have been pleased because she smiled, and said, "Strip."

Well. That was unexpected, but she didn't need to tell him twice. Isaac tore off his T-shirt, then his jeans, and finally his boxers. Each brush of fabric against his suddenly-sensitive skin felt like a caress. His cock sprang free, heavy and swollen and so fucking desperate for her, but she didn't even blink. Certainly didn't look. Her eyes were pinned to his as she murmured, "On your knees."

He sank down to the floor before her. Didn't even pause to consider what he was doing. If he had, he'd have been horrified; Isaac Montgomery did not kneel. Not in spirit, and certainly not in fucking body. Not for anyone. Not even for her.

Only he did. Blood pumped painfully through his cock, but the need in his gut had nothing to do with her beauty and every-thing to do with the way she looked at him. Isaac had no time to think. For once in his fucking life, his mind was as blissfully silent as his mouth. All he could do was feel. And he felt so fucking much.

Lizzie lowered her leg, hooking her knee over his shoulder. Now the space between her thick thighs lay open, exposed, right in front of his face, and he thought he might die at the sight. His eyes ran over her hungrily, taking in the way her leggings stretched over her body, the way the fabric moulded against her flesh, displaying the plump outline of her pussy. Jesus fucking Christ. He felt dizzy. Isaac dragged his gaze up to her face, and his voice was rough and pleading when he said, "Let me."

She cocked her head. "Let you what?"

"Lizzie..."

"You will give me words, Isaac. Because I want them." And then, her tone softening, she added, "It's just me. Alright?" She reached down to cup his cheek, and that first real touch was almost painful in its perfection. Isaac pressed his face into her hand, revelling in its cool softness.

"Alright," he acquiesced, his breathing harsh. "Alright. I want to touch you. I want to taste you. I want to make you come. Let me."

She stared at him for a moment, biting her lip, as if she were really thinking about his words. And then she said, "No. I don't think so."

Isaac was silent for a moment, certain he'd misheard. But she looked at him steadily, and he realised that she wasn't taking it back. She would deny him, and she would enjoy it.

"You can make yourself come, though," she added, as if it was an afterthought. "In fact, I think you should. I'm sure you want to." Finally, she let her honeyed gaze dip to his cock, and then—he wasn't imagining it—her control slipped for a moment. He saw her lips part, saw her eyes widen. But within seconds, she composed herself again, looking firmly away. "You definitely want to," she drawled.

He wrapped his hand around his aching shaft as if he'd simply been waiting for her permission. Maybe he had. "You can't be fucking serious," he ground out, pumping his fist slowly.

And she giggled. She fucking giggled.

Isaac's control snapped.

He met her eyes, held them, let her see every ounce of the lust coursing through him. "If I kiss you now," he said through gritted teeth, "will you stop me?"

She shrugged.

"If I rip off your fucking clothes and put my mouth on your pretty cunt, will you stop me?"

She wasn't smirking now. She was wide-eyed, and though she remained silent, the leg she'd hung over his shoulder tightened as if to pull him closer.

He resisted, as much as he wanted to take that hint and run with it. Setting his jaw, Isaac rasped out, "Answer me." His hand worked his cock faster, gripped his shaft tighter.

"No," she whispered.

He deflated. "You're saying no?"

She reached forward, running her fingers through his short hair. "I'm saying I won't stop you." Then she pulled him up, and he came gladly, pushing her across the desk with a growl.

———

LIZZIE GASPED as Isaac forced her down over the desk, her head protected by the cradle of his hand.

But that hand wasn't still for long. He surrounded her, his weight pressing her into the unyielding mahogany, his hands everywhere at once as though making up for lost time. He kissed her, just as he'd threatened to do, and she didn't stop him. She didn't tell him no. She'd rather fucking die.

It wasn't supposed to be like this. She'd had a plan. She'd devised the perfect way to get what she needed without the sexual submission Mark had hinted at earlier that day. It was all about control, Lizzie had decided; so she would stay in control. And *he* would submit.

When would she accept the fact that Isaac destroyed even the best-laid plans?

Somehow, she'd ended up exactly where she hadn't planned to be: on her back. And it was rather wonderful.

His tongue slid against hers as the firm pressure of his lips massaged her own. His fingers sank into her thighs, and his naked erection brushed against her clothed pussy, and then he shuddered above her and oh, Jesus Christ, she would never be the same.

Isaac dragged his mouth from hers, grazing his lips over her jaw, down the line of her throat. His touch set off fireworks within her, sparks flying behind her closed lids. He'd probably smudged her lipstick to high heaven. The lipstick she'd applied so carefully, thinking there was no way he'd get close enough to kiss it off.

She should tell him to stop. This was probably the most unethical thing she'd ever done. But being with Isaac was like drowning beneath of a wave of bliss; all she wanted was five more minutes, every five minutes, for the rest of time.

Lizzie abandoned her self-control, letting her hands run over every inch of him. His skin was burning hot as if the fire kindling between them was heating his blood as much as it did hers. There was no mistaking the way he wanted her. He pressed his big palm between her legs, against her aching clit, and she stifled a cry at the sweet pressure.

"Don't," he panted in her ear, rubbing her pussy through her clothes in a slow, easy rhythm. "Don't stay quiet."

"I can't possibly—"

"You do whatever you want with me," he interrupted, his voice fierce. "If you want to scream, you scream." He hooked his fingers beneath the waistband of her leggings and knickers at once, yanking them down her thighs. Then he continued stroking, his calloused fingers grazing the hood of her swollen clit, with nothing between them to dampen the touch. Lizzie almost *did* scream.

His other hand pushed up her jumper, squeezing her hip as if the feel of her body alone could get him off. Maybe it could. The thick head of Isaac's cock grazed the sensitive crease at the top of her thigh, the slick drops of his arousal moistening her skin. Her pussy clenched desperately, the rising wave of need within her reaching its peak.

"Isaac," she panted. "I need you to..."

"What?" His hand moved from her hip to her belly, cradling the soft flesh. "Tell me what you want."

But she couldn't. Not anymore.

Lizzie stiffened as he ran his fingers over the tender spot where she'd last injected. It didn't hurt; not really. But the soreness burst through the cloud of desire surrounding her, and suddenly she felt sick. He was touching her because he wanted to, and she...

She had no idea what she was doing. But whatever it was, he didn't deserve it.

Isaac saw the change in her immediately. "What's wrong?" He frowned, pulling away slightly. "Are you okay?"

"Get off." It was all she could say.

He pushed himself off the desk, his biceps shifting. Standing before her, still gloriously naked, he frowned. "Did I—"

"You did nothing wrong." He was the victim here, actually. And with that thought came shame, heavy and hot. Lizzie stood, pulling her clothes into place. Patted her hair even though she knew from experience that all the sex in the world couldn't dislodge it.

Not that they'd had sex. Thank God.

"I'm sorry," she said, the words sticky as caramel on her tongue. But nowhere near as sweet.

"For what?" he asked, his confusion palpable. "What's going on?"

"Nothing. Nothing's going on." She should correct this. Smooth it over, keep him close. But the reminder that she needed him for reasons he could never understand—and would never forgive—only made Lizzie want to push him away.

Rebelliousness is your worst trait, Elizabeth. Don't convince yourself that it's charming; it isn't.

"Lizzie..." He reached for her, hesitant, obviously wary of rejection. Which made it even harder to back away from his touch. But she did it anyway. It was for his own good.

"I have to go," she muttered.

He didn't speak. Didn't move. But she felt his eyes on her as she scurried through the room, yanking open his door.

And she felt his hands on her for the rest of the night.

CHAPTER FOURTEEN

"ISAAC'S LEARNING TO SKI."

Lizzie dunked her biscuit carefully into her tea, ignoring the girls' chatter as best as she could. Isaac's name was coming up far too frequently, and it felt like a slap every time.

The memory of yesterday refused to fade, and she wasn't sure if it ever would.

"He's adorable. I saw him out there with John shouting orders at him. And he was wobbling around like a baby duck!"

Audrey's *Superior Elder Sibling* voice stepped in. "Ducks don't wobble, Ava."

"Yes, they do."

"No; they waddle."

"Girls," Lizzie interrupted, finally looking up from her cup. "Don't bicker." And then, before she could give in to the urge to ask about Isaac, she popped the biscuit into her mouth. It crumbled against her tongue, gingery and delicious.

Beside her, Candy was dunking her own biscuit enthusiastically. She'd lose half of it in the cup, if she wasn't careful.

"He wasn't going to ski at all, but I convinced him." Ava said smugly.

"No, you didn't. It was Alex."

Ava snapped, "It was both of us."

But Audrey remained firm. "No. It was Alex."

Alexandra, of course, was silent.

"Crap," Candy muttered. She'd lost her biscuit.

Lizzie looked around the hotel's quiet little cafe as though searching for strength, a break, or God Himself to aid her. None of the above appeared. So she lured in a waiter with a wave of her hand and murmured, *"Plus de thé, s'il vous plaît."*

"Bien sur, Mademoiselle," the waiter nodded, disappearing for her tea. She could only hope that he returned soon. All this talk about Isaac had her nerves shot.

"What are you going to do this week, Lizzie?" Ava asked, her gaze bright and innocent as ever. "Audrey says you won't ski."

"Certainly not. I haven't since I was a child."

"So what will you do?"

Uncomfortable, Lizzie shrugged. She should be spending her time luring in Isaac, as Mark had made horribly clear. And she'd only made her job harder after yesterday's fiasco. A sexually satisfied man was easy to manipulate. A confused and frustrated man... well.

"I don't know," she admitted, and the girls couldn't begin to understand just how much she meant that.

"You should go to the spa like Mummy," Audrey offered, nibbling on her third truffle. Lucky cow.

"Maybe," Lizzie murmured. It was a good idea, really, but she wasn't sure about wandering around half-naked in front of people. Definitely not Clarissa, with her weekly spa trips and her pedicures and God only knew what else. But still, Lizzie filed the idea away. It would be a nice replacement for the baths that Mark had ruined. And she had to get over this odd disconnect with her body somehow.

She hadn't felt disconnected with Isaac.

"Oh," Ava cried. "Look!"

All at once, the sisters sprang to rapt attention, their noses lifting slightly as though they were dogs scenting the air. Baffled, Lizzie turned to follow their direction of their collective gaze—

Only to have Alexandra of all people hiss "No! Don't be so obvious, Lizzie!"

Well. That was her chastened, then.

Exchanging an incredulous look with Candy, Lizzie turned back to face the girls and said, "What on earth are you three doing?"

Alexandra flushed beet red. Audrey's gaze slid to the white, linen tablecloth. Ava, however, was completely shameless.

"It's a boy," she grinned. "And he's French. And he likes me."

"No he doesn't," Audrey argued. "He's seventeen."

"He *could* like me," Ava muttered.

"You're a child."

"I'm a teenager."

"He likes Audrey," mumbled Alexandra. "Everyone likes Audrey."

The quiet hopelessness in the girl's voice made Lizzie frown. But no-one else seemed to notice.

"Lizzie," Ava was gushing. "Won't you teach us that Parisienne accent you do? It's so sophisticated."

"Perhaps another time," Lizzie said, still watching Alexandra. The middle sister appeared to be deflating breath by breath, like a pin-pricked balloon. Lizzie remembered this part of adolescence well. But had she herself looked so desolate, back when she'd been going through it? Hopefully not, for poor Olu's sake.

"Alexandra," Lizzie murmured, leaning forward to capture the girl's attention. "Seventeen is far too old for you. But you must know that you're very lovely, and charming, and talented. You do know that. Don't you?"

Awkwardly, Alex shrugged. She looked left and right, checking that her sisters were still enraptured, or bickering, or some combination of the above. And then she leaned forward too and said, "Ava and Audrey are both more interesting. I'm... boring."

"You're quiet," Lizzie corrected. "And do you know who else is quiet?"

Alex shook her head.

"Isaac," Lizzie said. She leaned back, watching as that single word sank into Alexandra's mind and brought with it a tremulous smile. The girl looked down into her lap, biting her lip. She was pleased by the comparison, then. Apparently, even though Lizzie wasn't able to galvanise herself half the time, she had managed to say the right thing.

"Oh, he wants us to come over," Audrey said brightly. "Lizzie, Candy do you mind if—"

"Of course not," Candy smiled. "Go for it, babe."

"You two are the best!" Audrey stood, sending a little wave to the mysterious boy behind Lizzie's head, and her sisters followed. As they left the table, Alexandra threw a small smile over her shoulder that warmed Lizzie's heart.

Then Candy said, her voice wry: "I heard that."

Lizzie blinked. "Heard what?"

"*Isaac*," Candy echoed, in a fair imitation of Lizzie's crisp tones. "What was that about?"

"Oh… You know. Just, the girls admire him so much. They spent half the day with him yesterday."

"I know," Candy grinned. "Poor fucker."

Despite herself, Lizzie laughed. "I think he likes how much they—"

"Talk? Probably. Fills all his brooding silences." Then Candy's smile grew sly. "But you like his brooding silences, don't you?"

"Oh," Lizzie murmured absently. "The tea is here."

"You drink more bloody tea than my nan."

They paused as the waiter settled a fresh tea set onto the table with a flourish. But then, as soon as he left, Candy started again.

"Why don't you just admit that you like him?"

"I don't like him," Lizzie insisted.

"Yes you do. You at least want to sit on his you-know-what."

Shocked, Lizzie put down the teapot. It wouldn't do to drop it. "Candice!" she gasped. "I can't believe you just said that."

The younger woman gave her an embarrassed smile. "To be fair, it comes a lot easier when I'm writing it down."

"Good Lord, woman. How old are you, anyway?"

"Twenty-one," Candy grinned. "But don't forget, I am a best-selling relationship expert."

"I ought to ring your mother."

"My mother's worse than me."

Lizzie snorted. Then she clapped a hand over her mouth, mortified. But when her eyes met Candy's, she snorted again, before the both of them broke out into peals of laughter. The kind of laughter that only makes sense to those in on the joke, and makes everyone else extremely irritated. Usually, Lizzie would rather die than cause such disruption in a public place.

Today, she didn't give a damn.

CHAPTER FIFTEEN

LIZZIE TIGHTENED the belt of her robe as she peered through the doorway. It was an unnecessary precaution, but paranoia had been her closest friend since Mark's visit to her room.

Of course, she wasn't in her room right now. And this, she hoped, would be even better than a bath.

Confident that the coast was clear, Lizzie stepped out of the changing room and into the wide, low-lit corridor that would take her to the spa.

Audrey had been right earlier that day; Lizzie needed something to do. A way to relax. And hopefully, since it was well past 11 p.m., there wouldn't be anyone around to interrupt her as she luxuriated in the steam room. Or the sauna. Or the hot tub. Or the rain room.

She'd been impressed by the spa's brochure, to say the least.

Padding across the warm, stone floor, Lizzie felt the air heat as she drew closer to the spa's open facilities. Terracotta walls became dark wood, then a thick, translucent wall of glass bearing the hotel's swirling logo. And then, finally, she came to the archway that would lead her into wonderland.

Oh, my. This would definitely do the job.

Lizzie gazed with growing pleasure at the open space before her. The heated room was almost entirely taken up by a huge, round pool, surrounded by smaller pools with built-in stone seats —or were those hot tubs? The bursting jets seemed to indicate so. At the far end of the pool there was even a cascading faux-waterfall. She'd like to try that out, for sure.

But first, she'd take her time peeking through the slim glass doors scattered about, chic metal plaques above the doorways making each room's purpose clear.

The whole place was completely empty. She could certainly take her time.

Grinning, Lizzie eagerly untied her robe and hung it up by the archway. Her sunshine yellow bikini would do just fine. She shucked off her flip-flops, placing them neatly beneath her hanging robe, before moving further into the room, giddy as a child on Christmas Eve.

She'd already planned out her spa schedule. Looking around, she realised that there was no clock on the wall—annoying. But that was okay; she was good at judging time on her own, anyway. She'd start with the sauna and give herself about ten minutes, if she could handle that long. She tightened her grip on the little bottle of water she'd carried in from the changing room, which was already sweating. It'd be her second in the last thirty minutes, but she couldn't risk dehydrating while she was alone in here.

Unscrewing the lid, Lizzie crossed the room slowly, basking in the relaxing sound of running water and the soothing nature soundtrack that played gently from hidden speakers. Her aching feet felt like putty against the smooth floor, and already she felt her worries slipping away—for now, at least. She'd give herself one night to relax; to forget all the bullshit she was dealing with. Mark's twisted demands, her worries about Olu, the… the Isaac issue, could all wait until tomorrow. She was absolutely determined to relax. She would not fail.

Taking a final sip of water, Lizzie opened the heavy door to the sauna and stepped inside, the heat hitting her like a brick wall. The hiss of water in the air told her that the sauna's steam had just been refreshed; a fact she'd have known by the thick cloud obscuring her vision, anyway. Allowing herself to grow acclimatised to the temperature, Lizzie stood and waited for the steam to calm.

She peered at the tiered benches around the perimeter of the room as her vision cleared, deciding where to sit—or rather, lie. Since she was alone, she'd happily spread out and hog all the space. There—she'd take the highest spot in the corner of the room, just because she liked the neatness of its angles. Her vision clearing, Lizzie moved forwards, ready to clamber up the wood-hewn benches to her right.

But then, suddenly, she realised that the sauna wasn't empty at all. A long, broad body lay across the lowest bench, its contours clearer now as her vision sharpened. It seemed to be a man, with a little towel was spread over his face. His shoulders were so wide, they didn't fully fit on the bench. The rest of him wasn't much smaller, either. She stared, oddly entranced by the golden hair covering his chest, a slim trail pointing the way to his—ah, lower body. Which was covered by another, scandalously small towel wrapped around his hips. It may hide the necessaries, but she could see far too much of his thickly muscled thighs to be decent. She was struck by a wave of heat as intense as it was unwelcome. Because this liquid fire wasn't the sauna's doing: it was desire.

Lizzie stood as if hypnotised, her gaze skipping over the stranger's body like a pebble over smooth waters. She should leave. Right now. Salivating over someone who thought they were alone was unacceptable. She would turn around and give him his privacy. Immediately. This minute.

She stared a moment longer at those muscular thighs, at the scrap of fabric protecting him from full exposure. Her lids lowered as indecent images rose like sauna steam in her mind.

Wait! No! She was leaving. Now.

Gritting her teeth, Lizzie grabbed hold of her senses and turned away, dragging a hand across her face. She was already sweating. The sauna was probably a bad idea, anyway. Dehydration was something she needed to avoid at all costs.

Stiffening her spine, Lizzie opened the sauna door and stepped out, the main room's air now seeming deliciously cool against her skin. She paused for a moment, her fingers wrapped around the door handle, savouring the contrast of the rooms' warring atmospheres.

Then, suddenly, a hand caught her forearm. A broad chest was pressed against her back. An arm wrapped itself around her waist. She stiffened.

And then a low, gravelly voice said, "Lizzie."

"Isaac," she breathed. Because of course it was him. Of course it would be. For Christ's sake, was she tied to this man by some invisible cosmic leash?

But her indignation faded as the weight of his touch sank into her bones. The molten heat in her core—the heat that had risen for *him*—sparked, catching fire. He tightened his arm around her, dragging her close until she felt the press of his hard cock against her back. Lizzie was jolted fully into her own body, conscious of herself in a way she hadn't been for months. This was how she felt when she danced, hitting every beat, holding every position, riding the music and tearing out her own heart.

Connected. Grounded. Herself.

Isaac opened his palm against the soft skin of her belly, as though he needed to feel every inch of her—and this time, the touch didn't pull her out of the moment. In fact, it dragged her under. The rasp of his calloused hand sent a snap of desire through her, as sharp as the sudden lighting of a candle. One minute, she was waiting eagerly for the spark that would push her over the edge—and the next she was burning, burning, burning.

Conscious thought disappeared as she turned, wrapping her arms around his neck. His high cheekbones were flushed, his skin glowing, and his eyes—his eyes were like twin mirrors, reflecting her own need. And fuck, did she need. Lizzie rose up, up, up onto her toes, and she thought he'd lean down to meet her. Instead, he made a rumbling noise deep in his chest and picked her up, his hands gripping her thighs. She wrapped her legs around him and ground her bikini-covered pussy against the thick column of his erection, and he groaned. She flicked her tongue over the throbbing pulse at the base of his throat, and he swore. She rocked against him again and again, each movement catching her clit just right, making her light headed—

"Jesus Christ, Lizzie," he rasped. He stepped back into the sauna, bringing her with him, letting the door swing slowly shut.

He backed up until they hit the bench, and then he sat down, letting her straddle his lap. She reached between their bodies, searching for him, but he caught both her wrists in one hand, holding them tight.

"Lizzie," he murmured. "Look at me."

She dragged her gaze up from his lap—which somehow remained covered by the little towel he wore. Then she rolled in her lips, suddenly shy.

It had all been fine. Great, actually. But then he had to go and say her name like that—soft as a secret. And now she felt that indescribable *presentness* fading, felt the worries and quibbles of her conscious mind popping up to take over.

He put his fingers to her chin, pushing until she was forced to look up fully, to meet his gaze. And the gentleness she found there made things even worse.

"Don't," she said. "Just—let's just—"

"I don't know what you're trying to do," he interrupted, "but I like it. I just need one thing. Yeah?"

She swallowed. "What?"

"Look at me." He slid his fingers from her chin along her jawline, cupping her cheek. "Say my name."

"I..." Suddenly, she felt self-conscious. She was barely-dressed. Her hair wasn't even done, for Christ's sake! She'd let it down in the shower earlier, and now it hung between her shoulder-blades, still dripping. She probably looked like a wet dog.

He smiled slightly, making her foolish heart leap, and when he spoke again, his voice was rich with amusement. "I know you were looking at me before."

"Oh." She felt herself flush. "I'm sorry. I—I didn't know it was you. I mean, I didn't realise that anyone was in here—"

"It's okay," he whispered. His free hand came to rest against her hip, holding her as though she belonged to him. The touch, small as it was, had her shifting in his lap again, the ache between her legs reignited. And he gritted his teeth and thrust up to meet her, as though he couldn't help himself.

There. *That* was what she wanted.

Lizzie did it again, settling into a languid rhythm. She rolled her hips, riding his thick cock through the barriers between them, holding his gaze since he wanted it so fucking badly—why not? She'd give him what he needed, and he'd do the same. An exchange. Fair enough. So she stared into his eyes as she chased her pleasure, using only her thigh muscles, since he still held her wrists in one hand. Didn't matter; she was strong enough to keep this up all night.

Usually, he was impossible to read—he might as well be made of stone—but all of sudden she could see his every emotion. And there were many. So many. His harsh features were raw, animalistic, a twist of passion and need that spurred her on just as much as the pressure of his cock against her clit. But soon, that dull, rough friction wouldn't be enough. Soon, she'd need more. She wanted to know that he would give it.

"I'm sorry," she panted, the steaming air around them stealing her breath. "About yesterday."

He replied through gritted teeth. "You want me?"

"I think I'm making that obvious."

But he shook his head. His hand moved to the mass of her hair, and he wrapped its length around his fist, pulling her head back slightly. "Pretty," he murmured, almost to himself. "So pretty." He meant her hair, she realised with a jolt. He liked her hair. Then he leaned forward, and his lips brushed against her ear as he repeated, "You want me?"

"Yes," she whispered.

"Sure?"

"Isaac. I'm not using you." It should've been a lie, but in that moment, it was the truest thing she could say.

He paused. And then, in the space of a second, she felt the air shift, as though something vital had just clicked into place.

He let go of her wrists and wrapped an arm around her waist, pushing her down on the long, wooden bench. She watched with a slight frown as he stood, gazing down at her with an expression that might have seemed like anger, if she didn't know any better. In truth, this was how he looked when he wanted her—*really* wanted her.

With a flick of his hand, he pushed away the towel that hung low on his lean hips. It fell to the floor, landing in a heap around his feet. And Lizzie was left to stare with satisfaction at the hard column of his cock. It curved proudly up towards his tight ab, the head already shining with pre-cum. She hadn't let herself enjoy the sight yesterday, but today... today, she'd bask in it.

When he wrapped his fist around himself, stroking lazily, she thought she might bloody pass out.

"You looked at me," he said coming to kneel by the side of the bench. "I want to look at you."

She stiffened, waiting for the familiar tightening in her chest, the tempest of anxiety in her gut that always came with exposure, with scrutiny, with the act of being consumed.

But it didn't come. She felt nothing but frantic desire and desperate need at the sight of him on his knees, looking over her like she was dessert.

He studied every inch of her, so slow and methodical that she could almost follow the path his eyes took. First, adorably, he looked at her face. And then he bent forward and kissed her cheek, her brow, her jaw.

"Tiny ears," he said, before biting gently down on one lobe.

"I know. Everyone says that."

"Never—"

"You never saw ears so small, yes, I know." She let out a strangled laugh. She was on the edge of desperation and he was going on about her bloody ears. "Everyone says that."

He chuckled. But then humour faded as he pulled back and continued his exploration, tracing his gaze down to her chest. Still stroking himself slowly, he reached forward and tucked a finger beneath one of the cups of her bikini. His fingertip brushed against the stiff peak of her nipple, and she gasped. Isaac withdrew his finger, looking up at her face. "No?" he asked.

"Yes," she told him, biting her lip. Arching up beneath his hovering hand, straining for more. "*Yes.*"

The corner of his mouth kicked up in a smirk so deliciously arrogant, she didn't know if she wanted to smack him or kiss him. But then he hooked his finger beneath her bikini again and tugged the cup right down, exposing her breast, just like that. And now all she wanted was more of his touch, all of it, everything he had to give.

As if he could hear her thoughts, he pushed away the other side of her bikini top, leaving her completely uncovered. He swirled his thumb around her right nipple, his touch deliciously rough. "Tell me," he said gruffly, and for once she had no idea what he meant—until he bent his head and captured her other nipple, sucking it deep into his mouth, his hot tongue caressing her skin with each pull.

"That," she gasped, writhing helplessly beneath him. "Like that. *Fuck*—"

He raised his head, setting her nipple free with a wet pop, and Lizzie almost screamed in frustration. But all he said was, "I still can't believe you swear."

"Of course I fucking swear," she huffed. Then she grabbed the back of his head and pushed it down toward her breasts again. She heard a snatch of his chuckle before he returned to duty, torturing her sensitive nipple, then drawing as much of her into his mouth as he could, the sweet pressure driving her need everhigher.

Her head curiously light and simultaneously heavy, Lizzie bent her knees, placing the soles of her feet against the hot wood. She reached down with one hand, shoved her bikini bottoms aside, and slid a finger along the wet satin of her slit, adding to the delicious lust that Isaac's lips and tongue ignited. With a sigh, she brushed her clit lightly, so lightly—

Isaac rose up again, but this time he looked down her body, watching as she touched herself. And then, after a moment, his hand slid from her breast, over her belly, to ties that held her bikini bottoms together. He undid them with a few tugs and pulled away the bright material, exposing her completely to his gaze.

Lizzie's fingers stuttered, then halted completely. But he shook his head. "Don't stop," he ordered, and when he turned to look at her, she saw nothing but lust in his eyes. Breathless, Lizzie nodded. She stroked delicate circles around her sensitive clit, drawing out her own gasps, teasing out her own pleasure. And he watched with hunger written all over his face, his hand moving compulsively on his cock, faster and faster.

Then he reached out and slipped a hand beneath her bent leg, his fingers going directly to her pussy. Lizzie's breath hitched as he eased his thumb inside her, just an inch, barely stretching her. Somehow, it was enough to make her head spin.

"I told you," he said, "that I wanted to lick your cunt." The harsh words send a shudder through her, but he continued calmly, his thumb still teasing her entrance. "Do you want that?"

"Yes. Please—"

Before she could finish her sentence, he grabbed her leg and slung it over his shoulder, angling her toward him. He kissed her thigh, his tongue tracing the lightning-bolt stretch marks that decorated her skin. Moving slowly, he dragged his lips higher, his gaze pinned to hers. All her life, Lizzie had been something to stare at—because of her family name, or because she was often standing under a spotlight, demanding attention. She'd gotten it, too: attention, and adoration, and admiration.

But no-one had ever looked at her like this.

Isaac finally reached his destination, and she felt his tongue—hot and wet and firm, and *fuck, so good*—brush against her clit, stroking the aching nub. He forced his broad shoulders between her legs, spreading them wider, and then the teasing pressure of his thumb at her pussy was replaced by his thick fingers. Isaac eased into her steadily as he lapped at her clit, hitting the rhythm she needed. Her body beyond her control, Lizzie's hips jerked against him—but he pressed a palm to her belly, pinning her down. Holding her still while he tortured her with lips and tongue and long, long fingers.

The wave of desire finally broke, sending sprays of pleasure through her blood. She cried out, unable to silence herself—or perhaps, with him, she was simply unwilling. Lizzie slumped against the wood as her climax faded, aftershocks rippling over her skin.

She felt Isaac's fingers slide from between her thighs; felt him kiss the corner of her mouth softly. But the sensations were distant, as if she were on the edge of sleep. Christ, that had been intense; she was ready to pass out.

And then she heard him say, "Lizzie? Are you okay?" But his voice was all muffled. Remote.

Oh, fuck. She *was* going to pass out.

Jolted toward consciousness by the realisation, Lizzie dragged herself up. Isaac wrapped his arms around her and stood, and she barely noticed her bikini bottoms slipping onto the floor, or the fact that he was completely naked and she wasn't far from the same state.

"Out," she gasped. "Water." And predictably, he had no trouble deciphering that fragmented speech. Swearing furiously, he yanked open the sauna door with one hand and strode out into the main room, carrying her in his arms like a rag-doll bride. The cool air soothed her feverish skin and brought her brain closer to working order, slicing through the fugue that had settled over her. She wanted to ask where he was taking her—because they were still moving, though all she could see was the ceiling and his hard-set jaw. But she didn't think her tongue was working properly.

In the end, she didn't have to try. Within seconds, he was opening another door and carrying her into another cool room, one thick with soothing mist. A gentle shower, like summer rain, fell from the ceiling, gliding over her skin. He lay her on a raised stone dais, one designed just like the wooden version they'd defiled minutes ago. And then he pressed his palm to her head and looked down at her with frantic concern in his eyes.

"What's wrong?" he demanded.

"Dehydrated," she managed.

He cursed, stood, then paused, as if he wasn't sure he should leave. But she waved him away—because she felt fine now, really, or at least in control. So he strode off out of the room, and she stared up into the falling mist, blinking when it gathered along her lashes.

Almost immediately, he returned, with several of the red water bottles that the hotel handed out like sweets. He unscrewed the cap of the first, then raised her up in his arms like she was an invalid.

"Stop that," Lizzie muttered, batting him away. Rolling her eyes, she sat up properly and took the water, downing the lot. She felt better already. "Next," she said, holding out her hand for more.

He unscrewed another bottle and passed it to her. "You should've had a drink before you came in," he said.

She guzzled down the rest of the bottle before answering. "I did. Actually, I think I dropped the bottle back in the sauna. Oops."

"Never been in a sauna before?"

"Of course I have."

He eyed her knowingly. "Recent, then?"

"Recent?" She frowned.

"Your diagnosis." His gaze flitted down to her stomach, and she looked down too. Even though she knew what she would find there. Littered over the soft bulge of her belly were countless bruises. Faded mixed with fresh to create a dark rainbow against her brown skin. *Fuck.*

"I… I'm naked," she said foolishly.

"Not completely." He smirked up at her useless bikini, still pushed aside around the mounds of her breasts.

"Oh, bugger," she muttered, pulling the cups back into place. "Jesus! You're naked too!"

"Yeah. Because we just—"

"I know what we did. What if someone comes in?!"

He shrugged. She waited for him to speak. Of course, he did not.

"Oh, for God's sake," she snapped, standing up. And then she wobbled slightly as her world slipped to one side—which rather undermined the impression of authority she'd been trying to create. He steadied her effortlessly, wrapping a hand around her upper arm and holding her in place until her balance was restored.

"Careful," he said.

How helpful.

Infinitely irritated, Lizzie pulled away—as soon as her wavering senses would allow—and stalked toward the door, intent on recovering their clothing from the sauna. Or rather, his towel and her bikini bottoms. He followed quietly, walking as though he wasn't buck naked in a public place. Lizzie, meanwhile, practically ran across the smooth, stone floor.

How ironic that she'd come here intent on relaxing. *Alone.* Now her heart was pounding, her head was spinning, and God damn it, her pussy was still tingling like a traitor. Now was really not the time for this sort of thing.

But Christ, Isaac was rather magnificent, wasn't he?

When he wasn't filling her with impotent fury.

No; that wasn't fair. It wasn't his fault that she'd come over all damsel in distress. It wasn't even his fault that he apparently knew, based on nothing more than a near-faint and a few bruises, that she was diabetic.

Maybe he was psychic. Maybe he'd broken into her room and found her insulin. Maybe she needed more water.

Sighing, Lizzie opened the door to the sauna—only for Isaac to drag her back into his arms like he was pulling her from the path of a speeding car.

"Stay," he grunted, letting go of her. Then he went in, quickly returning with their things.

Her nerves completely raw, Lizzie arranged the scrap of fabric around herself before fumbling with the ties. Everything slipped tragically south at least five times before Isaac gently pulled her hands away, replacing them with his own. In a humiliatingly short space of time, he had her covered up again.

"Thank you," she whispered, avoiding his eyes. Worrying that her own would spill over with the hot, embarrassing tears that had been threatening for the past few minutes.

"Hey," he murmured, nudging at her chin again. Reluctantly, she looked up at him—and was shocked to find not an ounce of pity on his face. In fact, he looked the way he always did. Calm, controlled, slightly intimidating and entirely Isaac.

"Don't worry," he said. "Okay?"

She should've scoffed, or pulled away, or asked him what, exactly, he meant by that. She should have told him that these days, she couldn't do anything *but* worry.

But when she opened her mouth to reply, all that came out was, "Okay." And the word must have been an incantation of some kind because it cast a spell over her pounding heart and aching head and battered pride. As soon as she said it, it became true.

She was okay.

"You need to eat?" he asked.

"Maybe. I'll check."

"Want me to come?"

"No." Granted, this conversation wasn't nearly as painful as usual—it didn't make her want to sink into the earth, or hit something, the way it did every time she visited her doctor. But talking about an illness was very different to living it. And bringing Isaac into her new world of blood sugar tests and insulin shots and controlled chaos was not something she could do right now.

She could barely stomach the thought of involving her own brother, for God's sake.

"Okay," he said.

And that was it. She rolled back on her heels for a second, shifting her weight like a child killing time. He simply stood, that towel back in place on his hips—and it was even more arousing than it had been before, because he wasn't some anonymous figure now. Lizzie knew exactly what lay beneath that towel.

And she wanted more of it.

But that was an entirely different problem, one for a different day.

"I'll just… go, then," she muttered. Graceless as a bloody hippo. Blushing slightly, she turned and hurried toward the archway that would take her away from this entire experience.

"Lizzie," he called after her. She paused, looked over her shoulder in question. And now, if she didn't know better, she'd think that he was nervous. But when he spoke again, his voice was as steady as ever. "Tomorrow, yeah?"

Somehow, she smiled. "Yes. See you tomorrow."

He gave her a sharp nod. And by the time Lizzie reached the changing rooms, she wasn't embarrassed or worried or annoyed anymore.

She was smiling.

CHAPTER SIXTEEN

THE NEXT MORNING, Isaac wandered the corridors of the hotel's vast gym, its contemporary decor and high-tech equipment making the little wing of the elegant building seem like an entirely different world.

This was their fourth day at the hotel, but he hadn't entered the gym until now. Isaac wasn't a big fan of gyms. He thought all the fancy machines and mirrored walls were more of a hindrance than a help; unnecessary trappings that would do nothing but distract him. His routine had been honed from boredom and a determination to improve himself somehow, in some small way, after the disaster he'd made of his life. He focused on weight-bearing exercise because he didn't take tools of any kind for granted.

You never knew when you'd find yourself in a 7-foot square cell without a thing to your name. Not even your dignity.

So gyms weren't his bag. Which suited him fine; the thought of voluntarily spending time in an enclosed, public space made his skin crawl, anyway. But today, instead of following John out onto the slopes for another lesson—like the last one hadn't been painfully unsuccessful—he was making his way down to the little room Audrey had described to him the other day. The studio, she called it.

Because, though he could barely believe it himself, Isaac wanted to talk. Specifically, to Lizzie. Even more specifically, about *them*. And he knew, thanks to the girls' tendency to dump information onto any passing soul, that Audrey's daily practice would finish at eleven.

So, he thought as he meandered closer to the final door in the hall. Right. About. Now...

It was open, just a crack, and music danced through the gap between door and frame, soothing his anxiety. This would be fine, he told himself. Isaac had studied the map that came in his little welcome package; this was a side entrance. He'd wait here until the music stopped, until they wrapped up whatever complicated shit they were doing in there, and then when Audrey left through the main door, he'd go in and talk to Lizzie.

And maybe she'd do that thing she did—maybe she'd retreat into coldness after the events of last night. He was starting to realise that distance was her knee-jerk reaction to vulnerability. But that was okay. Because he knew what to do when she got all prissy.

He knew how to make her laugh.

Isaac leant against the doorframe, and a slice of the room came into view. He saw a mirror along one wall, and in its reflection, a desert storm, spinning with sharp precision across the floor. Lizzie. She flashed in and out of view, and despite his attempts at subtlety, Isaac strained forward, desperate to see more.

She was magnificent.

Her movements were both demure and seductive, delicate and powerful. She rose up in that way ballerinas had, right on their toes, which he'd never understood—it must fucking hurt. Her entire weight rested on that perfectly pointed foot, balanced in a way he'd never seen outside of cartoons, as she whipped around and around. Then, just as suddenly, her turns stopped. She took tiny little fluttering steps on her tiptoes, and now he could see her face—just enough to register deep yearning and raw pain. It was in her creased brow, her desperate mouth, the curve of her shoulder. She crumbled perfectly, folding in on herself, and Isaac had to work to remember that this was just some dance she'd learned—it wasn't real. She wasn't falling to pieces right in front of him. It was a performance. A performance with no audience.

No audience but him.

Except, if it wasn't real—why did it hurt so much?

The music faded slowly, not into silence, but into calm. The tempest had passed and now the raging waters stilled, and Lizzie's body caressed the floor itself like a lover. Isaac watched, transfixed, squinting through the gap, not knowing or caring where the hell Audrey was, just needing to see more, more of this brilliant, magnetic strangeness…

A slow clap began, crashing through the music like a hammer. One, two, three hollow blows, destroying the magic that had unfolded before Isaac's unbelieving eyes. He watched as the reflection that was Lizzie stiffened, fell out of perfection and into reality. She looked up, and he expected to see his own confusion in her brown eyes. But there was no confusion. Only fear.

What the fuck was Lizzie afraid of?

The clapping stopped, replaced by slow, purposeful steps. They clicked across the wood floor, and Lizzie scrambled to her feet as though the devil himself was coming toward her.

Then a figure stepped within the mirror's reach, and with a sinking feeling in the pit of his stomach, Isaac recognised the source of Lizzie's fear. It was Mark.

"Very well done," Mark said wryly. "Beautiful, in fact."

Isaac should step forward. Show himself. In the last few seconds, this had gone from innocent observation to something like spying. And he wasn't going to eavesdrop. He had *some* manners.

But something kept him frozen, kept his muscles locked into place.

"Thank you," Lizzie said. Her voice was empty; her spine stiff. Isaac had thought he understood her, but at this moment, he had no idea what was going on in her head.

Mark seemed to, though. He stepped even closer, a thin little smile on his sharp face, and then he held out a hand, as if to touch her. His fingers hovered over the bare curve of Lizzie's shoulder the way one might trace the air above a work of art. "So, my dear," he began.

That was enough. Isaac didn't want to hear whatever was coming next.

Gritting his teeth, he pushed the door open and entered the room with more noise than he'd thought himself capable of. Two sets of eyes swung to stare at him, and he felt his face heat. Great. So he'd announced his presence. Now what?

He was saved from deciding when Mark stepped abruptly away from Lizzie, the sly expression on his face disappearing like mist. "Montgomery, m'boy," he grinned, all good-nature and welcome.

But Isaac saw something slimy and cold beneath the other man's smooth veneer.

"Morning," he nodded. And then, turning to the centre of the room, the centre of his consciousness right now: "Lizzie."

She nodded in turn. "Isaac."

Ah, the way she'd said his name last night. Would he ever hear that again? Right now she was more wooden than the floorboards beneath their feet.

"What brings you here?" Mark asked, his tone deceptively light. His eyes were heavy, heavy, heavy.

"Looking for Audrey," Isaac said. "Told her I'd help with her homework." Which wasn't a lie. Only he hadn't planned on helping today.

"Her personal study, you mean?"

Isaac shrugged. He didn't understand the intricacies of the girls' many extra lessons. He just helped them with their geography and listened to them moan.

"Well, she's not here," Mark said. "Didn't you hear? She went out skiing with some boy yesterday and sprained her ankle."

This was the part where Lizzie sniffed something about having warned Audrey countless times. Only, Lizzie was silent. Completely silent.

Suddenly, Isaac felt the need to get her away from Mark. Or rather, get Mark away from her.

"Right," he said. "That's a shame. Where is she?"

"I believe she's holding court in the drawing room," Mark chuckled.

"Tell her I'll come up and see her, yeah?" He stepped further into the room, moving with purpose, heading straight for Lizzie. His eyes remained pinned to Mark, and he displayed his message clearly. *Off you go, mate. Do one.*

Mark stilled for a moment, his jaw tightening almost imperceptibly. But then he seemed to brighten, like an old penny made temporarily fresh by rain.

"Of course, of course," he smiled. "I'll tell her now. I was heading up to see her myself. Have a nice day, you two." His smile twisted slightly, a smirk breaking through as he swept through the room's main doorway with an airy wave of his hand. Huh. For a man who'd seemed reluctant to leave seconds ago, he'd certainly had a rapid change of heart.

Shrugging off that weirdness—everything about Mark set off his internal alarm these days—Isaac drew Lizzie into his arms. He almost passed out when she came to him immediately, docile as a lamb. There wasn't a moment's resistance or sarcastic comment to be found; she just folded herself against his chest, burying her face in his T-shirt.

Perplexed, he peered down at the top of her head. She looked fine. Normal. But then, all he could see of her right now was that enormous bloody bun. He pushed her back slightly, just enough to see her eyes. They were… troubled. Dim. There was no laughter, no passion, not even a spark of annoyance. Just an empty desolation that inspired something close to fear in him.

"What's wrong?" he asked.

She shook her head as if emerging from a dream. "Nothing," she murmured.

"Lie."

She gasped, looking up at him in outrage—but then, after a

beat, her anger faded into a smile. "You're right," she admitted. "I just… you know I used to work in Paris?"

"Really?" Clarissa said something like that. About seeing Lizzie perform in France.

"Yes. Not that long ago. I was… well. You don't need to hear that story. But being here is reminding me of things. People."

"People?"

She huffed out a laugh. "I made a lot of friends there. But I ruined everything when I left. Burned all my bridges. Blazing glory. You know. It was all very me."

Huh. Isaac didn't know the circumstances, but that did sound very Lizzie. Only…

"Why'd you leave? Must've been bad."

She looked up at him, startled. "What do you mean?"

"You don't give up. You don't just… leave. So it must've been bad."

"Yes," she said slowly. "I suppose it was."

He wrapped his hands around the soft flesh of her bare upper arms, rubbed them soothingly, warming away their goosebumps. "Tell me?"

"I…" She took a deep, shuddering breath. "You know what? I think I will."

"Good," he murmured. But… not yet. She couldn't tell him yet. Not while her eyes were haunted and her hands were shaking. Suddenly, Isaac was desperate to bring back her spark, to make her smile again. That seemed even more important than learning her secrets.

And so he took a step back, looked down her body until he came to those pale pink shoes. "How'd you do that thing?" he asked, nodding at her feet. "Up on your toes like that?"

She licked her lips. "There's a box. Like a block of wood, right here." She picked up one foot and tapped the toe against the floor.

Isaac's brows shot up. "And you just… stand on it?"

"Yes." As if to emphasise the word, she rose up onto her toes again. She was almost as tall as him, now. Much easier to kiss…

"Doesn't it hurt?" he asked.

"I suppose. It doesn't really matter." Then she laughed, covering her mouth with the tips of her fingers. "Stop looking at me like that!"

"Like what?"

"Like I'm talking nonsense."

Isaac felt himself grin. "You kind of are."

She rolled her eyes.

"Show me," he said impulsively. Because he wanted more of the beauty he'd seen before Mark had ruined everything, and he had a feeling that it would make her happy.

He was right. She looked pleased, even though she tried to hide it. "Alright," she murmured, and held out a hand. Isaac took it, his fist swallowing up her slender fingers.

She raised her left leg, perpendicular to her body. The limb twisted strangely so that her heel was pushed up toward the ceiling. It should've looked uncomfortable, unnatural—but it was oddly beautiful. And he knew it must be hard, but her face was a picture of serenity, and the lines of her body were so smooth and graceful, he could almost forget the sheer strength she possessed.

Her eyes met his, crackling like twin flames. She raised her leg even higher, until her pointed toe was hovering above her head.

"Jesus," he muttered. Then he remembered that all of her weight was still balanced on one foot. "*Jesus*," he said again.

"I should dye my shoes," she said conversationally, as though she wasn't defying gravity before his eyes. "Walk around me in a circle."

He blinked. "What?"

"Walk."

"Uh…" He did as instructed, still holding her hand… and she turned with him, rotating like a figure in a music box.

"But I don't bother anymore. No-one's going to see them anyway."

Lost, Isaac shook his head. "What are you talking about?"

"My shoes," she said patiently. "They should be brown."

"Why?"

"To match the rest of me, of course." She smirked. He was still walking, and she was still spinning.

"Oh," he said. "So they're supposed to be... flesh-coloured? Not pink?"

She shrugged. "Unless your flesh *is* pink."

Over their voices, the music still played. As it swelled into yet another crescendo, Lizzie lowered her leg, bringing it behind her in an angle that seemed at once impossible and perfect.

"This is an arabesque," she said, because somehow she could tell that he wanted to know. Had Isaac always been so easy to read? Was he slipping? Or did she simply see the things no-one else could?

"Dance for me?" he asked.

Just like that, the music stopped.

No; it was still playing. But the swirl of magic that surrounded her, the beat that seemed to hum through her very body, was snuffed out like a flame. Lizzie sank onto flat feet, her hand slipping from his.

"No," she said hoarsely. "I don't dance for people to watch."

Fuck.

But then, as quickly as it had come, her dark mood seemed to pass. She shook her head, smiling up at him. And even though it was weak, it was real. She meant it—or she was trying to.

"Sorry," she murmured. "It's not you. Just... a decision I made."

Ah. He nodded, because he understood that. And because he'd achieved his goal: whatever she was feeling right now, it wasn't fear. That was all that mattered.

"So," he began, searching for a way to clear the awkwardness between them. "Need to eat?"

She bit her lip. Which, he already knew, meant *yes*.

"Lunch?" he offered.

"I need a shower."

Lizzie, naked, hot water cascading over her body as she scrubbed herself, soapy bubbles foaming over her slick skin—

"Be quick," he said gruffly. "And we can meet at the uh..."

"La Pièce Verte?"

"Yeah. That one."

"Okay," she said softly. "It's a date."

Oh. Damn. A date.

Isaac felt himself smile.

CHAPTER SEVENTEEN

HE WAITED for her in the bright, airy space of the restaurant, the mountain sunlight glowing gently through the windows. When she came, she was as glorious as the view. He watched her make her way through the maze of little tables with unconscious elegance. Even in casual clothes, she stood out like a queen amongst subjects. And some time in the last few days that had stopped making him resentful.

Now it made him hard.

He rose to greet her, and she inclined her head slightly, the thick coil of her hair gleaming like a crown. But it had been even more beautiful last night, loose and wet and swinging around her waist like stolen ocean. Which was an awkward memory to latch onto at this precise moment, because it made him even harder, and if she didn't sit down soon he was going to disgrace them both.

"How very gentlemanly of you," she murmured as she finally sank into her seat, allowing him to follow suit.

He shifted in his chair, rearranging the inconvenient bulge in his jeans. "Mam raised me proper," he said gruffly. "Just didn't make it easy on her."

"I'm sure." She laughed as she rearranged her napkin, and he copied her movements because he had no idea what the fuck was expected in a place like this. "She must be a formidable woman."

"She was," he said quietly. Then he waited—waited for the sensation of drowning to take over; waited to feel as if he was forcing his lungs to take in briny water. But just as the twin spirits of regret and loss rose like the tide, she leaned forward to rest her hand on top of his.

"I see. I'm sorry for your loss," she said, her voice softer than ever before. He hadn't even known she could sound like that.

There'd been no-one to say those words to him, when it had happened. Some people found them cliché, or cheap. Isaac never could. He'd been absolutely desperate for condolences—for someone to acknowledge the depth of what had been stolen from the world, when his mother's light went out. No-one did. Because the pricks he'd thought of as friends had all disappeared when he'd gone straight, when he'd made it clear his priorities had changed. When she got sick.

He swallowed, shook his head. Was unspeakably grateful when a waiter arrived, interrupting the moment with drink orders and menus.

Lizzie greeted the guy in French—that much Isaac could understand—and the waiter must have assumed they were both fluent, because he reeled off the rest of his spiel in a language Isaac had never even begun to learn. He sat in silence, preparing for the feeling of woeful ignorance that often overtook him in places like this. With people like the ones sitting in this room, people who probably didn't notice that the tableware was silver, and the china was real—but would sure as hell notice if it wasn't.

But then Lizzie interrupted the waiter with another incomprehensible stream of words. "*Je suis désolé. S'il vous plaît, parlez anglais pour mon ami.*"

The waiter said, "My apologies, *Mademoiselle. Monsieur.*" And he began again. In English.

Isaac stared at Lizzie as the waiter spoke. She studied her menu avidly... Until the moment when she slid her gaze shyly up

137

to his. Like a baby playing peekaboo, she looked down the moment their eyes met. But a smile curved her lips. He liked that smile. He liked it a lot.

"I'll have the ratatouille and the Niçoise, no dressing," she said at last.

Crap. He should've been listening. "Uh... I think..."

"The same?" she suggested innocently.

He looked up gratefully. "Yeah. The same."

The waiter nodded and moved to leave, but a thought struck Isaac suddenly. "Hold on, mate." He looked to Lizzie. "You want anything now? Something small?"

She bit her lip. Looked firmly down at the bright white table-cloth. "Yes, please."

Isaac nodded. "Alright. Can we get some bread or something, please?"

"Of course, *Monsieur*," the waiter nodded.

"Cheers."

They were left alone again, or as alone as they could be in a room full of people. But at least the tables were set metres apart. With Lizzie, that felt like enough space to constitute a safe little bubble. If he only looked at her, it was easy to forget everyone else in the room.

"Why didn't you ask?" he murmured, suddenly curious. "You don't mind asking for what you want." He knew that well. Knew it and loved it.

She shrugged, and though she rarely seemed as small as she was, something about the movement made him conscious of her size. Of how little space she took up, despite both her strength and softness.

"Weakness is private," she finally responded. Shocking the shit out of him.

"Weakness?" he echoed. She nodded. Now it was his turn to reach for her hand. He slid a palm over hers, wrapping his fingers around her wrist. "No weakness here," he said, even as he felt the delicacy of her bones beneath her skin. He meant it.

She sighed heavily, with the kind of exhalation that spoke of a thousand thoughts that had nowhere to go. "How did you know?" she asked. "About…"

"My dad was diabetic," he told her.

"Really?"

"Yeah. And an alcoholic. Not a good combination." Ah, crap. Why had he said that? Only now the questioning tilt of her head was making him want to continue. "Sometimes he was good. Mostly he wasn't. He always seemed… angry. With himself. With his body."

He watched her closely. And he wasn't at all surprised when she murmured, "I know the feeling." Sadness took over her features, her whole body.

Often, she was a brick wall, but sometimes she became emotion itself, living and breathing. He could never guess which Lizzie she'd be at any given moment. But he found himself wanting to learn more about her, wanting to be the one who could predict this unpredictable woman.

"Hey," he said softly, determined to chase away the shadows in her eyes. "My mam always said, no point being angry about something you can't change. Sometimes, you've got to adapt. Move forward. For your own good."

She took a deep breath, biting her lip. But then she offered him a weak, shaking smile. He took it gladly, held it close to his heart like a candle in the wind. Thought that he'd do anything to help it grow.

"Most people tell me it's not that bad," she said. "All the doctors I've been to, anyway. I have Type 1. They say I'll learn to manage, the first year is the hardest, it'll get better or I'll get used to it." She shook her head. "I've done enough learning in my life. Enough trying. I had everything under control. And now I'm back to square one."

He shook his head. "You should be kinder to yourself."

She blinked up at him, clearly surprised. But then she shrugged. "That's not how I operate. It's just... I'm far from perfect.

But my body was perfect. It was the only thing I could rely on. And now even that has failed me."

"That why you left Paris? Can't perform anymore?"

She snorted. "I should never have left Paris. I should have powered through. Made a fuss. But the truth is I..." She swallowed, her gaze flitting down to the tablecloth. "I was weak. I wanted an excuse to leave because I wasn't strong enough to stay."

"It was... too difficult?" He frowned.

"Something like that," she answered. But it wasn't the whole truth. He could tell. She was holding something back.

Ghosts haunted her, clinging to her happiness like parasites. He swore they hadn't been there the day they'd met. Or maybe she'd just hidden it better. Maybe he'd been too wrapped up in his own feelings to see it. Didn't matter. He saw it now, and he wanted it gone.

"What's wrong?" he asked. He'd asked before. Been denied an answer. But now—surely she'd tell him now. Surely she felt the thing growing between them, rising like the dawn. Surely...

He knew, the moment before she spoke, that she would lie to him.

"Just..." she sighed. "Thinking about Ellen."

"Ellen?"

"A friend. In Paris. I... didn't treat her very well."

"Ah." He leaned back in his seat as the bread arrived. Lizzie thanked the waiter before grabbing a soft roll and nibbling on it delicately, no butter. "One of the bridges you burned?" he asked.

"Yes. She... tried to help me with something. But I was too proud to be helped."

He shrugged. "If you're sorry, you should tell her. Even if it's not enough."

"Even if she doesn't forgive me, you mean?"

"Yeah. People deserve apologies. We don't deserve forgiveness. It's not an exchange."

She chewed thoughtfully. "That's true." And then, a moment

later: "Maybe I'll talk to her. At some point." She gave him a teasing smile. "Is this the kind of sage advice that's gotten you where you are today, then?"

Isaac shook his head, a smile of his own threatening to break free. "Nah. You really haven't read 'em?"

"Your books? God, no. You look so intimidating on the cover."

"Had to."

"Oh, don't act like that isn't your resting expression." She laughed, and he found himself joining in. Because really, he looked miserable as fuck on both of those bloody covers. And he had been. Photoshoots weren't his thing.

She leaned forward, her brown eyes sparkling now, all hints of sadness gone. For the moment. "What do you write about, then?" she asked. "I imagine it's all very dramatic."

He shook his head. "'Gritty realism.'"

"Who said that?"

"*The Times.*"

"And you think?"

He shrugged. "Just life."

"Life in prison."

"In prison. After prison. The shit that leads up to prison. For some people, that's just life."

She leaned back, her gaze assessing. And then she said, "Maybe I should read them."

"Don't think you'd like it."

She shrugged delicately. "Some things aren't meant to be liked."

Well. If she hadn't hit the nail on the fucking head. The gleeful enjoyment of his books by people who would never walk that path had been turning his stomach for the past few years. He'd take their money, sure. He was no saint. But he didn't have to like it.

"How did you end up published, anyway?" she asked.

Huh. She really hadn't read a damned thing about him, beyond a few screaming headlines. That was… interesting.

"I left my diary," he said quietly.

"I'm sorry, pardon?"

He cleared his throat, spoke louder. "I left my diary. When I was released. Warden read it. Cousin's brother-in-law worked in publishing."

"Really?" She blinked. "How... fortuitous."

"Something like that."

"So you keep a diary? Is it that little book I've seen you with?"

He shrugged, suddenly embarrassed. Technically, the whole world knew he kept a diary. When his first book was published, that had been a huge part of the marketing. True stories. Real perspective. Blah blah fucking blah.

But telling Lizzie felt different. It wasn't that he still clung to the bullshit he'd bought into as a kid—that there was a certain way to be a man, and writing shit down wasn't it. He knew better than that. It was just that everything he said to this woman seemed to mean more than it usually would. Everything between them was... intimate.

Still, he found himself finally saying, spurred on by her questioning stare: "Yep."

"And what do you write about now?" she asked. "How to spend a fortune in ten days?"

Ah. So she'd read some things.

He shrugged. "That was an experiment."

"An experiment?"

"Wanted to see if it really helped. If money really helped." One year, on the anniversary of his mother's death, he'd spent a fucking fortune in a single week, doing his best to emulate the lifestyle of the rich and witless, blazing a trail through the tabloids at the same damn time. *Dark Angel Rebels*, they'd said. That had cemented the bad boy angle more than his fucking record.

The thing was, his tactic hadn't worked at all. Spending all that fucking money had only made him feel worse.

She gazed at him as if she knew. "And did it? Help, I mean?"

"What do you think?"

She shrugged. "I have no idea of the impact of money on

happiness. I have never been without money. I have certainly been unhappy; but I imagine I'd be even more so if I had to worry about bills on top of everything else."

He blinked. "…Yeah."

"Have I surprised you?" She laughed. "Most dancers aren't like me, you know. Not the ones who make it. Privilege like mine usually encourages laziness, and laziness doesn't sell tickets. So I've seen enough of the way other people live to know that I'm lucky."

He nodded, digesting that information.

When their food finally arrived, the conversation turned to lighter topics for a while. His attempt at skiing—never to be repeated, he assured her. The royal engagement: "My brother adores Harry. It's funny; we have friends marrying in the spring, too." And Audrey's twisted ankle, a topic dogged by uncomfortable silences. Perhaps Mark's appearance that morning weighed heavily on both their minds. Though in her case, he couldn't imagine why.

Finally, after a bite of her ratatouille, she asked the question he'd been quietly anticipating.

"So," she murmured. "You mentioned the things that lead up to prison."

He nodded.

"I don't suppose you'd tell me what led you there?"

He didn't know if he should be happy she'd asked. On the one hand, it might show that she saw him as a person instead of a statistic. On the other, she might just be hunting for tragedy porn in an attempt to justify whatever it was that made her want him.

No. That wasn't fair. That wasn't Lizzie.

He chewed slowly, his food turning to lead in his mouth. But eventually, he forced it down past the lump in his throat and began.

"Never had much money. Dad was a piece of shit. Used to make my mam steal for him."

She put down her fork with a precise click.

Clearing his throat, Isaac continued. "Food, fags, booze. But eventually she got spooked. Said she wouldn't do it anymore. So when she was out at work or whatever, he'd… ask me. Send me out to go and get whatever he wanted. Made me swear not to tell her."

He still remembered the look on her face, the day she found out. The day the owner of the corner shop caught him red-handed and dragged him home by the ear. Shame. Shame deep enough to reach hell itself.

"It all came out soon enough, though. Got caught. Never been a good thief. So she left my dad. Never occurred to me that she would. In fact, I don't think she would've, for any other reason. But… it made things better, in the end. We had more without him leeching off her all the time. Not a lot, still, but more.

"We moved, though. Because it was his house. The council put us in these flats…" He could still see them now, four huge, hulking blocks grazing the sky, barely a stone's throw apart. "She had to work a lot. So I was left to my own devices. Fell in with the wrong people. Thought I could make things better for her—for us. All she ever did was work, and we had fuck all. So I thought, work isn't the way then, is it? Gotta do something else.

"Started working for one of the dealers in my area. Just delivering. She knew something was up, and she begged me to stop, but I wouldn't. I had money to give her now, so why the fuck would I stop? I told her she could reduce her hours. Stay at home. But she wouldn't. We were always arguing. And then… she got sick." He shrugged, as though it was nothing. As though they were just words. As though he wouldn't remember the day of her diagnosis for the rest of his life, like a kick in the fucking gut that had ploughed straight through to his spine.

"What was it?" Lizzie asked. She wasn't eating. He should remind her to eat. He nodded towards her fork, still abandoned on the table, and she looked down as if she'd forgotten it was even there. But she nodded and picked it up and poked at her food as if it were rotten.

"Breast cancer. Metastasized. Spread to her spine. Within a few months she could barely walk."

Lizzie's lips parted. Probably to say *I'm sorry*. But if he stopped talking, he might never start again—so he ploughed on.

"I gave up the bullshit I was involved in. All I could think was that I'd get caught, locked up, and she'd have no-one to look after her."

"And they just… let you stop? Just like that?"

He gave a humourless laugh. "It's not like in films, Lizzie. Drug dealers aren't the mafia. Pay what you owe, be respectful, and you can do whatever the fuck you like. It's just that most people never want to stop. No pension, no job security, but it pays better than stacking shelves."

She nodded, her eyes wide. She probably had a father or a brother who'd beat him senseless for telling her any of this. But there were little girls all over the country who'd known nothing but this life since childhood. The silent majority didn't have to be silent if only somebody would listen.

Lizzie was listening.

"So I stayed with her. I stayed with her until—until she died. And I promised her that I'd stay straight. I swore I'd try to do something with my life."

"What happened?" she asked softly.

He smiled, though there was no pleasure in it. It was more a thin stretching of the lips, a pathetic attempt at emotion. Because it was all so fucking ironic.

"I kept my word. I was doing well. I found a college that did bricklaying courses. I was okay at it, too. Things were… calm. Boring. I liked that.

"I started to make some friends. So, one Saturday night, we all went out. The usual. But one of my mates got into an argument with some guy. Next thing you know, we're all fighting. Someone comes for me; I swing. Punched him square in the face. He went straight down. Smacked his head on the concrete. Killed him." Isaac chose a spot on the snowy tablecloth, a square inch just as pristine as the rest. He focused on that spot, clung to it like a lifeline as he finished the story.

"When he didn't get back up, I took a look at him. Realised he wasn't breathing. Then I saw the blood, spreading around his head. Like a halo. My mam—she used to collect these cards, with pictures of angels. They had little sayings on the back. He looked just like that. Only his halo was red.

"Called an ambulance. Wasn't fast enough. I even tried fucking CPR, like that would help. The guy's brain was painting the pavement and I started breathing down his mouth like a fucking idiot."

"Isaac," she said. "Don't treat yourself so harshly—"

"Why not?" he gritted out. "I'm alive to do it. He's not. So why fucking not?"

She bit her lip. "What was his name?"

"Ben Davies," he said, the words falling from his lips like a habit. "He was twenty-two. Had three little sisters. His mother cried every time she saw me. His father never said a word."

Lizzie leaned forward, squeezing his hand. "I was wrong," she murmured. "When I said that you profit from it."

"No." He shook his head. "You weren't."

"I was. Because you suffer, too, don't you?"

He gritted his teeth against the searing pain of her words, of her gaze, so soft and understanding.

"I know you," she said. "I know that you've probably done all you can to atone for that day. So ask yourself this: what else can you give? If the answer is nothing but more of this pain... Maybe consider the fact that it's not helping anyone."

He swallowed, his throat suddenly dry. And then, unable to help himself, he said, "Why do I want to tell you everything? How do you make me feel like this?"

She stiffened. Not a lot. Just enough that a man who felt her the way he felt gravity would notice. And in an instant, he saw that she was pulling away. That the shutters were falling. That the shadows had returned.

She gave him a little smile, valiant and utterly fake, and returned to her food as if it wasn't freezing cold by now. "I'm sure I don't know," she said lightly. "How is your ratatouille, anyway?"

He hesitated, just for a moment. Then he picked up his fork and said, "It's good."

Because he'd let her do this, if it was what she needed. He'd let her pull away.

But he wouldn't stop hoping that one day she'd let him in.

CHAPTER EIGHTEEN

LIZZIE SANK into the soft embrace of her room's double bed with a sigh. A tiny pillow fell from its grand arrangement to land on her face. She didn't bother brushing it off.

Its presence helped with her wallowing.

She'd never felt so low in her life. Not when she was twelve, and she'd accidentally told seven-year-old Yen that Santa wasn't real. Not when she'd broken up with her first boyfriend and he'd cried. Fuck, not even when she'd said those awful things to Ellen.

She dug her nails into the palms of her hands, trying to chase away the memories of Isaac. His kindness, his understanding, the aching intensity of his gaze. It had been hours since their lunch date; hours since she'd pushed him away for what felt like the hundredth time. He'd let her go when the meal was over, but she almost wished that he hadn't. She almost wished he'd push.

He never would.

He wasn't the man she'd believed him to be. And when Lizzie had agreed to all this, as much as she'd despised the subterfuge, it hadn't been a difficult choice. Her brother, or a stranger with a bad reputation? No contest. Except he wasn't a stranger anymore. And Lizzie was starting to realise that, despite all she'd been raised to believe, reputations didn't mean a damned thing.

Full of anxious energy, Lizzie sat, pushing the pillow off her face. Moping was a waste of time. She should be glad that things were turning out this way, that he was opening up to her. Soon, she'd find the perfect moment, and she'd get the information she so desperately needed. And then this would all be over. And he would never forgive her.

Restless, Lizzie unlocked her phone. She needed to talk to someone—but there was no-one left.

Olu was miles away, further in spirit than he'd ever been in body. Yen soaked up other people's moods like a sponge; if Lizzie called the younger woman now, they'd both end up in pieces over something or other. And Ellen… She'd ruined everything with Ellen.

But then she remembered Isaac's words. *If you're sorry, you should tell her. Even if it's not enough.*

Biting her lip, Lizzie decided he was right. It was past time to apologise.

She pulled her suitcase out of the wardrobe and unzipped it, rifling through the few things she hadn't unpacked. At the bottom was her laptop and charger, as yet unused; she'd been strangely busy on this trip, despite not being busy at all.

Manipulating men took serious energy. Who knew?

A pathetic voice in her head argued that it wasn't manipulation. That voice was a liar. Because whether Lizzie wanted to or not, enjoyed it or not, she knew what she was doing. She would get close to Isaac, she would learn his secrets, and she would use them against him.

That was the bottom line.

Lizzie unlocked her laptop and pulled up Facebook, typing Ellen's name into the search bar. Her friend's familiar, smiling face came into view, along with a cover photo of what looked like half the *corps*, grinning in their leotards.

Oh. Lizzie was in that picture too; at the back, on the right, side-on to the camera. She was talking to someone—Mario, another dancer. Neither of them appeared to notice the photograph being taken just metres away. And she looked… awful.

She was painfully thin, her calves barely the width that her arms were now. Her joints protruded, giving away the fact that her body was carrying less weight than it should. Her head looked far too big for her bowed shoulders, almost cartoon-like. And there were heavy circles under her eyes.

She clicked the image, bringing up its details. It was uploaded nine months ago. Before she'd committed to looking after her body, back when she'd been free-falling.

God, no wonder Ellen had snitched.

Feeling slightly sick at the prospect of what she knew she had to do, Lizzie closed the picture and brought up a chat box. She typed three different versions of the same sentence before finally settling on the right one.

I'm really sorry.

She stared at the words. They didn't seem adequate. She had no fucking idea what else to say. Apologising always made her want to vomit. The more necessary it was, the worse she felt.

Before she could change her mind, Lizzie hit 'send' and closed the little window. There. Ellen and Lizzie weren't Facebook friends anymore, so she had no idea if Ellen would even see this message. But she didn't have the other girl's number—Lizzie had deleted every trace of her old life in a ridiculous fit of temper. So this was the only way.

She just hoped it would be enough.

A ding came from the laptop, and her gaze flew to the corner of the screen. Ellen had replied already?

Oh. No. Crap. It was Olu.

Biting her lip, Lizzie clicked on the notification, opening the chat.

Olu: I see you online, sis.

Lizzie tapped her fingers against the side of her laptop. It was a simple sentence, but it felt like an accusation. She could hear his unspoken questions: *Where have you been? Why have you been avoiding me?*

When he'd first started his never-ending world tour, she'd wanted so many times to ask the same questions. But she never had.

Maybe she should've.

Olu: You free?

Time to be a big girl. Straightening her spine, Lizzie typed back simply:

Yes.

A second later, her phone rang.

She picked it up, dread pooling in the pit of her stomach. Just like it did every time she spoke to Olu now. It bubbled, acidic and disgusting, as if she was moments away from throwing up her guts.

"Hello?" she croaked into the phone.

"Liz." His familiar voice filled her at once with comfort and anxiety. She missed the days when she'd been free to love her brother without reservation. Now every interaction was laced with guilt, and it was all so fucking tiring. She was sick of it. She couldn't fucking stand it. Suddenly, Lizzie was so furious with the entire situation, she felt dizzy.

"How are you?" he asked, his voice cautious.

She blurted out, "I'm diabetic."

Shit.

He paused. And then, his voice laced with shock, "What?"

Sighing, Lizzie dragged a hand across her face, kneading her suddenly throbbing temple. "I'm diabetic. I have Type 1 diabetes."

"But—what? Are you okay? When did this happen?"

"Um… February. Last year."

There was another pause. Longer, this time. And then he said, his voice pure iron: "Elizabeth Adewunmi Olusegun-Keynes. Did I mishear you?"

Uh-oh. His Substitute Parent Voice. But for once, the sound didn't make her nervous.

In fact, for the first time in months, she felt lighter than air.

"No," she said. "I'm sorry."

"Is this why you left Paris? Not that bullshit line you fed me about *diversifying your craft*?"

"Kind of. I mean… they got rid of me."

"What? Why? Those pieces of shit—"

"No, no! Not like that. I… I wasn't coping well. So they put me on a break. But I just... left."

She could almost hear him grinding his teeth. "What do you mean, you weren't coping well? Did you tell anyone about this? Did you tell Mother?"

"Don't be ridiculous."

"Who, then?"

She was quiet. "Well. No-one, really."

"Oh, Lizzie." He sighed, and the depth of sadness she heard in that single exhalation brought her guilt rushing back. But without the added weight of such a huge secret, it was a lot easier to bear.

"I'm sorry," she said again. "I should've told you. But I didn't want to—you know, to get in the way of what you're doing."

"Get in the way?" he repeated, incredulous. "Lizzie. You're my sister. I could be saving the planet from fucking aliens and it wouldn't matter. As soon as you need me, that's my priority. It's not like I'm out here splitting the fucking atom."

"You're helping people," she said. "Or… animals. I can't remember what you're doing right now."

"I'm in the Ukraine. But forget about that. You're more important than everyone else in the world, Lizzie."

"That's not true."

"It is to me," he said, his voice soft. Then he cleared his throat as though leaving the emotional part of the conversation behind. He was far better with feelings than she was, a thousand times better than their parents—but it still didn't come easily to him. "Are you at home?" he asked. "I'll come and see you."

"Actually," she said, staring up at her bed's canopy, "I'm in the Alps."

"What the bloody hell are you doing over there?"

"The Spencers are on holiday. They decided to take me with them. But I'll be back soon. In… three days, I think?"

"Alright. I'll come home too. We can actually see each other in person for once."

She giggled. "That might be nice."

"I know you said you weren't coping, before, but how are you doing now? Better?"

"Yes," she said. And it was true. "I'm much better. I'm getting the hang of it."

"So you have to… inject yourself, and everything?"

"Oh, yes. It's kind of gross, actually. You know I hate that sort of thing."

"I'm impressed, to be honest. You've been doing this all on your own?"

"Well… at first I tried to avoid doing it at all. I just kept thinking, you know—you can train your body to do anything, if you work hard enough. So maybe I could… fix myself."

"You don't need fixing," he said. "That sounds like Mother. Not everything needs to be fixed, Liz. Some things just need to be taken care of."

"I like that," she said softly. "I like that a lot. But anyway… I'm managing now."

"Are you?" he asked.

And in that precise moment, she felt completely confident when she said, "Yes." Alone in her room, she felt herself grin with pure happiness. "I got an invitation to Theo's wedding, by the way."

"Oh, yeah! Aren't they perfect?"

"They're lovely. But how do you know? Yours is at my house."

"Oh, I helped choose the stationery. I've been texting the maid-of-honour."

In the past, this would be the point where she made a sly comment about him texting strange women. He did, after all, have a reputation as a ladies' man. But right now she had no idea if that reputation was one side of a half-hidden coin, or a complete fabrication. A smokescreen designed to keep the world out.

No matter which option was true, the fact that she didn't know for sure made her wary of the whole topic. So she let the moment slide.

"Is the location anything to do with you?" she asked. "I know you like Greece."

153

"Oh, yeah. La Christou. It's a beautiful place. They don't usually do weddings so early in the year, but I know the guy who owns it."

"He's a friend?"

"Pretty much. And he owes me a favour."

She rolled her eyes. "Everyone owes you a favour."

"True." She could hear his smile. "Listen, Liz, I've got to go. I'm meeting with the head of this orphanage in twenty minutes."

"Alright. Love you."

"I'll see you soon, okay?"

"Okay."

"Love you. Bye."

The call ended, and Lizzie let her phone fall onto the bed. Then she did the same, laying back against the mountain of pillows with a smile on her face.

Wasn't it funny how the things that *seemed* so difficult often turned out to be so easy?

CHAPTER NINETEEN

ISAAC PUT on his briefs and then his jeans, dragging the worn denim up his still-damp thighs. He didn't know who spread the rumour that cold showers helped with raging fucking hard-ons, but they were wrong. Showers didn't do shit.

All he'd thought about since returning from lunch was Lizzie. Should he have pushed her? Should he go to her now? Should he fantasise about sucking on her tits while he came in his own hand, or would that be the moment he really hit rock-bottom?

Jesus Christ, he had no idea what to do with this—this multi-layered lust. Wanting a woman was so much easier when you didn't *also* want her every thought and feeling.

Maybe he was just out of practice. Maybe he was back in teenage-boy-mode, and a good fuck would get his mind into working order.

Yeah, and maybe tomorrow morning pigs would fly past his bloody window.

He wandered into the suite's sitting room in search of his note-book. But as he passed the hotel room's door, he heard… foot-steps. Muffled, light, but hovering back and forth along the same stretch of corridor. Right outside his room. Slipping into stealth like a pair of worn-in shoes, Isaac crept closer to the door and turned off the suite's lights. Though the windows still let soft, mountain sunshine through, he could now see the play of light and shadow in the crack at the bottom of his door, where it wasn't quite flush to the carpet. As whoever was out there moved around, the strip of light fell into shadow. Light. Shadow. Light…

Shadow.

He counted to three. There was no movement; the shadow remained, right outside his door.

Whip-sharp, Isaac pulled the door open, ready to take advantage of the element of surprise. But the tables turned when he found wide, whisky eyes and soft lips parted on a gasp, waiting for him.

Fuck.

He reached out and grabbed her arm, dragging her into the room before shutting the door behind them.

"I—I wasn't sure if you were busy," Lizzie said, stumbling over her words. "I didn't want to—"

"Don't care," he grunted. Then he pushed her back against the closed door, cupping his hands beneath her arse, pushing her up, up, up until her mouth was right where he wanted it.

She wrapped her legs around his waist as if they belonged there. They *did* belong there. She belonged with him in any and every way. He knew it when she put her hands to his cheeks, gently as though he were actually something precious. "Kiss me, then," she whispered.

Her wish was his command.

He kissed her slowly, achingly slowly, his lips moving over hers as if spelling out the secret of how much he needed her. It might be the one thing he could never say to her out loud. But he showed her. He traced his tongue over hers, and he showed her. He pressed his body against her, poured himself into her, and he showed her. He let his every touch scream the contents of his enchanted mind. *You. Only you do this to me. Only you make me so hungry and yet so satisfied. You.*

He showed her.

She touched every inch of him she could reach, as if his body was worth exploring, as if she might need him as much as he

156

needed her. Her soft palms traced over his ridges and hard planes, leaving trails of cleansing fire in their wake. And she whimpered into his mouth, rocking against his growing erection as if daring him to move faster, to speed this up—but he absolutely would not. When a blessing came your way, you didn't rush through it. He had her, right now, in the safety of his own fucking room where no-one could interrupt, and he wouldn't let her go until he'd watched her come for him at least a thousand times—

Fuck. He pulled back, his heart falling fifty feet.

"What's wrong?" she panted.

"No condoms."

She blinked. "What—none?"

"Nah."

"Seriously?"

He didn't answer. Just looked at her. He wasn't about to tell her he hadn't been with a woman since he got out. Hell, before then—since the days when he'd had the time and energy spare for human contact. Which was a long fucking time ago.

"Well, that's okay," she said. "I've got one."

Isaac felt a grin spread across his face, relief and disbelief merging. "Yeah?"

"Of course. Safe sex is very important. I only brought one, though. You know, just in case."

This fucking woman.

"Now take me to bed," she said imperiously.

His pleasure. He pulled her away from the door, carrying her through the suite until they reached his bed. He dropped her in the middle of the luxurious quilt and she looked like a work of art, like another priceless masterpiece in a roomful of shit too fancy for him to touch. But God help him, he was going to touch. Breaking the rules had never scared Isaac.

He unbuttoned his jeans, and shoved them off, turning away from her for a minute as he undressed. But when he looked up again, she was somehow already naked—except for a pair of lacy, blue knickers he wanted to tear apart. He stared at her tits for half a second, hypnotised, before snapping to attention.

"How did you—?"

"Practice." She smiled. Her bra was hanging off the century-old lampshade. She held a single condom in her hand. He might want to marry her.

Laughing, his chest lighter than it had been in years, Isaac joined her on the bed. Pushing her backwards, he knelt between her legs and hooked his fingers under the edge of her underwear. Then the smile was wiped from his face as he pulled them slowly down, revealing heaven inch by inch.

He'd been dreaming of this. Ever since that night in the sauna when he'd tasted her for the first time, he'd been dreaming. His hands shaking, he pulled the sky-blue fabric from her muscular calves. Everything about her was so fucking beautiful.

But this…

Pushing her further up the bed, Isaac sprawled onto his stomach, his face at a level with the ultimate prize. He spread her soft folds with his thumbs, exposing her pretty little cunt, all wet and swollen. For him. Her clit was stiff, demanding attention, begging him to take exactly what he wanted.

So he did. He lowered his head, desperate to taste her sweetness—but before he lost control completely, he forced himself to rasp out, "Okay?" He was too far gone to bother with sentences, or to make any fucking sense at all.

But she always knew what he meant. She put her hand on the back of his head and pushed, spreading her legs wider, and she was panting and breathless when she spoke—even though he'd barely touched her.

"Now," she moaned.

He loved the way she sounded when she was like this. When she was with him. She fell into desire utterly, without reservation, coming completely undone. A princess unravelled. All because of him. He wanted to make her fall apart completely; he wanted to put her back together again. He wanted everything.

Isaac let go of his tightly wound control, burying his face between her legs and feasting, weak with lust. He bathed in the rich, earthy scent of her desire, worshipping her tender flesh with

158

desperation. Her taste, the way her wetness pooled against his tongue, the plump folds of her cunt—everything was dragging him under, like a tidal wave of pleasure he would happily drown in. As she writhed beneath him, her soft thighs tightened around his ears with a strength that should be alarming. But it wasn't.

He was suffocating in pure Lizzie, and fucking loving it.

When she came, he kept licking lightly at her clit, dragging out her soft, keening moans, just because they made his balls ache. But eventually she shuddered and twisted her hips, pulling away, so he tore himself from the sweetness of her pussy. Resting his head on her thigh, he looked up at the magnificent landscape that was her body. Every roll and curve was even more beautiful than the mountains surrounding this place, and he had her all to himself. Holy shit.

He was hard as fuck, desperate to get inside her—but the soft, sated look on her face made him pause. He could stare at her forever. She looked like heaven.

She looks like mine.

———

LIZZIE STARED up at the ceiling above Isaac's bed, wondering how the hell she got here. Hardly caring. It was ungracious to reject life's blessings. Never look an orgasm in the mouth.

She'd dropped the condom somewhere in between seeing galaxies and flying through them. But now she had regained her senses, and still she needed more. She needed everything.

Perhaps she'd never get enough of him.

She sat up, barely noticing that the self-consciousness she'd been struggling with was gone. She was utterly naked and completely unbothered, the way she used to be, before everything had changed. It felt like another part of her old self, the girl who'd grown up dressing and undressing in the wings beside fellow performers, had returned.

She found the condom, tearing open its foil wrapper with her teeth, and then she said, "Come here."

Isaac's eyes widened slightly before he obeyed, coming to his knees before her. The rippling muscles of his thighs bulged. His cock, thick and long and gorgeous as she remembered, stood to attention, almost painfully hard. Maybe it *was* painful. She wouldn't know. But she was about to help him with it.

She rolled the condom onto him in one smooth stroke. Then she cupped the heavy weight of his balls in her hand, squeezing slightly, running her nails over the soft skin. He swore, his abs tightening, and Lizzie smiled. She liked this part—knowing that she was exactly what he needed. She liked it very much.

He grabbed the back of her head and pulled her to him, taking her mouth in a bruising kiss. His weight pushed her back onto the bed, and she slid her legs over his shoulders, spreading herself open for him.

He pulled back to look between their bodies with some surprise. Then, a little smirk twisting his lips, he muttered, "Forgot. You're flexible."

"I'll show you how flexible I am..." She reached beneath him and wrapped her hand around his cock, gratified to hear a strangled gasp leave his lips. "...Some other time. But right now, you should concentrate on fucking me." She brought the swollen head of his erection to her pussy, letting out a moan of her own as the touch sent a spark of pleasure through her.

"Ah, fuck," he grunted, pushing forward, easing his way inside. Lizzie rolled her hips as he stretched her wide, desperate for more, for everything. But he maintained control, pressing soft, teasing kisses against her gasping lips, refusing to fill her completely.

"More?" he asked as she clutched his broad shoulders.

"Don't tease me," she warned. "I'll make you pay for it."

He just laughed. She didn't blame him. It was hard to sound threatening when a dick the size of Big Ben was blowing your fucking mind.

But then, when he finally settled in her to the hilt, the weight of his balls resting against her arse, his smile disappeared. He

160

bumped his forehead against hers, finding her eyes amongst the shadows between them. And he whispered, "You're perfect."

"No such thing," she whispered back, as if she hadn't spent her whole life pursuing it. As if perfection didn't haunt her like a memory, far more real than a ghost.

"You're perfect," he said again. One of his hands found hers, and their fingers laced together. His other hand reached between their bodies. She felt the pad of his thumb press firmly against her aching clit, and then he rubbed slow, even circles. The ragged, desperate sound she made might have embarrassed her, if she'd been capable of embarrassment at that moment.

Then he began to move, pulling back slowly before he thrust, steady and hard and deep, stroking every inch of her fluttering pussy. Jesus, God above, this was better than anything she'd ever felt. Anything. Better than the ache in her calves after a hard days' practice. Better than the moment when her tired body surprised her with a perfect performance. Better than chocolate melting on her tongue. Whatever she'd been doing before now, obviously it hadn't been sex. Because *this* was sex. This was the thing people killed for and died for, sold their souls for, left everything behind for.

If she wasn't careful, she'd become addicted.

He rose up, shifting the angle of his thrusts so they brushed against some devastatingly sensitive place inside her she hadn't even known about before now. And he rubbed her clit faster, fucked her harder, stared down at her with a look of unrelenting determination that told her he wouldn't be offering mercy any time soon. He gritted his teeth, his muscles clenching and releasing as he rocked above her, becoming the only thing in her world that mattered. Finally, Lizzie felt herself go under, a ragged scream leaving her lips as incandescent pleasure burst through her.

Isaac lowered himself until his weight was pushing her into the mattress. As the vestiges of her orgasm faded, he squeezed her hand in his. And then he gripped her thigh and ploughed into her, faster and faster, panting with each thrust. A guttural roar tumbled from his throat, and then he truly collapsed over her, the harsh lines of his face fading into a gentleness she wouldn't have thought possible.

After a brief moment in which she was thoroughly squashed, Lizzie felt his weight shift. He rolled over slightly, pulling her with him, wrapping an arm around her. They lay side by side, their faces a breath apart, as their heart rates slowed. She was ready to fall asleep. Her body hummed, heavy and sated. The bed was so soft, and his arms were so warm...

But then he spoke. "You're the first woman I've been with since—since I was... nineteen?"

Lizzie stared at him in pure astonishment. "That's not possible."

He huffed out a humourless laugh. "It is."

"No, I mean—of course. Wow. Okay." She smiled as a thought hit her. "So you're out of practice?"

"I suppose."

"Good Lord. If you get any better, my brain might melt."

He grinned, and the sight sent a thrill of pleasure through her. There was no sweeter sight than Isaac's smile.

He rolled over, pushing her onto her back, settling between her legs. "More, then?"

"Down, boy. No more condoms, remember?"

"Fuck." He shifted to lie on his side, tracing circles over her bare ribs. She caught his hand, touched the signet ring on his little finger.

"What's this?" she asked.

"Mam's."

"Ah." She kissed his knuckle. "It's lovely."

"Thanks," he smiled. Then his expression grew thoughtful. So thoughtful that she almost laughed when he said only, "Where do we find condoms in a place like this?"

Lizzie snorted. "I have no idea, sadly." She smiled up at him, at the gentle happiness on his face. He was so relaxed right now, so open.

And then her pleasure evaporated. Because she knew what she had to do.

Though Lizzie had thought the room warm, she was suddenly freezing. Her nakedness, so decadent a moment ago, was now uncomfortable—as if she were Eve after the Fall, suddenly discovering shame.

But she couldn't cover herself. She couldn't do anything that might alter the mood. She had to taken advantage of this moment before it passed.

She had to take advantage of him.

Lizzie trailed a finger along the stubble of his jaw, and her heart nearly broke at the way he leaned into her touch. "Isaac," she said, and she swore she heard her voice shaking. But it must be in her head, because he didn't say anything. Just raised his brows in question.

She moved a hand to his chest, because men liked that, didn't they? Fuck. All of the movements that had come so naturally five minutes ago now seemed stilted, ridiculous. But Isaac pressed his hand over hers, and now she felt his heartbeat. She was definitely going to hell.

"I…" She had no idea how to go about this. But she had to, had to push and probe in a way that felt entirely foreign. Then, thank God, inspiration struck. "I Googled you."

He looked surprised. "Yeah?"

"Yes. And this thing came up about… about something you did last summer."

For a second, he stiffened. Her heart pounded as she worried that she'd blown it, that she'd overestimated her abilities. But then, just as quickly, he relaxed. Because he trusted her. Because he'd tell her anything.

Lizzie hadn't even known she could hate herself this much.

"The journalist," he said.

She nodded. "Is it true? Because the articles said that he refused to comment."

"He refused to comment because…" He trailed off.

Lizzie bit her lip. *Close.* So close she could taste it. One more question, one more push, and she'd have what she needed to keep her brother safe. To stop his life from falling apart.

"What happened?" she asked softly. Her voice said quite clearly that Isaac could trust her. After all, she was in his arms, in his bed, and vulnerable.

That wasn't true, of course. She was mirroring him; that was all. It was just part of the performance.

And it worked. It worked beautifully.

Isaac told her.

CHAPTER TWENTY

SHE HADN'T STAYED the night.

In fact, she'd barely stayed two hours. Claimed she had a dinner date with Candy. Isaac had watched her dress with a sinking feeling in the pit of his stomach. She was smiling, but he didn't believe it. She touched him, but he hadn't felt it fully.

He'd had the oddest impression that she was leaving. Leaving him. That the first time he ever had her would be the last.

But his mind had always run to the dramatic.

Now, in the morning light, he saw things much more clearly. There was nothing weird going on with Lizzie yesterday. Nothing weirder than usual, anyway. Emotions were high, and he was a miserable bastard. Expecting the worst was a habit that had been beaten into him by life. But Lizzie would change that. Lizzie had been the best surprise of his life.

Isaac laced up his boots and grabbed his keycard, ready to face the day. Ready to find his woman. And some condoms, wherever they hid them in this fancy place. Rich people had sex too, after all.

And they were pretty fucking good at it, if Lizzie was anything to go by.

He strode through the halls like he was king of the damn world. If he'd bumped into anyone he knew, they'd probably have passed out in shock at the grin on his face. He didn't care. Today would be the start of the rest of his life; he could feel it. He was going to grab what he wanted with both hands.

And what he wanted was Lizzie.

Since he didn't like it when she left, he'd have to give her a reason to never leave again. He'd have to make it clear that she was his, and he was hers, if she'd have him. And she would. She *would* have him. He saw in her face the same thing he felt in his heart.

After taking the stairs two at a time—the lift would be too damned slow—Isaac marched up the corridor that would take him to the little row of rooms where Lizzie had been put. He turned the corner, lost in his cloud of anticipation. He didn't even notice that Lizzie's door was already open.

But he did notice when a man stepped out of it, backing into the hall.

Isaac stopped in his tracks, frozen. Completely still, right down to his suspended pulse. For a heartbeat, he saw red.

But then his good sense returned. It was only a man. Men were just people. Lizzie was also a person. Sometimes, people interacted. Often, in fact. This was fine. This was absolutely fine.

Then the man spoke, and all of Isaac's fury came rushing back. Because he realised who it was.

"Don't overreact," Mark was sneering. The charm and joviality he usually cloaked himself with were utterly absent. There was only venom now, dripping from his every word, and all Isaac could think was: *It better not be Lizzie he's talking to like that.*

It was. Because she answered with a roar to rival a lion's. "Get OUT," she bellowed. "OUT!" And then she followed him into the hall, pushing at his chest, shoving him as far from her room as she could. She was wearing a long, silk robe, but her feet were bare, and her hair was floating around her head like a cloud.

"Careful, sweetheart," Mark said, something dark and sinuous in his voice. Something that sounded too much like a threat for Isaac's liking.

Suddenly, he could move again. He surged forward, intent on

something—he didn't know exactly what. But it felt bad. It felt really fucking bad.

They noticed him at the same time, their heads turning in tandem, and the poisonous air around Mark instantly receded. Everything from his posture to his expression to the look in his fucking eyes changed in seconds. Isaac had seen hints of this dual nature before, but watching the man literally transform…

It was unnatural. To be so manipulative—to be a liar in everything you did, in every single breath, to your fucking core. Isaac felt slightly sick.

"Why are you here?" he gritted out, still stalking toward them.

"Isaac," Lizzie warned. "Don't."

"What? Don't what?"

"Just don't," she snapped. Then she stepped away from Mark —toward Isaac. Where she belonged. He felt himself relax, just a bit. She reached out a hand, and he took it.

"Good morning, Lizzie. Isaac." Mark gave them both a genial nod, as if nothing untoward had happened, as if this was any other day. He strolled off, and as he passed them, Isaac had a vivid vision of himself ripping Mark's head off of his body.

Then Lizzie squeezed his hand, and he came back to the real world. He pulled her through the open doorway, shutting the two of them safely inside her room. Away from whatever the fuck had just happened out there.

"What the hell was that?" he asked.

"Nothing." Her voice was terse. Strained. He loved her hair down, but for some reason the sight was making him uncomfortable right now. Maybe because it seemed like a sign of vulnerability on her. A sign he didn't want someone like Mark to see.

Too late for that.

"Why was he here?" Isaac asked.

"Can we… can we just leave it?"

He stared in disbelief. "What the fuck? No, we can't just *leave it*. Did he do something to you?"

"Of course not." Her robe was coming undone, and she tugged the halves together, holding them close to her chest. But he saw enough of her smooth, brown skin to realise that she was naked beneath.

Bile rising, he looked wildly around the room. She didn't have a suite like him. Just a bedroom and a bathroom. Her sheets were rumpled, but she'd probably just woken up. And yes, the pillows were all over the floor, and there wasn't an inch of the bed that didn't look like it'd been turned upside down, but maybe she was a rough sleeper.

He wouldn't know. She'd never slept with him. She'd never come close to spending her nights with him. And she'd never brought him to her room.

Isaac stormed through to the bathroom, pulling up short when he found that the lights were off, candles glowing seductively through the darkness. He could just make out what looked like rose petals floating atop the steaming water that filled the bath. His face grim, Isaac returned to the bedroom, spearing Lizzie with his gaze.

He waited for her to rush at him with explanations, but she didn't. Of course she didn't. She'd never lower herself.

And so, it was his own voice that broke the silence. "You fucking him?"

She turned her head toward him, so, so slowly. And then she said, her tone unyielding: "I know you did not just ask me that."

Grinding his teeth, Isaac shrugged. As though there wasn't a ten ton weight on his shoulders, dragging him down, sweeping him beneath the surf. "You could be anywhere in the world," he said. "But you're here. Teaching a few kids—"

"*His* kids," she said. "His children. With his *wife*. What do you think of me?"

Fuck. Isaac dragged a hand over his face, his brain moving slower and slower by the second. Almost as slow as his mouth, as his useless tongue.

"I'm sorry," he said finally. "Out of order."

"Yes you fucking are." She wrapped her arms around herself as though holding pieces together, and he realised he'd never seen her do that before. He'd never seen her appear broken or even splintered. Either she was perfect, formidable—or she was wild beneath him, flawless in a different kind of way.

"What did he want?" Isaac asked, jealousy fading, concern stampeding to the forefront of his mind. "You didn't invite him here. Why did he come?"

She ignored him, walking to stare out of the window. Usually he'd be just as eager to see the view. Today all he could do was watch the column of her spine, stiff as always.

"There's something wrong with him," Isaac said. Because as always, she dragged the words from him without even trying. "Always has been. But it's worse now. Closer to the surface. Can't ignore it anymore."

She turned, probably outraged that he'd dare accuse the golden man. Her old family friend. Connections were everything to these people.

Only she didn't look outraged. She was staring at him with something he couldn't quite identify. Her lips were slightly parted, and her eyes were suspiciously bright.

His face heating, he finished gruffly: "Just... be careful with him. Alright?"

"You really do see everything," she muttered. "Like Blake, wandering through London."

"Don't," he gritted out. "I'm no poet." But then, when she arched a brow, he realised his mistake.

"You read the Romantics?" she asked.

Fuck. "Not much to do when you spend all day locked in a cell."

A gentle smile softened her face as she moved toward him. "You think I don't know you. I do. I didn't mean to, but I do." She slid her arms around his shoulders, and he held her close as though it were automatic. A reflex. And fuck, didn't everything feel better now that the air he was breathing tasted of her?

She was close, so close he could see those sweet little freckles beneath her eye. She moved closer still, pressed her lips lightly to his. When she spoke, she spoke into him.

"You are a poet, Isaac Montgomery, whether you like it or not.

I know there are entire galaxies inside your mind, and I know that you pour them into that little book of yours—"

He kissed her. He wrapped a hand around the back of her neck and felt the clouds of her curls against his fingers and forced his lips roughly into hers with no delicacy and no art and no sophistication. He had to show her somehow, the only way he knew, that he was hers. Whether it made sense or not. She'd branded him in a way he couldn't shake.

But just as he started to feel anchored again, just as the frantic panic of confusion faded, she pulled away. Put her palm against his chest, as if to push him back. He let go of her and his confusion returned. He felt like he was floating away. Like he'd be lost in the sky forever, unable to get down again, because the woman he needed refused to ground him anymore.

"I can't," she choked out.

"What?"

"I'm sorry. I can't." She looked up at him, and her expression was so empty. She was barely recognisable. He couldn't bear to see it.

Fuck. He squeezed his eyes shut, running his hands over his hair. "I shouldn't have done that."

"Done what?" she asked dully.

"Kissed you. I thought you—"

"Isaac. I'm not talking about that." Something in her tone made him look at her again. The sight was like a punch to the gut.

She was different. Completely different. Just like Mark. A minute ago she had been smiling for him, teasing him, telling him she knew him. Whispering exactly what he wanted to hear. Now she looked disgusted. She pressed a hand to her stomach as if she might be sick, and her warm, brown skin seemed grey and waxen.

"What's wrong?" he asked, his voice a whisper.

She shook her head. "*This* is wrong." Her breath shuddered through her body, and for a moment he thought he saw tears in her eyes. But it was just a trick of the light. She looked right through him as she said, "I need you to leave."

Isaac stood there, the words playing over and over in his head.

She opened her mouth to speak again, and the sight spurred him into action. He wouldn't make her ask twice.

He turned away from everything he'd ever wanted, heading straight to the door without looking back.

Apparently he'd been alone this whole time.

He was Lizzie's. But Lizzie would never be his.

CHAPTER TWENTY-ONE

EVERYTHING WAS RUINED, and it was entirely her fault.

She knew that. She accepted it. She wanted to cry and scream and punch a wall because of it, but she'd never do anything so utterly ridiculous.

There was no time for childishness. She was going into battle.

As Isaac shut the door softly behind him, Lizzie threw off her robe. She grabbed her phone from the bedside table before heading to the bathroom, turning on the lights.

Dialling with one hand, she used the other to put out all these fucking candles. Each one burned for a precious instant before it snuffed out beneath the pressure of her finger and thumb. The whisper of pain was necessary. This was all necessary. She needed to remember that.

As she sank into the bathwater, her brother finally picked up the phone.

"Keynes," he said, voice brusque.

"I'm coming home early."

"Liz." She could hear the frown in his voice, the surprise. "You are?"

"Yes. If you'll lend me the money so I can fly home today."

"I'll give it to you," he said, as always.

"I don't want it. Lend it to me."

"Whatever. You okay?"

She wouldn't bother answering that. "I need to talk to you."

"Ooookay…" She heard voices in the background, what sounded like cars passing in the distance. "Do you need me to come home now?"

He was probably busy. In fact, he was definitely busy. And she didn't like to bother him, didn't like to interrupt the little place he'd carved out for himself in the world—or rather, the places he'd carved out worldwide.

But he was her brother. Somewhere along the line, the real meaning of that word had become lost to her. Only now, she was starting to remember.

Us against the world. Together.

"Yes," she said. "I—I need you to come home." Her voice cracked, and hot tears prickled at the corners of her eyes.

"Lizzie," he muttered, lowering his voice. As if he were in the middle of something. Whoops. "Are you crying?"

"No," she sobbed.

"I'm coming home. Heathrow. Wait for me."

"O-okay," she gasped, trying to catch her breath. Trying to fend off the tears. Too late. They were there to stay, it seemed.

"See you soon. Love you."

"Love you," she sniffed.

The call ended. She reached up to put her phone on the counter. Then she sank beneath the hot, scented water, the water she'd thought might help her sleep after last night's painful insomnia.

She didn't need to sleep anymore. What she needed now was to continue with her plan. Of course, she wasn't entirely sure of the plan just yet. But she had a goal, and the sadness she'd just seen in Isaac's eyes—the sadness *she'd* put there—was motivation enough to achieve it.

Lizzie gave herself five seconds to remain immersed, surrounded by the water, a world apart from the mess that was her reality. On the sixth second, she rose up, her hair streaming down her back. Her hair was the first thing she needed to deal with. The first part of her armour.

She grabbed a comb and some conditioner, almost emptying the bottle as she squeezed it over her head. Dragging her way through the tangles, Lizzie combed and combed until her hair was as soft and sleek as it was ever going to get. Which wasn't very. But it was enough.

She washed herself, got out, stood before the mirror armed with a hair-tie, a thousand grips, and half a ton of hair gel. She scraped her hair back, brushing it into submission, remembering the look of grim determination on her mother's face every time Sunday—wash day—came around. The nanny didn't know how to do Lizzie's hair. Said it was too much to handle. So Mother had learned, and hated every minute of it.

Lizzie held that hate close to her heart as she pulled and tugged and twisted until her hair was devoid of texture, tightly bound atop her head. She smiled at her reflection, the expression sharp. Already she felt like herself. Like the kind of woman who could deal with this situation. Not just do as she was told to survive—but *handle it*.

Next, she tested her blood sugar. Her body was her ally, not her nemesis; she knew that now. And she couldn't charge into battle unprepared.

She ran through the now-familiar motions: pricking her finger, watching as crimson bloomed, spilling her blood onto the test strip. Numbers were good. She was in control. She'd been looking after herself, and now her body was looking after her. Lizzie almost felt proud.

Almost. But not quite. All these tiny victories didn't mean she'd won the war.

She would, though. She dressed carefully, methodically, in the kind of clothes she hated to wear—the kind her mother loved. A neat little skirt suit, patent leather heels, a cardigan to soften the look. She should wear pearls, but she hadn't brought any with her.

She folded her comfortable leggings and leotards up neatly,

arranging her luggage with care. Then she called the front desk and asked for someone to come and collect it. Then she called the airport and booked a one-way ticket on the next flight to Heathrow. And *then* she called a taxi company and arranged for them to pick her up.

There. All of her phone calls were done. Now it was time for some real conversations.

———

IT WAS BEYOND PAINFUL, smiling and air kissing the girls as if nothing was amiss.

Audrey reigned supreme over the drawing room, her sprained ankle propped up on a velvet-upholstered stool, her sisters crowding around her. For once, she and Ava weren't even bickering. And Clarissa was present too, because that was just Sod's Law, wasn't it? The girls were often too wrapped up in themselves to notice the little things, but Clarissa, for all her airy ways, was sharp as a fucking tack. She hadn't married Mark by accident, after all.

"You're leaving early, then?" she murmured, her voice languid —but her eyes like a hawk's.

"Unavoidable, I'm afraid," Lizzie replied. "Family emergency. And since Audrey is indisposed—"

"Oh, of course, of course." Clarissa waved her hand. "It's no issue. I do hope your emergency is resolved."

"I'm confident that it will be." Lizzie swallowed, hard. "I was hoping I might speak to Mark, before I go?"

"If you run up to our suite, darling, you might catch him before he hits the slopes."

Lizzie winced internally. She didn't want to be anywhere so private with Mark—not after he'd let himself into her room yet again this morning, and never mind the fact that he swore he didn't want her. A man didn't have to *want* in order to take.

But this was her only chance. And she had to do this just right, perfectly, if she was going to buy herself some time.

"Thank you," she nodded stiffly. "I'll be off, then."

"Do you have to go?" Ava pouted.

"*Yes*," Audrey said. "It's a family emergency. We'll see her soon, anyway, won't we Lizzie?"

All three girls looked up at her, eager as puppies. Lizzie smiled woodenly. "Of course."

But the truth was, she wasn't certain. She wasn't certain at all.

———

THE SPENCER SUITE was on the hotel's highest floor, and there were only four doors to choose from. Of course, Lizzie didn't have to guess—she knew their room number—but still, she hesitated.

And the memory of the last time she'd hesitated outside a hotel room brought heat to her cheeks.

Isaac.

She stiffened her spine. No time for that now. No time at all.

Lizzie knocked firmly on the Spencer's door, waiting for an answer with her heart in her mouth. She almost hoped he wouldn't be there. But she needed him to be.

And he was. After a few long minutes, the door swung open, and Mark appeared. He scowled, probably still smarting over the events of that morning. But she didn't have the time to soothe his ego. Lizzie pushed her way past him into the room, walking with purpose. Mother always said that a woman who walked with purpose could take over the world.

The narrow doorway widened into a charming little sitting room, and she helped herself to a seat, watching Mark as closely as she would a viper.

He let his gaze flit insulting over her body before he followed her, coming to sit in the loveseat that faced her chair. "To what do I owe the pleasure, Ms. Keynes?" He asked, sounding almost bored.

The patience that he'd been wearing on for so long finally tore.

"*Olusegun*," she corrected sharply. "My name is Elizabeth Adewunmi Olusegun-Keynes, and I'll thank you to use it."

For a moment, Mark appeared slightly unbalanced—though he tried valiantly to hide it. Didn't matter. She saw through him. Oh, his lip curled derisively, but her senses were suddenly so sharp, her nerves so on edge, that she couldn't miss the way he hesitated before speaking. "Quite," he murmured finally. "Miss... Olu..."

"O-lu-se-gun." She sounded it out slowly, as though speaking to a child. "Don't worry. Your tongue may be lazy, but you'll get the hang of it." She gave him an acidic smile, and in that moment she felt just like her mother.

In the best possible way.

He cleared his throat. "Why are you here?" he demanded. As though he hadn't been invading her space every chance he got.

But she couldn't let her disgust run wild now, even in her thoughts. If there was one thing she knew, it was that a performance must be done with the whole heart, or not at all.

So Lizzie forced fear and subservience into her own soul, and let it shine through as she spoke. "I—I need to leave early."

He arched one dark brow, imperious. "Have you completed your task?"

"No," she admitted.

"Then why should I allow you to go?"

"Because it's an emergency. And because I can prove to you that I'm close."

"Close?" He leaned forward, and she resisted the urge to shy away. "What do you mean?" he demanded, his gaze lit with something grasping and desperate.

"I know what happened with the journalist."

Mark grinned. Not the cheerful, open smile she was used to seeing—the one that she now realised had always been fake—but the horrifying, face-splitting grimace of a monster closing in on its victim.

"Well then, that's it," he said, almost breathless with excitement. "We have what we need!"

"Not quite. You see, this particular journalist was planning an exposé. A tell-all about Isaac's childhood, with the help of his estranged father's sister. It relied quite heavily on less than flattering stories about Isaac's mother—the implication being that she had raised him cruelly, that her influence had turned his gentle soul toward a life of crime—you get the gist."

Mark's face fell at her words. "You mean... He beat the journalist to defend his mother's honour?"

"Oh, no." Lizzie shook her head. "He didn't beat the journalist at all."

"I-I beg your pardon?" Mark gaped. He looked almost as shocked as Lizzie had felt, when the truth came out.

I haven't hit a man since the night I killed Ben Davies. And I never will again.

Lizzie forced herself to speak around the lump in her throat. She kept her tone measured, her face impassive, as she snatched away the backbone of Mark's plan. "Isaac intimidated the man, certainly—but there was no violence. He paid Mr. Wright off. Had the man sign a contract. And then he engaged his publicist to ensure that nothing similar would ever occur. I have no idea where the man's injuries came from, but if he treats people so poorly, I'm sure there are plenty of possible culprits."

Mark blinked, as though his mind was struggling to comprehend this new reality. Because it was so very *shocking* that Isaac should use his intelligence rather than his fists, Lizzie supposed. God, she didn't know how Isaac could stand the way people saw him.

The way she'd seen him.

She was no better than Mark.

Clearing her throat Lizzie moved on. She couldn't become distracted. Not if she wanted every piece on this chess board to move in her favour. "This isn't exactly the scandal you were hoping for," she said, trying her best to sound sympathetic.

"No." Mark folded his hands, turning pensive. "No, not at all."

"But don't worry," she said brightly. "I've won his trust. That much is clear. Yes?"

Slow and lazy as a lizard, Mark nodded. "Yes. I suppose that's true…"

"And there's so much more for me to find out," she said, her tone low, beguiling. "I just need a few days to help with my—my family issue. He'll miss me. Absence makes the heart grow fonder, as they say. I'll get what you need soon enough."

Mark's gaze sharpened. "You'd better. Because if you don't—"

"I know," she snapped. And then, dragging back her self-control, she smiled. Smoothed her hands over her lavender, cashmere skirt. "Don't worry. I'm fully aware of my obligations. And I won't let you down."

"Excellent," he said crisply.

And when she left, they almost parted on good terms. Mark certainly seemed happy, anyway. And so did Lizzie, right up until his door closed. Then she let every inch of her worry and fear run free—but just for a moment.

She couldn't lose herself to emotion just yet. She had one more thing to do.

CHAPTER TWENTY-TWO

FOUR DAYS. Four days they'd been here, and Isaac felt like he'd spent every single one of them wrapped up in the kind of intense emotion he usually felt once a year, if that.

But he hadn't minded so much when those emotions had all been the warm and fuzzy—or red-fucking-hot—kind. He certainly hadn't minded when he'd been lying in this very bed with Lizzie just yesterday, thinking that for the first time in his life, he'd managed to secure something worth having. Something that filled him with a dangerous kind of joy.

Dangerous because he'd known, deep down, that he'd fuck it up. And he had.

The look on Lizzie's face when she'd pushed him away played on a loop in his head. Somehow, he'd ruined things. No surprise there.

He should've known it couldn't last. She was delicate and precious, and he'd always had clumsy fucking hands.

Isaac stared blankly up at the ceiling as his phone rang for what felt like the hundredth time in the last half hour. He should answer it. But he didn't have the energy. Better yet, he should switch it to silent, so he could ignore the world in peace.

And now he was thinking like a teenage boy. Clearly, this mood was getting out of hand. He sat up with a sigh and grabbed the phone. The call stopped as soon as he touched it—because that was just how his life worked—but a moment later, it rang again. It was Jane, he saw, but he'd already known that. Only Jane would call fifty fucking times in a row. And she'd rip him to shreds when he finally answered, too.

Still, he hit 'accept' and put the phone to his ear. "What?" he barked.

"Where the fuck have you been?" demanded his publicist, her voice steely. "I've been calling you all day!"

"You've been calling me for half an hour."

"At *least* an hour."

He sighed. There was no arguing with this woman. He'd do better not to waste his breath.

She began a tirade about his awful lack of manners and professionalism, but it was interrupted on Isaac's end by a knock at his door. A knock that made his heart stop, made his blood freeze in his veins. It was her. It had to be her.

"Hang on, Jane," he said, getting up to answer the door.

"Hang on? What the fuck do you mean *hang on*? We need to talk! There's—"

Isaac pulled open his door and found her standing there, dressed like some political wife. Her hair was up, her eyes were sharp, her shoes were shiny and her skirt was far too long for his liking. She was still the most beautiful thing he'd ever seen.

"Jane," he said. "I'll ring you later."

"What? Isaac—"

He hung up.

Lizzie stared at him. He stared at her. He didn't know how long he stood there in silence, but it was probably too long. Only, when he got like this—when his mind was full of words demanding release—those were the times he really struggled to speak.

Luckily, she never struggled to speak. She didn't struggle with anything.

No; that wasn't true. She wasn't in control all the time. It simply seemed that way.

"Can I come in?" she asked tightly.

He nodded, stepping back to let her through. She strolled into the little sitting room like she owned it, like the carpet beneath her feet was there only by her grace. He shut the door and watched as she sat, every movement perfectly composed, her face a careful mask. And his heart dropped, tore right through his stomach, and sank into the fucking floor.

Everything about this was wrong.

"What is it?" he asked.

"I think you should sit down."

"Just fucking tell me, Lizzie. Don't drag it out. Tell me."

She sighed. A sigh that said, *I wish you'd just be reasonable about this.* Or maybe he was imagining that. Maybe he was projecting. Being fatalistic.

Probably not.

"There's no easy way to say this," she said, her voice low. Almost a whisper. His first instinct was to move closer—but he couldn't. He couldn't be close when she held herself so carefully, as if one touch would shatter her into a thousand pieces. When she might not welcome his nearness the way she had only yesterday.

When you'd touched the moon itself, would moonlight still be enough to move you? Or would it feel like an insult?

The latter, Isaac thought. But that, he knew, was a personal flaw.

"I lied to you," she said.

Isaac swallowed. Wet his lips. Forced himself to ask, "What do you mean?" But he already knew. The blank, unfeeling mask of her face was enough to tell him *exactly* what she meant.

The whole thing. The whole thing had been a lie.

"I was invited here to get close to you," she said, her words slow and painfully clear. As if she were giving a speech, a presentation: *All the Ways I Owned Isaac Montgomery.*

"I used you," she said. *I owned his body.* "I manipulated you." *I owned his heart.* "I betrayed you." *I owned his soul.* "And I'm very sorry for it."

Isaac took a deep, shuddering breath, air catching on all the words stuck in his throat. But then she stood, as if to leave, as if she were done, and that eased the way for all those pent-up words real fucking quick.

He stepped forward, felt fury's bite, and revelled in the pain. "Where do you think you're going?" he gritted out.

She pursed her lips.

"Well?" he demanded. "You can't—you can't just leave. You have to tell me why."

"What's the point?" she asked quietly. "You won't care. You won't forgive me—"

"You don't deserve forgiveness," he spat. "But *I* deserve an explanation."

She swallowed. He saw the motion, watched the delicate line of her throat, remembered the taste of her cinnamon skin, and wished he could burn it from his brain. He'd been so fucking right about this woman. She was always meant to ruin him.

Biting her lip, she sat down again. Folded her hands neatly in her lap. Crossed her ankles. He remembered when her hands were all over him, when she couldn't keep them still. When she'd looked at him like she needed him. And that was all a lie too. The only time he'd truly known her was the first fucking day they'd met.

"I have a brother," she began. He wanted to say, *I know.* He wanted to say, *You never mention him.* But that was part of the act too, wasn't it? He'd assumed that they must not be close. From the look on her face, he was willing to bet he'd been wrong.

She took a deep breath before she continued. "I love him more than anything else in the world."

What would that be like? To have her love? Her loyalty? Isaac folded his arms to hide his clenched fists.

"He has done more for me than anyone. Been more of parent to me than our own parents ever were. Whenever I need him, he's there. Always." Her voice was soft, haunting. Her eyes were unfocused, as though she were far from here. Far from him. "My

183

mother forced me to study ballet when I was a child, for discipline. She always said I had no discipline."

Isaac blinked, stunned. Lizzie was the epitome of discipline. It was hard to imagine that she'd been any other way; that she hadn't emerged from the womb complete with perfect posture and social graces.

"When it became clear that I had talent," she said, her voice bitter, "I became Mother's walking trophy. Finally, she could be proud of me. I had to be the best. I had to take the world by storm. So, when I was fourteen, she sent me away. Away from London, away from my friends—to train. It was a prestigious dance school. An honour." She looked up at him, and for the first time, he understood. A vital piece of the puzzle that was Lizzie clicked into place.

She didn't want to be a ballerina.

"I was terrified," she said. "But I had to do it. I already knew that. My mother is not to be disobeyed. Only... I couldn't do it alone. So I called my brother.

"He's a lot older than me. He was twenty-five, he was free, and I was stuck at home with them. But he came back, and he fought for me. I don't know how, but he convinced our father that we should move together. That I should stay with him, instead of at the school. So I went, and Olu came with me. He looked after me. Mother spent so much time teaching me... control. Perfection. Everything I'd need to succeed. But Olu to taught me how to be fearless. I couldn't have done it without him."

Isaac drifted toward her, even though every step sent a blade through his heart. But she was hurting, and it pulled him closer. Her eyes were shadowed, not by the ghosts he'd caught glimpses of, but by her true demons. For the first time since they'd met, Lizzie's posture slipped into something less than perfection. And even though he hated every word she was saying, hated this, he felt glad. Because at least he'd finally know her, now. He'd finally know the woman he'd almost fallen in love with.

"You don't want to dance?" he asked.

Her head shot up and she looked at him as if he'd just said the sky was green. "Of course I want to dance!" she gasped. "I love to dance. It's all I have."

You could've had me.

Isaac took a breath, tried again. "But you don't want to perform." She'd told him so in a thousand tiny ways, but he hadn't understood until this moment. Until the moment it mattered least.

She deflated, shrinking before his very eyes. "No," she said, her voice bleak. "I don't. I *should*. What else can I do? What else can I do that isn't somehow... beneath me? *Ordinary*?"

The words felt like a slap. Like she was talking about him. About the way things were between them, and the woman he'd thought she was. The woman he'd cared for so fucking much.

But then she whispered, "There must be something wrong with me. Because I *want* to be ordinary."

And that filled him with something new. Something that felt too much like hope.

Isaac squashed it. He'd learned his lesson.

"Get on with it," he said, leaning against the wall. Lounging, as if he were bored, when really he needed its solid presence to stop him from falling. "You lied. Because...?"

He expected her to bristle. He waited for her posture to stiffen, for the broken desolation on her face to disappear. He waited for her to become flawless again; untouchable. Something more than human. Something too cold to love.

It didn't happen. Her walls didn't come up. She looked at him, and he saw every scrap of despair in her eyes. And he knew it was cruel, but he wished she'd stop. Wished she'd hide. Wish she'd perform for him the way she did for everyone else, even as she told him how she hated it.

"My brother is the best person I know," she said. "My parents taught me how to be proud. He taught me how to be a person. I have always known that he'd do anything for me. But now... now he needs *my* protection. Someone is threatening him, and I had the chance to eliminate that threat. All I had to do…" Her voice cracked—but of course, she didn't break down. She didn't allow herself to falter. She powered through, meeting his gaze as she said the words: "All I had to do was get close to you."

Isaac turned away. He couldn't look at her, not when her eyes shone with devotion, with the kind of pure, unconditional love that no-one had held for him since the day his mother died. It was the thing he'd been searching for without even knowing it, and he'd thought... he'd thought that he'd found it in Lizzie.

And he had. He'd found real love, devoted love, selfless love. It just wasn't for him.

He bit the inside of his cheek, hard. And then he said, "This is about that fucking contract, isn't it?"

"Yes," she murmured. "I don't know what's in that thing, but you can't sign. You once told me to be careful with Mark. Now I'm telling you the same." She stood, and this time he let her. Let her skirt around the furniture, let her come to him. But when she reached out to touch his cheek, Isaac grabbed her wrist.

"Don't," he choked out.

"Isaac..." Tears glistened in her eyes, and she didn't try to hide them. Why wouldn't she hide them? "Please listen to me," she whispered.

He clenched his jaw. Remained silent. For the first time in his life, it was a struggle. But he did it.

"I'm sorry," she whispered. "It was wrong, and I was desperate, and I'm sorry." Her wrist was still trapped in his hand. She didn't pull away. *He* should pull away. He should let go. Touching her was dangerous. But soon, she would walk out of the door, and after that moment he'd never touch her again.

Just a second. Just one more second. He'd give himself that much.

The tears that had been threatening for the last few minutes finally spilled over her long lashes. He watched as the little moles under her right eye were drowned in something like sorrow. "You have to know," she said. "I wasn't faking anything. I wasn't. When we're together, I—"

"*Don't*," he roared. As soon as the rage burst from him, he wanted to apologise, to reassure her. But he didn't have to. She stood firm, unafraid. She'd never been scared of him. At least that had been real.

Unlike everything else.

"Isaac," she continued. Because of course she'd ignore him. "Isaac, I'm falling in love with you."

For a moment, everything was still. Suspended, as if time itself had ceased to exist. As if he'd be trapped in this moment forever.

But then, just like that, reality restarted. And something in him snapped.

He jerked her forward, his grip on her wrist tightening. By rights, she should be avoiding his gaze. But she wouldn't; too fucking proud to back down, always. And it made him furious.

"Why," he began, his voice low and barely controlled, "should I give a fuck?"

That got her. She blinked up at him, shock taking over hopelessness. "You believe me?"

"Let's say I do," he said. "Let's say I believe you. Okay; you could love me." He felt a smirk twist his lips. "Why should I give a fuck? You're a liar. You're manipulative, and you're fake. I see it all the time. I watch you handing out false smiles and bullshit like lollipops. And I was arrogant enough to believe that you'd treat me differently. That I was special." He pushed her away. She stumbled, but he knew she wouldn't fall.

Lizzie never fell. Not unless it was choreographed.

"I won't make the mistake twice," he said. "Love is only worth as much as the person who gives it. All this time I told myself that you were perfection and I was just lucky." He shook his head, letting her see every inch of his disgust. "You had me fooled. You really did. But not anymore. Your love doesn't mean *shit*. Show's over. Now get out."

She finally retreated, wrapping ice around herself like a blanket. Her jaw clenched, and her spine was like a church spire, but there was desolation in her gaze. With a slow, stiff nod, she turned away.

Lizzie sailed past him like a queen to the guillotine, and he heard the door swing open behind him. Couldn't look back.

In the stifling silence of the room, she spoke for one last time. "I kissed you because I wanted to. Even though I knew it would hurt."

Before he could even begin to process that, she was gone.

He stood, unmoving, in the silence, letting it soak into his skin. Letting it suffocate him. Allowing numbness to spread, to take over his body and shut it down, a welcome virus.

But then his phone rang. Again.

His movements slow and calm, Isaac walked across the room. Picked up the phone.

Then he turned and threw it at the door with such force that the screen shattered, broken shards raining down onto the carpet.

Silence reigned. The phone landed on the floor with a hollow *thump*.

And then it rang again.

CHAPTER TWENTY-THREE

"HEY."

Someone was poking her. Which was impolite, to say the least.

Usually, Lizzie would spear them with her most scathing look until they regained their senses and removed themselves from her person. But currently, she couldn't be bothered. She couldn't be bothered to do anything, actually. Doing led to thinking, which led to remembering, which led to—

"Hey. Weirdo."

Well, that was *definitely* unacceptable. The poking continued, and mild irritation rose from the fugue of Lizzie's mind. As it awakened, other, less welcome emotions followed suit. Shame. Regret. Utter devastation.

See, this was why she didn't want to move.

"Wake up," the voice demanded. And then she felt a hand squeeze her bun like it was bicycle horn, and the voice said, "*Bloop.*"

Her eyes shot open. And despite the storm of emotion swirling in her chest, Lizzie managed to smile. "Olu."

"Good evening to you, sister. Why are you sleeping in Arrivals?"

"Why did you take forever to get here?"

"It's all about making an entrance, Liz, you know that."

Olu was flashing his usual charming grin, the one that always got him out of trouble. His green eyes sparkled against his glowing skin, which had tanned to a nut-brown shade that would absolutely scandalise their mother. His golden, curly hair was slightly longer than usual, and he was wearing the old, worn clothes that he always travelled in. Despite the outfit, he still looked like a supermodel. As Mother would say, at least one of her children had been blessed with beauty.

"Is the car here?" Lizzie asked.

"Of course. But before we go…" He sank down beside her, settling comfortably into the first class lounge's cloud-soft chair. Pulling out his second phone—the smartphone, not the one he used while he was abroad—Olu tapped at the screen before turning to show her a news article. All she could see was the headline, and a single image. But that was enough.

"This isn't why you needed me to come home, is it?" he asked. "Because I am happy to commit murder at your request. Just let me know."

Stifling a gasp, Lizzie snatched the phone from his grasp. Oh, sweet Lord.

NATION'S BAD BOY GETS STEAMY WITH EXOTIC MYSTERY WOMAN!

The picture was slightly grainy, either taken from afar or with a very poor camera. But it was her. She and Isaac, together, thankfully not touching… but beneath the pixilated blurs, clearly naked.

And he was clearly holding her yellow bikini bottoms. She scrolled down, just an inch, to find that there were several more pictures.

Oh dear.

Lizzie's mind worked rapidly, fluttering back and forth. How could this have happened? Had they really been so distracted? Or was it because she'd been so out of it? But Isaac noticed everything.

No, not everything. Not all the time. Not when she was with him.

A single sob burst from her throat, but she covered it with a loud cough, slapping a hand over her mouth.

Olu wasn't convinced.

"Jesus Christ, are you crying? Again? What the hell happened?"

"Nothing," she squeaked.

He gave her a sceptical look, reaching for the phone. Blushing furiously, she shoved it beneath her backside, sitting on the damning little device. "You can't look!" she snapped.

"Unfortunately, Liz, I've already seen more than I wished to." He wrinkled his nose.

"How did you know it was me? The quality's awful."

"You're my sister!" he said grandly. "I should hope I'd know you anywhere."

She raised a sceptical eyebrow.

"Oh, alright," he huffed. "Your hair tipped me off."

"My *hair?*"

"It's 2018. No-one has hair that long anymore. But really, Liz, what in God's name were you thinking?"

Lizzie maintained a dignified silence.

"You know if Father finds out, he'll flip his fucking lid."

"Never mind that!" she said. "Not important. Let's move on."

"*Let's move on?* Are you high?"

"Fuck off, Olu!"

"Oh, charming. I come all the way back home to mend my sister's broken heart—"

"This is not about my broken heart!" she barked. A woman a few seats away gave them an alarmed look, and Lizzie cleared her throat, wiping her face of all emotion. Arguing in public: item 1,684 on the list of things that she and Olu couldn't get away with. Class didn't always trump colour.

"Can we do this at home?" she asked through gritted teeth.

Olu sighed. "Probably for the best. Okay; come on." He picked up her suitcase, and she stood, retrieving his phone. But before she handed it back to him, she removed the article from his virtual newsstand.

No need for them both to be traumatised.

———

AN HOUR LATER, they finally tore through the traffic to arrive at Olu's Shoreditch flat. It took him so long to find his key that Lizzie gave up and searched for her own, which was languishing in the depths of her handbag. Eventually, they got inside, and Olu turned on the heating and hot water while Lizzie prepared the tea. They'd need a lot of it, she was sure.

Olu spent little time here, though it had been his official place of residence for five years. Lizzie had to rinse out the teacups before pouring, but she still had everything ready in record time. Settling into the living room, she tucked her feet beneath her on the sofa, feeling none of the softness that leather acquired with frequent use. In front of her, mounted on the opposite wall, a flat-screen TV gleamed. Olu had never turned it on.

"Right," her brother said, striding into the room. "I was going to grab some ice cream but... Well. I suppose you can't do that, anymore, can you?"

Ah, their infamous ice cream binges. She shook her head. "No. Afraid not. At least, not with Haagen Dazs."

"Not to worry, not to worry. Oh—you made tea. Is that, er—? Is that okay? Do you need to eat something, or..."

"Don't worry about it," she said, with a smile that almost felt real. "I'm fine."

"Right." He came to sit beside her, scratching the back of his neck awkwardly. "I did Google—you know. Diabetes, and what have you. I'm just not sure I've wrapped my head around it yet. But I will!"

"You don't need to," she said quietly. "I have everything under control."

"And I'm your brother," he said, his voice censorious. "We're in this together. You know as well as I do that control can be a heavy burden. So you'll share it, and I'll help. Okay?"

Her eyes wide, Lizzie gave a slow nod. If she spoke, she'd probably do something unforgivable. Like cry.

She'd expected support from her brother; of course she had. But what she *hadn't* expected was how good it would feel to know he had her back. What a relief it would be to share her condition with him instead of hiding it away like a dirty secret.

"Thank you," she finally whispered.

He smiled, giving her an awkward little nod. "Well," he said, his voice a touch too loud. He was uncomfortable. She didn't blame him. This interaction was far more emotional than they were used to.

For a second, Lizzie's mind dragged her back to that morning —had so little time passed?—when she'd been quite sickeningly emotional. For Isaac. And he'd thrown it in her face.

She didn't blame him.

"You're looking well," Olu continued brightly.

Lizzie gave herself a mental shake, leaning forward to pick up her cup and saucer. "Mother wouldn't say so."

"Mother's a hag, Liz."

She almost spat out her tea.

"What? It's true, and you know it."

"Stop!" She waved him off helplessly. "You'll make me choke."

"You'll be fine," he grinned. But then his smile faded, replaced by a familiar expression: brotherly concern. This was it, then; he was about to go into full-fledged parent mode. "Lizzie," he said sternly. "Will you tell me what's going on?"

Ah. Biting her lip, she put her tea safely back on the table before her suddenly shaking hands could result in a ruined carpet.

"I… I didn't want to do this," she said carefully. "I didn't want to put you in this position. I just thought I could take care of it on my own, and you'd never even know, and you could do everything how you wanted to do it. If you ever *did* do it."

He frowned. "Do what? What are you babbling on about?" And then, when she hesitated: "Come on, Liz. You know you can tell me anything."

She looked up, meeting his eyes. "And you can tell *me* anything. Do you know that?"

He stared at her for a moment too long. The colour leached from his skin, leaving behind an ashy pallor, and she saw his jaw clench. He began to tap his foot rapidly against the thick, cream carpet. He'd always done that when he was nervous. Mother had rapped his knuckles for it more than once, and now he mostly kept it under control.

But not always.

For a moment, she thought he was afraid. But then the dark cloud hovering over him passed. He sighed, and there was resignation in his eyes. "You know, don't you?" he asked.

"Yes," she said. "I'm sorry. I shouldn't have found out this way." And then, after a little pause, she clarified. "We are talking about—"

"I only have one secret, Lizzie." He managed a smile. "From you, anyway." Olu reached for his teacup, tracing its polka-dot pattern. "I always planned to tell you, you know. But the longer you leave it, the stranger it feels. As if I were hiding it in the first place. And I wasn't, not from you. Just from— "

"I know," she said quickly. "I understand."

He nodded, his gaze skating away from hers. He stared intently at the carpet under their feet, and there was something indescribable on his face. A look of loss. As if he'd been cheated.

Well, Lizzie thought, he had been. But maybe…

The idea was ridiculous, but that didn't matter. This was her brother, and they had always been ridiculous together, and she had to try *something* to make him feel better. To give him back control of the situation. Even if she failed.

"Olu… If you want to tell me, just tell me."

He looked up at her, a frown creasing his brow. "Tell you? But…"

Leaning forward, Lizzie took his hand. "Yes. Tell me. This is for you. It's about you. It belongs to you. So if *you* want to tell me, then tell me. Your words are the only ones that matter anyway."

And he understood. She'd known he would. A little smile

quirked his lips, and he sat up straighter. "Okay," Olu said. "Okay. Lizzie..." His smile grew wider. "I'm gay."

The fact that such a dark situation had led to this conversation didn't stop her from grinning back. It didn't stop her from blinking away tears, and it didn't stop her chest from swelling with pride. Before she could think better of it, Lizzie pulled her brother into a hug.

For a second, his familiar warmth transported her back to their childhood. Not the terrible moments, or the stressful moments, but the ones filled with joy. They'd had a few, somehow, despite the frigid household they'd been raised in. That was the power true family held: lighting up darkness.

It was easy to think, while her brother patted her back with such dear, familiar awkwardness, that everything would be okay now. That he was safe.

But he wasn't. Not yet.

Olu must have felt her stiffen, because he pulled back slightly, his expression suddenly hesitant. "Lizzie," he said slowly. "How did you find out?"

"Well," she said, straightening up. Putting away her softness and her love, because now the conversation would turn to evil things, and she had to be prepared. "That's the problem, actually. Mark Spencer told me. He... blackmailed me, I suppose."

Olu clenched his jaw, his eyes flashing dangerously. "Mark Spencer *blackmailed* you?"

"Yes. To put it simply, he made it clear that if I didn't follow his wishes, he would out you to our parents. He possesses some... sensitive photographs." Lizzie let out a humourless chuckle. "God, aren't we a pair? Wouldn't the whole family just die?"

But he didn't laugh with her. "It's not the same, Liz." Olu leant forward, resting his elbows on his knees. His posture was one of desolation, but his face held fury. Fury, and a determination she recognised.

"No," she murmured. "I suppose it's not." Because, somehow, unlike him, she'd managed to build a life that didn't rely on their parents' good graces.

Wait. Not *somehow*. She'd done it because Olu had been there at every turn, making sure she did. Making sure she *could*.

Would she ever fully understand all of the things her brother had done for her?

"But why blackmail *you*?" he asked suddenly, looking up at her with sharp eyes. "What did he want?"

"Ah…"

"If it was money, why didn't he come to me?"

"It's all a bit… well, complicated, actually." She looked away, avoiding his gaze.

"Lizzie," he said, his voice urgent. He put his hands on her shoulders, forcing her to face him. "Please tell me he didn't do anything…" His voice trailed off, painfully uncomfortable, and it took her a moment to realise what he was saying.

"Oh! No. No, don't worry."

He let out a sigh. "Thank fuck. But… Liz. You didn't do anything awful, did you?"

"Well, yes," she admitted, her throat tightening. *The worst thing I've ever done.* "But that doesn't matter. What matters is that I failed. I wanted to look after you, and I wasn't good enough. I wasn't smart enough. I can't handle things like you do. And now I've interrupted your life yet again because I need help."

He stared at her as though she'd sprouted an extra arm. "What on earth are you talking about?"

She sighed. "You say we're in this together, but the truth is… you're always the one making sacrifices. Doing the work. Helping *me*. I dragged you back to England when we were younger, when you'd just managed to escape. And now I had the chance to pay you back, to be the one protecting *you*. And I couldn't do it. If we fail—if I've ballsed everything up and Mark tells our parents— your life will change forever. They'll take away all of this." She waved a hand around the luxurious room. "They'll take away your power. They'll take the life you love. And it'll be my fault."

But despite her explanation, his frown didn't fade. His confusion didn't appear to abate. He stood up, shaking his head furiously.

"Lizzie," he said slowly, as though searching for words through a fog. "This isn't how I want my life to be. This isn't what I love."

"Well, no," she agreed. "Obviously not *this*. But I mean, all your travelling and—"

"I don't want to travel," he said, the words tumbling out of his mouth.

She stared. "What?"

"I don't want to travel." The second time around, the words were clearer, more confident. "I don't want to float about all the time like a piece of bloody fluff. I don't want to go months without seeing my best friend or my little sister. And I fucking hate airports," he muttered, as an afterthought. "Awful places."

"But—I don't understand," she said. "As soon you turned eighteen, you left. You started flying all over the world and—"

"Of course I did!" he cried. "*Think* about it, Lizzie. Every fucking day in that house—if Father spoke at all it was to spew some hateful bullshit about… about who was going to hell and who God should strike down and—"

She put a hand to her lips, unable to find words as he broke off. He took a shuddering breath, his head falling back, his face twisted with pain. Or perhaps just the memory of it. Sometimes, the two were equally potent.

Lizzie had never spent much time with her father. He had given her a perfunctory once-over every evening at dinner—on the evenings he was present, anyway—and made sure that her grades were high at the end of term. That was it.

But Olu… Father had spent plenty of time with Olu. *Plenty.* Trying to mould his son, to teach him how to be a man, he'd always said.

Apparently, all he'd really taught Olu was the need to hide.

She wanted to hug him. To offer him safety, the way he always had for her. Before now, it had never even occurred to her that he might need it. He was her big brother. He was the king of the world.

But he was human, and he was hurting.

"I'm sorry," she whispered.

"It's not your fault," he sighed, his hand coming to rest on her shoulder. His face hardened. "But I'll tell you one thing: *nobody* blackmails you. Nobody blackmails us." There was a familiar thread of steel in his voice. It gave her comfort.

Her brother was beautiful and charming, a true social butter-fly. Nobody saw him as dangerous. But they should. Beneath his peacock's feathers lay a razor-sharp mind and an iron will that no-one on earth could escape.

Lizzie felt calm settle over her like a fresh blanket of snow. "I know you'll handle this. I know you'll think of something."

He turned to face her, his hands on his hips, his trademark grin creeping across his face. "Actually," he said, "I already have."

Of course he had. "Okay. What's the plan?"

He came to sit beside her, his eyes alight. She knew that look. He was in control now. He was on a mission.

"First things first," he said. "We need reinforcements."

CHAPTER TWENTY-FOUR

"OUCH! YOU NUDGED MY ANKLE!"

"I didn't nudge your *ankle*—"

"You nudged my leg! My leg is connected to my ankle!"

Alexandra, who had been gazing dreamily out of the window, turned to stare reproachfully at her sisters. "Ava, you're doing it on purpose. Audrey, Lizzie told you not to ski."

And Isaac, slumped into one of his room's fancy chairs like a broken toy soldier, tried to control his reaction to the sound of Lizzie's name.

It didn't work.

"What's wrong with you?" Ava asked sharply, forgetting the sisterly discord. "Why did you make that noise?"

Isaac shrugged.

"It sounded like a dog when its tail is stepped on," Alex said. "A stray dog."

When the hell had she gotten so bloody talkative?

Isaac maintained his silence since it was the only scrap of dignity he had left. He wouldn't have let the girls in at all—he hadn't let John in, or Candy, when they'd come. But he couldn't ignore the girls.

Still, that didn't mean he had to entertain them.

"You're very boring at the minute, Isaac," said Ava, in the

manner of a scientist observing some strange phenomenon. "I thought you were only boring when grownups were around."

"I'm a grownup," Audrey argued.

Alex snorted. "You certainly are not."

Audrey sniffed. "You wouldn't understand."

"What does that even mean?"

"Just..." Audrey floundered. "Shut up."

"*All* of you shut up," Isaac snapped. The words burst from his chest without thought, without warning, without permission from his brain. But then, his brain had been sluggish since the events of yesterday.

Oh. Fuck. It was only yesterday.

And already he was shouting at children.

The girls stared at him, matching expressions of shock on their faces. Alex remained by the window, Audrey's bare foot rested on the coffee table, and Ava had her shoes on the no-doubt priceless sofa as if it were a bloody park bench. Thus frozen, they blinked in matching bafflement, creating an almost comical picture. But Isaac couldn't have laughed if you'd paid him.

"Sorry," he gritted out. "I'm sorry. Didn't mean that. I'm—I'm in a bad mood. You should probably go." He forced a weak smile, dragged his facial muscles into position with every scrap of will he had left. It was no doubt a poor effort. "Better tomorrow."

"Hmmm," Ava said, peering closely at him. "I don't know if you will be. I rather think our news will make things worse, actually."

Isaac frowned, blind-sided. "News?"

"Yes," Audrey nodded. "We came up here for a reason, you know."

The slight quirk of his lips caused by that sentence was, at least, one hundred percent real. "Thought you wanted to see me," he said dryly.

"Oh, we did," Ava nodded, her wheat-coloured hair swinging about her little face. "But Candy said that you'd be wallowing in self-pity because something was wrong with you and Lizzie—"

"Ava!" Alex snapped. "You have the biggest mouth in England!"

To her credit, Ava managed to look regretful as she slapped a hand over her lips.

But it was too late for that.

Isaac sat up straight, his dulled senses suddenly springing to attention. "Why did she say that?" He could hear how frantic his own voice sounded, how pathetic he must seem, but he couldn't stop it. "Did Lizzie say something to her?" Because for some reason, even as he told himself that Lizzie was exactly what he'd first judged her to be—a manipulative brat, not to be trusted— Isaac was desperate to come up with some explanation that would completely exonerate her. That would allow him to overcome his pride and his humiliation and his pain, that would allow him to forgive her, and mean it.

Thus far, he'd come up with fuck all. And pissed himself off in the process.

Ava just shrugged. Which was enough to have him sinking back into his chair.

"I don't think so," Audrey added. Her voice was vacant, distracted, her eyes glued to the phone that she'd just produced from her pocket. "I think she guessed. Because Lizzie left so suddenly. And you wouldn't leave your room. And then... well."

All at once, a stillness fell over the girls. Isaac marvelled at the effortless connection between three people who seemed to spend most of their time arguing. But too late, he realised he should be thinking less about the eerie similarities between the sisters and more about the cause of their sudden silence.

He looked at Ava, who was fiddling with a thread from her jumper. She pulled at the cashmere, avoiding his gaze. He looked at Alex, who had overcome her sudden verbosity and was once again staring out of the window. And then he looked at Audrey, who was still clinging to that phone.

"What?" he demanded. His mind flew to dark places. Force of habit, always expecting the worst. But now, instead of the house fires and family illness that had haunted his teenage fears, his mind went immediately to Lizzie. Lizzie in a plane crash; Lizzie in a car accident; Lizzie missing her insulin.

Audrey held out the phone, and he took it, his heart in his mouth. When he saw the words on the screen, he nearly laughed with relief. It was nothing. It was fine. Just another bullshit gossip column about him and...

And a mystery woman?

Fuck. Swallowing hard, Isaac scrolled down the screen, tapping to enlarge the image.

The blood drained from his face as the picture ballooned, showing he and Lizzie in the spa, naked, and far too close. His face was barely visible in this picture.

Hers wasn't.

He looked up, his cheeks burning. Why the hell did it have to be the girls who brought this to his attention? He wanted to jump out the fucking window.

His voice gruff, he asked awkwardly, "Everyone seen this?"

"Well, I assume so," Alex said. "It is a national newspaper. I'm not certain of the circulation, but—"

"I mean," he interrupted tightly, "have your parents seen this?"

"Oh," she said. "Um. Yes."

"And they said...?" he asked, working hard to keep his irritation hidden.

"Well, they didn't really talk about it in front of us..."

"Kate says Lizzie should be sacked," Ava murmured helpfully.

"I bet she fucking does," Isaac growled. "Jesus. Okay. I... thanks. For telling me. I need you to go."

"So you can call Lizzie and ask her to marry you?" Ava grinned.

"No." Three faces fell at the harsh finality in his voice. Suddenly self-conscious, Isaac cleared his throat. "I mean—I don't have her number. Need to call my publicist."

"Oh," Ava smiled. "Of course! Well, don't worry about that." She stood and skipped over to the side table, snatching up his phone. Fractured shards of screen fell like snow as she picked it up. "Um—did I break it?"

"No," he said tersely. "What are you doing?"

She ignored him, tapping away at the half-destroyed screen. "There. Now you have her number." As if it were the easiest thing in the world. Well; clearly it was. She put the phone on the table in front of him, and Isaac stared at the slim, battered piece of metal. The piece of metal that now had as much power as a fucking black hole. One slip and he'd be sucked in. Should he ring her? He shouldn't. He should. He had to, now, surely? Or was he just making excuses? He had no idea. It would've been a lot fucking easier if he simply couldn't.

But what did children like Ava know of *couldn't*? When had she ever heard the word *can't*?

Suddenly, Lizzie's stuttering words returned to him, as clear as if she were still in his room, holding back tears. *"It was wrong, and I was desperate, and I'm sorry."*

He shook the memory away.

When he returned to his senses, it was to see the girls standing in a tight little trio, Audrey's arms slung around her sisters' shoulders as she leaned dramatically on her good foot.

Despite the urgency coursing through his veins, Isaac took a moment to glance sceptically at her ankle. "That bad?"

Audrey blushed. "Not really. But Lizzie said—" She broke off at the look on his face. "Are you okay?"

"Fine," he said. "I'm fine. Later."

"We'll see you at dinner?" They began hobbling toward the door like a line of can-can dancers.

"Maybe."

"I don't think he's going to come," Ava whispered.

"I think he can hear you."

"He can't; I'm whispering." And then, raising her voice, she chirped, "Bye, Isaac!"

He directed a half-hearted wave to their backs. Blessedly, they left and shut the damn door behind them.

Finally alone, Isaac released all the emotions that had been

203

swelling painfully in his chest—the hurt, the worry, the anger, the pure exhaustion. It came tumbling out in a sigh as vast as a tidal wave. He rubbed his hands across his face, scrubbing at his eyes to relieve the splitting headache he'd developed some time in the past ten minutes. Like a lightning bolt, pain scorched its way through his brain. This was too much.

Lizzie was gone. She was never truly there in the first place. His arrogant fantasies of belonging, of partnership, of something like love, lay burnt-out on the ground—and the devil on his shoulder laughed at the embers. He had no idea what to do about this fucking contract, or about the warning Lizzie had given him. He couldn't fathom what in the hell was going on with Mark. His phone kept fucking ringing, his chest was burning, his head was dull, his fingers clumsy, he couldn't write a goddamn word, he spent all night dreaming of her—

And now this fucking mess. Because of him, Lizzie's privacy was torn to shreds. Maybe he shouldn't care, all things considered; maybe he should shrug and say it served her right. But God, he couldn't think like that. Even if he'd hated her, he couldn't think like that.

Why didn't he hate her?

His movements slow and painful, as if he'd woken from a century's sleep, Isaac leaned forward and picked up his phone. The battered screen displayed his brand new contact. *Lizzie*, it said, with little hearts at the end. He had no idea how Ava had added those hearts. For a moment, he considered editing the contact, just to delete them. But he couldn't make his fingers move.

He should call Jane. Clearly, this was why she'd been harassing him non-stop. And he owed her an apology, anyway. She probably wouldn't make that easy. He didn't have any excuses for his rudeness recently. *I fell for a frozen woman; she became a forest fire.* Had a nice ring to it, but Jane wasn't one for poetry.

Resigned to a verbal scalping, Isaac found his publicist's number and hit 'Call'. She answered on the first ring.

"Finally. What the fuck is going on with you?" Her words were right, but her tone was all wrong. She didn't sound furious or caustic but concerned. Isaac's gut tightened uncomfortably.

"Nothing."

"Mmhm. Sounds like bullshit. But I'm not your therapist. Have you seen the papers?"

"Yeah."

"You okay with this?"

He frowned. "Why would I be okay with this?"

"Well, y'know. The bad boy image does you good. Some people find this sort of attention worthwhile."

Isaac's jaw set as fury burned at his chest. "Not just about me. Lizzie."

"Oh, so it's true? According to my contacts in the city, that's Elizabeth… Elizabeth O… How the fuck do you pronounce this?"

"Uh…" Isaac stood, wandering over to the window. Squinting into the sunlit snow, remembering the night he'd held her in moonlight. "I don't think I know her full name."

There was a pause. Then Jane barked out a laugh edged in disbelief. "You fucked this girl in a spa and you don't know her name? What's up with you right now?"

Isaac closed his eyes. Took a deep breath. *Inhale, exhale.* He opened his eyes again, and let the calm, white view soothe him. Followed the jagged soar of the mountains up into the sky. Then, finally, when his anger was under control, said, "Please don't talk about her like that."

"Oh," Jane said. "Oh. Sorry. Well... what do you want me to do? Have you two spoken about it?"

"No."

"I know you're not big on verbal communication, but I'm gonna need some more direction here."

Fair enough. "Can you tell me—?"

"What happened? Yep. It was that fucking blogger. She's some upper-middle-class time-waster, it turns out. Found out about the retreat and booked a bed-and-breakfast in the village. I threatened to slap her with a court order so she spilled, but she'd already published the pictures, so. Oh, and I dealt with the hotel." Jane's voice took on the dark, robotic cadence she used when dealing with business. It was the tone that had cowed a thousand men and would likely cow a million more. "They've refunded the whole party's stay. They're *deeply* ashamed that such an invasion occurred due to their lack of security."

"I bet."

"Mark sent me a very grateful email. He also refused to confirm or deny the girl's identity, which I guess is good for our purposes. The papers still haven't published a name. But there are whispers. You know her dad is some Nigerian oil tycoon? And her mother is the daughter of a viscount?"

Isaac sighed. "Heard something like that."

"A viscount! I didn't even know we still had that shit." Jane cackled. "Inbred fuckers. Oh; sorry. Anyway, I've got things under control for now. But I wanted to check in with you since you're always so unpredictable. Not that you made it easy," she added, her tone suddenly severe.

"I know. I'm sorry."

She paused, probably waiting for more. But the familiar anxiety was clawing at his throat, sending his mind into a panic, like a deer spooked by wolves in the shadows.

"You should talk to this woman," Jane was saying. "I mean— does she talk? Or is she like you?"

"She's nothing like me." *Understatement of the year.*

But all Jane said was, "Good. Should make my life easier. Call me back, okay? Keep me updated."

"Okay."

"You promise?"

"Promise."

"Good. Look after yourself, chick. You sound like shit."

He barked out a laugh. "Thanks, Jane."

"No problem. Don't ignore my calls again or I'll carve my initials into your balls." She hung up.

Isaac really wished she hadn't. He wished she'd stayed on the phone, badgering and berating and threatening him, for at least another hour.

But things never happened the way you wanted them to; he should know that by now.

Still, Isaac put off the next step for as long as possible. He went to the bathroom, filled the sink with cold water, dunked his fucking head in there and held his breath til his lungs burned. When he emerged, his nerve-endings sang in icy contentment. He felt something close to clarity. It helped. Chasing the feeling, Isaac changed his clothes and shoved on his boots, lacing them up tight. Then he left his room for the first time all day, skulking through the corridors with a scowl on his face, no doubt scaring the shit out of the other patrons. A couple speaking rapid Italian gave him a wide berth as he stormed through the hotel's foyer, but it wasn't enough to make him pause. He couldn't control himself at times like this, times when he felt savage. He didn't have the energy to zip everything up tight inside of himself, to choke on his own pent-up feelings for everyone else's comfort.

He had to get outside.

———

THE COLD SLAPPED him hard and he welcomed the blow, stamping through the crystal-sharp layers of fresh snow. He could follow the salted paths to the ski slopes, or down into the village, but he didn't want to. He wanted to storm across untouched territory, towards the army of firs that edged the hotel's land, because that was where he felt strongest. Solid. Ready.

But when he finally reached the mess of pure, untouched nature—pressed his palm against the raw fucking bark, for Christ's sake—it *still* wasn't enough. He still wasn't ready.

He rang her anyway.

It didn't take long for her to pick up. Not long at all. Almost as if she'd been waiting for him. Despite himself—despite the betrayal that hung around his neck like an iron chain, the humiliation that shackled him—Isaac's heart leapt as the call was answered.

Until a man's voice said, "Keynes."

Isaac swallowed, hard, grinding his teeth. The last thing he needed right now, when he was at the edge of humanity, was to speak to someone who wasn't Lizzie. Someone who *should* be Lizzie, by rights. Because as much pain as her voice would cause him, it was all he'd been ready to hear.

So he didn't hate himself too much when he replied, his voice harsh, "Who the fuck is this?"

There was a slight pause, heavy and stiff. And then the man said, "I already told you. Keynes."

"Where's Lizzie?" Isaac demanded, and he could hear himself as though from a distance, sounding like a fucking caveman or worse. Didn't help. Didn't stop him.

"Lizzie isn't available at the moment, I'm afraid." And there was something—something in the purposeful cadence of those words, in the icy stiffness each syllable was imbued with, that was so familiar it felt like a punch to the gut.

"You her brother?" Isaac asked.

"I don't see how that's any of your concern," the man said. Yep; definitely Lizzie's brother. "I should be asking who *you* are. But I believe I already know. Isaac Montgomery, I presume?"

Isaac pressed his hand so hard into the trunk of a nearby tree that its bark grazed his skin, carving right through his callouses. "Yeah. Where's Liz?"

The man—Keynes—let out a sharp laugh. "What on earth makes you think that I would *ever* let you speak to my sister?"

"I think," Isaac said tightly, "that your sister is a grown woman who doesn't need your permission to talk to me."

"I suppose that's true. And yet, I find myself unable to care. I returned to London to find my sister in pieces. She won't tell me what it is that makes her look so hopeless; all I know is that she has been embarrassed in the national news because of you. When I spoke to her last, she was doing well. Now she's a ghost. Am I wrong to think that it's your fault?"

Shit. Isaac took a deep breath, wishing—wishing for so many things. But most of all, wishing he could speak the way this man did. With confidence, with eloquence, with surety. Every word precise and powerful. Because there was nothing Isaac could say to make Keynes seem even close to wrong.

"I need to speak to her," he finally, foolishly said. "I made a mistake. And I want to tell her that."

"I see. Well, Montgomery, here's the thing: you say my sister is a grown woman. You're correct. She is intelligent and capable and accomplished, and I am proud of her. But she is also in love with you. Lizzie would happily lay down and die for the people she loves. And the thing is—I see no evidence that you are worth her devotion. None whatsoever. So this is how it will happen: you will put the phone down. I will delete this call. I will block your number from her phone—not that you'll ever contact her again. Because if you do, Montgomery, you will find yourself in difficulties of the kind you have never even imagined. There's more than one underworld in London, you see. And mine is much better funded than yours. Do we have an understanding?"

Isaac stared at nothing, his mind churning. Keynes waited silently for an answer—no, for submission.

He could keep fucking waiting. Isaac ended the call.

He stood for a moment, imagining the look that might be on Keynes's face right now. Thinking about the fact that the other man probably thought he'd won. That Isaac was intimidated by his threats, so familiar and yet so strange. That Isaac was giving up.

And perhaps Keynes's speech might have worked. Perhaps Isaac might have agreed, might have left Lizzie alone, might have accepted that the differences between them, and all that had happened, meant they could never work.

But in the face of the other man's anger, Isaac realised something.

He admired it. He admired Keynes. And more than that, he admired Lizzie for protecting her brother just as fiercely.

When he was a teenager, Isaac had broken the law. He'd done

it again and again, with no remorse, because he'd had to. He saw his mother fading faster than a woman her age should, watched her work three jobs to put food on the table, and he'd just fucking had to.

Sometimes, the wrong choice was the only choice that made sense.

"Isaac, I'm falling in love you."

He'd rejected the love of a woman who'd do anything for those she cared about. He'd told her she wasn't good enough, for fuck's sake.

Some people—people who'd never sinned a day in their lives—might have the right to be so high and fucking mighty.

He didn't have that right, and he didn't want it. Because he was just like her. And she was just like him.

Isaac turned, marching back towards the hotel.

Let Keynes block his number. Didn't matter. Isaac made another call as he walked, and Jane picked up after the first ring.

"What's up?" she barked.

"Need information."

"And you called me? Darling. I'm flattered."

Isaac jogged up the steps to the hotel's entrance, grim determination on his face. "You know everything."

"Just what a lady loves to hear. What do you need?"

"Lizzie and her brother. Keynes. Think they're in London." He took a deep breath. "Find out where."

CHAPTER TWENTY-FIVE

"WERE YOU ON THE PHONE?" Lizzie asked, emerging from her bedroom. "I thought I heard you talking."

Olu sat with the paper propped over his knee, his arms spread wide as he read the broadsheet. Why he still read paper news, she had no idea. "Just Theo checking in," he murmured absently.

"Oh, wonderful! Will they be here soon?"

A knock sounded at the door. For a second, Olu became unnaturally still, every muscle in his body freezing. But then, like a computer getting over a glitch, he swung smoothly back into motion, folding the paper with sharp flicks of his wrist. "They're here now," he said.

Lizzie frowned slightly. Perhaps she was imagining it, but her brother seemed slightly… on edge.

But her confusion was pushed aside almost immediately, replaced by anticipation. The others were here. The plan was in motion. And of course Olu was on edge; he must be so nervous. But it was her job to support him now. They were in this together.

He strode into the hall to answer the door and Lizzie followed, her socked feet practically bouncing with every step. She was wearing her pyjamas despite the fact that it was only mid-afternoon, and she hadn't re-done her hair since yesterday. For some reason, she simply hadn't had the energy to make herself presentable since... Well. Since everything. She felt safer now that she and Olu were together, but that didn't help with her other problem. The problem she'd rather die than articulate.

I held something precious in the palm of my hand. Now it lies shattered on the ground, and I'm the one who threw it.

It was embarrassing, this feeling of utter hopelessness in the face of what should be happy moments. And it was even more embarrassing when Olu opened the front door to reveal a group of familiar and unfamiliar faces, all grinning.

She was not dressed for visitors, Lizzie realised at once. Not at all.

But no-one seemed to notice that as they streamed into the hall, sharing greetings and hugs.

Theo led the way, pulling Keynes into a huge bearhug. "It's been a bloody century!" he cried.

Yen followed, and her familiar smile soothed some of the discomfort in Lizzie's chest. It was only Yen, only Theo. They didn't care about all that. The Chamberlain household had been like an alien planet to Lizzie and Olu during childhood. The Chamberlains didn't have a dress code. They didn't insult each other's appearance. They ate breakfast in their slippers, for goodness' sake!

"Lizzie," Yen gushed. "How nice to see you!" And she sounded like she meant it. Her smile warm, she drew Lizzie in for a hug.

"I've missed you," she whispered.

And tears filled Lizzie's eyes as she realised that she'd missed Yen too.

"I brought cake," the younger woman added, pulling back. "And you must meet Jennifer! And Aria!"

"Oh," Lizzie nodded, blinking rapidly. Because the tears in her eyes could not spill over, especially not while she was introduced to Theo's future wife.

The men appeared to have finished their hug, which had gone on for rather a long time, involved gentle swearing, and turned slightly violent towards the end. They were now clapping each other jovially on the back as they faced the rest of the group.

"Keynes, Lizzie," Theo said. "This is Jenny. My fiancée." He stepped forward to grasp the hand of one of the women who stood awkwardly by the door, a polite smile on her face. She was strikingly beautiful, with dark skin and elegantly arranged hair that Lizzie quite envied. Her dress and coat were subdued in style, but the way they fit her generous frame caught the eye.

"Jennifer," she corrected, giving Theo a long-suffering look. And as she turned her head slightly, the light flashed off of the scars on the right side of her face; a scattering of teardrops that almost looked like decoration. But then she gave a little wave, and Lizzie's curiosity was immediately set aside by the sight of her ring. It was bloody enormous.

"And this is Aria," Theo said, putting an arm around the woman on his other side.

Aria… Ah. The maid of honour.

Her appearance matched her handwriting: bold, intense, and apparently unbothered. She was tall and statuesque, taking up a hell of a lot of space with both her body and the sheer force of her personality, which practically vibrated around her. Her long, dark hair emphasised her high cheekbones and kohl-lined eyes. A plethora of silver piercings stood out brightly against her brown skin, hoops sparkling in her nose and eyebrow. And as she unbuttoned her long coat in the heat of the hallway, Lizzie saw a maze of jet-black tattoos snaking their way across the other woman's shoulders. She was… an unusual character.

Then she grinned and said, "You got my note, yeah?" And for absolutely no reason at all, Lizzie liked her at once.

"Yes," she nodded. "I did."

"Nice one." The woman turned to Keynes. "And did you get my texts? Cuz you've been airing me."

"Calm yourself, woman. I called you down here, didn't I?" Lizzie blinked at the easy familiarity in her brother's tone. He and Aria were friends?

Then Olu stepped forward and pulled both Aria and Jennifer

into a warm hug. "It's nice to finally meet you two in person," he said. "Come in."

They all made their way into the living room, everyone chattering about the journey, the traffic in London, the weather. Lizzie floated in the midst of it all, vaguely disorientated. So many voices, so much happiness. The flat was warmer than ever with the combined energy of all this bloody good cheer.

And she stood apart from it all. Watching through glass, trapped by something the others couldn't even see. *Sorry I'm so quiet; I'm just coming to terms with the fact that I might never be happy again.*

God, that was dramatic. At least, she hoped it was dramatic. But right now it felt like the truth.

"Hey," Yen murmured, nudging her gently. "You okay?"

Lizzie looked up, startled. "Yeah. Just a bit overwhelmed, I suppose."

"Don't worry. It'll be like old times. When we were kids." Yen tucked the dark waterfall of her hair behind one ear. It immediately slid forward again, and she rolled her eyes. The familiar tick made Lizzie relax, just a little bit. Dragged her out of regret and into the moment, if only for an instant.

"Yes," she agreed. "I suppose it will."

"You want cake? I brought lemon tart. Jenny loves it. I think Theo left it by the door—" She moved to fetch it, but Lizzie held up a staying hand.

"No cake for me."

"What? You love cake. Don't tell me you're on a diet."

"Not exactly," Lizzie hedged.

"What are you two muttering about over there?" Olu called. "Come and sit down. We're holding a war council."

"Oooh," Aria grinned. "I like that. Please, tell us: who do we need to destroy?"

"You're so bloodthirsty," Jennifer muttered, rolling her eyes. Aria elbowed her in the ribs. But the women shared a gleam in their brown eyes as they bickered, one that spoke of years of teasing and laughter. It reminded Lizzie of the Spencer girls, bringing a sad smile to her face as she moved to sit beside Olu.

"Right," he began, his voice firm. He sounded like their father when he spoke this way. Authority rang through his every word. "I called you all because I need… well. Truthfully, I don't *need* anything. But I want your support."

The little gathering quieted immediately, solemnity falling on the group. Theo sprawled in the room's only armchair as if he owned it, and his voice was a drawl when he asked, "But really, Keynes: who *do* we need to destroy?" His casual posturing did nothing to hide the concern in his dark eyes.

Olu shook his head. "Before we get into that, there's something I want to share with you all." His words were strong and sure, without a moment's hesitation. "I'm gay."

There was a moment of silence, as if the air itself was absorbing that information. And then the room erupted all at once.

It took a moment for Lizzie to realise that the eruption was one of happiness.

"Oh, Keynes!" Jennifer cried.

Yen grinned, clapping her hands like a schoolgirl.

Aria crossed the room to clap Olu firmly on the back. "I'm kind of flattered to be included in your grand coming out," she winked.

Olu rolled his eyes. "Well, since you dragged yourself along…"

"You invited me, you cheeky fucker!" But she was laughing through her mock-outrage.

Then Theo stood too and held out a hand. Lizzie watched in confusion as her brother rose, his face serious. The two men shook firmly, as if closing a business deal—but then Theo pulled Olu into a hug.

Lizzie shared a look with Yen, who appeared equally baffled. Maybe this was some kind of manly emotional ritual. Whatever it was, when the best friends separated they were both smiling widely.

"Thank you," Theo said softly. "For telling us."

Olu nodded, swallowing hard.

"We should talk later. Okay?"

"Alright." The men shared a long look full of nuances Lizzie couldn't begin to understood. But she knew that her brother looked truly happy, truly relaxed, for the first time in…

Well. A long time.

Maybe ever.

"Well, then," Jennifer said, folding her hands neatly in her lap. "Should we get back to the death and destruction?"

"Oh, *I'm* bloodthirsty?" Aria scoffed.

"There will be no death," Olu, said, drawing the attention back to him. "But things are about to change for me. For us." He shot Lizzie a smile. "I am about to lose my inheritance. I'm aware that I've had the luxury of avoiding real life for some time. I won't be able to do that for long. And I might need help while I figure out how to… navigate normality."

"You know we will always help you," Yen said softly. "We're family."

Lizzie looked around the room and saw that sentiment echoed in every face, both the familiar and the new. And as her brother began to share the details of Mark's plot with everyone, Lizzie realised that Yen was more right than she knew.

This. This was what family meant.

CHAPTER TWENTY-SIX

IT TOOK ALMOST three hours to drive from the Midlands to the capital. So of course, the visitors stayed the night.

Despite the malice that had brought them all together, it was a happy evening. It would be the happiest in Lizzie's memory, in fact. If it weren't for the time she'd spent at *Charmonix-Mailet.*

It was strange, she thought, arming herself for battle the next morning. She hadn't even spent a night with Isaac—had known him for mere weeks. And yet, the beautiful fragments of whatever they had been formed a moonlit mosaic in Lizzie's mind. One that would stand out amongst the staid tapestry of her life forever.

But this wasn't the time for such thoughts. This was the time for utter invulnerability.

Her parents demanded nothing less.

Lizzie noted down her breakfast, her dosage, her blood sugar for the morning, pausing to admire the growing uniformity of her numbers. Once the measurements had been so sporadic, and wildly unpredictable when she did record them. She'd resented her body, resented its reliance on anything other than her own force of will. But that was a foolish attitude. She could see that now, as clearly as she could see the positive changes her care was causing.

Yes, her illness was exhausting. Yes, she wished she could eat without thought, dance without pause, leave the house without checking and double-checking that she had her insulin.

But when she got things right, it was rewarding. So rewarding. And today, of all days, Lizzie needed all the positivity she could get.

"Ready, Liz?"

She looked up to find Olu at her door, leaning against the frame. He looked charming in his checked suit, an emerald pocket square matching his eyes. She was similarly overdressed in her pastel twin set. And this time, she'd remembered the pearls.

It wouldn't help. They both knew that. Nothing would help.

But still she smiled and set her journal aside and said, "Ready."

The rest of the house was quiet. Jen and Theo were in the spare room while Yen and Aria bedded down in the lounge like children at a sleepover. But the Olusegun-Keynes household rose bright and early, thank you very much. So Lizzie and Olu left the flat for the winter-bright, grey-tinged sunshine of a London morning, holding hands as they went. Like Hansel and Gretel.

Off into the woods…

————

THE ROOM WAS WARM. Its walls were red as blood, shot through with gold, and the curtains and upholstery matched. The effect was unsettling, to say the least, but that was what Mother had intended when choosing the decor.

Despite the unmistakable fact that this visit was unwelcome— this *was* Mother's least favourite parlour—tea was set out on the table before them. Or rather, between them. Lizzie and Olu sat on one side of the room. And opposite them sat the enemy.

Their parents.

It was barely 10 a.m., but Mother was dressed beautifully. Far better than Lizzie. The woman could barely hold herself back from saying so, Lizzie knew; her ice-blue eyes ran over Lizzie's figure with thinly veiled disgust.

Father, for his part, seemed annoyed that they were in the same room at all.

"Lizzie," Mother said, her voice sickeningly sweet. Which meant that an insult was coming. "What on earth is the matter, dear? You're absolutely huge."

"It's true, Elizabeth," Father said, crossing his legs. He looked at her seriously. "Are you in disgrace?"

Lizzie jolted. "I beg your pardon, Father?"

"Are you pregnant, child?"

"No!" She felt Olu's warning hand come to rest on her shoulder. Careful. Control. Because their mother would take vicious advantage, should Lizzie come undone. "No," she said again, disguising her outrage with a delicate laugh. "Certainly not. I have gained some weight—"

"At least three stone," her mother sniffed.

"I don't think it matters," Olu cut in, his tone firm. "We've come to talk to you about something serious."

"You know," Mother murmured, "my friend showed me something the other day." Her voice was soft. Her gaze was sharp. "A girl in the papers, cavorting with a criminal abroad. Quite scandalous. She said that the girl resembled you, Lizzie, but I told her that she was mistaken of course. Only now that I see how your figure has… increased," she said, lowering her voice on the final word as if it were a curse. "Well! I understand her confusion."

"Lizzie has been in England," Olu said tightly. "With Yen."

"The Chamberlain girl?"

The only Yen we know, yes, Mother, Lizzie thought acidly. But she simply smiled and nodded.

"Well. That's certainly gratifying to hear." She didn't look gratified. But then, when had she ever? Lizzie gazed at her mother's pinched face with something close to pity in her heart. This woman had been born with everything, and life had only given her more. Yet she was constantly wanting. Never satisfied. Empty on the inside, it seemed.

And Father was no better. Clinging to his trophy, as though the pinnacle of breeding by his side would make all of England forget the colour of his skin.

"Mother," Olu said. "Father. I came home because I have something to tell you."

At this, their father perked up, his obvious boredom with the conversation fading. "Yes? You have news, my son? Perhaps you wish to come home again, to work with me now, like a good boy, ah?"

"Certainly, I will," Olu said. "If you want me to."

"Of course I want you to!" Father cried. "You know this! Long, I have wanted you to—"

"I'm gay," Olu interrupted.

Silence fell. It wasn't like yesterday's silence; this was no pause of surprise.

This was a silence of finality.

"Impossible," their father whispered.

"Well, no," Olu said dryly. "It's really not."

"Impossible," Father repeated, his voice stronger now. Harsher. Like barbed wire. "No son of mine could be an abomination," he spat. His face was alight with fury, and when he stood, Lizzie thought she saw violence in the tightening of his fists.

Olu stood to face him, and the two men stared each other down: the father visibly shaking with rage, the son perfectly still, jaw set, eyes a challenge.

After a beat, Father turned away with a shout of disgust. Lizzie felt her tension ease, just a little, as he stormed from the room, cursing in Yoruba. Olu sat down slowly.

There. It was done. Now they had only their mother to handle. Lizzie found Olu's hand beside hers, held it tight, but she couldn't risk looking at him right now; if she saw hurt on his face, she would most definitely lose control. Instead she turned to their mother, the woman who's approval had always hung just out of reach, like a carrot dangling from a stick. A carrot Lizzie had long hated herself for always, always reaching for.

No more.

"Say something," Lizzie whispered. And then, when no answer came: *"You will speak."*

Because her mother could hold a silence for days. Weeks, even. She often had, when it suited her.

But not this time. No. Languid as a lizard, her eyes rolled down to where Lizzie and Olu's hands met. There was no decoding the expression on her face; there never was.

But her words were clear enough.

"Why did you bring him here?" she asked, looking at Lizzie now, as though no-one else were in the room.

"I—what do you mean?" Lizzie faltered, blessedly confused for a moment.

Until Mother made everything crystal-clear. "Why did you bring him here?" she repeated, her voice a hiss as she jerked her head toward Olu. It was the most uncontrolled movement Lizzie had ever seen from the woman. Fine strands of golden hair fluttered free from her chignon and her pale eyes blazed. "Have you no consideration for your father? No respect?"

"Have you no love for your son?" Lizzie shot back, forcing the words past the lump in her throat.

Mother's eyes were cold. Colder than Lizzie's could ever hope to be.

"I have no son," she said, in the same sort of casual tone with which she might order a gin and tonic.

Lizzie surged to her feet. She had been so good for so long; had controlled her temper beautifully. This might be the moment it snapped.

But then, at the mocking tilt of her mother's lips, Lizzie hesitated. Reigned in her rage. Took a deep breath—and remembered Mother saying, long ago, *Don't flare your nostrils so, darling. You already look like a horse.*

Took another.

And then she spoke as calmly as Mother had done.

"You have no daughter either, then. You are childless now. And I for one, will not miss you."

She thought she saw a flicker of something—something indefinable but most definitely out of place—in Mother's eyes. But just as quickly, it was gone. Because Mother didn't have Lizzie's flaws. Mother was *always* in control.

Let her remain that way, then; untouchable. Perfect, and alone. She was welcome to her precious restraint, her discipline.

But Lizzie was tired of it.

Before she and Olu reached the door, Lizzie turned back, sparing her mother one last glance. "By the way," she said, "I'm not going back to Paris. I'm not going back to Europe at all, and I will never perform again. You'll have to find yourself another family trophy."

Mother said nothing. Nothing needed to be said.

Olu and Lizzie left the house peacefully, hand in hand, just as they had entered. Nobody tried to stop them. Nobody ran after them to say that it was all a mistake, that of course their parents would accept Olu, because what kind of monsters wouldn't?

Nobody said anything like that.

But it didn't matter. Not anymore. Because now, they were free.

Finally, finally, free.

CHAPTER TWENTY-SEVEN

ELLEN HAD REPLIED.

"We don't deserve forgiveness. It's not an exchange." That's what Isaac had said. And he'd been right. So when Lizzie had apologised to the friend she'd so cruelly pushed away, it certainly hadn't been in anticipation of this moment.

And yet, here it was. Lizzie stared at her phone screen, at the little blue bubble she'd never expected to see.

"Are you okay?" Jennifer asked, coming to sit on the sofa with a bowl of sweet popcorn. Aria and Yen followed closely behind, carrying their own treats.

Lizzie clutched her bag of plain peanuts self-consciously as she looked up. "Yeah! Fine."

"You're looking at your phone like it just tried to bite you," Jennifer observed, disbelief colouring her voice.

"What's up?" Aria prompted, throwing herself into the nearby armchair. "Sharing is caring."

"Um…" Lizzie found three pairs of eyes gazing at her expectantly. Even worse was the hint of worry in Yen's. And yet, though the attention should make Lizzie uncomfortable at least— and irritated at best—instead she felt… oddly pleased. These women were concerned. For her. As if they were friends.

Well; they were about to sit down to a Netflix marathon while

Olu and Theo ran around London taking care of mysterious 'business'. Perhaps they *were* friends.

"It's this girl," Lizzie heard herself say, as if from afar. "Ellen. We were close. But I made a mistake and... I wasn't very nice to her."

"Ah," Aria said, nodding sagely. "Happens to me all the time."

"It really does," Jennifer piped up. And then, when Aria reached over to smack her arm, "Ow! What? It does!"

"So what's going on?" Yen asked. "Are you arguing?"

"Ah, no. I sent her a message over Facebook. You know, to apologise. And she just replied."

"What did she say?"

"I don't know. I haven't opened it yet."

Jennifer rested her hand on Lizzie's shoulder, a soft smile plumping her cheeks. She really was uncommonly pretty. And unusually sweet. She and Yen would make perfect sisters. "Do you want to open it together?"

Lizzie took a deep breath. "Actually, that might be nice."

Which is how she ended up surrounded by a small crowd of women, pecking like mother hens, as she opened Ellen's reply.

Hey, Lizzie. I only just saw your message. I'm sorry I missed it. I'm really happy to hear from you.

Lizzie's face dissolved into a grin of disbelief.

"There you go!" Aria crowed, reaching over to slap her on the back. "Everything's gonna be fine."

I feel really bad about what happened, but I was so worried about you. I'm glad to hear you're doing better now. And I most definitely accept your apology. How are things? What are you up to now?

"She forgives me," Lizzie murmured.

"Of course she does," Yen smiled sunnily. "You're a good person. I don't think you'd ever do something unforgivable."

And just like that, Lizzie's good mood evaporated. Because she *had* done something unforgivable... to the person whose forgiveness she wanted more than anything in the world.

Her smile feeling rigid and plastic on her face, Lizzie put away her phone. "Alright then! What are we watching, ladies?"

224

Distracted, the other women launched into a discussion of their options. It didn't take long to settle on *Buffy*.

"How long do you think the guys are gonna be?" Asked Aria, tearing open a grab bag of Maltesers.

"I don't know," Yen said. "I mean, obviously Keynes was upset after the um… the visit with his parents this morning. Maybe they're drinking."

"I think it has something to do with this Mark person," Jennifer murmured. All eyes swung to her.

"You know," Aria said, her voice certain.

"No." Jennifer shook her head firmly. "No idea! Total mystery. I know as much as you lot."

"Liar," Aria snorted. "Fine. Whatever. Keep the secrets of thy marriage bed."

"Shut up," Jennifer said, grabbing a handful of popcorn. "Lizzie, do you want anything to eat?"

Great. Here came the awkward moment. Lizzie gave her airiest, most unaffected smile as she murmured, "Oh, no thank you."

"You're not just going to eat nuts, are you?" Aria demanded. "Are you on a diet?"

"Um… I… I'm diabetic." Lizzie waited for the awkward silence.

But none came.

"Ohhhh," Yen said. "That's why you didn't want the lemon tart!"

"Ah, yeah."

"Hm…" She looked thoughtful. "I wonder if I can make it with artificial sweeteners…"

"Shall we start from the beginning?" Aria cut in, waving the TV remote around. "Or just choose the best episodes?"

"You know I have to start from the beginning," Jennifer sighed. "I hate watching TV out of order."

"Fine, God. You're so anal."

As *Buffy*'s familiar theme tune began to play and the women settled down, Lizzie sat in slightly dazed silence. That… That was it? That was all? After all these months of treating her illness as some kind of painful secret, of telling only those who absolutely *had* to know—she announced her weakness to the world, and the response was a mumble about sugar-free lemon tart?

But then she remembered what Isaac had told her. *"No weakness here."* And he'd seemed so sure.

Maybe he'd been right, she thought as she turned her attention to the TV.

It seemed he'd been right about a lot of things.

————

BY LATE AFTERNOON, the boys still weren't back and Aria was practically bouncing off the walls.

"We have to be home by tonight!" she kept saying. "I have a Skype call with the wedding planner."

"We'll be back in time," Jennifer soothed, patting her friend's tattooed hand reassuringly. "Don't worry, love."

"Whose wedding is this anyway?" Lizzie chuckled under her breath.

"I'm still not sure," Yen murmured back with a smirk of her own. "You know, Jenny's not even in the group chat."

"The group chat?"

"Aria made it. It's called *The Wedding Avengers.* Me, her, your brother, and my mum. Jenny's not invited because she wants to keep things low-key, which Aria says is a 'scandalous waste of a wealthy husband'."

Lizzie almost choked on her laughter—but the humour came with a side of pain as the headache that had dogged her all day sharpened. She hissed, putting a hand to her temple.

"You okay?" Yen frowned.

"Yeah, just a headache. I think I need to… I'll be right back." She rushed out of the room, heading down the hall to the bedroom that Olu always referred to as hers. He'd certainly decorated it for her, back when he'd moved in. Now the purple walls and posters of her favourite ballerinas felt slightly OTT, but she still loved the place.

Lizzie found the little kit that contained her metre and readied the needle, grabbing a fresh test strip. She must be high. She'd had this headache since lunch. Somewhere in the background, she heard the front door open and the murmur of multiple voices; Olu and Theo were back. But she couldn't go to greet them until she knew what was going on with her blood sugar.

Only… it appeared that *nothing* was going on with her blood sugar. She blinked at the number on the monitor, confused. It wasn't perfect, but it was within the range she'd expect before dinner. Certainly not high enough to cause the pain in her head. So what was going on?

"Hey," came Olu's familiar voice from the doorway. "You okay? Yen said you have a headache."

"Ah, yeah." She gave him a quick smile before returning her attention to the metre. "I'm fine, thanks. Everything go okay today?"

"I have a lot to tell you," he said dryly. "Put it that way. And Theo helped, like I knew he would. Seriously, Liz, are you okay? Why are you looking at that… What is that, anyway?" He came into the room, frowning with concern.

"It's how I test my blood sugar," she told him.

"Is it bad?"

"No. It's fine. But I have this awful headache and if it's not that…"

"Oh," Olu said, sounding relieved. "It's probably just your hair."

She squinted at him. "What?"

"Yeah, remember. You used to get headaches all the time, because Mother did your hair too tight. And you really went for it today."

"Oh." She raised a hand to her scalp, realised that it did feel slightly tender. "Maybe… Maybe you're right."

"I don't know why you wear it like that, anyway. Your hair's so pretty."

"It's out of control. It's messy."

"No it's not," Olu said calmly. "It's exactly how it's supposed to be. And Mother isn't around to drip poison in your ear anymore, Liz. She's not going to drop in with a list of all the reasons why you're a failure. Not ever again. So maybe relax, for once." He gave her a small smile before wandering back into the hall.

Lizzie stood and walked over to her dressing table, resting her palms against its pale wood surface as she gazed at her reflection in the mirror. She looked… okay. Fine. The same as usual. Except for the little line between her brows, the furrow that marked her unconscious frown. Pursing her lips, Lizzie smoothed the line away. *Now* she looked fine. But her head still hurt like a bitch.

Maybe she should take her hair down. She often did that when she was at home, alone and trying to relax. But she hadn't wanted to since she left France. Because… because it felt like setting her hair loose would mean setting everything else loose. Like releasing the band that held her curls tight would release the grip she had on her emotions. But then, everything was slipping through her fingers already. She knew that. She welcomed it, even.

Soon, she would face the feelings she'd hidden away inside herself. Soon, she would have to think about Isaac.

The acceptance was like casting a spell. Now his face filled her mind, memories smashing into her all at once. His hard-won smile, the curt rasp of his voice, his hands on her skin, in her hair. And the way he said her name…

She sat down, hard. Now her reflection was at eye level, unavoidable, and suddenly the sight of her hair filled her with something like hate.

No—resentment. And weariness. She was so fucking tired.

Lizzie reached up and went through the familiar process of taking down her hair, unpinning this and unwinding that until finally, she was left with a tabletop drowning in oversized hair grips and a dark cloud of brushed-out curls floating around her face. She looked like a storm. The pounding in her head had abated slightly. Perhaps this was the moment where she cast off her insecurities and embraced her hair.

But she didn't fucking like it.

Lizzie sank a hand into the dark, springy mass. It was cotton-soft, with a dull sheen like wet earth. Pretty, really. But there was far too much of it. It floated around her head like a maelstrom, and though her scalp sang with relief at the freedom, she simply wasn't used to this. Everywhere she looked, her own hair floated at the edge of her vision. It surrounded her, grazing her cheeks, brushing her back. She felt like she was suffocating.

The problem was the length. Or rather, the size. She'd never actually had a haircut, she realised. Every place her mother had taken her, they'd been met with terrified, rictus grins and murmured apologies. *We don't do Black hair, I'm afraid.*

Well; fine. She'd do it herself.

Lizzie pulled open the dressing table's second drawer, producing the tailor's scissors she'd once used to alter costumes. They were slightly small for the job, perhaps, but they'd do.

She grabbed a chunk of hair by her left ear and pulled, stretching it out until it reached her hips. Her reflection watched her, wide-eyed. The Lizzie in the mirror wasn't entirely sure about this, it seemed. Her face seemed to echo the whispers sliding through the real Lizzie's mind: *You can't cut your hair. What else do you have?*

Lizzie opened the scissors, let them hover close to the section of hair, just a few inches away from her scalp.

You're not that pretty. You need hair.

"It doesn't matter," she whispered aloud. "It'll grow back."

Isaac likes it.

Isaac didn't like anything about her. She set her jaw and forced her fingers to move.

There was a sharp slice of sound. And then a length of fluffy, spiral curls floated to the ground.

Lizzie looked down at it for a moment, stark against the pale carpet. It was so very long. That hair had been with her since birth.

She chose another section and made the next cut.

LIZZIE," Olu called. "Everyone's leaving."

"Coming," she shouted back.

Her room's en-suite was small, with nothing but a toilet, a shower, and a little mirror over the sink. Usually, she'd do her hair in the main bathroom.

But she didn't need to do much to it now, anyway.

Lizzie stared at her reflection in the little square of glass, turning her head this way and that. She wasn't sure she'd done a good job of the back, but it didn't really matter. Water and a leave-in conditioner had her hair springing to life, and the way the tight little curls shrunk up appeared to be hiding her lack of skill. Really, it wasn't that bad. It might take some getting used to, but it looked fine.

It certainly *felt* fine. In fact, her head was deliciously light, so free that the slightest movement felt like dancing. God, she couldn't wait to dance like this. She had a feeling it would be a whole new sensation.

"Liz," Olu called again.

"Sorry!" With a last glance in the mirror, Lizzie turned and made her way out into the hall.

Everyone was packed and prepared, throwing on coats and scarves, chattering amongst themselves. But when they noticed Lizzie's arrival, all talk stopped.

Theo raised his brows, staring at her head as though it belonged to someone else. "You cut your hair?"

"Ah…"

"You've never cut your hair."

"Theo," Jennifer said. "You don't need to tell her that. She knows."

"Oh, yeah," he said awkwardly. "Sorry."

"I like it," Aria piped up. "You look like Rihanna!"

Despite her disbelief, Lizzie smiled. "Um… Really?"

"Yes," Aria said firmly. "Just like her."

"That's the highest compliment she could give, by the way,"

Jennifer added dryly.

"Anyway," Aria clapped. "We need to go! It's nearly six! Come on!"

At her words, the hallway filled with motion again. Both Olu and Lizzie flitted from guest to guest, giving out hugs and *thank yous* and promises to see each other again soon. And through it all, Lizzie avoided her brother's gaze like it was the plague.

But when the front door finally shut behind their friends and they were left alone in the emptiness of the flat, she held her breath and forced herself to face him.

"So," she said, smiling sunnily. Her voice wavered slightly, but she didn't think he'd noticed. "What do you think?"

He was looking at her with a mixture of concern and alarm. Which wasn't promising.

"Is this a cry for help?" he asked. "Like Britney Spears?"

She gave that a serious moment of thought. "No," she said finally. "I'm okay. I just wanted… a fresh start."

"Is this about him?" he demanded.

Wariness descended as she took in the subtle clues of her brother's temper. The tight control in his voice, the way his fingers tapped against his thigh. She frowned. "Why are you so angry?"

"I'm not." He ran a hand through his hair. "I'm worried about you. You haven't been yourself and I can tell that something's upsetting you. Something to do with that *person*—"

"His name is Isaac," she said sharply. "Don't talk about him like he's nothing."

"I don't know *what* he is, Lizzie," Olu snapped back. "Because you won't tell me. And I'm trying to be cool about this, but please consider my perspective. You go on this trip with him and Spencer, you get dragged into some sordid scheme and end up plastered all over the news in a very compromising position—"

"Is that what you think?" she asked. "That Isaac had something to do with all that shit? Because he didn't. He would never."

"How do you even know this man, Liz? He's a bloody murderer for Christ's sake—"

"Don't talk about things that you don't understand!" she

231

shouted, her voice rising as sharply as her temper. "You don't know him."

"Do you?" Olu demanded. "You know what they say about him. You know how he made his filthy fucking money—"

"There's no such thing as clean money, Olu," she gritted out. "Profit always hurts somebody. You know that. You're just clutching at straws to hide the fact that you're being a judge-mental twat."

He flinched as if she'd hit him. She might as well have done. Olu's throat bobbed as he swallowed hard, the anger in his eyes dimming until only regret and that ever-present worry remained. "I'm sorry," he murmured. "You're right. I..." He gave a self-conscious shrug. "I'm being a snob, I suppose."

At the apology in his voice, Lizzie's own fury faded. "Yes," she said, but her mouth lifted in a wry smile. "You are. But it happens to the best of us."

He smiled back, rolling his eyes at her words. But then he reached forward and ruffled a hand over her hair, no doubt messing up the neat little curls.

"I like it," he grinned. "You look like me now."

She snorted. "Charming. I look like my middle-aged brother."

"Middle-aged?! I'm thirty-six!"

"Oh!" She gasped in mock astonishment. "You should really wear SPF, Olu. You're starting to wrinkle like a walnut."

"Oi!" He grabbed her by the arm before she could get away and began rubbing her head as if she were a dog, absolutely destroying any semblance of a hairstyle she'd created.

"Get off," she laughed, stamping on his foot. Didn't work. Then she elbowed him in the stomach and he yelped, leaning back against the wall as he pantomimed a tragic death.

"How could you?" he rasped dramatically, his eyes wide. "My own sister!"

Before she could reply, a knock came at the door.

"I bet Yen forgot her cake boxes," Olu smirked.

"Probably." Lizzie unlocked the door and pulled it open. "What did you—?"

She stopped. Her smile faded. Because it wasn't Yen standing on the doorstep.

It was Isaac.

CHAPTER TWENTY-EIGHT

IMAGINATION WAS ALWAYS BETTER than reality.

When you spent hours bathing in the second-hand glow of a few precious memories, things changed. Fantasy took over. Feelings were exaggerated; beauty became perfection; mundanity was sacred. After all that, reality could never compare.

So Lizzie shouldn't have looked like heaven, standing in the doorway, her hair curling about her ears like a pixie's.

But she did. To Isaac's hungry eyes, she did.

In his fantasies, her hair was long, the way it had been at the spa. She'd been slightly damp, as though freshly risen from the mists. Fae. It suited her, the more he thought about it: she was all mischief and pride with a sharp edge of cruelty that only made her kindness more precious. He'd dreamed of her drawing him close and knowing, in that way she had, exactly what he wanted to say to her. He wouldn't even have to say it. That was the fantasy.

In reality, she was solid as an oak, real as anything. There were no mists and there was no magic. She stood in the doorway of her brother's flat, her face slack with shock, and she made no move to come to him. There would be no instant reconciliation.

"Lizzie," he said. Because the words he'd carefully prepared, the ones he'd drafted and memorised and thought perfect, had fled his brain completely. The only thing left in his head was her.

She remained still as a mountain, but behind her, there was movement. A second later another figure appeared, a frown of confusion on his face. He was taller than Lizzie, broader, his eyes and hair light where hers were dark. But he was clearly her brother. His sharp gaze, his cheekbones, the set of his mouth, all shouted out the connection.

And when he said, "Montgomery," in a voice dripping with disdain, Isaac knew for sure.

Ignoring the man, Isaac focused on Lizzie. He made his voice as gentle as he could. "Can I come in?"

She burst into tears.

Fuck.

His hands moving of their own accord, Isaac reached for her. But her brother—Keynes—was already there, wrapping an arm around her shaking shoulders, spearing Isaac with an accusing glare.

"I rather think that's a no," Keynes said acidly. "Don't you?"

He was right. He'd always been right. Isaac had made a mistake coming here—he'd made a mistake ever thinking he was smart enough to tangle with Lizzie in the first place. He should have walked away from her after that first kiss, when he'd tasted pure brilliance on her tongue. Because now he was in love and he'd already fucked it up, and he had no idea how to fix it.

Yep, that's what he was: hopelessly in love. Emphasis on the *hopeless*.

She looked so fragile, standing there, frantically wiping at her tears even as they raged like a summer storm. If just the sight of him made her cry, well—that was that. Maybe there were too many bad memories for her. Maybe it was because of how he'd treated her, the day she left.

Or maybe the whole thing really was fake. Maybe she'd forced herself to touch him and now she felt—

"No," she sobbed, and for a moment Isaac imaged she'd heard his thoughts. But then she finished, "Come in. Please." She gave her eyes one final, desperate rub, sniffed loudly, and then stepped back. Her brother was forced to step back too, following her movement, and Isaac took advantage of his good fortune before it could be snatched away. He entered the flat.

While he took in the sleek, modern decor, Lizzie managed to compose herself. Once again, that polite facade he knew so well was firmly in place—but tear tracks ran down her cheeks like cracks in a mask.

"Can I take your coat?" she asked, her voice light.

"I'll just… hang it up here," he said warily, nodding at the coat stand by the door.

"Oh, of course," she nodded. "Well... why don't you come through and we'll all sit?"

She led him to the spacious living room, full of the kind of impersonal, modern furniture that marked this place as a bachelor pad. The bachelor himself hovered after Lizzie and Isaac like a poltergeist intent on murder. Strangulation, specifically, judging by the way his fists clenched and unclenched. Not that Isaac could blame the guy. If he'd had a sister, he wouldn't want a man like himself sniffing around her.

Couldn't be helped. No matter what else happened this evening, he and Lizzie had to talk.

"Sit," she said. "Please. Make yourself at home."

Right. Since this was *such* a comfortable situation. Still, Isaac sank into one of the leather sofas, because she appeared so highly strung at this moment that the slightest conflict might send her into a meltdown. He'd never seen her so nervous. Of course, she hid it well.

But he saw it anyway.

"Have you had dinner?" she asked, sitting opposite him with a hostess's smile. Her brother leaned against the doorframe, glowering at them in sullen silence. If he was this quiet all the time, it was no wonder Lizzie had little problem with Isaac's own lack of communication.

"Don't worry about me," he answered. "Have you?"

She shook her head. *Hm.* With a wary glance at her brother,

Isaac leaned forward, meeting her eyes as he murmured, "Should you, then? When did you last eat?"

"Oh, for God's sake," Keynes burst out, throwing up his hands. "*He* knew? Before *me*? Really, Liz?"

Lizzie glared at her brother, a flash of her familiar fire burning through the mask. "Don't be childish."

"Fine," Keynes huffed. "You two do... whatever it is you're doing. I'm making that chickpea curry thing. Do you want some?"

"That would be lovely," she murmured. "Thank you."

"Is he eating?" Keynes demanded, jerking his head toward Isaac. Which was a surprise. The fact someone so high and mighty was cooking at all had Isaac somewhat confused, and now the other man was actually—if reluctantly—treating him like a human being?

"Well?" Lizzie prompted, looking at Isaac expectantly. "Are you?"

"Ah..." *Better not. Need to leave if things go south.* "No," he said shortly.

"Alright." Was he imagining a hint of disappointment in her voice?

Keynes left with a loud sigh, pointedly leaving the door wide open. He was... not what Isaac had expected. Dramatic where Lizzie was restrained. Though they appeared to be equally moody, at least. And despite the man's threats and overbearing nature, he seemed to treat Lizzie like... well. Like a person. There was an ease to all of their interactions that Isaac couldn't help but envy. An unspoken agreement that no matter what was said or done, their relationship would always remain the same.

Safe. Secure. Constant. Isaac found that he was glad. Glad that Lizzie had someone in her life who would never let her struggle alone. Who would make threats on her behalf. Who would hover menacingly. And who would cook her dinner even while she was doing the exact opposite of what they wished.

"So," she said softly, interrupting Isaac's thoughts. "You're here."

"Yes," he said. There was so much more he meant to say, and

he would, eventually. But right now he felt as if he could barely breathe. And for once it wasn't anxiety that choked him; it was the force of every word that he was desperate to set free, all battling to erupt at once. This was it; this was what she did to him. When he talked to Lizzie, the words he usually couldn't find almost fell over themselves in their eagerness to please her. And that was a dangerous thing.

Despite his best efforts, he'd always been drawn to the dangerous.

She was sitting there so primly, her knees and ankles drawn together like magnets, her back straight as a board. Even with the thick crown of her hair missing, she was royalty. Untouchable. Which only made him want to touch her more.

Standing suddenly, he stalked around the low coffee table to pull her up, drawing her to him. She let out a little gasp as they collided, but her hands settled on his shoulders like they belonged there, and then—ah. She rose up the way she always did, as if even the height distance between them was too much like separation. The panicked urgency in Isaac's gut faded with her nearness.

He put his hands against her cheeks and studied her face, searching for something—some hint that he wasn't alone in this. That he wasn't imagining things. That he wasn't the man she'd made a fool of, but the man she'd found in an unconventional way.

But that wasn't something he could find in her eyes, was it? She'd already told him how things were, and he'd rejected that. He was the one who needed to take a risk. He was the one who needed to believe.

And he was ready. He was ready to try.

———

LIZZIE HELD HER BREATH, as if freezing her own lungs could freeze time, too. When she'd seen Isaac on the doorstep her heart had stopped, petrified. It still hadn't started again. What if he were here to break it completely? To crush the barely beating chunk of scar tissue under his boot?

But that wasn't why he'd come. Surely not. His familiar hands, so rough and capable, were gentle as they cradled her face. A tempest swirled in the night sky of his eyes, and she thought she saw tenderness there. He was so handsome; the harsh features that made him seem intimidating were beautiful, really. Like fine art. You had to look the right way, to see him as he was, instead of what you expected him to be. And she saw him now. She really did.

Slowly, as if she might stop him, Isaac lowered his head to kiss her. Their lips met gently, like waking up on a bright Sunday morning. Everything was fresh; possibility stretched out for miles; calm, pure energy thrummed like a pulse.

Lizzie felt weak-kneed and light-headed with hope. There was a trapped dove inside her, fluttering its wings, rising up to find the sun. Familiar desire ignited, adding a wicked decadence to the moment, like strawberries dripping in dark chocolate. She clung to him, suddenly greedy. An hour ago, she'd been ready to spend the rest of her life starving. Now sustenance was here, and she couldn't let go.

But Isaac pulled away, even as she strained for more. Lizzie opened her eyes to find him smiling at her, and her heart leapt. She wanted to see that smile every day. Every morning, every evening. She wanted to tease out his joy from behind the stone wall he presented to the world. She wanted to be his haven.

"Lizzie," he murmured. The raw quality of his voice would always do this to her, would always tug liquid heat from her core like a touch. "There's so much I need to say."

"There is?" she breathed.

He nodded. "I have to... I have to tell you how sorry I am. About the pictures."

Oh. Oh. She stiffened. Her heart's premature somersaults fell flat. "The pictures," she said, stepping back. "That's why you're here. Of course."

Because he would want to apologise, to make sure she was

alright. Not because he needed to see her. Not because he'd changed his mind.

He still wanted her, but that didn't mean he *needed* her. Didn't mean he'd take her.

She had betrayed him, after all.

Lizzie swallowed, turning away from him—just for a moment. That was all she needed to deal with this flash of weakness, to swallow it ruthlessly down and present him with something better, something braver.

But she felt the touch of his hand on her wrist. "Don't," he said, pulling her back. Making her face him. "Don't do that, Lizzie. Please."

"Do what?" she asked flatly. *Please don't make this any harder.*

"Don't push me away." He tightened his grip, his thumb stroking over her pulse. "I'm not done."

She bit her lip. "Done with what?"

"All my apologies. I was wrong before. I thought I couldn't forgive you, but the truth was I didn't want to. I was angry, and I was embarrassed. And you have to understand, I never—"

He broke off, swallowing hard. His gaze burned into her, and she saw determination. Passion. Unable to stay away, Lizzie brought her hand to the sharp line of his jaw. A thrill swept through her as he leant into the touch, his eyes closing for a moment.

"I'm used to people using me, and looking down on me, and when you told me about this shit with Mark... I thought you were one of those people. That I'd been arrogant to think I could be with someone like you, when you're so flawless and I'm... I'm just me."

"Isaac," she began, because she couldn't let him say that. She couldn't let him think that.

He shook his head. "Let me," he said. "Let me tell you. Lizzie, you're not perfect." He smiled, and she did too. Because his smile was that powerful; she saw it, and her own joy grew in response. "You act like it," he continued. "But the truth is, you're not. You're irritable and you're sharp-tongued. And I like it. You're not loyal to ideas or rules—you're loyal to people. You know the difference between what should be and what *has* to be. I respect that, and I respect you. You're not perfect, but no-one has to be. Point is, you're perfect to me. And I don't care if you get it wrong sometimes. I don't care if you lose your temper. I don't even care that you lied to me because I understand why you did it. I forgive you."

Lizzie clutched at his hands like a lifeline, tears streaming down her face. She didn't wipe them away. Let him see. If it was the only way to show him, let him see.

"I'm sorry," she whispered, her voice shaking. "Even if you forgive me. I'm still sorry. I always will be. I ruined everything—"

"No," he said fiercely. "Don't say that. There's nothing in the world that can't be fixed."

She smiled weakly through her tears. "Or at least taken care of."

"Yeah," he nodded slowly. "Taken care of. Anything you want, I'll do it, because I can't let this go. Just being near you feels like medicine, and that's not something you can fake. *You* aren't fake, Lizzie. You're a brilliant performer, not because you make things up but because you make things *real*. That's who you are. That's where your power lies." He took a deep breath. "You said you were falling in love with me. I didn't really believe you. But I should have… because I'm already in love with you, and love means expecting the best from someone, not the worst. That's why love is for the brave. I should've been brave, Lizzie. I'm sorry that I wasn't."

Her heart soared with his words until it felt like she was really flying; like her spirit was dancing amongst the stars, and nothing could touch her. Nothing could bring her down.

"I love you," she whispered, because she still felt oddly shy about the fact. She'd never loved anyone like this—with such speed and such surety. The feeling was still strange. It was like ballet had once been: slightly uncomfortable, a challenge she'd never faced before, but one that she already knew she was made for.

Isaac bent down, resting his forehead against hers. "I love you, too," he whispered. "Is it weird if I say it again?"

"Oh, now you're all talkative?" she teased.

"I just gave you the longest speech of my life." He grinned. "Maybe I'm chatty now. Maybe you've changed me."

"No-one will ever change you, Isaac. And that's just the way I like it." She closed her eyes, breathing in the perfection of the moment. Safe inside a darkness of her own making, Isaac's soft exhalations warming her cheeks, she showed him the contents of her heart.

"I admire you," she whispered. He wrapped his fingers around her wrist, squeezed slightly. That was all the encouragement she needed. "No matter what life throws at you, you always make something of it. You could survive anything. In fact, you've survived practically everything. That's the kind of strength I want to have."

"You do," he whispered back. "We're not so different, Lizzie. Not really."

"Maybe. I just wanted you to know that I was wrong about you, when we met." She frowned, shaking her head slightly. "No. I wasn't wrong. You are who you've always been. But I was wrong to see you as anything other than brilliant. You're like..." Her mind searched for the perfect words, but for once she couldn't find any. So she borrowed them. "You're like the rose that grew from concrete."

Isaac huffed out a little laugh, the puff of air bringing a smile to her face. "Lizzie..." he said slowly. "That was corny."

Her eyes shot open, and she found him grinning at her, his eyes dancing. She snorted, and then giggles overtook her, and he laughed too, the sound warming her heart.

"You aren't impressed with my poetry?" she asked between chuckles.

"If you're going to plagiarise you should try something less popular." But he was pleased. She could tell. When he was happy, his face transformed from intimidating beauty to adorable sweetness.

God, she loved him.

Lizzie wrapped a hand around the back of his neck, pulling him forward to steal a kiss. This time there was no hesitation, no worry to dampen the spark between them, to gentle the passion. They burst into flame as they always had; Isaac's hands roamed over her hips, her arse, taking ownership of whatever he wanted. Lizzie did the same.

After nights spent without him, pushing away even the memory of the way he made her feel, she finally drank him down like air itself. She tugged up his T-shirt, running her palms over the heat of his abdomen, tracing the sensitive skin over his narrow hips. Electricity coursed through her, a spark ready to surge at any moment. He bent and hooked a hand beneath her thigh, pulling until she wrapped a leg around his hip. Now she was deliciously open to him, and he took advantage, pressing himself against her—

"Lizzie! Fifteen minutes!"

They broke apart, gasping and breathless. Isaac leapt back as if he'd been burned, whipping his head to the door—but no-one was there. Olu had been shouting from the kitchen.

Lizzie felt herself smile, even as she adjusted her rumpled clothing. "Are you scared of my brother?" she asked, incredulous.

"No," Isaac said gruffly. "Just…"

"Just what?" she laughed.

"Well, he's your brother." Isaac shrugged. "I know you love him. I don't want him to…" He trailed off.

She softened at the worry on his face. "Don't worry," she said. "Olu trusts me, and he'll see that I trust you. He'll come around."

"Lizzie!" Olu called again.

"Okay," she shouted back. "Thanks!" And then, to Isaac: "I need to go and take my insulin."

"Alright," he nodded. "See you in a sec."

Feeling giddy as a schoolgirl, Lizzie headed for her bedroom. But not before pressing a kiss to Isaac's cheek as she passed.

And she was almost positive that he blushed.

CHAPTER TWENTY-NINE

ISAAC SETTLED onto one of the room's fancy sofas and waited. He'd have to leave soon; they were having dinner. But even the prospect of parting with Lizzie couldn't dampen the joy shooting through his bloodstream like a comet across the sky.

The old worries nipped at his heels, of course. *This can't last. It's too perfect. Blink, and it'll disappear.*

He kicked them away, sent them whimpering back into the shadows. Because fuck everything else that had ever happened to him. This was different. This was Lizzie.

But even amid his happy haze, Isaac's instincts remained razor-sharp. He felt a presence in the doorway and looked up to find Keynes watching him, his gaze like a laser.

Isaac nodded in the other man's direction, grunting a greeting. This was Lizzie's brother, after all. And they were in the man's home.

Keynes stepped into the room, his arms folded and his stride slow but sure. Like a prowling lion.

"You ignored my warning," he said, his voice a wall of neutrality. So like Lizzie. And yet Isaac couldn't read this man at all.

"Yes," he said carefully. "I needed to see her."

"Apparently so," Keynes murmured. He wandered over to the

floor-to-ceiling windows, gazing down at the city's twilight streets. If his silence was an attempt to break Isaac, it would fail. If the man wanted answers, he'd have to ask the fucking questions too.

Apparently, after a while, Keynes realised that. He turned away from the window and came to the centre of the room, sitting opposite Isaac. Which was interesting. Isaac had expected the other man to remain standing, to employ whatever cheap power play he could.

But of course, Keynes wasn't cheap. He was expensive.

"You have developed an obsession with my sister," he said. "Is that it?"

"No." Isaac gritted out. *Not in the way you mean.*

Keynes ignored that, studying his nails with great interest. They were perfectly manicured, no doubt. "You wouldn't be the first," he continued. "Lizzie is considered quite beautiful."

"I know she's beautiful," Isaac said slowly. "But that's not why I'm here."

"We have no money," Keynes went on. "As of today, actually. We've been cut off."

"Good thing I'm loaded then, isn't it?" Isaac said, leaning back in his seat. The man was an amateur. The only thing he'd ever had over Isaac was his money, his power, and he'd just admitted to losing it. This would be an easy win.

Except, Isaac realised suddenly, winning wasn't the point. This wasn't a battle. This was Lizzie's brother, her family. So if he wanted to remain in her life without tearing it apart... Well. He'd better change tactics.

"Listen," he said. "I don't want to argue with you." The sudden change in his tone seemed to startle Keynes. The other man shifted, perhaps unconsciously, but such simple body language was easy enough to decipher. He was intrigued. He was listening.

"I'm in love with your sister," Isaac told him. "And you're important to her. She'd do anything for you. I experienced that firsthand. So I'd like it if we could get on. Yeah?"

Keynes's eyes narrowed as he leaned forward. "What do you mean, you *experienced that firsthand*?"

Isaac shrugged.

"You know about Spencer," Keynes said slowly. "That he was blackmailing Lizzie. Don't you?"

"Yep."

"Did Lizzie..." Keynes hesitated, clearly struggling with his words. "Did Lizzie hurt you to protect me?"

Isaac shook his head. "I'm not telling you about that. That's her business."

But apparently, Keynes needed no confirmation. His foot tapped compulsively against the thick carpet as he stared at Isaac. "She did, didn't she? That's why she's been so upset. Not because you hurt her. She hurt *you*. And... here you are." He studied Isaac with the kind of curiosity usually found in scientists discovering a new species. "You do love her, don't you?"

Isaac said the only thing he could. "Who wouldn't?"

Before Keynes could answer, the sound of footsteps reached Isaac's ears. Both men turned as one toward the door, just in time to see Lizzie appear with a smile on her face. Her real smile. The one that made his heart sing.

"Hey, you two," she said, coming to sit beside Isaac—and just that little gesture filled him with pride. She was his. They were a pair. She felt it, just the same as him. "Are you having a nice chat?" she asked drily.

"Yes," Keynes said, to Isaac's surprise. "We are. In fact, we were just about to discuss tomorrow."

They were?

"You were?" Lizzie asked brightly. "Is Isaac coming? I think that's a great idea!" She turned to look at him with sparkling eyes. He had not a single fucking clue what was going on, but he nodded enthusiastically. "Oh, brilliant," she grinned. "It'll be even better. I think Mark's scared of you."

Mark?

"The Spencer family are due to return to their estate tomorrow morning," Keynes said, his voice businesslike. "We will go in the early afternoon and have a little… *chat* with Mark."

Ah. "Right," Isaac said. "Good. Want to speak to him."

"Lord, don't say it like that," Lizzie murmured. "You make *speak* sound like a euphemism for *strangle*."

Isaac simply shrugged.

Keynes checked his watch and said, "Dinner should be ready in five minutes. Will you stay, Isaac?"

"Uh…" he studied the other man's face. The offer appeared genuine, if grudging. "Okay," he said finally.

"Good. You should sleep here. We're leaving early."

"…Okay?"

"Excellent." Keynes slapped his palms against his knees. "You'll have the sofa."

"Oh," Lizzie said. "But what about—?"

"The sofa," Keynes repeated firmly. "I haven't had time to change the sheets in the spare room. We had friends over," he added to Isaac. As if this were a normal conversation. As though the two of them were accustomed to casual chats.

"But Isaac can just sleep wi—"

"The sofa!" Keynes said again, standing up abruptly. "Anyway! Dinner! Off we go, everyone."

Isaac didn't bother to hide his smirk.

———

KEYNES TURNED out to be a good cook, which was unexpected. In fact, over the course of their dinner, Isaac found himself surprised by the man again and again.

"You should be my personal chef," Lizzie moaned around a bite of chickpeas. It *was* delicious. But Isaac really needed her to sound less fucking sexy if he was gonna have a chance in hell of finishing his food.

"We'll get you a personal chef," Keynes answered. "I meant to talk to you about that, actually. You need a dietician."

There was a pause, but Keynes didn't seem to notice. He took a sip of his wine as if nothing out of the ordinary had been said.

"Olu," Lizzie murmured, her voice gentle. "We can't do things like that anymore. Remember?"

Keynes shook his head dismissively. "Don't be silly. A personal chef is only—what, forty grand a year? That's fine. It's important."

"I thought you didn't have any money?" Isaac asked baldly.

"We don't," Keynes said. "Just my savings. And my property. I don't know; I'll talk to my accountant at some point."

Isaac's jaw dropped. "*That's* your idea of no money?"

Keynes shrugged. "What's a million pounds, when you get down to it?"

Suddenly, Isaac felt a weight on his thigh. Lizzie's hand, beneath the table, pressing hard into the muscle of his leg. Snatching his attention. He met her eyes and saw a message there, full of humour: *Don't bother.*

Then she turned to face her brother and asked brightly, "What's the plan for tomorrow?"

"Well," Keynes said, clearing his throat like a politician. "As you know, Theo and I engaged in some reconnaissance earlier today. It was fruitful, to say the least. Lizzie, do you have any idea what Mark was trying to gain when he blackmailed you?"

"Well... he wanted me to get information that he could use against Isaac. In case Isaac refused to sign his contract."

"I see." Keynes turned his intelligent gaze to Isaac. "Your books are popular, correct? You make a lot of money?"

"Some," Isaac hedged. Old habits died hard.

"They're very popular," Lizzie said. "He's a bestseller." Was that... pride in her voice? Isaac's heart warmed at the thought. Her hand remained on his thigh, and now its slight weight reminded him of other touches. Touches he was determined to claim tonight, everything else be damned.

"But you haven't signed this contract," Keynes said. His voice snapped Isaac out of the beginnings of a lustful reverie. "Why not? It isn't your typical boilerplate?"

"Uh… No." Isaac pushed down the vestiges of his desire, avoiding Lizzie's gaze. It did dangerous things to his composure. "My guy looked at it. Told me not to sign. Said Mark was trying to cheat me."

"I see," Keynes murmured. "Who is your lawyer?"

"Kev Palmer. But he's not a lawyer. He just reads a lot of books."

Keynes arched a brow. "And you trust his opinion?"

"He's been locked up for twelve years. When I say he reads a lot, I mean a *lot*."

"Ah," Keynes said. "How… interesting. Maybe I could speak with him about—well, never mind that. I'm your lawyer now."

Isaac stared.

"Still, your man's quite right about the contract. In fact, it wouldn't surprise me if Mark has been pulling similar scams for at least the last six months. The man is absolutely drowning in debt; clearly, being at least moderately intelligent, he decided to milk his current income for all it was worth rather than running around blackmailing folks willy-nilly. Keep things tight-knit, you know."

"Oh, God," Lizzie whispered. "Candy. We have to tell Candy."

"I wouldn't worry about telling anyone," Keynes said. "After we visit Mark tomorrow, I believe this whole thing will be nicely ironed out."

Isaac arched a brow. "Really?"

But Keynes seemed completely confident as he tore up a piece of naan. "Oh, yes. You'll understand when we explain the plan after dinner. But for now, know this: Mark Spencer will wish he'd never even set eyes on my sister."

And the threat in his voice was so very dire that Isaac believed him.

―――

HE'D BEEN WAITING for her.

Lizzie knew as soon as she saw him, standing by the room's

wall of glass and staring out into the moonlight, his broad back to the door. He was in nothing but his briefs, and she saw his muscles tighten as she crept into the room, her movement unnaturally loud in the pre-dawn quiet. But he didn't turn. He didn't speak. He simply waited.

And looked damn good doing it.

Lizzie padded across the carpet on bare feet, her silken robe cool against her fevered skin. She swallowed as her eyes followed the sweeping lines of his body; the dips and ridges of his muscled flesh. He was so strong.

But he'd kneel for her.

She rested her palm against his shoulder, and he exhaled as though he'd been holding in a long breath. His head fell back, and she saw that his eyes were closed, his expression pained.

"Did you shut the door?" he rasped.

"Yes."

"Good." In one swift movement, he turned and pulled her against his body. His hands slid beneath her arse, lifting her up into his arms until their faces were level—until his thick shaft grazed the core of her desire. She whimpered at the pleasure that spiralled through her at just that small touch.

"Shh," he whispered, right before he claimed her mouth with his.

Somewhere in the back of her mind, Lizzie registered the fact that they were moving. But she barely felt Isaac's slow steps; all she could focus on was the feel of his lips against hers, of his tongue teasing its way over her own until she surrendered, opening to him completely. He growled against her mouth and the kiss deepened, gradually descending into a chaotic desperation that matched her need perfectly. Holy fuck, she wanted him.

He sat down, and the sofa beneath them gave Lizzie leverage. She rose up on her knees and rolled her hips, grinding her aching clit against his erection. When she undid the belt at her waist and pushed off her robe, Isaac's touch became frenzied. His hands roamed her naked body, rough and possessive, and he thrust up to meet her movements.

"Missed you," he whispered against her lips. "So fucking much. Thought I'd never touch you again. Thought—"

She took his face in her hands and bit his lower lip. When he moaned, she pulled back. "Don't think about that," she whispered. "You have me. Now what are you going to do?"

———

ISAAC WATCHED as a wicked smile spread across her face. She was magnificent. She was everything. She was testing him. And she knew it.

"Please tell me you have condoms," he muttered, unable to answer her question—to *show* her—without them.

"You still don't have any?"

"Didn't think we'd end up like this."

"Why not?" she asked, her eyes adorably wide. "We always do."

He laughed, his chest light despite the current of desire sweeping him under. His cock was so fucking hard it almost hurt, and still, she made him laugh. Always would.

"I have some," she relented, reaching down to pick up the waterfall of her silk robe. She produced a few foil packets from the front pocket. "But you have to earn the right to use them."

"Yeah?" The imperious tone of her voice made his cock harden further, and he hadn't even thought that was possible. His balls tightened as she looked down at him, her eyes a spark of light in the darkness. They caught up every drop of moonlight in the room and reflected it, mesmerising him. Like magic.

"If you want to fuck me," she whispered, her words deliciously precise, unflinching clear, "work for it."

He turned, pushing her back onto the sofa. Her head landed neatly on the pillows he'd laid down to sleep—though he'd never gotten around to the sleeping part. Not with Lizzie just rooms away, within his reach but untouchable. Always, she was untouchable. And yet, she allowed him the honour.

She was so beautiful, laying before him, her legs spread

around him, her arms over her head. Outstretched, as if in surrender. But the way she watched him, the confident curve of her lips, the tempting roll of her hips, designed to steal his good sense—she wasn't the surrendering type. That was why he wanted her so fucking much.

Isaac pulled off his briefs, finally freeing his aching cock from the restraint of cotton and elastic. Then he covered her body with his own, caging her, surrounding her. The moonlight was locked out of their intimate embrace; he rested on his forearms, his lips inches from hers. In an instant, his senses were overtaken, his world shrinking until it could balance on the tip of a knife. There was only the flutter of her panting breath against his lips, the softness of her thighs around his hips, the scalding heat of her wet cunt, open to him, teasing his cock with its slickness.

"Could fuck you right now," he murmured in her ear. She shivered beneath him, arching up, and the movement pushed his shaft against her folds. The sweet friction sent sparks up his spine, and she whimpered beneath him. "You want it," he told her, and never mind the fact that his own voice was frayed with lust.

She bit his throat lightly, right over his pulse, and he thought he would come on her belly like a fucking teenager. "Work. For. It."

But her voice shook. At least she was just as desperate, just as needy. Filled with satisfaction, Isaac thrust his cock between her folds again—not into her pussy, no matter how much he wanted to sink into her. No; he wrapped a hand around his shaft and guided it over the sweet, swollen nub of her clit. She let out a broken little moan, so he did it again. And again. And again.

She threw her head back, sinking her nails into his arse, urging him on. Forcing him against her, harder, faster, as her face twisted in ecstasy. The sight was too much. He felt himself sliding closer and closer to the edge, but he'd cling on. He had to.

Only it would be a lot fucking easier if she didn't look so damn beautiful all the time.

"Your hair," he murmured, searching for something to distract him from the way her slick skin felt gliding against his. "I like it."

She opened her eyes, let out an agonised little laugh that held as much need as it did humour. "You're telling me now?"

"Mmhm. Pretty."

"Just pretty?" She arched a brow.

"Sexy as fuck."

"That's better."

He rose up slightly, slowing his thrusts just because he knew that she wanted them faster. Sure enough, she whimpered, rolling her hips beneath him. He loved that. Loved the fact that she wanted him so much, and that she'd take what she wanted without hesitation. He could feel how wet she was, dripping for him, and the knowledge made him want to howl at the moon like a beast. He ran his hand up her ribcage, capturing her breast, kneading roughly. She put her own hand over his, squeezing. Hard. *More.*

"Now," she gasped, her eyes fluttering shut. "Fuck me now."

He leant down to whisper in her ear. "Work for it."

"Fuck you."

"Come for me," he said softly, circling the sensitive head of his cock over her clit. She felt so fucking good it had him grinding his teeth. But she wouldn't give in.

"Say please," she gasped, teasing him even as she shivered under his touch.

"Nope." He let go of his cock to grab her hip tight, pinning her in place as he played with her. She moaned beneath him, her fingers closing around his wrist, so tight she almost cut off his circulation. Urging him on, as if he needed encouragement. He knew the look on her face, recognised the way her breath became ragged. She was close.

He swooped in to kiss her just as she began to cry out, silencing her pleasure with lips and tongue. She poured her satisfaction into his mouth instead, kissing him desperately as her body was wracked with shudders of ecstasy.

"I want you," she said finally. "Now."

Like he needed prompting. Like he hadn't already died and gone to heaven five times over just from needing her. Isaac grabbed one of the little foil packets and sheathed himself as rapidly as he could, considering he hadn't had much practice over the years. It took just a few seconds, but any amount of time was too long. His whole fucking life had been too long. Like a prologue. And this woman was the main event.

He looked into her sunshine eyes as he leaned over her, easing two fingers into the soft heat of her cunt.

"Please," she whimpered, and he felt her walls tighten around him. "Just—please."

He kissed the tiny little moles beneath her lower lashes, even though he couldn't see them in the dark. He knew they were there, and he loved them. That was all. His fingers stroked her melting core, and she spread her legs wider as if begging wordlessly for more. Telling him she could handle it. He knew that. But teasing her was almost as good as watching her fall apart beneath him.

Finally, when her nails scored lines across his back and her pleads turned into demands that went straight to his cock, Isaac relented. He eased his fingers from her velvet grip and replaced them with his aching shaft. The relief he felt as his cock parted her folds made him light-headed. He pushed into her slowly, savouring every moment of delicious friction, revelling in the way she stretched around him, the way she drew him closer, the way her breath hitched with every inch he thrust forward.

"I love you," he whispered in her ear. "I love you, and I love this. So fucking much. How did I breathe without you?"

She wrapped her arms around him, her touch tender. "You were waiting for me," she whispered. "And I was waiting for you."

"Yes." He filled her to the hilt, his every nerve-ending singing with pleasure. Their chests were pressed so closely together, he could feel his own heartbeat. Or maybe that was hers. Maybe they were the same. Slowly, so slowly, he pulled back, and she shivered in his arms as the friction sent sparks through them both.

He loved her steadily, thoroughly, catching every sigh and whimper and gasp with his lips, taking them as sustenance. His thoughts scattered, ran into one another like dominoes, so simple and yet so frantic. *Need her, want her, will never have enough of her, keep me here forever I'm so happy I could die in her —*

"Isaac," she whispered, clutching his shoulders tightly. "I'm going to—"

"Yes," he gritted out, moving faster. Letting go of his control. Giving her everything.

She bit her fist as she came, muffling her own cries, and as he followed her over the edge, he buried his face into the dip where her neck met her shoulder. His vision was dark, full of her, the way she was full of him. Her warmth surrounded him, her pussy squeezed him, and he was coming so fucking hard he thought he might pass out.

But he didn't. Instead, stars still shooting across the night sky of his vision, he kissed her. And he tasted forever on her lips.

CHAPTER THIRTY

"DO you think we caught them at a bad time?" Keynes muttered under his breath, eyeing the hustle and bustle of the Spencer mansion warily.

"I don't think there'll ever be a good time for this," Lizzie replied grimly. "Come on. Let's go."

She strutted up the Spencer's icy garden path, and Keynes followed closely. But Isaac trailed behind, keeping his steps short. Perhaps now wasn't the best moment to watch the sway of his woman's arse, but she made it bloody hard to ignore.

She was a general leading her army into enemy territory, but this was the most charming of guerrilla warfare. The staff rushing in and out of the house might have paused at the sight of Isaac or Keynes striding alone with such purpose. But Lizzie was like a shield. The staff loved her, clearly. Just a smile or a friendly hello from her was enough to lull the workers into a false sense of security. They grinned back, waved, paused in their duties to ask after her health. And just like that, the trio sailed into the Spencer house. They breached enemy walls, detected—but unchallenged.

"His office is this way," Lizzie murmured. "He's always in there. So that's where we'll start."

God, he wanted to kiss her.

She undid her coat as she walked, her heels clicking sharply against the polished wood floors. The Spencer mansion was as vast and intimidating as ever, especially with an army of staff marching through it, their uniforms giving them an almost robotic appearance. A train of young women charged down a nearby staircase in the black and white outfits, *Spencer* embroidered over their breasts. They carried a mountain of luggage with them, their arms straining.

"What are they all doing?" Keynes whispered.

"I don't know," Lizzie murmured back. "It's not usually like this. Maybe because they've just arrived home—?"

"Nah," Issac said. "Should be unpacking. But they're taking shit outside."

"Odd," she replied, but her voice was so distant, so thoughtful, she might as well have been talking to herself. "I wonder…"

By the time they reached the door to Mark's office, Isaac was beginning to feel on edge. There was an eerie silence to this part of the house, an emptiness that belied the excess of grand furniture and busy decor. Mark's door, dark and shut tight, gave Isaac the impression of a portal to some other realm.

One that wasn't friendly.

Lizzie put her hand on the brass doorknob, but Isaac stopped her, placing a hand on her forearm.

"No," he said. "Let me."

She rolled her eyes. "He doesn't bite. He might not even be in there."

"He's in there," Isaac said, suddenly certain. "And something's not right."

"Do as he says," Keynes murmured. Isaac flashed the man a look of gratitude. Lizzie was far from weak, but this situation was no longer predictable. Which made it dangerous.

"Fine," she sighed, stepping back. "Go on."

Nodding, Isaac opened the door, peering into the emptiness of the room. It was dark, the thick, burgundy curtains drawn, but a lamp on the edge of Mark's huge desk glowed through the gloom. The light it cast did little to improve visibility and sent strange shadows dancing across the walls.

But Mark stood out amongst the darkness. His pale skin and colourless eyes flashed like a blade. He sat slumped in his vast, leather chair, gazing sightlessly at the papers strewn across his desk.

Isaac looked over his shoulder, nodding at Lizzie and her brother. They nodded back, eerily in sync, their faces distant echoes of each other.

The three of them entered the study, shutting the door tightly behind them.

Mark finally looked up, his eyes settling on Isaac. They lit with something close to fear before the shark-like man smoothed away every hint of expression, his mask in place once more. But it was slipping. His usually slicked-back hair was limp and oily, hanging over his narrow brow. Sweat gleamed on his forehead and his hands shook slightly as he stood, spreading his arms wide.

"Guests," he said, his voice cracking. "I have guests. What an... interesting development."

"He's off his tits," Keynes said, his words clipped.

Isaac raised his eyebrows, turning a questioning glance on Lizzie's ever-surprising brother.

The other man shrugged. "Coke. I know the signs."

Hm. Isaac studied Mark's blown pupils, his shaking hands, the manic edge to his welcoming grin. Yep. High as a kite.

Might make things easier. Might make them a hell of a lot harder.

Isaac moved closer to Lizzie, shifting slightly so that he was in front of her. Maybe he was paranoid; but it was better to be paranoid than fucked.

"What can I do for you, then, gentlemen?" Mark asked grandly, flopping back into his seat. His gaze flickered as it passed over Lizzie's brother, his already-bleak face tightening. As if he were afraid. "It's certainly nice to see you again, Keynes. How long has it been?"

"Since Vienna?" Keynes asked, his tone mild. "Or since we last spoke?"

"Ah, yes. That conversation was, what... Six months ago?"

Mark raised his eyebrows, but the effect was somewhat ruined when he let out a light burp. "You called me about your sister. I'm sure you appreciate the favour I did you, allowing Lizzie to teach my girls. We could have enrolled them into a proper school—"

"No-one could do better than Lizzie," Isaac interrupted, his temper flaring. "Cut the shit."

"I don't know about that," Mark blustered, sweat gathering on his upper lip. Funny; Isaac thought the room was quite cold.

"You were going to sack me anyway, I'm sure" Lizzie said sharply. "So the *favour* is done with."

"Well! Those pictures—I'm sure you understand." Mark was sweating, just a little. He pulled the pocket square from his blazer, patting at his hairline, staining the silk. "The girls need a positive role model—"

"But she did exactly what you wanted," Isaac said quietly. Mark's sudden silence was loud as an anvil. "You told her to get close to me. Didn't you? In fact, you forced her."

For a moment, Mark's mouth worked soundlessly, his thin lips opening and closing like those of a gasping fish. Then he croaked out, his eyes panicked, "I don't know what she told you—"

"Enough," Keynes snapped, as though his fraying temper had finally torn. "Be quiet, before the hole you're digging turns into a grave." He strode closer to the desk, slamming his briefcase onto its surface, and Mark flinched.

"We know what you've been up to," Lizzie said. Her voice was light as air, her lips curved into a sweet smile. Only those who truly knew her might detect the undercurrent of icy menace in her voice, the violent gleam in her brown eyes. Isaac heard. Isaac saw. Isaac loved it.

She moved forwards too, but she reached for Isaac as she did so. Their hands clasped tight as a promise, they stood side by side, facing the pathetic shell of the man who'd tried to ruin them.

"You're desperate for money," Lizzie continued. "Cash disappears fast when one develops such expensive habits. You could've blackmailed my brother directly, but a more roundabout plan suited your needs better. You've always been ambitious, haven't you? And you are a businessman. So you knew that you had to secure a greater income, to think long term. Which I admire, honestly. Dream big, and all that."

"Plus," Keynes added, rifling through the contents of his now-open briefcase, "extorting lump sums from individuals is all a bit sordid, isn't it? Not to mention risky. Meeting in dark little corners, exchanging secrets for money. You needed cash cows to pump out a steady, hefty income, since your own hasn't been cutting it for some time. It's difficult, isn't it, marrying the aristocracy? Personally, I don't recommend it if you're anything less than a billionaire. The standards these people expect..." He cast a look around the room. "Shocking, really."

Mark clenched his jaw, his gaze narrowing. "You think you have it all figured out?" he hissed. "How clever you must feel. But don't forget, Keynes—I still have power over you. Or didn't your sister tell you?" He turned his venomous gaze to Lizzie, and Isaac's fists clenched of their own accord. "Well, Elizabeth?" the snake continued. "Were you too embarrassed to bring up your brother's dirty little secret?"

"What secret?" Keynes interrupted, his voice innocent. "The fact that I'm gay, you mean? Old news, my friend."

Mark faltered. He blinked slowly, as if he'd been hit over the head. "I-I beg your pardon?" he stuttered finally.

Keynes shrugged. "I have come out, as they say. I've been disowned and disinherited too, I'm afraid. So I'm hardly worth inclusion in your nasty little plots anymore."

Mark stared, his mouth working in silent desperation. Isaac felt satisfaction settle over him, a quiet triumph filling his soul. *That* was Keynes's 'secret'? All of this—the blackmail, the lies, even Keynes and Lizzie being cast aside by their own parents—it was all because Keynes was gay?

The world was a twisted, unbalanced place. But they were about to adjust the scales, even if the effects spread no further than this little room.

Lizzie moved to stand beside her brother, shoulder to shoulder. She flashed Mark a smile as she leaned forward, bending over the desk—and damn if Mark didn't lean back, practically cowering from her.

This was definitely an inappropriate moment to be turned on. But nonetheless, Isaac's dick leapt to attention as Lizzie spoke in a voice dark and threatening.

"What you failed to anticipate, Mark," she murmured, "is the size of our family's brass fucking balls. So now you will find out the hard way that no-one messes with an Olusegun-Keynes. Or," she added, a smile in her voice, "with a Montgomery."

"What do you want?" Mark whispered hoarsely.

"It's very simple." Lizzie sat down in one of the stiff-backed chairs before Mark's desk, her posture perfect as always, her hands folded primly in her lap. "You are going to sell Spencer Publishing. To Isaac."

Isaac frowned. *What?*

But he maintained his composure. They were a united front. There could be no break in the ranks. And while this was a slight deviation from their agreed plan—well. He trusted Lizzie. Completely.

"For a reduced fee, of course," Lizzie continued. "Next to nothing, in fact. In return, my brother and I will deal with your outstanding debts, which I'm sure will be a great relief. Apparently there isn't a dealer left in London who'll take your empty promises. I bet you're getting desperate. Aren't you?

Isaac hadn't thought it was possible, but Mark grew even paler. His hands shuffled pointlessly over the papers strewn across his desk as he muttered, "I-I don't know about all this. I'll have to speak with my lawyers."

"Oh, no," Keynes said cheerfully. He produced a sheaf of papers from his briefcase. "This is for you. Don't read. Just sign. I'll summarise."

"I couldn't possibly—"

"Do you know what dealers do with customers who cannot pay?" Keynes interrupted, his voice bland. "I've heard it's dreadful. I'm sure Isaac would be happy to give you a few details."

Mark's eyes flicked desperately up to Isaac's face before skittering away like dusty cockroaches. "No," he said weakly.

"Good. Now sign. Here's the short version: Isaac will own Spencer Publishing and all related assets, in their entirety—which includes any of those awful contracts you may have conned writers into over the past few months. We'll be rectifying that situation immediately, I'm afraid. In return, we will deal with your outstanding debts."

"But... how will I live?" Mark whispered.

"Your wife is a wealthy woman in her own right," Keynes shrugged. "You'll hardly be out on the streets."

"You don't understand," Mark cried, surging up from his seat. "She's leaving me!"

"I beg your pardon?"

Isaac blinked. *That* he had not seen coming.

"She found out," Mark whimpered. "She found out..."

"About your addiction?" Keynes frowned.

Mark shook his head slowly. "About the girls' trust funds. Bloody Audrey, plotting her move to Paris, of all places. Wanting to be like *you*." He shot a venomous glare at Lizzie. "The three of them started snooping. Found out. Told their bloody mother." He rolled his eyes—but the action was less sophisticated cynic, more panicked horse trapped in a burning barn. "I just took a little here and there, you understand, for—"

Isaac's blood became white fire. He clenched his fists, fury singeing his nerve endings. "You stole from your *children*?" he growled.

Mark scowled through his tears. "It isn't stealing. I borrowed. You sound just like Clarissa." But then he seemed to crumple like paper. "I'll be nothing without her," he whispered.

For a moment, Isaac's heart softened.

But then Mark continued: "Unless I receive a settlement in the divorce..."

Ah.

"I'm bored," Lizzie said, her tone dry as ash. "Sign."

Mark hesitated, his eyes wild, and for a moment he took on

the frenzied panic of a cornered animal. This, Isaac knew, was the fraught moment that hung like an impending storm, the moment before a man lost his head and did something everybody would regret. In an instant, things could go south.

And he absolutely could not allow that to happen with Lizzie in the room. In a flash, Isaac stalked around the desk, grabbing Mark by the collar of his deep blue blazer. He dragged the man up like the rat he was. And then, forcing as much menace into one word as he possibly could, Isaac said, "*Sign.*"

He dropped Mark back into the chair.

And Mark picked up a pen and signed.

"Initial here, please," Keynes murmured politely. "And here."

Mark did as he was told, scratching out the letters with barely controlled fury.

"There," Keynes said. "Was that so bad?"

The other man didn't respond, slumping down in his chair as though drained.

"I think that's our cue to leave," Lizzie smiled.

They filed out of the room peacefully, as though nothing untoward had taken place. But just before he shut the door behind them, Isaac turned back, giving Mark a slow, dangerous smile.

"Pleasure doing business with you mate," he said. "Just so you know; if you ever contact Lizzie again, I'll rip off your head and shove it up your arse."

He shut the door on Mark's strangled whimper.

Lizzie and Keynes stood in the hallway, their faces lit up with twin smiles of triumph.

"We did it," Keynes breathed, betraying his lack of complete confidence for the first time since they'd left the city that morning. "We actually fucking did it. It's handled. It's over."

"Almost," Isaac corrected. He took Lizzie's hand before he asked them both, "What was that?"

Lizzie blinked up at him innocently. "I don't know what you mean."

He shot a look at Keynes and found the other man shifting awkwardly in his perfect suit.

"You *know* what," Isaac growled at the pair. "I'm buying the company?"

"I hope you don't mind," Keynes said. "Only, it's a cracking deal. And you're the writer, after all."

Well. That was true. *I* am *the writer*. And they were both looking at him with such calm confidence…

"I'll need help," he said slowly. "Someone I can trust. Like you."

Keynes blinked. "Me?"

"Yep."

"Well…" Isaac didn't think he was imagining the hint of pleasure on the other man's face. "Okay," Keynes said finally. "It's a deal."

They shook hands, and Lizzie looked on like a proud mother. But then her slight smile faded, and she turned to gaze down the hallway, towards the rest of the house.

"We should find Clarissa," she murmured. "And the girls. They must be upset." She bit her lower lip. "I'm really not looking forward to this part."

"It's okay," Isaac said softly, wrapping an arm around her shoulders. "We'll do it together."

"Yes," she said, her eyes softening as she looked up at him. "Together."

Beside them, Keynes made a dramatic retching sound, shattering the moment. "If you two could be less in love for a minute, that would be fantastic."

"Grow up," Lizzie snorted, rolling her eyes and heading down the corridor.

"I'm older than you," Keynes shot back as he followed.

"Clearly not in spirit."

"Oh, please."

Isaac stood for a moment, watching them with a smile on his face.

He'd thought family was over for him, the day his mother died. But he'd been wrong, hadn't he?

Family was more than blood. Family was love.

CHAPTER THIRTY-ONE

TWO WEEKS LATER

HE WAS SO PALE.

The cold had leeched away the natural warmth beneath his skin—but the tip of his nose was bright pink. It was so delightfully incongruous that Lizzie couldn't stop herself from laughing.

"What?" Isaac whispered with a smile of his own. He held her tighter, shifting her in his lap, and the rusty garden chair they sat on squeaked dangerously.

"Your nose," she whispered back. Dusk was so beautifully silent out here in the country. As they watched the sun stain the sky in a glorious parade of blood-orange and plum purple, Isaac and Lizzie held the silence as close as each other.

"What about my nose?"

"It's pink."

"Kiss it, then."

Giggling, she pressed a kiss to the tip of his nose. And then to his chin. And then to the corner of his soft lips...

He cradled the back of her head and took her mouth, his tongue sliding against hers in a raw, earthy rhythm that snatched the laughter from her chest. Lizzie felt heat unfurl, deep between her legs. She pressed her palms to his cold cheeks and kissed him back, helpless to resist. By rights, this man's touch should be mundane. It had become a part of her routine over the last couple of weeks: wake with Isaac, come for Isaac, work with Isaac, come for Isaac, eat with Isaac, come for Isaac—

And yet, she wanted more. Always, always more.

She pulled back, their quiet evening dissolving like the mist as lust slammed into her. "Let's go inside," she breathed.

He stood, his strong arms lifting her, and walked back into her cottage. Though technically, it was their cottage now. Because she had to stay here to set up the dance school she was starting—with Clarissa's support, thank God. And Isaac? It turned out Isaac refused to be anywhere that Lizzie wasn't.

So here they were.

He carried her through the house, his steps quick, his jaw set.

"Are you in a hurry?" she asked teasingly, arching one brow.

He looked down at her, and the intensity of his gaze—of his sharp, fierce features—sent a thrill of desire coursing through her. "Yes," he said shortly. But then his phone beeped, and he pulled up short.

"What?" she asked. "What's up?"

"Just…" He trailed off, and then he put her down. Actually set her on her feet. Lizzie blinked in astonishment. He never did that. The minute he had her, and he got that dark look on his face, there was no escaping his arms.

But there he stood, fumbling through the pockets of his coat, searching for his phone.

"What are you doing?" she asked.

"Candy," he muttered.

"Candy?" she repeated. "Why would Candy be texting you? She's *my* friend."

He looked up at her for a moment, flashing a smile so achingly handsome she almost forgot what they were talking about. "Jealous?" he asked.

"Shut up." She rolled her eyes.

"Yep. Jealous." But before she could whack him, he finally found his phone. He studied the screen like it was a holy text, and then his face lit up. "It's ready," he murmured. "Come on."

"What's ready?" she demanded as he grabbed her hand, pulling her through the house. "Isaac! What's going on?"

He led her into the dining room, where he'd left his laptop on the table earlier. Pulling out a chair, he settled her in before bending down to flip open the computer, typing in his password.

She watched as he opened an Internet browser and navigated to Candy's website. The familiar stylised cartoon appeared, alongside a logo that read *Aunt Candy*. Isaac clicked on the website's blog and then, with a flourish, he turned the laptop to face her.

She read the blog post's title, her mind moving as though through treacle.

You Know You're In Love When…

Her eyes flicked to the byline.

A guest post by Isaac Montgomery, author of *Catching Time*.

She looked up to find Isaac watching her with something in his eyes that looked like… nerves?

"You write blog posts now?" she asked. "Are you diversifying?"

"Maybe," he said, his voice gruff. "Read."

"Okay…" She turned back to the screen.

Love is tricky. The more you give it and receive it, the better you become at recognising it. But for those of us who, for whatever reason, have been shut off from the world, love often becomes a stranger. It can be hard to recognise love when you haven't seen it in a while.

I've recently become accustomed to the feeling, though, and I think I know how to spot it now. So I thought I'd share some handy tips with all of you. Just in case there's someone else out there who's having trouble recognising love these days.

You know you're in love when…

5. A few minutes in their presence stirs more emotion than you've felt all day. Might be soft and fuzzy; might be a little more passionate. But the point is, they make you feel alive.

4. You find yourself opening up to them for no reason. As if they have the key to some locked-away part of you, a part you didn't even know was there.

3. Their happiness becomes more important to you than your own. When watching someone else smile brings you more joy than a thousand years of laughter—that's when you know you've got it bad.

2. Your dreams of the future include them. Whatever your goals, wants, wishes—this person changes everything. Your fantasies begin to shift, to make room for the one who'll be by your side through it all.

1. And finally… You know you're in love when you need them with you. Always. Forever. And you don't care about how long it's been or how these things should go, because you already know that you can't do this thing called life without them in it.

So, with all that in mind…

Elizabeth Adewunmi Olusegun-Keynes, I am most definitely in love. Will you marry me?

Lizzie stared at the final line, her heart pounding. This… this couldn't be real. Could it?

She turned to find Isaac watching her, his whole body vibrating with nervous energy. He tapped a hand against his thigh compulsively, and she followed the movement, her gaze catching on the little, black box held loosely in his fist.

"Is that a ring?" she choked out.

"Can't propose without a ring," he said, his voice raw and scratchy, as if he hadn't used it in days. "Want to see?"

"Yes," she breathed. But then she caught herself, shaking her head with a frown. "Wait—no."

Isaac's face fell. He hadn't been smiling—his features had been twisted into more of a grimace, if anything—but now everything about him seemed to droop, wilting like a flower in a drought.

"Oh," he said, his voice gruff. He lowered his gaze, the muscles in his jaw working tightly. "I thought…"

"I want to say yes first," she whispered.

His eyes shot back to hers, and in that moment his face was more expressive than ever. In his impenetrable features she saw hope, disbelief, exhilaration, and more than anything—love.

"You do?" he asked, his voice cracking.

"Of course," she said, and her words were no better, wavering terribly as the first tears spilled over her cheeks.

He sank to his knees in front of her, taking her face in his hands. "Yes?"

"Yes." She nodded firmly. "Yes, yes, yes, yes—"

He pressed his lips against hers, cutting off her joyous chant, and she wrapped her arms around him and let herself revel in the knowledge that somehow, impossibly, this man had become hers.

"Wait," he whispered, pulling back. "The ring."

"Isaac, I don't give a fuck about the ring," she grinned. "Kiss me."

So he did.

Every day, for the rest of their lives.

EPILOGUE

ONE YEAR LATER

"ARE you sure you want to do this?"

Jane was asking the question, but for a moment, Isaac heard Lizzie's voice. She'd said the same thing to him last night. Under far more intimate circumstances.

Blinking himself back into the present, Isaac nodded firmly.

His publicist gave a wry smile as she adjusted his tie. "You know you're gonna have to talk, right?"

"Yep." The knowledge made him want to vomit, but he'd do it anyway. It was necessary.

Especially considering what he'd learned last night.

"You remember what we practiced?" Jane stepped back as a crew member darted forwards, attaching a tiny microphone to his lapel.

"Yep," Isaac said again, trying not to feel uncomfortable about the proximity of the crew member's shiny, bald head to his face. Things were about to get a *lot* more uncomfortable than that.

Like, *spill your guts in front of the nation* uncomfortable.

He gritted his teeth. Just like he'd told Lizzie last night—he could do this.

And she'd agreed. She believed in him. So it must be true.

A stern-looking woman strode toward him, her curtain of shining hair pushed back by the headset she wore. Something about the purposeful way she moved and the impatient look on her face reminded him of Lizzie.

"Two minutes!" the woman snapped. "Get over here!"

Her severity was… comforting. She turned on her gleaming high-heels and marched away, and Isaac followed her like a duckling after its mother. This might not be a battle, but it sure as shit felt like one. At least he was following a formidable general onto the field.

"Good luck!" Jane called after him. He raised a hand in reply.

The woman with the headset parted the bustling hubbub of staff around them like it was the Red Sea, waving her clipboard like a beacon. Crew members scuttled out of her way, and Isaac trailed obediently in her wake, barely noticing the nervous stares his presence inspired.

Okay, so he *did* notice them. He probably always would. But these days, he really didn't care.

He'd made peace with himself and with his crimes. The rest of the world could follow suit or get fucked.

"Here we go," the woman hissed, leading him along a dark, narrow corridor. A doorway of light shone at the far end, cut out from the passage's imposing facade. The sound of exuberant voices and friendly laughter floated through, soothing Isaac's nerves. That didn't sound so bad, not really. He'd been more intimidated the first time Lizzie's friends had come over for coffee.

But then the woman with the headset brushed something off his shoulder, fiddled with his microphone, and whacked him lightly on the back with her clipboard. "Go!" she said.

Well, shit.

His heart pounding, Isaac took the final steps toward that glowing doorway. And then, with a deep breath, he went right through it.

Out of the darkness, into the light.

"...Isaac Montgomery!" an exuberant, feminine voice cried. "The best selling author of *Catching Time* is here to discuss his brand-new release, *Mountains!*"

Applause rang out, and Isaac stood still for a moment as his eyes adjusted to the light. *Don't squint*, he remembered Jane saying. *We need to capitalise on your face, just in case you fuck up.*

Because, apparently, he was handsome. Or something like that.

His vision clearing, Isaac gave himself half a second to gaze out at the studio audience, who were clapping enthusiastically for… him. They were clapping for him.

Then his sense returned: he was supposed to be walking. Walking toward that infamous sofa, the big red one parked squarely in the centre of the stage on which he stood.

Pete and Charli Morning stood in front of it, clearly waiting for him to sit down. Pete's affable grin was firmly in place, and Charli looked cheerful as ever with her plump cheeks and long, blonde hair. The married co-hosts of *Wake Up with the Mornings* were so very bloody *pleasant.* Isaac had once thought they were faking it.

But as he'd learned while preparing for this TV appearance, they absolutely weren't. They were just that sweet.

Isaac went over to join them, remembering at the last minute that he was supposed to smile too. He shook Pete's hand and kissed Charli on the cheek—which felt kind of personal but was apparently what *normal* people did. Then, at their friendly insistence, he took a seat on that famous red sofa.

"So," Charli said, leaning forward. She was somehow utterly average and completely compelling all at once. It was an effective combination. "Isaac Montgomery. The nation's bad boy. Our dark angel. Do you ever get tired of the nicknames?

What had Jane said? *Be yourself. Out loud.*

Okay.

"Yes," he said simply.

There was a pause, and then Pete looked out at the audience and said, "He's a talker, this one!" He laughed, and the audience laughed with him.

Isaac waited for his skin to crawl… but the moment never came. There was nothing mean-spirited in this particular joke, he realised. No sneering sting in its tail. Or maybe he wasn't as sensitive as he'd once been. With that thought, he did what he'd been desperate to do since stepping out on stage.

He looked for Lizzie.

And there she was, sitting in the front row, a wry smile on her face. Their eyes locked, and the last of Isaac's anxiety drained away.

He could do this. He *could*.

Crossing an ankle over his knee, Isaac allowed himself to settle back into the sofa. He relaxed, really and truly, feeling his throat loosen up and his leaden tongue become something close to silver. As close as he'd ever get, anyway.

"The truth is, none of those things are really me. Tabloids like a bit of drama." He shrugged. "I'm not a dramatic guy."

Charli reached forward, picking up a copy of his new book from the nearby coffee table. They'd been arranged in an artful pile, and apparently the camera would get them into shot as much as possible. Isaac hoped so. Because he was really fucking proud of this book. And he wanted it to sell.

For the sake of the people he now called family, the dark rumours surrounding him needed to stop. Or at least slow down.

"You say you're not dramatic," Charli said, waving the shiny hardback, "but the story within these pages has a lot of ups and downs. I will confess, I cried through Chapter Four. You know, when—"

Pete gave her a playful tap on the thigh. "Spoilers, love!" he scolded with his trademark cheeky smile. Then, his tone slightly more serious, he turned to Isaac. "Your books are always non-fiction, but this new release is more autobiographical than anything you've done. Tell us about that."

Isaac nodded. "Well, my other books were about the system, life in prison, the reality of being a convicted criminal. Used case studies. Didn't always talk about myself."

"You seemed to *avoid* talking about yourself," Charli said. "You became a very mysterious character."

Isaac smiled, catching Lizzie's eye. She smiled back. *Mysterious* sounded far better than *shy*, at least.

"Yeah," he agreed. "I wasn't ready to talk about myself. Still coming to terms with some stuff. But I'm okay now, and I want people to know who I really am. So… here it is." He nodded towards *Mountains*.

"The account of your childhood, the thought process and lack of options that led you into a life of crime; that was fascinating," Pete said. Teasing. Giving the audience just a taste. "But those concepts aren't exactly new. It's later in the story that things really take a turn. The situation surrounding your conviction for manslaughter; that was especially harrowing."

Isaac forced himself to nod. "I guess so. More for the victim's family than for me."

"Of course," Charli said quickly. "And—I have to ask—can you tell us anything about the rumour that surfaced recently?" She looked out into the audience, as though checking to see if they followed. They fucking followed. It had been all over the papers. But Isaac let the woman speak. "Supposedly, since your first book you've been giving a percentage of your royalties to the family of Ben Davies, the man who unfortunately passed away after an altercation with you back in 2005. Is that correct?"

Isaac forced himself to shrug. "Not my story to tell."

She raised her eyebrows, looking back towards the audience. As if to say, *There you have it, folks.*

He hated assumptions. Assumptions had caused a lot of problems in his life. But as Jane had told him once: *Playing the game isn't a matter of principle. It's a matter of common bloody sense.*

So this was common sense, in his new world. He'd get used to it.

With a smile, Charli continued. "Now, the fascinating thing about *Mountains*—beneath your brilliant style, that raw and gritty tone you have—is your attitude toward the hand that life has dealt you. You mention 'peace' a lot in this book. It's clear that things have changed since your earlier releases. Is there anything in particular that's triggered that transformation in you?"

This was his favourite question. It was one he'd been prepared for, one he was actually eager to answer. Isaac grinned, his eyes going to Lizzie once again. Her hair was still short, and she was fiddling with a tiny curl by her right ear. She was self-conscious. Because she knew what he was about to say.

"Yes." His voice was bold, full of pride, clearer than it had ever been. "I met someone. It's briefly mentioned toward the end of *Mountains*. We fell in love in the French Alps." He held up his left hand, displaying the plain, gold band that glinted alongside his mother's signet ring. "And we got married a few months ago."

Charli clapped her hands while the audience gave a little *Awwww*.

"There were rumours!" Pete cried. "And we're very happy to confirm those rumours today! We wish you every happiness."

"Thanks," Isaac smiled.

"Now, we don't want to talk too much about your lovely wife, but I think we all remember certain photographs appearing about a year ago…" Pete trailed off with a good-natured grin, and the audience burst into laughter.

Lizzie had a hand over her mouth, hiding a smile—but her eyes were dancing. Then, as a camera swung towards her to capture her reaction, she giggled outright.

"Yes," Isaac admitted. "We were a little careless."

"It's all very romantic," Charli said sweetly, patting his thigh as though they were old friends. "So tell us about her!"

"She's… a dancer. She runs a school out in the country, near our home. She's very smart. Kinda terrifying. Knows what she wants."

The audience laughed again, and Isaac felt like chuckling along with them. He hadn't expected this whole experience to be so… well. *Fun.*

"Would you say love has changed you?" Charli asked.

Instinctively, Isaac shook his head. "Didn't change me. Just showed me who I was always meant to be. Once you see the path, it's easier to follow."

"Oooh!" Charli cooed. The audience echoed her dutifully. "Now, that brings me to *another* rumour we've been hearing… That you're moving away from non-fiction and into poetry!"

Isaac smiled, rubbing his jaw reflexively. "Don't think I'm allowed to confirm or deny that just yet."

She leaned forward, giving him a conspiratorial look. "You can't give us a little hint?"

""Fraid not. My publisher's a scary guy." That got a laugh out of both Charli and Pete—because of course, as everyone knew, Isaac owned his publishing company.

"Well!" Charli threw up her hands. "Can't blame a girl for trying."

"A *lot* of people describe you as scary," Pete added. "And some of the scenes in *Mountains* support that, but there are plenty of vulnerable moments too. So, one last question for you today: who *is* the real Isaac Montgomery?"

"It's funny you should bring that up," Isaac said, his expression suddenly serious. "Because I've been thinking about that a lot, recently. Especially in light of…" He trailed off, considering his words. "Well, I'm a married man now. I want to start a family." He couldn't look at Lizzie right now, or he'd completely lose his head. His mind would travel back to last night. And he'd get caught up in the fact that they *were* starting a family. He'd get caught up in those four perfect words:

"We're having a baby."

"My children will never experience the things I did," Isaac said. "That's a relief. They'll always have choices. They'll always have options and support. But I don't want to just… give them money and act like it's enough. That can't be my only legacy. I want to be the kind of man my kids look up to. And I want to be the kind of man who shares his blessings. I want to give people the tools they need to walk away from the life's darker paths. So I think the real Isaac Montgomery is… human. And trying. And hopeful." He shrugged. "I don't know. That's really all I've got."

"Oh, that's plenty," Charli said solemnly, her blue eyes wide. "What an inspiring answer from an inspiring man." Then, just as quick, her cheerful smile returned, and she faced one of the four cameras hovering around the edge of the stage. "*Mountains* by

Isaac Montgomery will be available tomorrow morning from all major retailers. It's an absolutely amazing read."

"Thanks so much for joining us this morning, Isaac," said Pete.

"Thanks for having me," Isaac smiled.

"Ladies and gentlemen, give it up for Isaac Montgomery!"

To Isaac's surprise, the studio erupted. The audience stood, clapping and whooping and cheering.

And there, at the very front, was Lizzie. His wife. The woman carrying his child.

The love of his fucking life.

He'd found peace, alright. And he would never let it go.

THE END

SWEET ON THE GREEK

READ ON FOR A PEEK AT ARIA'S FAKE RELATIONSHIP
ROMANCE.

CHAPTER ONE

Three Months Ago

La Christou needed a better photographer, or better marketing or something.

From the wedding packages the hotel had sent over, Aria had believed it to be a jewel of a find: a luxurious but intimate venue on the western coast of Greece, famed for its ravishing gardens. But now that she was here, she what it truly was: a fantasy come to life.

Good. Good. Jennifer deserved nothing less.

The ceremony was held in the ballroom. Aria had spent countless hours over the past few months on video calls with La Christou's events manager, and they had decided that the vast, cool room of marble and aged gold would be best. They had been right.

The ballroom seemed smaller now, filled with friends and family, elegant floral arrangements spilling from every available fixture. Orchestral music filled the air as

Aria and Keynes, the best man, walked down aisle arm in arm.

Keynes gave her a wink as he moved to stand beside the groom, Theo. Aria tried not to grin back. He was impossible.

She took up her position, breathed out, breathed in, breathed out—and on cue, the music changed. Swelled into something achingly romantic, a touch dramatic, the violins easing out a gentle, courtly welcome.

The double doors at the far end of the room swung open for the last time, the only time that counted. And Jennifer appeared.

She stood for a moment, framed by the doorway and the golden light spilling through it, her dark skin gleaming, her smile radiant. A bouquet of peach roses and pure white lilies was clasped in her hands, trailing like a waterfall, but even that couldn't draw attention away from how utterly stunning Jen looked.

Aria tore her gaze from her best friend, just for a moment, to take a peek at the groom. Theo was watching his bride with rapt attention, his eyes wide, his lips caught half-way to a smile as if joy and disbelief warred inside him. When the handsome, older man raised a hand to swipe hurriedly at one cheek, Aria realised that Theo—powerful, wealthy, always-in-control Theo—was crying.

She rolled her lips in to hide a smile. Damn right he better cry. He was about to marry Jennifer Johnson. There wasn't a luckier man on the planet.

Jen reached the altar and flashed Aria a smile, her own eyes as teary as her husband-to-be's. Aria grinned back, too ecstatic to bother with a demure expression, and never mind that the ceremony was being filmed. Her shamelessly cheesy smile would have to remain immortalised, because this might be the happiest she'd ever been.

Until Jen turned to face Theo and the scars on the side of her face caught the light. Just a few small, dark, teardrop-shaped marks scattered erratically over her skin. No attempt had been made to cover to cover them. Jen was proud of them.

Aria wasn't. Those scars had come, after all, from her ex-boyfriend's backfiring gun.

The priest began the ceremony and Aria watched the glowing couple, pinning a smile onto her face. She wouldn't ruin Jenny's wedding video by allowing even a hint of her disquiet to show. No-one could ever know.

Aria took a breath and heard Theo say, "I, Jyu Theodore Chamberlain, take you, Jennifer Abigail Johnson…"

She took another breath and let the words calm her. Felt the strength of Theo's love, his incandescent happiness, and let it fill her heart with gladness. There. That was better.

Crisis averted. For now.

———

"Aren't you a *vision*," Keynes drawled. "Skulking in the shadows, admiring your handiwork."

Aria narrowed her eyes as the best man drew closer. His suit jacket was nowhere to be seen. His bow-tie hung loose around his neck and his shirt sleeves were rolled up, revealing caramel skin dusted with tawny hair.

"Fuck off," she said.

He came to lean against the cool, marble pillar beside her. "You first. Got a light?"

"Nope."

"Doesn't matter; I have. Got a fag?" The word sounded preposterous, uttered in his private-schoolboy accent, but she'd gotten used to Keynes over the months since they'd first met. In fact, if this were primary school, he'd be her second-best friend by now.

Still, she glowered at him. "You're interrupting my brooding."

"That's the idea, love. Got a fag, or not?"

"You know I have."

"Yep." He produced a lighter from his pocket—a sickeningly slick little thing, silver and gold. No common-or-garden plastic Bic for Mr. Olusegun-Keynes.

With a sigh, Aria hiked up the gauzy skirt of her sunshine-yellow gown.

Keynes averted his eyes with all the drama of a stage dame. "Behave yourself, madam. You know I'm immune to your wiles."

"More's the pity," she muttered, snatching a cigarette from her garter. "I've only got one. We'll have to share."

"One, because?"

"Because your sister scared me into almost-quitting, and I'm trying to be good."

"Don't listen to her." Keynes lit the cigarette as Aria held it to her lips. "She's all talk. Once she's had a few drinks—"

"Stop enabling. I'm quitting, and so should you."

Keynes plucked the cigarette from her fingers and took a drag. Then he said, smoke trailing from his full lips like dragon's breath, "I *have* quit, love. But enough about me. What are you doing over here?"

Good fucking question. Aria was usually the life and soul of any party—and this wasn't just a party. It was her best friend's wedding. One *she'd* organised, with Keynes's dedicated assistance.

But it was all over now, and the prospect of long, uneventful months without a reason to force herself into Jen and Theo's happy life was... unappealing, to say the least. Not that she'd ever admit that. No-one needed to know how pathetic she'd become.

So instead, she offered a secondary truth. "Scouting for boys."

"Me too. But the pickings are slim."

"They are not," Aria snorted. She nodded towards a table of young men at the edge of the terrace, where marble floor turned into La Christou's glorious patio. They were clearly appreciating the atmosphere, lounging around with casual grace, drinks in hand. Part of Theo's family; cousins, she thought. They shared his razor-sharp bone structure, and some of them were almost as handsome as he was. "They're gorgeous," she said. "Tell me they're not."

Keynes scoffed. "I've known those boys for too many years to take one to bed. I vaguely remember sharing a bath with the eldest."

Right; because Keynes and Theo's families were tight like that.

Although it might be more accurate to say that Theo's family offered Keynes and his sister a respite from their nightmarish home life.

Tomato, tomato.

"But," Keynes said, "any of them might do well for you. Don't you think?"

No. She didn't think. Which was one of her many, many problems. "No-one here is doing it for me."

"Rubbish," he said. "You're just thinking too hard. You're not even drunk, are you?"

Stone cold sober. "Whatever," she replied, rolling her eyes. "You know, since I'm the maid of honour, I *should* be sleeping with the best man."

Keynes grinned, full lips parting to display American-white teeth. Honestly, the man had no right to look the way he did. If they were actors in a teen movie, he'd be the bad guy. He was too beautiful to be anything else. "Oh, love," he said. "If I were so inclined…"

"Blah, blah, blah. Stop trying to charm me. I'm not even close to your type." Gender aside, Aria knew for a fact that Keynes preferred his partners… clean-cut.

Aria was as far from clean-cut as a country singer's mullet.

"Listen," he said. "You're moping, and we both know it. But look at all this." He swept a hand through the air, indicating the beauty around them—and the figures of Jenny and Theo, intertwined on the dance floor, swaying to every song as if it were a waltz. "Frankly, that slapped-arse expression is bringing down the mood. Want to take a break?"

The tip of Aria's tongue worried the silver ring bisecting her lower lip. "A break?"

"Yeah. Let's wander off. Go on an adventure. It'll be very Enid Blyton."

"Only Greek," she added, pushing off of the wall.

"Only Greek," he agreed, already leading the way.

"You know where you're going?"

"I know that you're following."

Well, she supposed. Fair enough.

CHAPTER TWO

Nikolas Christou had a problem.

He wasn't really used to problems—which might be why he was handling this one so poorly. In fact, it *definitely* was. That was the downside to a charmed life, he thought, as he jogged through his family's flagship hotel: a chronic inability to deal with one's own bullshit.

Eventually, he'd have to learn. Maturity yawned out ahead of him, tapping its metaphorical foot, reminding him that his glory days were officially over. He'd have to grow up, now, wouldn't he?

But Christ, not tonight.

Nik had just retired—prematurely, to some, but not to his bank account—from football. The beautiful game had done something to his left knee that was, unfortunately, rather ugly. He'd come home to annoy his mother, harass his little sister, and decide what to do with the rest of his life, since he had no useful skills. He had not expected to bump into Melissa fucking Bright while licking his wounds.

Although, *bump into* seemed too generous a phrase. It was more accurate to say that she'd hunted him down like a gazelle.

He could hear her voice now, echoing off the marble walls behind him. "Nik! Where are you? Did you see him, Perry?" There was a pause, and then she practically shrieked, "NIK!"

His name on her lips had sounded so much better in bed. Strange, really.

He took a sharp right and hurried along the corridor. He certainly wasn't going to *run*—he did have some pride—but he couldn't be fucking bothered with this woman. Honestly, of all the questionable people he'd ever made the mistake of sleeping with, she was the absolute worst. Bloody exhausting, bless her. Though really, a part of him admired her tenacity.

But dealing with that tenacity usually gave him a migraine

and made her, after she was done screaming, burst into tears. Nik hated to make a lady cry, even if that lady was a grasping, manipulative dingbat who couldn't take no for an answer. Just the thought of making someone feel unwanted made him imagine his tutting mother and scowling sister saying *God, Nik, you're so insensitive! Now look what you've done!*

He took a left, then a right, then another right, until he was tied up in knots. It was horrifying to realise how little he remembered of the hotel he'd grown up visiting; clearly he'd been living and playing in England for too long. Melissa's voice chased him no matter which way he turned, growing closer and closer until she might as well be on top of him.

By the time he came across the deep, shadowed alcove bracketed by classical statuary, he was practically frantic. And by the time he noticed the two people *standing* in that alcove, staring at him as if he were a headless chicken, he was literally desperate.

He almost fell over in shock when he realised that one of the people was Keynes. Or rather, Olumide Olusegun-Keynes, man of the world, mystery, and excellent practical jokes.

Keynes's lips twitched as he took in Nik's panicked expression. "You alright, mate?"

"No," Nik said. He never had been one to prevaricate. "I am being ruthlessly corralled by a pair of lionesses."

Keynes gave in and allowed himself a full-blown smirk. At any other time, Nik might pause to admire the lips involved in that smirk. The man as a whole was worthy of admiration, actually; he looked like a model. But that didn't matter, because Nik was putting his days of carefree sluttery behind him.

Tragic.

"That's rough," Keynes said. He looked over at his companion, so of course, Nik did too. Which is when his jaw almost, very nearly, dropped. Because the woman standing in the shadowed alcove was unlike anyone he'd ever seen.

He'd heard of people being called *striking*, and he certainly felt like he'd been struck. Her dress, long and buttercup-yellow, was pretty, but it was the rest of her that affected him most. Everything about her commanded attention, from the contrast between her platinum blonde hair and dark skin, to the tattoos that covered every visible inch of her. A silver ring glinted down the centre of her glossy lower lip, accompanied by little studs on either side of her nose and what looked like a thousand tiny gemstones decorating the curves of her ears.

She watched him with eyes rimmed in pitch-black makeup and glinting with amusement. There was a sardonic tilt to her lush mouth that made him think she was laughing *at* him, rather than with him. Then he heard Melissa's strident tones from just down the hall, and the woman's slight smile turned into a full-blown, wicked grin.

That grin was giving him ideas. But, worse than that, *something* about her was giving him fucking heart palpitations. He couldn't even describe the feeling that overtook him at the sight of her. It was like… like running onto a pitch and sprinting through icy drizzle, eyes narrowed, feet fast, the earth soft beneath his studs, knowing absolutely nothing could stop him.

Weird.

"In trouble?" she asked. And Jesus Christ, her low, teasing voice alone did more for Nik than porn ever had.

"You could say that," he managed, his eyes flitting from the smirk on her lips to the arch of her brow. She was tall, but the way she stood made her seem taller—or maybe it was the energy that surrounded her, strong enough to suffocate the weak.

Nik wasn't weak. But he wouldn't mind giving up his oxygen for her.

Which was possibly the strangest fucking thought he'd ever had.

"If you're a friend of Keynes's," she said, "then whatever's happening here must be your fault. He only likes disreputable people."

Nik heard, as if through a tunnel, the sound of Keynes snorting out a sarcastic response. He barely registered the words. He didn't register a damned thing except her, bright like sunshine, burning him alive in the most beautiful way. "If you're his friend, too," Nik said, "doesn't that make you disreputable?"

"Of course," she smiled. It was a real smile, so brilliant it set him off balance. Her brows arched as she grinned, one slightly higher than the other, and her eyes tilted up at the corners.

Nik didn't know if he'd just felt the earth shake or if he was tragically losing his mind. Phantom or real, *something* jarred his bones and his brain all at once, until everything felt... different. He blinked slowly, readjusting to this slight shift in his world. The first thing his gaze focused on was her. An unfamiliar need hummed through his blood stream, growing stronger with every beat of his heart. Something inside him unfurled; it was the monster that took over him on the pitch, its demands a low growl. This time, though, it wasn't telling him to win.

Her. Take her.

Wait, what?

Before he could grapple with that alarming thought, he heard the sharp click of footsteps, too fast and too close. Melissa. His panicked caveman brain set in again. Actually, maybe it wasn't caveman brain, because a caveman's solution to this problem would be fight or flight, right?

As opposed to Nik's solution, which was to lock eyes with the tattooed woman and say, "Can I kiss you?"

Her brows shot up. "Me?"

"Yes."

"Now?"

"*Yes.*" When she didn't answer, he turned to Keynes. "Or you. If you're into that." He knew very well that Keynes *was* into that, but the woman beside him might not.

Keynes gave him a slow, catlike smile. "I certainly am." He stepped forward, hooked an arm around Nik's shoulders, and kissed him.

It was an excellent kiss, all things considered. But it didn't have the desired effect. Melissa didn't, it seemed, find Nik kissing someone else and finally take the fucking hint.

Instead, she saw him kissing someone else and hollered, "Nik! *There* you are!"

————

Aria had tried a lot of things, but she'd never bothered with voyeurism. It just didn't ring her bell.

She also knew that she wasn't the slightest bit attracted to Keynes. She had been, at one point, because he was drop-dead fucking gorgeous, but friendship had dealt with that lust rather swiftly.

Yet, as she watched Keynes kiss Mr. Tall, Tan and Terrified, she felt a hot, tight stirring in her belly that had been conspicuously absent for some time. And if it wasn't related to voyeurism, and it wasn't there because of Keynes, she supposed that only left one other source.

His friend. The stranger.

Which made sense, considering the way her eyes were currently devouring him. Her gaze danced feverishly from the swell of his biceps as he grabbed Keynes's arms, to the firm grip of those big, long-fingered hands, to the ferocious frown on his dark brow. A few seconds ago, his features had seemed sweet and friendly, despite his obvious panic. Now his profile was sharp, intense, hungry. She noticed abruptly that he was taller and more muscular than he'd seemed. She wouldn't have said, thirty seconds ago, that this guy was bigger than Keynes—but now she could see quite clearly that he was, because the two men were plastered together from mouth to hip.

You'd think that situation would put off the blonde woman who appeared a few feet away, with a pair of friends lagging just behind. But it didn't. Instead she stood for a moment, transfixed, her pink mouth forming a perfect *O*. Rather like a prim little version of Aria's own, she imagined.

But the woman's fixation didn't last quite as long as Aria's had. She pulled herself together much more quickly, a smile taking over her face as she trilled, "Nik! *There* you are!"

At the sound of her voice, the stranger—Nik, apparently— stiffened. He broke the kiss, easing gently away from Keynes, a sort of grim resignation taking over his features. It was pretty obvious he'd hoped to make the woman disappear, for some reason, but she clearly wasn't that faint-hearted.

Typically, Aria was highly suspicious of men who ran from women. In her experience, that kind of situation suggested that a man had taken something, or else that he owed something, and in order to avoid dealing with his responsibilities, he was leading some poor cow on a merry chase.

But something about this particular man seemed so disturbingly… genuine. Or maybe she was just making excuses for herself. Maybe he was quite clearly scum, but her libido had taken over her brain. Whatever the reason, Aria did something deliciously reckless.

She stepped forward, caught the man's face in her hands, and brought her lips to his.

It wasn't difficult. Not just because she was tall and wearing killer heels besides—although that helped—but because he seemed totally onboard. Clearly, he was pretty fucking eager to avoid the woman standing a few feet away. Aria had just enough time to note that his eyelashes were ridiculously long and his brown eyes looked almost black. Then his mouth was on hers and raw, needy, impossible lust rolled through her body like a tidal wave.

Kissing wasn't supposed to feel like this. Or rather, it was *supposed* to, but it never, ever did. In her nightly fantasies, a kiss would be enough to heat her blood, to sensitise her skin and send a shiver through her body, but in reality, it never was.

And yet, kissing the stranger did just that.

Maybe it was the way he held her; not settling his hands somewhere polite, but wrapping both those thick arms around her waist and hauling her against him. Maybe it was the feel of his broad chest, his abdomen, his hips, pressed tight against hers. Maybe it was the fact that, despite the insistence of his touch, he kissed her almost gently. His lips moved over hers in a series of soft caresses. He didn't stick his tongue down her throat like an overfriendly dog. He didn't put his tongue in her mouth at all.

Even though she kind of wanted him to.

That inappropriate want reminded Aria that she was doing this for a reason. This guy wasn't kissing the hell out of her for kicks; he had an audience to perform for. To what end, she had no idea—but this kiss definitely made her Top 3 of All Time list, so Aria decided she owed him.

He wanted to put on a show? She could do that. She could definitely, definitely do that.

Aria slid her hands from his jaw to the thick, silky strands of his hair, raking her fingers through it as she rolled her hips against his. She wasn't expecting him to release a soft groan against her lips, so quiet she almost missed it, but she certainly wasn't complaining. Not at all. She also couldn't complain when one of his hands began to roam, sliding down the small of her back, skipping her arse—*boo!*—but grabbing her thigh—*yay!*—and dragging her leg high. At that point, her brain powered down completely to accommodate for all the extra blood her other body parts were demanding. And by 'other body parts' she meant her clit, which might as well be a bloody landmine. One touch and she'd explode. She'd better stop things here, because the arousal dancing along her nerve endings was starting to get out of hand.

Aria broke the kiss. Her vagina literally wept, but she did it anyway. Her vagina, after all, did not make the decisions here.

Her breath came in soft pants as she studied the face in front of her. The face of the man who'd just given her at least a month's worth of wanking material. He had golden skin, a broad nose and broader cheekbones, a square jaw and deep-set eyes that mirrored the shock she felt. Aria's gaze flicked down to his mouth without permission. His lips were full, slightly parted, bracketed by laugh lines. She wanted to taste them again.

"Gamóto," he breathed, the word harsh like a curse. "You— you're…"

Nice to know she wasn't the only one whose thoughts had

been scattered by that lust tornado. But now probably wasn't the time for startled stuttering.

She tore her gaze away from him and turned to give the blonde woman a look. It wasn't her scariest look—not even close—but it *was* A Look. And it had the desired effect.

The woman didn't seem quite so unconcerned anymore. Her blue eyes were wide, her mouth tight, her hands curled into fists at her sides. She started to speak, a strangled, choked sound emerging from her lips. Then she snapped her mouth shut again. Finally, as Aria had expected, she turned on her heel and hissed, "Let's go!"

Her friends hurried off after her, tossing disgusted glares over their shoulders. As soon as they all disappeared, Aria took a step back, breaking free of the stranger's embrace—no matter how good his hands felt. He let her go, but the startled expression on his handsome face had turned into something more like awe.

"How did you *do* that?" he asked.

Aria shrugged. "Minor intimidation tactics. I'm a lot scarier than Keynes."

Keynes huffed out a laugh. "On sight, sure."

"But…" The stranger shook his head, frowning down at her long, yellow skirts. "You're not scary at all. You look like a princess."

Aria's brows flew up. Beside her, Keynes gaped at the man standing in front of them, his jaw as slack as hers felt. This guy must be taking the piss, right? But he looked genuinely confused, and completely earnest, and…

And it didn't fucking matter if he needed his eyes testing. She had a conscience to soothe and places to be. "Listen, before I rush back to the ballroom—" that quip was rewarded by Keynes's snicker "—I kind of want to know what just happened. You aren't, like, avoiding child maintenance payments, are you?"

The stranger wrinkled his nose. "What? No. I'm avoiding Melissa. She's not great at taking no for an answer. But this tactic went *much* more smoothly."

Aria digested that nonsensical speech, decided it was bullshit, then turned to look at Keynes. To her surprise, he didn't offer a mocking smirk, or roll his eyes. Instead, he nodded subtly, as if to say, *"The bullshit you just heard is actually totally legit, by the way."*

Aria puzzled over this for a second before deciding that Keynes, despite being her friend, was a man, and therefore not entirely trustworthy.

Ah, well. She didn't need to know the truth, anyway. "We should get back to the reception."

"We certainly should," Keynes agreed. He slung an arm over her shoulder, and they walked away.

"Wait!" the stranger called. "Hang on a second." He had a slight accent, and it seemed to grow more pronounced as he followed them. "What's your name?"

"Aria," she said, still walking. It wasn't exactly classified information.

"I'm Nik. Nikolas. Aria, I want to—"

"I'm busy," she called over her shoulder. "Hence the whole *walking away* thing."

"Tomorrow, then!"

She laughed as Keynes propelled her down the hall. "If you can find me!"

The sound of his heavy footsteps behind them ceased. Just before she turned the corner towards the ballroom, he spoke again. "I will. I will find you."

Beside her, Keynes gave a quiet snort. "Oh, Nik. That boy. He sounds like a bloody Disney hero."

Aria laughed softly, and they shared a congenial smirk at the stranger's expense. Only, she couldn't help but remember that, five minutes ago, he'd called her a princess.

So it made sense that he sounded like a prince.

Available Now: SWEET ON THE GREEK

AUTHOR'S NOTE

The world we live in has its issues. I'm lucky to write in a genre that lets me acknowledge those issues—between all the jokes and magical penises, I mean.

This book features some things that have affected me personally. For example: the threat of being outed; coming to terms with a lifelong health condition; classism and the criminal justice system.

I didn't intend to put these issues into a story. They just kind of... happened. You know how it is!

But something I'd like to mention in more depth is Lizzie's body positivity journey.

Lizzie is fine with her size and appearance throughout the book, so you might wonder what I mean by 'body positivity'. It's a popular phrase these days, but it's often used in an incomplete way. Many 'body posi' messages tell us that we should love our bodies for what they can do instead of how they look.

"Your body lets you laugh, sing, dance, listen to music, watch the sunset, walk a mile! It deserves your love!"

Okay, great. And what about the deaf bodies? The paralysed bodies? The bodies that cause their owners pain with every breath? The inconvenient bodies that require expensive medication and constant doctor's appointments? What about those bodies? Do they deserve love?

At the start of this book, Lizzie isn't sure. She sees her unwell body as her enemy, as something dragging her down.

But her perspective changes over time. She has a happy ending with Isaac, but she also has a happy ending with herself.

My body positivity means treating yourself kindly, for no other reason than because you deserve it. There are no conditions or caveats. You are a human being, and you deserve happiness.

Aaaaand… now I'll stop being all mushy! Ahem.

Undone by the Ex-Con is book 2 in my Just for Him series (book 1 was, of course, *Bad for the Boss*). I'm happy to tell you all that I'll be writing Olu's love story, too, as part of an upcoming queer spin-off series. So look out for that!

Thank you so much for reading this book, guys. I really, really hope that you enjoyed it.

Love and biscuits,

Talia xx

ABOUT THE AUTHOR

Talia Hibbert is a *USA Today* bestselling author who lives in a bedroom full of books. Supposedly, there is a world beyond that room—but she has yet to drum up enough interest to investigate.

She writes steamy, diverse romance because she believes that people of marginalised identities need honest and positive representation. Her interests include makeup, junk food, and unnecessary sarcasm.

And, as Talia would say... that's all, folks. Love and biscuits!

https://www.taliahibbert.com